Dear Reader,

I love masks. There is something sexy and mysterious about a man or a woman in one. That's why I was delighted to see *Reunion at Cardwell Ranch* and *The Masked Man* together in this edition.

First we return to the Cardwell Ranch. The last of the Texas cousins, Laramie Cardwell, buys a house at Big Sky, Montana. Of course there is trouble instantly. While he was only planning to stay for the holidays— he finds himself chasing an elusive "masked" cat burglar.

You have probably guessed that this is not your usual cat burglar. Laramie is stunned to discover that the masked, black-clad figure he tackles to the snowy ground is a young woman. To his surprise, she kisses him and manages to flee. But surprise! The artwork she was attempting to steal is apparently not what anyone thought it was. One kiss and Laramie is in deep. The Texas tycoon can't help but try to solve the mystery surrounding the painting and its alluring would-be thief.

In *The Masked Man*, a fling with a handsome masked stranger and a case of mistaken identity land Jill Lawson in more than hot water. Now she is being framed for murder. She can't imagine what came over her, but there was something about the masked man's kiss...

We've all been there. Or wish we had, huh?

I hope you enjoy these two books with some of my favorite fun characters,

B.J. Daniels

B.J. Daniels is a *New York Times* and *USA TODAY* bestselling author. She wrote her first book after a career as an award-winning newspaper journalist and the publication of thirty-seven short stories. She lives in Montana with her husband, Parker, and three springer spaniels. When not writing, she quilts, boats and plays tennis. Contact her at bjdaniels.com, on Facebook or on Twitter, @bjdanielsauthor.

Books by B.J. Daniels

Harlequin Intrigue

Cardwell Cousins

Rescue at Cardwell Ranch
Wedding at Cardwell Ranch
Deliverance at Cardwell Ranch
Reunion at Cardwell Ranch

Crime Scene at Cardwell Ranch
Justice at Cardwell Ranch
Cardwell Ranch Trespasser
Christmas at Cardwell Ranch

HQN Books

The Montana Hamiltons

Wild Horses
Lone Rider
Lucky Shot

Visit the Author Profile page at Harlequin.com for more titles.

REUNION AT CARDWELL RANCH
&
THE MASKED MAN

New York Times and USA TODAY Bestselling Author

B.J. DANIELS

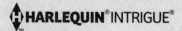

ISBN-13: 978-0-373-83809-7

Reunion at Cardwell Ranch & The Masked Man

Copyright © 2016 by Harlequin Books S.A.

The publisher acknowledges the copyright holder of the individual works as follows:

Reunion at Cardwell Ranch
Copyright © 2016 by Barbara Heinlein

The Masked Man
Copyright © 2003 by Barbara Heinlein

Recycling programs for this product may not exist in your area.

Printed in U.S.A.

HARLEQUIN®
www.Harlequin.com

CONTENTS

There are books that seem to write themselves. And there are books that try to kill me. This one drove me crazy. But thanks to an escape to the Bahamas with people I love, I was able to finish the book. This one is for Danielle, Travis, Stelly, Leslie and, always, Parker. Your faith in me keeps me going.

REUNION AT CARDWELL RANCH

CHAPTER ONE

THE MOMENT SHE'D stepped into the dark house, she could feel the emptiness surround her like a void. The owners wouldn't be coming to Montana for Christmas this year. The couple was getting a divorce. The man's third marriage, the woman's first.

She'd gotten her information from a good source, but she'd learned, though, that you can never be certain of anything, especially the rumors that ran more wildly than the river ran through the Gallatin Canyon past Big Sky.

Standing stone still in the dark, listening, she waited for a few moments before she snapped on her tiny penlight. There were no other homes close to this one. The owners of these expensive spacious second homes wanted to feel as if they had the mountainside to themselves. Because of that there was little to no chance that anyone would notice if she turned on lights. But she didn't like playing against the odds when it came to the chance of being discovered.

As she moved through the house, she saw sculptures that she knew had cost a small fortune and paintings like some she'd sat for hours studying in museums back East. She hurried on past them, reminded that time was never on her side. In and out as quickly as possible was her personal motto. Otherwise she knew all too well things could go very badly.

She found the painting in the master bedroom on the third floor. A twenty-by-sixteen-inch signed Taylor West original depicting a rancher on horseback surveying his herd. It was one of her favorites. She stepped to it quickly, admiring the brushstrokes and the skillful use of shading as she let the penlight move over it until she found what she was looking for.

Lifting it off the wall, she checked the time. She was running a little over five minutes on this job because of the three stories she'd had to search for this piece.

Quickly she replaced the painting with the one she'd brought, noticing that the bag she'd carried it in had torn. Wadding up the bag, she stuffed it into her coat pocket and tucked the painting from the wall under her arm.

She made her way back through the house, pleased. If only they were all as easy as this one. She'd barely completed the thought when a set of headlights washed over the room.

LARAMIE CARDWELL MENTALLY kicked himself for driving up this snow-packed narrow mountain road in the dark. But according to his sister-in-law, and the real-estate agent for the property, if he wanted a house in the Big Sky area, he had to jump on it the moment it became available.

"Why would you want to buy a house up here when you can stay in one of our guesthouses on the ranch whenever you come?" his cousin Dana Cardwell Savage had argued.

While he appreciated her hospitality at Cardwell

Ranch, as much time as he found himself spending in Montana, he wanted a place of his own. It had been family that had brought his brothers back to Montana. But it was love—and barbecue—that had them staying.

He often marveled that it had all started with barbecue—the one thing all five brothers knew. They'd opened a small barbecue joint outside of Houston. Surprisingly, it had taken off and they'd opened others, turning a backyard barbecue into a multimillion-dollar business. It had been his brother Tanner "Tag" Cardwell who'd first come up with the idea of opening their first Texas Boys Barbecue restaurant in Montana in Big Sky.

While some of them had balked at the idea, it had proved to be a good one. Now his brothers were talking about opening others in the state. His four brothers had all returned to their Montana roots, but Laramie was a Texas boy who told himself that he had no desire to live in this wild country—at least not full-time.

With his entire family here now, he wanted his own place, and he could darn sure afford a second home. Though he suspected the one he was on his way to check out would be too large for what he needed.

But there was one way to find out. He figured he'd get a look at the house from the outside. If it wasn't what he wanted, then he wouldn't waste his sister-in-law McKenzie's time looking at the interior.

As he topped a small rise in the road, a moonlit Lone Mountain, the peak that dominated Big Sky, appeared from behind a cloud, making him catch his breath. He'd seen the view numerous times on his other visits to the area, but it still captivated him.

He had to admit this part of Montana was spectacular, although he wasn't so sure about staying up here for the winter. While the snow was awe inspiring in its beauty, he still wasn't used to the bracing cold up here.

"You wouldn't mind it if you had someone to cuddle with at night," his brother Tag had joked. All four of his brothers had fallen in love in Montana—and with Montana—and now had wives to snuggle up to on these cold winter nights.

"I only want a house up here," Laramie had said. "I can kick up the heat when I spend time here during the holidays."

As he topped the rise in the road, his headlights caught on a three-story house set against the mountainside. Laramie let up on the gas, captivated by the design of the house and the way it seemed to belong on the side of the mountain in the pines.

That's when he spotted the dark figure running along the roofline of the attached garage.

CHAPTER TWO

LARAMIE REMEMBERED HEARING that an alleged cat burglar had been seen in Big Sky, but so far the thief hadn't gotten away with anything.

Until now.

Slamming on the brakes, he threw open the door of his rented SUV, leaped out and took off running. It crossed his mind that the robber might be armed and dangerous. But all he could think about was catching the thief.

The freezing snowy night air made his lungs ache. Even though he'd been the business end of Texas Boys Barbecue, he'd stayed in shape. But he felt the high altitude quicken his breathing and reminded himself he wasn't in Houston anymore.

The dark figure had reached the end of the roofline and now leaped down as agile as any cat he'd ever seen. The thief was dressed in all black including a mask that hid his face. He was carrying what appeared to be a painting.

Laramie tackled the burglar, instantly recognizing his physical advantage. The burglar let out a breath as they hit the ground. The painting skidded across the snow.

Rolling over on top of the thief, Laramie held him down with his weight as he fumbled for his cell phone.

The slightly built burglar wriggled under him in the deep snow.

"Hold still," he ordered as he finally got his cell phone out and with freezing fingers began to call his cousin's husband Marshal Hud Savage.

"You're crushing me."

At the burglar's distinctly female voice, Laramie froze. His gaze cut from the phone to the burglar's eyes—the only exposed part of her face other than her mouth. The eyes were a pale blue in the snowy starlight. "You're a...*woman*?"

In a breathless whisper, she said, "You just now noticed that? Could you let me breathe?"

Shocked, he shifted his weight to allow her to take breath into her lungs. This was the cat burglar?

She freed one arm and wiped away the powdery snow from her eyes as she whispered something else.

He cut his eyes to her, suddenly worried that he had injured her when he'd taken her down. She motioned for him to lean closer. He bent down.

Her free hand cupped the back of his neck, pulling him down into a kiss before he could stop her. Suddenly her lips were on his, her mouth parting as if they were lovers.

The next thing he knew he was lying on his back in the snow looking up at the stars as the cat burglar took off. Her escape had been as much of a surprise as the kiss. He quickly sat up. He'd lost his cell phone and his Stetson. Both had fallen into the snow. He plucked them up as he lumbered to his feet. But by then she was already dropping over the side of the ridge.

He took off after her, but he had gone only a few yards when he heard the roar of a snowmobile engine.

Scrambling after her, he turned the corner of the house in time to see the snowmobile roar off through the snow-heavy pines and disappear. He listened to her get away, feeling like a fool. He'd let her trick him.

She'd taken advantage of his surprise and the extra space he'd given her to breathe. She was a lot stronger and more agile than she had appeared and she had a weapon—those lips. He groaned when he thought about the kiss—and its effects on him.

As he turned back, he saw a corner of the painting sticking up out of the snow. Laramie trudged to where it had landed. The only good news was that she hadn't gotten away with the painting.

Surprisingly the frame was still intact. He carefully brushed away the snow, thinking about the woman who'd gotten away. He'd known his share of women in his life. A few had tempted him, a couple had played havoc with his heart and several had taken him for a ride.

However, none of them had tricked him like this. He could well imagine what his brothers would say.

But would he be able to recognize her if he ever saw her again? She'd never spoken above a whisper and he hadn't gotten a chance to remove her ski mask before she'd dumped him in the snow.

Those eyes. Those lips. He told himself if he ever saw either again, damn straight he'd recognize her.

She thought she was smarter than he. She thought she'd gotten away. But he had the painting. And he would find her—if she didn't find him first, he thought, glancing at the painting in the moonlight.

To the fading sound of the snowmobile, he walked

back to his rental SUV. Placing the painting in the backseat, he called his cousin's husband, the marshal.

THAT HAD BEEN too close. As Obsidian "Sid" Forester pulled the snowmobile around to the back of the cabin, she glanced over her shoulder. No headlights. No lights at all. She hadn't been followed.

She'd taken a longer route through the trees. At first she'd thought the man who'd tackled her was the owner of the house. But she'd done her research on him and knew he was much older than the man she'd just encountered.

So who was that cowboy with the Southern drawl? Moonlight on snow did strange things to one's vision. But she had gotten a good look at him—a better look than he'd gotten of her, she assured herself. Thick dark hair. Ice-cold blue eyes. Handsome, if you liked that clean-cut, all-business kind of man. She did not.

The only thing that had thrown her was his accent. Definitely from down South. Definitely not the New Yorker who owned the house.

That wasn't all that had thrown her, she had to admit. The kiss. It had worked just as she'd planned and yet... She touched her tongue to her upper lip, remembering the electrical shock she'd felt when they kissed. Worse was the tingling she'd felt in her belly. True, she hadn't kissed a man in... She couldn't even remember when, but she'd never had that kind of reaction. She certainly hadn't expected to feel...anything.

Her pulse was back to normal by the time she entered the cabin. The air smelled of oil paint, turpentine and linseed oil. She shrugged out of her boots and coat at the back door, hung up her coat and kicked her boots aside as she moved to the painting she'd been working on earlier that day.

She gave it a critical perusal before moving into the small kitchen. Unfortunately she hadn't been to the grocery store in several days. She was always starved after one of what she called her "night jobs." With a bottle of beer—her last—a chunk of cheese and some stale bread, she stepped into the living area where a half dozen paintings were drying.

The cabin was small with only a living room, kitchen, bedroom, small bath and a storage room off to one side at the back. The moment the owner had shown it to her—and told her about all its peculiarities—she'd had to have it and had quickly signed the papers.

Sitting down now, she considered each of her paintings as she ate her snack and sipped her beer. It was hard to concentrate after what had happened earlier, though. She'd come close to getting caught before, but nothing like tonight. What would the man do?

Go to the marshal.

She considered that and decided she wasn't worried about the law catching up with her.

What did worry her was that he had the painting.

Taking another bite of cheese and bread, she chewed for a moment before washing it down with the last of the beer. She really did have to go to the store tomorrow.

Just the thought of going out in public made her wonder if she would run into him. That was the other thing about her cabin. It was nestled in the woods, far from urban Big Sky.

What if she did see him again? She had no doubt

that she would recognize him. She'd gotten a good look at him. He had high cheekbones, a patrician nose and generous mouth. She felt that ridiculous stirring again over that one stupid kiss.

She assured herself that there wasn't any way he could recognize her since she'd had the black ski mask on the whole time. Nor could he recognize her voice since she hadn't spoken above a whisper.

Shaking her head, she tried to put him out of her mind. There was more than a good chance that she would never see him again. Obviously he was a tourist, probably only here for the holidays. Once the holidays were over, he'd be on a jet back to wherever he'd picked up that Southern drawl.

Still, she wondered who he was and why he'd driven up to the house tonight. Probably lost. Just her luck. What other reason could he have had to be there?

But while she'd gotten away, it hadn't been clean, which upset her more than she wanted to admit. She prided herself on her larceny skills. Worse, she'd failed. She didn't have the painting.

Losing her appetite, she tossed the crust of stale bread in the trash and put the cheese back into the fridge before she returned to her work in progress. She always did her best thinking while she painted.

"SO, YOU DIDN'T see her face?" Marshal Hud Savage asked as he looked up from his report at the marshal's office later that night.

"She was wearing a ski mask with only the eyes and mouth part open. Her eyes were this amazing… bluish-silvery color." Laramie frowned. "Maybe it was the starlight but they seemed to change color." He realized the marshal was staring at him. "Just put down blue. If I ever see those eyes again, I'll recognize her." Or those lips, he thought, but he wasn't about to tell Hud about the kiss.

It had taken him by surprise—just as she'd planned. But for a moment, his mouth had been on hers. He'd looked into her eyes, felt something quicken inside him, then her warm breath on his cheek and…

He shook his head, reminding himself that it had only been a ploy and he'd fallen for it, hook, line and sinker. He'd kissed a *thief*! What annoyed him was that he had felt anything but disgust for what she'd done.

"How about height and weight?" Hud asked after writing down *blue*.

Laramie shrugged. "Small. Maybe five-five or -six. I have no idea on weight. Slim. I'm sorry I don't have a better description. It all happened too fast. But I have the painting. Maybe you can get her fingerprints—"

"Was she wearing gloves?"

He groaned.

"And you say she got away on a snowmobile?"

All he could do was nod.

"Did you get a make or model?"

Another shake of his head.

"And she overpowered you? Was she armed?"

Laramie groaned inwardly. "Not armed exactly. She was much stronger than I expected and she moved so fast… She caught me off guard."

Hud nodded, but he appeared to be trying hard not to laugh.

"You wait until you find her. She's…wily."

Hud did chuckle then. "I'm sure she is. Here. Sign this."

"So what are the chances you'll catch her?" Laramie asked as he signed the report.

"With a description like the one you just gave me…" Hud shook his head. His phone rang and he reached for it. "Marshal Savage." He listened, his gaze going to Laramie. "Okay. Yep, that'll do it." Hanging up, he picked up the signed report and ripped it in half before tossing it into the trash.

"What?" Laramie demanded.

"I just spoke with the owner of the house. He hadn't planned to come up this holiday, but apparently McKenzie called him yesterday and told him you would be looking at the house. Seems he's anxious to sell, so he flew in tonight." Hud met his gaze. "When I called the maintenance service and asked them to check the house, they found him there. He looked around to see what was missing and found nothing out of order."

"There wasn't anything missing? Was he sure?"

"It seems he has a painting, just like that one…" He pointed to the one leaning against the wall on the floor near Laramie, the painting the cat burglar had dropped. "It isn't missing."

"That's not possible."

Hud shrugged. "The owner says he has the original—the only one of its kind. Also, he said his house hasn't been broken into."

"That can't be right. I saw her coming out of the house."

"Or did you just see her on the ridge of the garage roofline?" the marshal asked.

Laramie thought back. "Maybe I didn't see her come out of the house."

"Since the first report we received about a cat burglar, we've had several sightings. But in all three cases, nothing was taken, the house showed no sign of forced entry…"

Laramie could see where this was going. "So it was a…hoax?"

Hud studied him openly for a moment. "You didn't happen to mention to your brothers that you were going up to that house tonight, did you? They also didn't happen to tell you beforehand about a cat burglar in the area, did they?"

He would kill his brothers. "You think it was a setup?"

Hud shrugged. "You know your brothers better than I do, but I'd say you've been had."

Had in more ways than the marshal could even imagine. He got to his feet. "I'm sorry to bother you with this, then. I just hope they haven't planted counterfeit money on me, as well." His brothers had told him that Hud was investigating a counterfeit operation that had been passing fraudulent money in the canyon.

"Let's hope not," Hud said with a groan. "I get a call a day about a bad twenty. Someone's churning them out," he said, getting to his feet. "In the old days it took a lot of expensive equipment and space along with some talent. Now, all you need is a good copy machine. A video online will walk you through the entire process. The good news is that these operations are often small. We aren't talking millions of dollars. Just someone needing some instant spending money."

"Well, good luck finding your counterfeiter and, again, I'm sorry about this. You have enough going on." But as he turned to the door, he said, "What about the painting?"

"The owner swears he has the authenticated original with paperwork on the back." Hud shrugged. "I would imagine this is nothing more than a cheap prop."

"Then you don't mind if I keep it?" Laramie asked.

The marshal chuckled. "It's all yours."

Laramie considered the painting on the floor. It was what he would have called Old West art, a rancher on horseback surveying his herd. It was titled "On The Ranch" and signed by an artist named Taylor West. The painting looked expensive to him, but what did he know?

"If someone comes looking for it, I'll let you know. But I have my doubts." Hud grinned. "If you ever see that woman again, though… I'd be curious just what color her eyes are since they seem to have made a real impression on you."

"REALLY?" LARAMIE DEMANDED when he saw his brother Tanner "Hayes" Cardwell at his house the next morning. "That wasn't funny what you and the others pulled last night." He couldn't help but wonder if the kiss had been planned, as well. It was a nice touch, something that would have had his brothers rolling on the floor laughing. "Hud got a real kick out of it since he has nothing to do but take bogus crime reports. I hope he arrests the whole bunch of you."

"I don't know what you're talking about," Hayes said as he poured coffee for them.

Laramie looked to his sister-in-law and real-estate agent McKenzie. He'd been staying with them this holiday and, while he enjoyed being with them, he was anxious to get his own place. McKenzie had been helping him find a house.

"Tell me you weren't in on it, too," he said to her.

"I abhor practical jokes." McKenzie shot a disapproving glance at her husband. "What did you and your brothers do?"

"*Nothing. Honest.* I have no idea what he's talking about," Hayes said holding up his hands. He looked genuinely innocent.

But Laramie wasn't buying it. He knew his brothers too well. They'd all treated him as if he was the bookworm who ran their family business, Texas Boys Barbecue. They would all have said he was the brother who never had enough adventure in his life.

So it would be just like them to set this up to add some spice to his life, as they would call it.

"Who was the woman?" Laramie demanded.

"There was a *woman*?" Hayes asked and grinned.

McKenzie shook her head. "You'll have to tell me about it on the way to the house, Laramie. I promised the owner we'd be there by nine. You can deal with your brothers later."

On the way up the mountain, he told McKenzie about what had happened last night.

"That doesn't sound like something Hayes would do," she said. "Are you sure your brothers were behind it?"

"It's the only thing that makes any sense. I saw her leaving with a painting. So, of course, I thought she'd stolen it. I guess that's what I was supposed to think."

"Are you sure the painting you have is a fake?"

"It doesn't look like it to me, but I'm no expert by any means. The owner says he still has the original. So maybe I stopped the woman before she could make the switch, but I could have sworn she was coming *from* the house."

McKenzie seemed to give it some thought. "Maybe she saw your headlights coming up the road and took off before she could make the switch."

"I suppose. If she really was a cat burglar. Or it could be just what the marshal thinks it is—my brothers' idea of a joke.

"I know an art expert if you're interested in finding out about the painting. Or, if it is by a local Western artist, you could take it right to the source," she said.

"Have you ever heard of Taylor West?"

McKenzie looked over at him in surprise. "He's a well-known artist in these parts. He lives farther up the canyon near Taylor Fork. I'm sure if you took the painting to him, he'd be able to tell you if it was his or not."

"I just might do that." He looked up the mountain road ahead and thought about what he'd seen last night as he'd come over the last rise. He couldn't help thinking about the woman. She'd certainly played her part well. If his brothers had been in on it.

He thought about what he'd seen in her eyes just before he started to call the marshal. She'd looked scared. But that could have been an act, too.

"First thing I want to do is see the original," he said to McKenzie.

"You think the owner lied about having it? Why would he do that?" she asked as the house came into view.

"I don't know. To collect on the insurance, maybe. He could be in on some scam involving the artwork if this artist is that well-known."

McKenzie raised a brow as she parked next to a

white SUV next to the house. "Cowboy art doesn't go for that much. A Taylor West might sell for near a hundred grand to the right market. But we aren't talking the Mona Lisa."

He didn't know what the original was worth, but he was anxious to see it. "I looked up the artist's website last night. Most of Taylor West's original work sells for twenty-five to seventy-five thousand depending on the size. Some of his older works are worth more."

"Did you see this particular painting on the artist's website?"

"No."

The owner, Theo Nelson, turned out to be an older distinguished man who'd apparently made his money in real estate back East. "If you have any questions, just let me know. I'll be in my study." Nelson disappeared up the stairs, leaving them alone.

"So what do you think, so far?" McKenzie asked as they stepped to the bank of windows that looked out on Lone Mountain. The snow-covered peak glowed in the morning sun against a robin's-egg-blue sky.

"The view is incredible," Laramie said. Then he dragged his gaze away to look at the paintings on the walls.

"This open concept is nice," McKenzie said as she went into the kitchen. "Great for entertaining. Granite countertops, new top-of-the-line appliances, lots of cupboard space, a walk-in pantry and even more storage for multiple sets of china and glassware—if you ever get married to a woman who collects both... You aren't listening to me," she said when Laramie didn't take the bait.

"Sorry. Let's see the second story," he said, already starting up the stairs.

The next floor had a large second living area, two bedrooms and a study. The study door was partially open, the owner at his desk, head down.

Laramie scanned the walls quickly. The painting wasn't there.

"Another great view," McKenzie was saying.

He agreed, taking a moment to notice the house. He liked it. "Let's see the top floor." He saw her shake her head, but she followed him up to the third level.

This, he realized, was a huge master bedroom. It cantilevered out so when he stood at the bank of windows, he felt as if he was flying.

"Impressive," McKenzie said. "But I'm not sure I could sleep in here. I have this thing about heights. The master bathroom is really nice, though. Check out this shower." She turned, no doubt realizing she'd lost him again.

Laramie stood in front of a painting, shaking his head. "This is the one."

"Does it look like the painting you took from the woman last night?" McKenzie asked in a whisper as she stepped closer.

"It looks *exactly* like it. How can he be so sure it's the original?"

"Because I had it authenticated." Neither of them had heard the owner come up the stairs to join them. Now the man stepped past them to take the painting off the wall and show them the back.

Laramie could see that it had a small card taped to the back. He realized how easy it would have been for the cat burglar to make the switch—including the authentication.

"You must be the man who thought you saw a burglar here last night," Nelson said as he put the painting back on the wall. "I'm glad it was a false alarm."

"Me, too," Laramie said, still not sure he believed it.

"So what do you think of the house?" the man asked.

"I like it."

"We'll be looking at some others," McKenzie said quickly. "How long are you going to be in town?"

"Only as long as it takes. So if you're interested…"

"You'll hear from us," she said, motioning to Laramie that it was time to go. "I have several other houses for us to look at this morning," she said once they were in the SUV heading off the mountain.

"Don't bother. I want that one."

She shot him a look. "But you haven't even—"

"That's the house. Find out what furniture stays. Also I want that painting."

As they dropped over the rise, the house disappearing behind them, McKenzie hit her brakes and skidded to a stop in the middle of the narrow snow-packed road. "You want the painting?"

"I'm pretty sure he'll part with it. If he's selling the house, then he's leaving Montana. His next wife won't want any cowboy art in her house."

McKenzie laughed. "You are definitely decisive once you make up your mind, but did you even look at the house or do you really just want the painting?"

He smiled over at her. "I want both. See what kind of deal you can get me, but don't take no for an answer."

She laughed and shook her head as she got the SUV

going again. "You're more like your brothers than I thought you were."

She had no idea. "I think you're right," Laramie said. "It wasn't my brothers who put that woman up to that stunt last night."

"I'm relieved to hear you say that," she said.

"I think she really *is* a cat burglar."

McKenzie shot him a look. "But she didn't steal anything."

He rubbed his jaw, surprised that he'd forgotten to shave. He'd been so anxious to confront Hayes this morning. "I'm not sure about that."

"Why am I getting a bad feeling that you're thinking of trying to catch this woman?"

He smiled over at her. He knew he could go to his brothers for help. Hayes was a private investigator and Austin, who'd been a deputy sheriff, now worked for Hayes at his investigative business.

But his cat burglar had made this personal. He wanted to catch her himself.

CHAPTER THREE

"I know Taylor West's work well," the art dealer said when Laramie called. "Who did you say gave you my name?"

"Local Realtor McKenzie Sheldon Cardwell. She said she's worked with you before."

"Oh, yes, McKenzie," Herbert Darlington said. "You have a painting you'd like me to authenticate?"

"If you can."

Darlington made an unpleasant sound. "If it is a true Taylor West work, I will be able to tell at once. When would you like me to take a look at it?"

"I'm parked outside your gallery right now."

The gallery was in a narrow building along the main street of Bozeman. Laramie had driven the forty-five miles first thing that morning. He was anxious to know about the painting. Even more anxious to know about the woman who'd gotten away.

Golden light shone on the paintings on the old brick walls of the gallery as he entered. He looked for any by Taylor West and saw several of Native Americans as well as one of cowboys. This one, though, was a cattle drive filled with longhorns and cowboys driving the herd through a canyon. It looked so real he could almost smell the dust the cattle were kicking up.

"Bring it back here," Darlington said, motioning to

a door at the back. The man was short and thick with thinning hair above a round red face. He wore a dark suit like an undertaker and sported a narrow black mustache above narrow thin lips.

Without another word, Darlington took the framed painting from him and moved over to a table. He snapped on a light, pulled on a pair of glasses and bent over the artwork.

"Where did you get this?" he asked after a moment.

"I picked it up from an unknown source."

Darlington shot him a look over one shoulder before returning to the painting. "It's quite good."

"But it's not a Taylor West."

"I didn't say that."

Laramie waited impatiently as the man pulled out a magnifying glass and went over the entire painting again. So much for being able to tell at a glance.

After a few minutes, Darlington let out a sigh, took off his glasses, snapped off the light and turned. "It's an original Taylor West."

Laramie let out a laugh as he raked a hand through his hair. How was that possible? How did any of this make sense? It didn't. "You're sure?"

The art expert gave him a pained, insulted look. "I'm guessing you picked it up for a song."

"Something like that." He reached for the painting.

"So you're interested in selling it," Darlington said. "I suppose I could make you an offer."

"It's not for sale." He reached again for the painting and this time the gallery owner handed it over, though reluctantly.

"I would be happy to authenticate it for you in writing," the gallery owner said.

Laramie wondered if he'd authenticated the one now hanging in the house he hoped McKenzie was getting for him. "I'll think about it." The art dealer walked him toward the front door.

Just then a tall, thin older man with a shoulder-length mane of white-blond hair and a handlebar mustache came in on a gust of wind. He looked like something out of an Old West movie.

"Cody can verify what I've told you," Darlington said.

Laramie eyed the man, wondering if he was also considered an art expert.

"Cody Kent is another of our Western artists," the gallery owner said. Then he turned to Cody. "Mr. Cardwell brought in a Taylor West painting. He was questioning its authenticity."

"Really?" Cody tilted his head to look at the painting in Laramie's hand as Darlington explained to him that while this was a one-of-a-kind piece, apparently there was another one owned by another collector.

That definitely got the man's attention. "So you're saying one of them is a forgery?"

"I'd stake my reputation that this is the original," Darlington said, puffing himself up. "Do you agree?"

Laramie handed the man the artwork and watched him as he inspected it. He noticed that the man's hands seemed to tremble as he stared at it.

The artist handed it back. "Sure looks like the real thing to me." Cody Kent's gaze met his. "Where did you get it?"

"Just picked it up recently," Laramie said. He took it back from the older man. "Glad to hear you both agree it is an authentic Taylor West."

As he headed for the door, Darlington followed. "Well, if you decide to get rid of it…"

Laramie shook his head but then stopped just short of the door to ask, "How much would you say it's worth?" He noticed that Cody Kent had moved to one of the paintings on display only yards from them, clearly listening to the conversation.

Darlington seemed to give a price more thought than was necessary since he'd just offered to buy it. "I could give you…thirty," he said, keeping his voice down.

"Thirty?"

"Thirty *thousand*," Darlington said. "It would be more but it's an older piece. His work has improved over the years."

Was that right? Laramie smiled to himself. From what he'd seen online last night, artists' older work appeared to have more value—especially if the artist was now dead. Taylor West was still kicking, apparently, but Laramie suspected the painting must be worth a lot more that what he was being offered.

"Thanks, but I think I'll keep it," he said as he tucked it under his arm. "It has…sentimental value."

SID PUT ON clean jeans and a sweater to go to the grocery store. Often she went in her paint-streaked pants and shirts. Anyone who paid any attention was aware that she painted since she spent most Saturdays at the local craft show selling her wares.

Not her paintings, but haphazardly done Montana scenes on everything from old metal saw blades and antique milk cans to ancient tractor parts and windmill blades. Amazingly, her crafts sold well, which proved to her that most people didn't know the difference between good art and bad.

But today she wanted to fly under the radar. No reason to call attention to herself as an artist. It might be too risky if the man from last night was still in town. She knew she was being silly. He'd probably completely forgotten about her.

She assumed he would have gone to the marshal last night with a story about her robbing that house. Since the painting wouldn't be missing, she wasn't worried.

Her only regret was losing the painting. She needed it. Which meant she had to get it back. Or taking all these chances would have been for nothing.

Where was the painting now? She'd learned at a young age to make friends where needed. Now she picked up the phone and called her friend who worked at the marshal's office as she drove to the grocery store.

After the usual pleasantries, she said, "So what's new down there?" Dispatcher Tara Kirkwood loved her job because she got to know everything that was going on—and she loved to share it.

"Counterfeit bills keep turning up," Tara said, keeping her voice down although the office was small and she was probably the only person down there right then. The marshal and detectives were probably out.

She and Tara had established long ago that anything Tara told her wouldn't go any further—and it never had. "The marshal is chasing one right now that was passed at the Corral Bar."

"No more cat burglar sightings?" she asked after listening to what Tara knew about the counterfeit bills.

"Actually, before Hud left, he said his wife's cousin who is in town caught the cat burglar last night." She laughed. "According to him, the burglar turned out to be a *her*."

"No kidding? So is she locked up down there?"

"Naw, she got away." Tara laughed again. "Hud got a chuckle out of it since apparently there was no crime and his cousin-in-law was quite taken with the woman."

Sid laughed even though this was not what she wanted to hear. The marshal's cousin-in-law? Just her luck. Not to mention "quite taken with her"? *Really?* She thought of the kiss. It might have been a mistake since she'd had a hard time forgetting about it, as well.

"What's the guy's name?" she asked.

"Laramie Cardwell."

Cardwell? Anyone who lived in the Gallatin Canyon knew that name. The Cardwell Ranch was one of the first established in the canyon. But she'd never heard of a Laramie Cardwell before.

"You said he was in town. So he's not from here?" she asked even though she knew his accent was way too Southern.

"His father is Angus Cardwell. Apparently his mother got a divorce years ago and took her five sons to live in Texas. Laramie's up here from Houston. He and his brothers own that new place, Texas Boys Barbecue."

"Huh."

"Have you tried it yet?" Tara asked.

"No. I've been meaning to, though," she said, realizing it was true.

"It's really good."

"So did the so-called cat burglar get away with anything?" she had to ask. "You said no crime was committed?"

"Laramie found a painting, but it wasn't stolen from the house. I overheard Hud say Laramie is hanging on to it. Kind of like a souvenir."

Sid mouthed a silent oath. She'd reached Meadow Village and the grocery store. "So now it's hanging at Cardwell Ranch," she joked.

"More than likely at his new house," Tara said.

"His new house?"

The dispatcher dropped her voice even further. "The house that he caught her allegedly robbing? He's *buying* it."

Sid pulled into a parking spot in front of the store. Tara was always a wealth of information. "Now that is a coincidence," she said. "So apparently he's staying."

"At least for the holidays I would think. You really should try their barbecue. It is *so* good."

"I just might do that. Got to go. Sure hope they catch those counterfeiters."

"Me, too. Hud is fit to be tied. It will be nice when things die back down around here."

Disconnecting, Sid parked in front of the grocery, thinking about everything Tara had said. How was she going to get the painting back? She'd never been one to push her luck and hitting the same house twice was more than risky, especially since now Laramie Cardwell might be expecting her. But did she really have a choice?

Her stomach growled. Still hungry and realizing it was almost lunchtime, she looked up the hill at the sign for Texas Boys Barbecue.

THE FAMILY HAD gathered at the Cardwell Ranch for lunch. Everyone but Laramie.

"What's going on with him?" Austin asked. For years he had been the no-show brother, the one who caught grief because he didn't play family well. Since meeting Gillian and returning to his birthplace, he'd changed. He loved these family get-togethers.

"He's looking for the cat burglar," McKenzie said. "And the four of you can blame yourself for that if you're behind this."

"What?" Austin asked, looking around the table. Hayes told him what he knew, Hud added his part and McKenzie finished it up. *"Seriously?* Laramie is trying to find this woman?" He turned to Hayes. "You told him we had nothing to do with this, right?"

"I swore we didn't."

Austin groaned. "So he might actually be chasing a real cat burglar."

"Only if the cat burglar is a young woman with silvery-blue eyes," Hud said, shaking his head. "This whole cat burglar thing started when a few residents saw a dark-clad figure sneaking around a couple of houses. But the bottom line is that no one has reported being burglarized. No valuables or paintings are missing."

"So you think it's a hoax," Austin said.

"I do," the marshal agreed. "Probably the local security company put the woman up to it to drum up more business. A lot of the people in Big Sky are from urban areas so security is a concern for them. The rest of us locals don't even bother to lock our doors."

"He told me he was going to visit the artist whose painting the woman dropped," McKenzie said between bites. "Taylor West. He lives up the canyon near Taylor Fork."

"Why didn't he come to us?" Austin asked his brother Hayes. "We are actually trained for this sort of thing." He'd gone to work for Hayes's detective agency after quitting the sheriff's department in Texas—he hadn't been satisfied being simply retired. Gillian had been right. He'd been miserable. He was too young to retire and he enjoyed investigative work.

"Seriously?" Dana asked. "You don't understand why your brother might want to solve this thing on his own? It involves an apparently attractive woman who tricked him and escaped. Laramie is related to all of you. Enough said. He probably thinks she's in trouble and is off to save her."

They all laughed, but Austin couldn't shake the bad feeling he had.

"I know that look in your eye," Gillian said to Austin. "Don't do it."

"She's right," Jackson said speaking up. "We need to stay out of this. I think Laramie's been getting bored running the business. Why not let him have a little… fun, since there is nothing to the cat burglar stories?"

They all agreed. Except Austin. "*Fun?* What if this woman is dangerous?"

"Laramie can take care of himself," Hayes said. "He hasn't just been sitting behind a desk for the past ten years. He's worked with some of us on cases. I think Jackson's right. He needs this and he needs us to stay out of it."

Austin couldn't help being protective of his youngest brother. While he and Hayes had both worked in law enforcement, Laramie had no experience dealing with criminals.

"I hope you're right," Austin said as he watched his family finish their lunches. Still, he couldn't shake the feeling that Laramie had no idea what he was getting into.

For the time being, he'd stay out of it since, if Hud was right, it had been nothing but a prank. But if a woman was involved…

CHAPTER FOUR

ARTIST TAYLOR WEST was a tall drink of water. At least that's how Laramie had seen him described on his website. The man who opened the door at the West home *was* tall. He'd aged, though, since he'd put his photo on his website. Laramie guessed he must be in his sixties and had once been very handsome. The gray hair at his temples gave him a distinguished look, but his complexion told the story of a man who drank too much.

"I don't usually meet clients at my home," West said, looking put out.

Laramie was glad he hadn't called ahead. "This was a matter that couldn't wait." A photograph on the wall behind the man caught Laramie's attention. It was of Taylor with a pretty young green-eyed blonde. He was staring at the photo more intently than he realized—especially at the eyes. Could this be the woman he'd tackled last night? She looked the right size but the eye color was wrong.

"My wife, Jade," West said.

Laramie blinked in surprise. Given the age difference between the artist and the woman in the photo, he would have thought it was West's daughter.

West's gaze went to the painting Laramie was holding in one hand. "Is that one of mine?" He sounded like a man worried that Laramie had come here to complain.

"That's what I'd like to know. I promise not to take any more of your time than necessary."

"What makes you think it's mine?" West asked.

"Because it has your name on it." He didn't mention that the so-called expert at the gallery had authenticated it.

"Well, fine, come on in out of the cold. This shouldn't take long." He didn't look less perturbed, but he did step back to let Laramie in.

But that was as far as the invitation was extended. Standing in the entryway of the house, Laramie uncovered the painting and handed it to the artist. Past West, he could see that the house was a huge mess. So where was the young wife?

West looked at it and said, "I don't see what the problem is," and started to hand it back.

"So it's yours?" Laramie asked.

"Obviously," the artist said with impatience.

"Then there *is* a problem." He told him about the one that Theo Nelson owned, the one that had been authenticated. "How do you explain that?"

"One of them must be a forgery since I only painted one."

"And you're sure this one is the original?"

West snatched the painting from him and with a curse headed down a hallway. Laramie followed, stepping over boots and shoes, jackets, dirty socks and assorted dog toys.

"The cleaning crew comes tomorrow," West said over his shoulder before turning into what was obviously his studio. It, too, was in disarray.

Laramie suspected the man didn't have anyone to clean the house. Or the young wife to do so, either, for that matter.

West snapped on a lamp and put the painting under it. "Where did you get this?"

"I picked it up recently."

"Nelson is right. If he has the original, then this one isn't mine," West said.

"Are you sure?" Clearly he wasn't. "I should tell you that before I came here, I took the painting to a local expert," Laramie said. "He confirmed it was yours and offered me thirty thousand for it."

The artist's eyes widened in surprise. "The original is worth over fifty."

Just as Laramie had suspected. "But the question is, which is the original?"

West swore. "If this is a forgery, it's a really good one." The man was frowning at the artwork, clearly angry and also seeming confused.

"I've looked at both. They appear identical. So if you didn't paint the copy, then who did?"

The artist shook his head. "How would I know?" He was upset now.

"It would take some talent, wouldn't it?"

West sighed impatiently. "Sure, but—"

"Otherwise, you're saying any art student could copy your paintings?"

"I see what you're getting at," the older man said angrily. "Yes, it takes talent. A *lot* of talent. They would have had to have studied their craft and have some natural ability, as well. Also they would have had to study my work. Not just anyone could make a reproduction this good."

"So has this person been hiding under a rock, or is it someone you know?"

West seemed shocked by the question. "It couldn't possibly be anyone I know."

"Why not? I would think the cowboy art market is very small. It must also be competitive. There can't be that many of you painting at this level, right?"

The artist nodded. "There are only twenty of us in the OWAC." Seeing Laramie's quizzical expression, he elaborated. "The Old West Artists Coalition."

Laramie considered that. "Only twenty? That sounds like a pretty elite—and competitive—group."

"We're all *friends*. We encourage and support each other. The only competition is with ourselves to get better."

"But some of you must make more money than others," he prodded. "Who is the best paid of this group of cowboy artists?"

West met his gaze with an arrogant one. "I am, but there are several others who do quite well."

"And you're telling me there is no jealousy?" Laramie scoffed at that. He knew too well, being one of five brothers, that competition was in male DNA. "So who are the others who are doing 'quite well'?"

"Cody Kent and Hank Ramsey, in that order. Rock Jackson quite a ways behind those two."

Laramie couldn't help but laugh. Just the fact that West knew that proved *he* at least had a competitive spirit. "So what exactly does this group do?"

"I told you. We support each other. We came together because of a desire to keep this art form alive in memory of the greats like the late Frederic Remington and Charles M. Russell. But also to ensure the work is an authentic representation of Western life. Without standards of quality and a respect for each other and the work…" He sounded as if he was quoting the group's bylaws.

"And you belong to this group?"

"I'm one of its founders along with Rock, Hank and Cody Kent," he said proudly.

Laramie had heard something in the man's tone. "What does it take to be a member?"

"You have to apply. The members decide if your work and your character meet our standards."

"Your *standards*?"

"Originally, you had to have cowboy experience as well as talent. That's changed some. Why are you asking me all this?" West demanded.

Laramie wasn't sure. "So it's an exclusive…club."

"None of my fellow artists would have any reason to rip me off by duplicating my work, if that's what you're getting at," West said. "Not to mention, most of them don't have the talent to copy my work."

Laramie tried not to smile. No competition here.

"Look," West said as if he knew he'd said too much. "There aren't that many of us. We're a dying breed of artists who care about our work. The satisfaction comes from painting and selling our own work—not copying someone else's and passing it off for money."

"Even if they needed money badly?" Laramie asked.

He saw something change in West's expression as if the question had made him think of someone. Laramie knew money could be the most obvious reason for making forgeries of Taylor West's work. Or maybe to rub West's arrogant face in it.

West picked up the painting, frowning harder as he

studied it again. "This is definitely the original," he said, but he seemed to lack conviction.

"If no one in your group is talented enough to make you question if this painting is yours or not…"

"I'm telling you," West snapped, "there's no one alive who could have copied my work well enough to fool an expert, let alone me."

Laramie thought that was a ridiculous statement given that someone obviously had, and he said as much.

West suddenly looked even more upset. "There is one man," the artist said after a moment. He'd paled. "H. F. Powell."

"Where would I find him?"

West didn't seem to hear him for a moment. He shook his head as if clearing away cobwebs from his brain. "Find him?" His laugh was more of a grunt. "Six feet under, last I checked."

TEXAS? SO THAT was Laramie Cardwell's accent, Sid thought. The barbecue restaurant had opened in Big Sky Meadows just last year. She'd heard it was owned by five brothers from Houston. Since she didn't get out much—at least during the day—that had been all Sid knew about the place.

Good sense told her to go into the store, buy some food and take it back to the cabin. The sooner she got home, the sooner she could get ready for tonight. Last night's close call was a good reminder that she needed to finish this and move on.

But barbecue sounded good. More than anything, she was curious. She quickly shopped for what groceries she needed, telling herself she would get a barbecue sandwich to go. She knew she was taking a risk, but then again, she'd been taking risks for some time now. Putting the groceries into the back of her SUV, she walked quickly up the hill to Texas Boys Barbecue on the recently plowed sidewalk. The sun glistening off the snow was almost blinding. It was one of those clear, cold winter days in Big Sky when she could see her breath as she walked. She looked up at Lone Mountain, momentarily stunned by how beautiful it was this morning.

Sometimes she got so busy she forgot to notice what an amazing place this was. Once she was done with all of this, maybe she would take a few weeks off and snowboard up on the mountain. She deserved it after this.

A bell jangled over the door as she entered the restaurant. It was early so the place was busy but not packed, and there were enough people that she didn't think she would stand out. Not that she believed Laramie Cardwell could recognize her.

The aroma of smoked meat filled the air, making her stomach growl again. Slipping into a booth, she pulled out a menu from behind an array of barbecue sauces with names like Hot in Houston and Sweet and Spicy San Antonio.

She'd just opened it when she heard a male voice with a distinct Southern accent coming from the kitchen. Looking up she saw a head of dark hair. The man was talking to another man with the same accent. As the first man turned, she realized he wasn't the one from last night, but the resemblance gave her a start even before she laid eyes on the second man.

It was him!

Suddenly, as if sensing her staring at him, he

glanced in her direction. Sid quickly ducked behind her menu as a young waitress approached her booth.

"What can I get you?" asked a teenaged girl with a ponytail and an order pad.

"I'll try the pulled pork sandwich with beans and coleslaw," Sid said from behind her menu. "Can I get that to go?"

"Great choice. What would you like to drink?" the girl asked.

Sid peeked out from behind the menu. Through the window into the kitchen she could no longer see the two men—nor could she hear them. Maybe they'd left.

"And a beer."

The girl nodded, then shyly asked if she could see her ID. "I'm sorry, but I have to ask."

Sid might have found that amusing since she was thirty. But she was aware that she didn't look a day over twenty. Behind the waitress, she heard the men's voices coming from the kitchen again. They sounded as though they were arguing.

She heard one say he didn't like what the other one was doing. "Austin, if I need your help I'll ask for it. I can handle this." Laramie Cardwell's voice. Handle what?

Sid looked up at the waitress. Today of all days, she didn't want to show her ID. She knew it was silly since Laramie Cardwell hadn't seen her face last night. But he might have a few moments ago. She remembered him above her in the moonlight and the way he'd looked into her eyes…and felt a shiver.

"You know, just make it a cola. I have work to do this afternoon."

The poor girl nodded without looking at her and wrote on her order pad.

"The owners of this place, are they really from Texas?" Sid asked.

The girl brightened. "They sure are. Five brothers. They just opened this place, but I heard there's another one going to open at Red Lodge."

"Really? Five brothers, huh?"

"Yep, all raised in Texas. They were born here, but left when they were kids. Four of them have moved back."

"The fifth one?" Sid asked, remembering how strong the man's Texas accent had been.

"Laramie still lives in Houston. That's where the main office is located. He's the one in charge of all the restaurants. They're cousins to Dana Cardwell of Cardwell Ranch, if you're familiar with the area."

Anyone who lived in the Canyon as the Gallatin Canyon was known had heard of the Cardwells of Cardwell Ranch.

"Their story is on the back of the menu, if you're interested. I'll get your order right out," the girl said. "You want that cola while you wait?"

Sid would much rather have had a beer and felt foolish for not showing the girl her ID. What were the chances that the waitress would remember her name or have any reason to mention it to her bosses?

Glancing toward the kitchen, she didn't see the men. Or hear them, but that didn't mean they weren't still back there. And if the man from last night had seen her a few minutes ago…

"Sure, I'll take the cola now, but make it to go," she said as she picked up the menu and turned it over.

The Cardwell brothers' story was on the back along with their photos. What surprised her was that Texas Boys Barbecue was a franchise the brothers had started. She'd just assumed they only owned this one restaurant.

Less surprising was that all five brothers were drop-dead gorgeous. In the photo on the back of the menu, the photographer had lined them up along a jack-legged fence, a ranch house in the background. Each brother wore jeans, boots, Western shirts and Stetsons. Each was equally handsome.

Her gaze went to Laramie. He was definitely the one who'd tackled her last night. She felt a shiver as she looked at his photo. His blue eyes stared back at her almost challenging. She told herself she had nothing to fear. He didn't know who she was or the marshal would have been to her door already. Even if he had bought that house, he'd be like most of the residents—staying only a few weeks of the year.

She wished she could wait for him to return to Texas. Unfortunately, she couldn't. Time was running out. She had to get the painting back—even knowing there was a chance of crossing paths with Laramie Cardwell again. She would just have to make sure that didn't happen.

CHAPTER FIVE

LARAMIE LEFT THE RESTAURANT, his mind on the painting and the woman, of course. The winter day sparkled under a blinding sun that ricocheted off the new-fallen snow. At loose ends waiting to hear if McKenzie got him the house, he went for a drive up the canyon.

Next to the highway, the Gallatin River snaked through the canyon under a thick layer of aquamarine ice. He tried to enjoy the beauty of this alien winter place. The snowcapped pines bent under the weight of their frozen burden, reminding him that it was less than a week until Christmas. His cousin Dana loved the holidays and went all-out surrounded by her family. He smiled at the thought.

Glancing in his review mirror, he realized he'd seen the large dark brown older-model sedan behind him before—right after he'd left Taylor West's house. It was behind him again.

He tried to laugh off the thought of someone following him. First cat burglars now this? Well, there was one way to find out, he thought as he neared the Corral Bar. He slowed and pulled in. The car went on past.

The windows on the vehicle had been tinted, so he hadn't gotten a good look at the driver. If he had to guess, he'd say male. As it disappeared up the road, he told himself the driver hadn't been following him anyway.

He thought about going inside the bar and having a burger and a beer. This was his father and uncle's favorite bar. Their band often played here.

But he was too antsy. He wanted to get back and find out if McKenzie had gotten him the house…and the painting. He pulled back on the road headed toward Big Sky again, his thoughts going to his cat burglar. The forgery at the house had to have been painted by someone with a whole lot of talent as Taylor West had said.

So if it was a forgery, who had painted it? Not some dead man named H. F. Powell unless he'd painted it before his demise. But the big question was why would his thief take it instead of the authenticated original?

She wouldn't. So if he was right and she'd been coming out of the house when he'd arrived, then she'd been in the process of stealing the original when he'd stopped her.

Which meant McKenzie was about to make a deal for a forgery.

Shaking his head at his own foolishness, he glanced in his rearview mirror. The brown car was back.

He felt a start at the sight of it behind him again. As he glanced in his rearview mirror again he saw that the vehicle was coming up fast. The canyon road had been plowed, but the dark pavement was still icy. Add to that the twists and turns the highway took as it wound through the Gallatin Canyon and the driver of the car was going way too fast.

Laramie had only a moment for his brain to take it all in before he realized that the driver had no intention of slowing down. A curve was coming up, one with a steep rock face on one side of the road and a precarious drop to the frozen river on the other.

He felt the vehicle's bumper connect with the back of his rental. Just a tap. But on the icy road that was all it took. The rental SUV began to fishtail on the ice as the dark car bumped into him again. He could feel the tires lose traction and the next thing he knew he was sliding toward the river. He felt the tires go off the pavement. A wall of snow rushed over the hood.

Expecting the SUV would be pitched into the river and break through the ice, Laramie braced him. Moments later, heart in his throat, he was shocked when the deep snow off the side of the highway stopped his descent just yards from the frozen river. He sat, so shaken he didn't notice the dark car backing up on the highway above him until he heard the roar of the engine.

Looking up, all he saw was the dark tinted windows on the passenger side as the car sped away.

THE PULLED PORK sandwich was to die for, just as Tara had said. Sid couldn't believe she hadn't been to Texas Boys Barbecue before this. The beans and coleslaw were quite good, too. She had downed the cola on the drive back to the cabin but had saved the rest until she'd reached home. Once there, she'd pulled a cold bottle of beer from the grocery bag and sat down at her kitchen table to devour the barbecue. She couldn't help licking her fingers.

Her father would have loved the food, she thought, and then pushed the thought away. While he was always with her, driving her more than ambition, remembering him often brought aching pain. One day that pain would go away, once she accomplished the job she'd set for herself, she told herself as she cleaned up the mess and changed her clothes.

Back at her easel, she considered the painting she was working on. It was one of her father. He was standing by a horse next to the corral. His battered straw cowboy hat was pushed back, sunlight on his weathered face. Behind him were the rocky cliffs and scrub pine of her youth. She was painting it from memory since all the photos had been lost.

She thought of the stash of original artwork she had hidden all these years. It had been years since anyone had seen those paintings—herself included.

Until recently.

LARAMIE CALLED 911 the moment he was out of the SUV and standing at the edge of the highway. He couldn't believe how lucky he'd been. Just a few more yards and the rental would have been in the river.

Marshal Hud Savage came on the line. "What's this about you being forced off the road?"

He told him and Hud promised to have a wrecker sent down to get his rental out of the snowbank.

Laramie had given him what little description he could of the vehicle that had forced him off the road. As with the alleged cat burglar, he had little information other than the car was large and brown with tinted windows.

"It happened too fast," he said. "But there was no doubt of the driver's intent." He could almost see Hud nodding.

"Had you passed the driver? Or had any interaction before this?"

"No. I saw the car earlier up by Taylor Fork, then again later when I went for a drive up the canyon." He could tell that Hud had little hope of finding the vehicle. "Can you do me a favor? Find out what Taylor West drives."

"Taylor West, the local artist?" Hud asked with obvious surprise.

Hud told him that West owned a large SUV and an older-model pickup. Neither matched the description Laramie had given him.

"What makes you think Taylor West had anything to do with running you off the road?" Hud wanted to know.

"Nothing really," Laramie said. "That's just the first place I noticed the car following me, after I visited the artist. I'm probably wrong about there being a connection." And yet he had a feeling that if Taylor hadn't been behind it, then someone he knew definitely was. But he had no idea why. "Maybe I ticked off the driver somehow."

"Maybe," Hud said. "You sure you weren't going too slow?"

"Maybe."

TAYLOR WEST PACED the floor after the Texan left. He'd been so shaken that he would have poured himself a drink if there'd been any booze in the house. But his wife had dumped every drop she could find down the drain before she'd left. He'd dug out enough from his hiding places that he'd been fine. Until now.

"When are you coming back?" he'd demanded as he'd watched her throw her clothes into two suitcases and head for the door.

"When you get some help with your drinking."

He didn't need any help. He drank fine without it.

The old joke fell flat. He knew it was more than his drinking. She'd been trying to let him down easy, he thought as he looked around the house. He hadn't realized what a mess it was until he'd seen it through his visitor's eyes. What had Laramie Cardwell been thinking, showing up unannounced at his door like that?

"It's that damned painting," he said as he opened one kitchen cupboard after another, not even sure what he was looking for—then he remembered where he'd hidden a bottle of bourbon months ago and felt better.

In the laundry room, he moved the washer out a little. Reaching behind it, he groped around, feeling nothing but air and cobwebs. Panic filled him. The drive to the nearest liquor store was a good ten miles. He couldn't go to the nearest bar since he'd been kicked out of it.

His hand brushed over the cold throat of the bourbon bottle. His relief rushed out in a laugh that sounded too loud in the small room. Clutching the bottle, he'withdrew it, wiped off the dust with one of his dirty shirts lying on the laundry room floor and headed for the kitchen.

Unable to find a clean glass, he took his first drink straight from the bottle. The liquor bathed his tongue in bliss, warmed his throat and quenched his thirst. He took another drink as the first one reached his belly and sent a golden glow through him.

That's when he knew he was in trouble. There was only one man who could have painted the forgery. He'd be kidding himself if he thought it was anyone but H. F. Powell. He thought of Powell's last words to him.

"I could paint one of your pieces and you wouldn't know the difference, that's how good I am."

Taylor shook his head. He hadn't let himself think of H.F. in years. Some things were best forgotten. Everyone knew that the painter had become a recluse in the last years of his life. No one had seen him for almost two years before the tragedy. There hadn't been a funeral—at H.F.'s request. No memorial service. No family.

H.F. must be rolling in his grave since his paintings were now worth a small fortune. Taylor admitted grudgingly, the man had been one hell of a painter. But look where it had gotten him. The arrogant old fool had died alone and miserable.

Just like you're going to die. Taylor snorted at the thought and the one that came after it. *What goes around, comes around.* He shuddered and took another drink, regretting the calls he'd made the moment Laramie Cardwell left. But he'd been so upset and he wasn't in this alone.

Rock Jackson had sounded as if he'd been asleep before the call.

"I'm telling you this painting was so good… I'm not even sure it isn't the original," he'd told Rock. "Tell me there isn't any chance—"

"Take it easy. You're jumping to conclusions. Who brought you the painting?"

Taylor told him.

"The guy's gone, right?"

"He just left."

"Then there is nothing to worry about," Rock had said. "Look, I have to go. Have a drink. Everything is fine."

Artist Hank Ramsey had told him pretty much the same thing, only Taylor had heard more worry in Hank's voice.

"If you had seen this painting…" Taylor had said feeling sick to his stomach.

Hank had asked the name of the man who'd stopped by and what painting it had been. Hank had tried to calm him back down. "Taylor, we're all painting cowboys, horses and Indians. We've all had someone copy our paintings. Since you're at the top of the heap, your paintings are going to be forged the most. Let me see what I can find out. In the meantime, don't do anything crazy."

He'd hung up, thinking about the other members of OWAC, picturing each of their faces and telling himself that none of them were good enough to paint such a perfect forgery.

He'd tried to call Rock back, but the number had gone to voice mail. "This is Taylor West. Call me. We really need to talk. If that painting is what I think it is… Call me." He'd disconnected, wondering where Rock was. Or if he just wasn't taking his calls after the first one. Which would make Rock look pretty suspicious, wouldn't it?

Now he took a long drink, admitting that he never should have trusted Rock. Rock wasn't that much different from H. F. Powell when it came to women. Now Rock was in trouble because of another woman. In the middle of an ugly divorce, he was probably desperate for money. But how far would he go?

Taylor knew his suspicion of Rock could also be because Rock had always been jealous of him—especially when Taylor had married Jade.

Jade. Where was his beautiful young wife? She'd probably gone to her mother's back in Indiana. He shoved the thought of her away as he took another drink. He had a lot more to worry about than Jade.

"THE HOUSE IS YOURS," McKenzie announced when Laramie stopped by her office after getting his rental SUV pulled out of the snowbank. He was still shaken, but even more determined to get to the bottom of whatever was going on.

"And the painting?" he asked expectantly. He told himself he couldn't be sure which was original and without it, he might never know.

She chuckled. "Yours, as well. He wanted extra for it, but I convinced him that you wanted pretty much everything in the house except, of course, any items that he couldn't possibly part with. If you don't want the furniture, I know a consignment place—"

"No, furnished is perfect. So what is he leaving?"

"Everything, including the kitchen sink, except for the other paintings and sculptures. He has an art dealer coming to take the lot of them this afternoon."

Laramie couldn't hide his relief. He wasn't sure why the painting was so important. But what had happened after he'd left Taylor West's house had him convinced the painting was at the heart of it. He thought about the house—where he'd seen his alleged cat burglar. "How soon can I take occupancy?"

"Right away, I suppose, if you're in that much of a hurry."

He'd been staying with Hayes and McKenzie and didn't want to hurt her feelings. "No hurry, just anxious to get settled."

"I can understand that. Since the house will come completely furnished, there won't be much that you will need. He's leaving bedding, all of which he said is brand-new. Apparently they haven't gotten to use this house much. I take it that his soon-to-be-ex wife didn't like it up here. Too isolated. Since you're paying cash, I can arrange a rental agreement until the sale is final. You should be able to move in this evening. The owner is in a hurry to get out of town."

"Great."

"But this…urgency to get settled, it wouldn't have anything to do with your…cat burglar, would it?"

Laramie smiled to himself. "You sound like Austin. I ran into him earlier at the restaurant. Like I told him, I know what I'm doing." He wished that was true.

But he didn't think the earlier incident was an attempt to kill him. Then what had it been? If the driver had wanted to scare him off, then he'd failed. Laramie was more determined than ever. He was counting on his cat burglar coming back for the painting. It was just a gut feeling, but a strong one, that for some reason she really needed that painting. And he really needed answers.

He stood to leave.

"Don't forget this," McKenzie said, reaching behind her. She handed him what Theo Nelson believed to be the original painting.

He stared at it, anxious to compare it to the one in his rented SUV. "Question, if I wanted everyone to know I'd bought the house, how would I go about getting the word out?"

McKenzie laughed. "In a small community like Big Sky? Are you kidding? Everyone knows everyone else's business. It's probably already out there since the owner informed me to go ahead and change the security information to yours. You'll need to change over the utilities and everything else as soon as you get into the house. But if you were to stop by the furniture store or the grocery and happen to mention you'd bought a house…"

"Let me know when you have my key, and thank you so much. Oh, and one more thing. Have you ever heard of an artist by the name of H. F. Powell?"

"Of course. In fact, one of his paintings is coming up for auction at the Christmas ball this year. It's expected to go high. This interest in cowboy art…"

"Just curiosity."

She laughed. "Uh-huh."

Laramie realized how little he knew about art in general as he left for Meadow Village. His plan was to do exactly what McKenzie had suggested. He had a feeling that his cat burglar kept her ear to the ground. How else had she known that the house was supposed to be empty last night?

CHAPTER SIX

SID RUBBED HER BACK. It ached from hours spent painting. She hadn't realized how long she'd been working. When she painted, time flew by. She hadn't even noticed that her back was aching until a few moments ago when she finally laid down her brush.

She also realized she was hungry. Going to the fridge, she peered in. She'd bought the basics at the store, but nothing appealed to her. The pulled pork barbecue sandwich came to mind. Why not go back there? Several good reasons came to her. Except once she thought of barbecue, nothing else would do.

This late in the evening, Texas Boys Barbecue was quiet. Only a few booths were taken. She slipped into one and was thankful when a different waitress came out with a menu.

"We have a special, if you're interested," the young woman said. She rattled off a variety of items, but all Sid keyed in on was the words *ribs*. Her stomach growled.

"I'll take the baby-back rib special." She started to say "to go" but stopped herself. "And a beer." As she started to whip out her ID, she realized the waitress wasn't even going to ask for it. With relief, she put it away, sat back and took in the place in a way she hadn't done earlier. It was nicely done. Comfortable and homey but without kitschy knickknacks. The atmosphere was warm and welcoming and the smells coming out of the kitchen were making her mouth water.

It felt good to be out of her cabin. She sat back, relaxing—until she heard voices in the kitchen as the waitress brought out her beer. Taking a sip, she watched the back, hoping to get another look at Laramie Cardwell. From where she sat, she could hear the conversation. This time there were three men, all of them speaking with a Texas drawl. But no Laramie.

"So he got the house?"

"He's moving in tonight."

"What was the rush?"

"Apparently he's anxious to get settled."

"I hope that's all it is."

"Bet Dana is already planning a housewarming."

Laughter before the three left.

Laramie was moving into the house *tonight*?

So Tara's information had been right, not that she'd doubted it. Sid thought about Laramie showing up so late the night before at the Nelson house on the side of the mountain. He'd only been interested in the house, but he'd stumbled onto her. Just her luck.

"I'm sorry," Sid said, getting the waitress's attention. "But could I have that order to go?"

Laramie was at the grocery store when McKenzie called to say she had the key to the house. "Do you want to meet at the house?"

"Sounds great. I'm picking up a few things. I can meet you there in thirty minutes."

He quickly got what he needed and headed for the checkout. In a matter of minutes he would have the key to his house. He owned a high-rise condo in Houston, but he had never been this excited about the purchase even though the condo had an amazing view of the city.

The house was perfect for him since he didn't plan to spend that much time in Montana. But he needed his own place when he did. If anything, he thought he might spend more time here—during the summer months.

Would he love the house as much if his cat burglar didn't come back for the painting? He pushed that thought away, telling himself he was in the market for a house long before he'd laid eyes on the dark-clad figure running along the rooftop. Long before the kiss.

At the checkout, he was impatient to get into the house. He had to wait in line behind a half dozen people and wished now that he hadn't bothered. Glancing around, he studied the other people in the line. The tourists were easy to spot in the latest ski gear or after-ski wear.

Out of the corner of his eye, he noticed a bulletin board. Dana had mentioned that there were always people looking for housecleaning jobs around Big Sky, if he needed help.

A poster with cowboy art on it caught his eye. A name jumped out at him. H. F. Powell. Leaving his basket to save his place in line, Laramie quickly stepped to the board. Western Art Exhibit at the Museum of the Rockies in Bozeman. H. F. Powell was one of the artists featured in what the poster said was a rare exhibit of the Western masters.

Hurriedly, he searched the poster for the date, fearing he had missed the exhibit. With relief, he saw that it opened tomorrow. Until today, he'd never heard of

H. F. Powell. Now he was curious about the man and his work given that Taylor West swore he was the only man who could have duplicated his work so perfectly.

His cat burglar had certainly piqued his interest in Old West art, he thought. After he checked out, he put his groceries in his SUV and walked up the hill to the restaurant for his dinner. The special tonight at Texas Boys Barbecue was ribs so the cook had saved him a slab along with sides.

As he entered the back door, he breathed in the smell of the food, still amazed that his and his brothers' love for barbecue had led to their Texas Boys Barbecue success. None of them ever had to work another day in their lives, but of course they all did have some job because that was the way they were raised. As promised, the cook had his dinner wrapped and ready to take home to his new house.

It was on his way out that he saw a woman as she came out of the front of the restaurant and climbed into a blue SUV.

The woman caught his eye because of the way she moved. No wasted motion, her steps so fluid—and familiar—as she hurried toward her vehicle. He stood there watching her get into the SUV, feeling like a man who'd just seen a ghost.

A thick, long curly mane of strawberry blond hair hung around her shoulders, catching the last of the day's light and making it shine like copper. He held his breath as he watched her slide behind the wheel. The engine revved. She seemed to be in a hurry to get somewhere. Just like that night.

It was her.

All common sense told him that he couldn't possibly have recognized her simply by the way that she moved. There must be dozens of slim young women like her in the area. And yet...

He looked down the hillside to where he'd left his vehicle as she backed up and sped off up the road toward the mountain. There was no way he could reach his vehicle in time. All he could do was watch her get away.

Which was good, he realized. His first impulse had been to go after her. And then what? If only he had been close enough to see her eyes. And those lips. He told himself that if he saw those again, he'd know for certain.

He was thankful he hadn't gone after her and made a fool of himself. He could just imagine what his four brothers would say if he shared this "sighting" with them.

"You need a woman," Tag would say. "Stalking is illegal," Hayes would warn him. "Get a grip," Austin would say. "I agree with Tag. You need a woman bad," Jackson would add.

As the blue SUV disappeared over a rise, he thought they would have been right. What was going on with him? This wasn't like him. He always thought things out before he reacted. And yet last night, he'd gone after what he believed to be a thief without any thought to the risk.

And now he'd almost chased that woman down, and yet what were the chances she was the same woman? Big Sky wasn't a large community. If McKenzie was right, then the woman might already know who he was. If that had been her... Would she dare go to Texas Boys Barbecue if she knew who he was, though?

He thought of the woman, of those silver-blue eyes, of those bee-stung lips, thought of how she'd tricked him and gotten away. Yes, she would go to the restaurant he and his brothers owned. The woman was a risk taker.

That thought sent a current of excitement through him.

What if she had gone there looking for *him* because she needed to get her hands on the painting—just as he'd suspected?

Laramie went back inside Texas Boys Barbecue. It only took a minute to find the young waitress who'd served the woman. "She didn't happen to use a check or credit card to pay for her dinner, did she?" he asked, crossing his fingers.

"Cash."

He couldn't hide his disappointment.

"Is there a problem?" the waitress asked.

"No, I was just hoping to get her name."

The teen laughed. "All you had to do was ask. I *know* her. That is, I've seen her at the craft shows. Her name is Obsidian Forester, but she goes by Sid for short."

"Obsidian." He nodded, silently cheered. He had her name. "Wait, you said craft shows?"

"Yeah, she's one of the exhibitors like me. I make candles and sell them. It's just something I like to do in my spare time since I like crafting."

"What does…Sid sell?"

"She paints scenes on stuff like handsaws, milk jugs, anything that is kind of old and rusted."

He couldn't help the thrill that moved through him.

Maybe that really had been her. "So she's an artist," he said more to himself.

"I think she's wasting her talent painting on old junk." The teen shrugged. "But what do I know? People seem to like what she does. She sells more of those paintings than I do candles."

"You don't happen to know where she lives, do you?"

As Sid drove home, she told herself not to let the Texas cowboy rush her. But she could feel the clock ticking. Any good thief knew not to play against the odds. She'd been lucky, but lately she'd been seen. Then last night, almost caught.

Once at the cabin, she ate her ribs. It was already dark. This time of year in the canyon it was pitch-black by five. The ribs were as good or even better than the pulled pork. She licked her fingers after finishing the last one, then cleaned up the kitchen and herself before dressing in all black. Picking up the black ski mask, she headed for her snowmobile.

The next house on her list wasn't far from her cabin, but she took the long way. The owners were spending the holidays in Hawaii. At least that was the intel she'd gotten on them. It would be easy to find out if it was true. The couple drove a huge ivory SUV and left it in the drive when they were there.

For months, she'd done endless research on the houses she planned to hit and the people who owned them. This one was owned by an older couple. He'd been a pilot, she a homemaker. The house was modest by Big Sky standards.

Sid had met both of them at the local art shows. She

often struck up conversations, especially with people who had a piece of art she was interested in. Art lovers were quick to talk about the artists they liked. It hadn't been easy to find the owners of the pieces she still needed, but she'd finally tracked them all down.

As she came over a rise, she saw the house. It loomed up out of the darkness. No lights on inside. No large SUV in the drive. The couple kept it in the garage for the next time they flew in.

She killed the engine on the snowmobile some distance from the house. There were no other homes around, one of the benefits of this affluent community. No one wanted neighbors. At least not ones they could see from their houses.

The snow was deep on this side of the mountain. She'd brought snowshoes for the last part of the hike up to the house. Strapping them on, she grabbed her canvas bag and started up the mountain. The moon had come up and now poured silver over the snowy landscape.

Sid could see her breath. The house sat on the side of a mountain at about six thousand feet above sea level. She stopped to catch her breath and look back down the mountain to where she'd left her snowmobile. Nothing moved in the darkness of the pines.

Ahead, moonlight shone a path to the house. Sid listened. Hearing nothing but her own breath, she headed for the house.

In and out. She set her watch. Five minutes. Then she slipped in through the back door that had been unlocked for her by Maisie at the precise time. She knew exactly where the painting she needed would be hanging and, turning on her penlight, headed right for it.

The exchange didn't take more than a few seconds. She put the painting into the large canvas bag, remembering the night before when the other bag she'd used had a hole in it. Another mistake. She was getting sloppy. Not because of overconfidence, she told herself. No, it was that she'd done this so many times it was becoming routine.

She thought of Laramie Cardwell as she locked the door behind her, texted Maisie "Lunch tomorrow?"— their code—and headed for her snowmobile. As she drove the snowmobile toward her cabin, she realized that once she had the painting she'd lost last night, she'd be done with these kinds of night jobs.

It filled her with a strange nostalgia. She'd been at this for several years now. When she'd started, she had questioned her sanity. Why do this when it could go so badly if she were caught?

Last night that had almost happened. Unfortunately, it wasn't in her nature to leave anything undone—even if she *hadn't* needed the painting to finish what she'd started. She would get that painting back and end this once and for all.

"So what do you think?" McKenzie asked as Laramie used his key to enter his new house.

"I love it," he said as he stepped in and took a deep breath. Through the wall of windows at the front of the house Lone Mountain glistened in the twilight.

"From what I can tell, he left everything but the artwork—other than the one you bought," she said. He looked around, realizing he would have to get more art for the walls, especially with these high ceilings. Walking through the house, he didn't see much that he would change. Theo Nelson's decorator had done a grand job of furnishing the house.

"He even left dishes, flatware and stemware," McKenzie said shaking her head. "He must not have been very attached to the house." She sighed. "There is a used furniture shop down the valley that we call the Second-Wife's Club. Most of it comes from Big Sky. New wife, all new furnishings. You can get some great deals, if you're interested."

Laramie shook his head. "I can't imagine anything more that I would want or need. It is clear that Theo and his wife didn't spend much time here. Everything looks brand-new. I expect to see the price tags still on everything. Let me get some things from the car and then let's take a look upstairs."

The second floor looked the same except for the study. Theo's computer was gone, but that seemed to be the only change. "He didn't even take any of the books on the shelves," McKenzie commented.

In the bedrooms, the beds were still made up with new linens, down comforters and expensive duvets, she noted. "He left all the linens in the bathrooms and the closets for the entire house."

Laramie glanced around and then headed for the stairs to the master bedroom with the two paintings he had acquired. The room looked much the same, save the spot on the wall where the Taylor West had hung. He took the painting he'd purchased from Theo Nelson and hung it back where it had been. On the wall next to it, he hung the one his cat burglar had dropped.

He turned on the small spotlights that shone on the paintings and stood studying the two, still unable to find anything to distinguish either of them.

"I'm glad you like the painting," McKenzie said, joining him. "I could have gotten the price of the house down another twenty grand without it."

He chuckled. "According to the artist, the original is worth fifty. Your art expert offered me thirty thousand for the one I acquired from my mysterious alleged thief."

She let out a low whistle. "Wow, so you got a deal on both of them. That makes me feel better. But I get the impression you would have paid even more for it and the house."

Laramie smiled. "You did great, McKenzie. I can't thank you enough."

"But which painting is the real McCoy?"

"That is the question, isn't it?" he said. "Meanwhile, I love the house." He walked over to the wall of windows. In the darkness of the winter night, the snow-covered Lone Mountain looked ghostlike.

He stood, admiring his view and wondering when his cat burglar would be back. *If* she would be back. He thought of Obsidian "Sid" Forester and wondered how he could make sure they crossed paths if she didn't come back.

Logic, something he'd always prided himself on, reminded him that he couldn't be sure Sid was his cat burglar.

"Not yet," he said to himself as he looked out at the Montana winter night. But all his instincts told him he'd already found her. Now it was just a matter of catching her in the act.

CHAPTER SEVEN

THE NEXT MORNING, after a rough night, Taylor West woke up hungover and upset. He hadn't gotten a moment's sound sleep last night, worrying that he'd been betrayed. Worse if the truth came out…

He picked up his cell phone and saw that it had been turned off. He had four calls from Cody Kent. He listened to the voice messages, then returned the man's call.

Clearly either Rock or Hank had called him—or they both had. And they'd both pretended to him that there was nothing to be worried about. He swore as he tapped in Cody's number.

"What's this about some forgery?" Cody demanded, sounding both angry and worried. Cody related that he'd been by the gallery yesterday and had run into a man with one of Taylor's paintings.

"Laramie Cardwell. I know. He came by my house."

"Was…it…*the*…original?" Cody asked.

"I don't know."

"What do you mean you don't know?"

"I would swear it was."

"So the other one is a forgery. Have you seen it?"

"I know what you're getting at," Taylor said. "The other one has to be a forgery, right? And anyone could have painted it."

Cody agreed. "So stop getting everyone all riled up over nothing."

"You're right." Still Taylor had a bad feeling about this.

"You'll let me know if there is a reason to worry, right?"

"Of course." He hung up and tried Rock's number. It went straight to voice mail. Where the hell was Rock? He'd gotten off the line so quickly yesterday…

Taylor felt sweat break out under his arms even though his house was cold this morning because he hadn't bothered to turn up the heat.

He'd had a long night to think about it. If anyone had betrayed them, it would be Rock.

LARAMIE HADN'T SLEPT well the first night in his new home. There was nothing wrong with the bed, the Egyptian cotton sheets or the house's ambiance. Still, he'd had trouble getting to sleep. Even after he'd dozed off, he'd awakened often thinking he'd heard something. All night he'd lain in the king-size bed, listening and waiting for the woman to return and thinking about the vehicle that had tried to put him in the river yesterday.

The incident had to have something to do with the painting, right? Which meant it had something to do with the cat burglar. What, though?

Before going to bed, he'd had a thought. Taking out his pocket knife, he'd carefully scratched a very small mark on the back of the canvas on the painting he'd purchased with the house.

He was sure she'd come back for one—or both—of the paintings. He figured if he ever saw them again after that, he'd know which was which. And if she only took one, he'd know which one she'd left behind. He was pretty sure she knew which one was the real one.

With that, he'd turned out the lights and gone to bed. When he'd opened his eyes this morning, he'd half expected to see the paintings gone. He wouldn't have been surprised if she'd sneaked in and taken them both.

But upon waking, he was almost disappointed to see both paintings right where they'd been when he'd gone to bed. She hadn't come for either one. What if he was wrong and she wouldn't be back?

His phone rang. Seeing it was from the marshal, he quickly took the call. "Do you have some news for me?" he said without preamble.

"Yesterday you asked me to check on vehicles owned by Taylor West," Hud said.

"Right. And you told me he didn't own a large brown car."

"No, he doesn't. But his wife, Jade, does. I got to thinking and checked to see if there were other vehicles that might be registered to someone other than Taylor."

"His wife?" Laramie remembered the photograph he'd seen of the pretty young blonde.

"I've put a BOLO out on it," Hud said. "We could get lucky. But why would Jade West—or someone using her vehicle—want to run you off the road?"

Laramie hung up convinced that it had something to do with the painting, but what, he had no idea. As he headed for the shower, he wondered if Obsidian Forester was indeed his cat burglar. The only way he'd know for sure was if she came back for the painting. He realized how much he was counting on it.

Showered and dressed, he went downstairs. He'd

just poured himself a bowl of cereal that he'd bought at the store yesterday when the security company he'd called rang his doorbell.

Theo Nelson had a security system but it hadn't gone off the night Laramie had seen the woman on the roofline. Which meant that the woman had disarmed the alarm before entering the house or she had outsmarted the system.

So he wasn't going to bother adding more security. All he wanted were cameras, and nowadays they made such small ones, she wouldn't know she was being captured on video.

He glanced at his watch. He needed to know more about cowboy art. McKenzie had handled everything including changing over the utilities and contacting the alarm company for him. Leaving the security people to do their work, he drove to Bozeman to the Museum of the Rockies. It was another beautiful winter day, not a cloud in the sky, the blazing sun bright on the snow.

He found himself watching his rearview mirror, looking for the large dark car that had run his off the highway the day before. But by the time he reached Bozeman, he hadn't seen it.

Parking near Montana State University, he entered the museum. While known for its dinosaur collection, the museum also held a variety of other exhibits throughout the year, according to the clerk who took his money, stamped his hand in case he wanted to come back later and handed him a map.

Since the museum had just opened for the day, there were only a handful of people in the new exhibit featuring Old West master artists. There were paintings by both Charles M. Russell and Frederic Remington, two well-known Old West artists from the 1800s.

They had apparently painted what they saw around them, capturing a lifestyle that they romanticized with their art. While four-wheelers had replaced horses at a lot of ranches, his cousin had told him, the cowboy life survived even to this day out here in the West.

Laramie had just stepped into an adjoining exhibition room when he saw a young woman standing in front of a large painting of a Native American chief in full headdress.

It was the same woman he'd seen coming out of Texas Boys Barbecue yesterday. Obsidian "Sid" Forester.

At seeing the woman again, his pulse jumped as excitement raced through his veins. He reminded himself that she was an artist in her own right, so of course she would be here. That didn't make her guilty of being the cat burglar.

She wore jeans and a canvas jacket over a rust-colored sweater. Her coppery hair was tucked up under a Cubs baseball cap, which pitched her face into shadow, making it impossible to see the color of her eyes at this distance. Nor could he get a good look at her mouth. But even in silhouette he could tell that her lips were full.

He remembered the taste of her mouth and felt an ache that had nothing to do with cowboy art. His reasons for wanting to find this woman had gotten all tangled up with a desire to kiss her again. He knew it was crazy and could just imagine what his brothers would say. But he couldn't wait to get his hands on her as if to assure himself that she was actually real. That what she evoked in him that night was real, as well.

Warning himself to take it slow, he moved closer. As if sensing him staring at her, she looked in his direction, then quickly turned away. He felt a start. Was it possible? He wouldn't know until he got a better look, but all his instincts told him he had her.

It didn't take Taylor West long to drive to Gallatin Gateway, a small, almost forgotten town at the mouth of the canyon. Once billed as the Gateway to Yellowstone, the town back then had a train that brought tourists to the beautiful large hotel, before ferrying them into the park.

Rock Jackson owned a small ranch against the foothills overlooking the Gallatin River. The place was run-down, the house small and old with some outbuildings behind it, including Rock's studio.

As Taylor pulled up and got out, he thought he saw movement at one of the front windows. But when he knocked hard at the front door, there was no answer from within.

"He probably saw me and doesn't want to deal with me," Taylor told himself. The drive had sobered him up since he'd been drinking before he'd left home. He hated that the drive might have been for nothing, until he reminded himself that he needed to go to a liquor store anyway.

He pounded again. Still no answer. Moving to peer into a front window, he saw that the place was neat and orderly inside. That made him all the more angry since his own house was a mess. Somehow that convinced him even more that Rock Jackson was guilty of something.

Walking around the side of the house, Taylor noticed Rock's art studio. Was he back there working? Raging inside, now positive that Rock had betrayed him, he stormed toward it. This time, he didn't bother to knock. He grabbed the door handle and turned it. Locked.

Cursing, Taylor cupped his hands against one of the windows. The studio was exactly like something he'd always talked about building on his property. He could see only one painting from where he stood. It appeared to be one of Rock's in progress.

As he started to turn away, he saw that there was another room behind the studio. When he got around back, the door into that part of the building had a padlock on it. That alone seemed suspicious.

He picked up a rock and tried to break the padlock but, failing, tossed the rock away and swore. The mellow he'd had earlier was starting to wear off along with the booze, leaving him with a headache and a worse mood. Furious, he stood outside the studio feeling as alone as he'd ever felt. The temperature had dropped with the appearance of clouds obscuring the sun. He shivered and looked around, not sure what to do then.

He could smell snow on the freezing air and wondered why he hadn't gone south this winter. Jade had wanted to go, but he hadn't wanted to make the long drive to Arizona. Now he wished he had. Laramie Cardwell wouldn't have been able to find him and he wouldn't have known about the painting.

Taylor knew that kind of thinking was crazy. Even if he'd been in Arizona, the painting would have surfaced. He'd seen it with his own eyes. He knew what that meant.

Behind him, he spotted an old barn on the property and walked toward it, thinking he'd look around and wait for Rock to return, since he now realized there was no vehicle here. He didn't want to have to drive all this way again if he could help it.

He pushed open the barn door and stepped into the dim darkness. It took a moment for his eyes to adjust, but he didn't mind. It was warmer in here and with the booze wearing off...

Taylor blinked as a large dark object in the barn took shape before him. At first he couldn't believe what he was seeing. He thought for sure it must have been the beginning of a hangover making him only imagine it.

But there was no doubt. The question was what was his wife's car doing in Rock Jackson's barn?

SID TRIED TO calm her racing heart. Her mind raced, as well. What was Laramie Cardwell doing here? Her first impulse was to flee, but that would be the worst thing she could do. Seeing him here had been so unexpected. She hadn't been prepared. That's why her pulse thrummed and skin prickled at the memory of his touch.

Why *was* he here? Maybe he was simply interested in cowboy art. She groaned silently as she moved from painting to painting, aware of him tracing her steps like a wolf on the scent of its prey.

Wasn't it possible that his interest in cowboy art had been sparked by the painting she'd dropped and nothing more? Which meant he hadn't forgotten about the painting any more than she had.

Was he here trying to find out more about the painting? Or was he looking for her? Her heart took off like a wild horse running in the wind. Was it possible he'd followed her? That thought turned her blood to ice.

Sid prided herself on her quick thinking when cornered—thus the kiss that had gotten her freedom two nights ago. But she was too aware of him—and vice versa. Good sense told her to leave, but she would have to walk right past him. Also, it might call more attention to her.

Even if she was right and this had something to do with the painting she'd dropped... Even if he was looking for her... He didn't know the importance of the painting in his possession any more than he could prove she was the woman he'd tackled that night.

Telling herself to play it cool, she forced herself to relax. She was safe and she had to admit, she was curious about the Texas cowboy. Wouldn't it be to her benefit to learn as much about him as she could? After all, she needed that painting.

As she moved through the exhibit, taking her time looking at each painting, she studied Laramie every chance she got out of the corner of her eye. He was taller than her few stolen glimpses of him had led her to believe. And since he was the business end of the Texas Boys Barbecue empire, she would have expected him to be some computer geek. But the man who'd tackled her had been anything but.

His dark hair was longer than she first thought. Was that designer stubble on his jaw? She smiled to herself, thinking that she might be wrong about him. He might not be as straitlaced and uptight as she'd thought at their first encounter. Either that or he'd loosened up since then.

Laramie moved slowly, studying each painting, stopping longest, she noticed, at an H. F. Powell painting of a cattle drive. The painting was beautiful, a masterpiece. Even someone without an artist's eye would see that.

He seemed so intent that she hadn't realized she'd been caught staring until he turned suddenly in her direction. She quickly swung back to the painting she had been pretending to examine. The intensity of his look had rattled her again. Could she be wrong about him not knowing who she was?

Just as she started to move away, he stepped up beside her.

"I know nothing about this kind of art," he said in his Southern drawl. "Do you really have to be a cowboy to paint it?"

She didn't look at him. "Sorry, but I wouldn't know. I'm not a fan of cowboy art."

"Really?" He sounded surprised. "And yet here you are." She could feel all of his attention on her. "So you just wandered in here like me?"

"It would seem so," she said, and quickly looked at her watch.

"Take this, for example," he said, clearly ignoring her subtle attempt to escape. "Is the idea to portray the life of the cowboy? Or romanticize it because these guys look too happy when you know they have to be freezing?"

Sid looked at the painting of cowboys standing around a campfire drinking coffee from tin cups as cattle milled in the background and snow began to fall. He was right. She couldn't help but smile.

Just as she couldn't help looking over at him.

He seemed startled for a moment as he met her gaze. Then his eyes shifted slowly to her mouth. She fought the urge to lick her lips as she recalled his mouth on hers. His gaze returned to hers. She tried not to shiver.

"I know this sounds corny," he drawled, "but I feel as if we've met somewhere before."

She did her best not to react to his words. "If that's your best pickup line—"

He snapped his fingers as if it had only just come to him. "Texas Boys Barbecue. I saw you coming out of there yesterday." While his intent gaze was still probing, his smile was all sincerity. "I'm betting you had the rib special. Tell me I'm right."

She tried to relax. "So you're a betting man?"

He laughed. "Not usually, but then again I'm a long way from home and out of my element. Right now I'm betting that if you agreed to have a cup of coffee with me, it would make this Texas boy feel more at home this far north."

She laughed, as well. "You seem very much at home to me."

"Laramie Cardwell," he said and extended his hand.

Sid felt she had no choice but to shake it. Her hand disappeared into his large, warm, suntanned one. She tried not to react to the jolt she felt. "Obsidian Forester."

"Obsidian? What a beautiful and unusual name."

"That's why I go by Sid."

"Well, Sid, I hope you take me up on the cup of coffee. I haven't met many people since I've been here."

She was tempted, which surprised her. Playing with

fire was one thing. Stepping into a blazing furnace was another. Still, he had no way of knowing—let alone proving—that she'd been the woman whose path he'd crossed that night. And if he did suspect, what better way to prove him wrong than by taking him up on his invitation?

Not to mention, he had the painting she needed. Maybe there was another way to get it, other than stealing it outright. Anyway, what would it hurt to have one cup of coffee with him?

CHAPTER EIGHT

VIOLET. IT WAS the color of her eyes. But Laramie realized as they walked the block to the coffee shop that her eyes changed colors in different light. No wonder he hadn't been sure that first night.

But there was no mistaking the lips. They were bow-shaped, wide and full, and a delicate shade of pink today. He'd remembered the feel of them against his the moment he saw them. Crazily, what he'd wanted more than anything right there in the museum was a repeat kiss. He couldn't be sure, with everything that had been happening that night, exactly what he'd felt when she'd kissed him. It had happened too fast. But the next time she kissed him…

Where had these thoughts come from? He reminded himself that she was a *thief.* His plan was to catch her. The chance of there being another kiss was beyond remote.

He was still surprised that she'd agreed to have coffee with him. He'd worried that he'd come on too strong. He'd never been like his brothers, who seemed to all have a way with women. He was more reserved. More cautious, usually. While he'd done his fair share of dating, he'd never met a woman he'd been serious about.

He figured he knew less about women than he did

cowboy art, which was saying a lot. So he felt he was out of his league if Obsidian "Sid" Forester was who he believed she was.

"So fess up," he said once they were seated in a small coffee shop a block from the museum. "You did have the ribs, didn't you?"

She had a nice laugh. An amazing smile. The woman was striking from her coppery hair to her heart-shaped face and the row of freckles that graced her cheeks. But it was her eyes that fascinated him. They'd been violet, but now in the winter light coming in from the coffee shop window, they were almost silver. Like a wolf's, he thought. Silver like they'd been in the moonlight the night they'd met.

"You caught me," she said. "I had the ribs. They were wonderful, but I guess I don't have to tell *you* that. I'm betting you're one of the Texas boys."

"Yep. My four bothers and me," he said, figuring she probably already knew that if she'd looked at their story on the back of the restaurant menu. Wouldn't only an innocent woman go to the barbecue restaurant after his encounter with the cat burglar?

No, he thought. This woman was gutsy. She'd go there almost as a dare.

"Barbecue was the only thing we knew, so we started cooking out behind a small house we turned into a restaurant in Houston." He shrugged. "The business just kind of took off."

"What brought you to Montana?" she asked and took a sip of her coffee. He could feel her watching him over the rim of her cup and wondered what game they were playing. She was definitely his cat burglar. He'd stake his life on it. The thought made him think of the car that had run him off the highway. If he didn't stop this, what would happen next?

Laramie knew he should be worried about that. But there was no way he was backing off. "My brothers and I were all born here in Montana. When my parents divorced, Mom took us to Texas where she had relatives. My dad still lives near Big Sky, so one after another my brothers have returned, and each has fallen in love with Montana and a woman… Opening a restaurant up here seemed like a good idea."

"It appears to be doing well. I heard you were opening another one in Red Lodge."

He smiled, nodding. "I handle the business end of it, so it's one reason I'm here, along with wanting to spend time with my family over the holidays."

"So you aren't staying?" she asked and took another sip of her coffee.

"As a matter of fact, I bought a house yesterday partway up the mountain."

"Really?" She didn't sound that surprised. "So you're planning to move up here?"

He shook his head. "I'll only spend part of the year here like most of the residents, it seems. I still own a condo in Houston and operate things from there."

She nodded.

"So tell me about *you*," he said.

Sid shrugged. "Not much to tell."

"Come on, I just told you my entire life story." He took a sip of coffee and asked, "You live in Big Sky?" She nodded. "What do you do there?"

Her silver-blue eyes met his. "I paint." Her full mouth quirked into an amused grin.

"Paint?" He pretended to be surprised. "You're an *artist*? Or do you paint houses?"

She smiled as she shook her head. "I'm more of a hobby-craft person. I paint Montana scenes on old rusty things I find like saw blades and old milk cans. I definitely wouldn't consider myself an artist."

"That explains what you were doing at the exhibit," he said studying her. "You really like cowboy art."

"I admire the artists, but cowboy art isn't my cup of tea, trust me."

"What is?" he asked.

The question seemed to surprise her as if no one had ever asked her that before. Maybe that was why it took her a moment. Or, he thought, maybe it took her a moment to come up with a lie. "Abstract. I like lots of color. I prefer impressionism over realism when I paint."

"My sister-in-law McKenzie would love one of your pieces, then." He studied her. She seemed to be relaxed, but he felt a tension just under the surface. He could feel it buzzing like a live wire between them. "I'd like to see your work sometime."

She said nothing as she finished her coffee and looked again at her watch. "I really need to go."

Laramie mentally kicked himself, but he'd never been patient when he wanted something badly. He pushed his coffee aside and stood as she rose. "It's been a pleasure meeting you. I do hope our paths cross again."

"Maybe they will," she said. He could smell the citrus scent of her morning shower. "Enjoy your new house."

"Speaking of my new house... I am in desperate

need of artwork. The ceilings are ten to twelve foot throughout. I have only one painting I'm partial to, but nothing else. With all these walls to fill, I need help. I sure would appreciate it if you could advise me." She started to decline. "Come on, who better than an artist who loves color to help me?"

DON'T DO IT. Sid met the handsome Texas cowboy's gaze. He'd just told her he had only one painting. She didn't have to guess which one that was.

"I doubt we like the same things," she said.

"You might be surprised," he drawled. "I'd love to show you my house whenever you can come by."

"There are plenty of designers around who could advise you on artwork. I'm not the person you want."

"Oh, I suspect you are exactly the person I'm looking for."

She looked at him, wondering how true that was.

"I have a confession," he said leaning toward her. "I have no artistic talent. I'm betting you have a better eye for art than you think. I'd love to see what you come up with."

Was he trying to tell her that he knew who she was? Or that he at least suspected? Or was he hitting on her? That thought almost made her laugh. Wouldn't that be her luck? A good-looking Texas cowboy interested in her and she had to avoid him for obvious reasons.

"You might not like what I come up with," she challenged.

He seemed to study her. "I think I might surprise you."

She feared that was definitely what might happen.

He walked her back to the museum where they'd

left their vehicles. A brief thaw had left the streets of Bozeman bare, but there was still plenty of snow in the mountains. Laramie commented on how beautiful it was.

"So do you ski?" he asked as they neared the museum parking lot.

"No." Sid wondered why she'd lied. But then again she was lying just being with this man.

"Snowboard?"

She shook her head.

"You must do something to enjoy winter since you live in Big Sky. Snowmobile?"

He had stopped beside a white SUV. She assumed it was the same one she'd seen the night he caught her leaving Theo Nelson's house with the painting.

"I hate how loud snowmobiles are," she said truthfully and mugged a face. "They ruin the winter quiet, don't you think?"

Laramie smiled at that. "But they seem to be a necessity if you're going to get around in the mountains in the winter and want to avoid the roads."

She looked away. She could feel her heart thundering in her chest. Oh, yes, he suspected her all right. "Don't you ski?"

He laughed at that. "I'm a Texas boy. I doubt I'll be staying here long enough in the winter to learn. But my cousin has invited me to do some horseback riding on her ranch. Do you ride?"

She thought of the horses she'd loved when she was younger and the many hours she'd spent in the saddle. Surprisingly, she hadn't realized how much she missed it until that moment.

"I love to ride." The words were out before she could bite her tongue.

Laramie's eyes brightened. "Then we have to go for a ride. When are you free?"

"With the holidays and all…"

"I'm staying until after the holiday masquerade ball that I'm told by my cousin Dana I can't possibly miss." He eyed her openly. "You don't happen to be going?"

She shook her head. "I wouldn't be caught dead there." And this time bit her tongue.

He laughed again. "I feel the same way, but my cousin is very persuasive. Listen, I'm serious about that horseback ride and about your help with artwork for the house."

"Speaking of being very *persuasive*." Their eyes locked for a moment and she felt a warning chill sprint up her back. *Be careful.* This was not a cowboy to fool with. Admittedly, he definitely had his appeal. She recalled the jolt she'd felt when she'd shaken his hand, not to mention the strange reaction to the kiss. "I'll think about both."

"Do that. This is mine," he said motioning to the SUV. "It was nice meeting you, Sid. Oh, I should tell you where I live in case you take me up on my offer. It's the three-story one off Lone Mountain Trail. You probably know it, right?" His gaze met hers and held it. She felt a shiver wind its way up her spine. One minute she was convinced he was hitting on her and the next she was positive again that he knew exactly who she was and was setting her up. "Why don't I give you my phone number in case you can't find it."

"I'll find it," she said as she turned and walked away, mentally kicking herself for this cat-and-mouse game she was playing since she was the mouse and the cat was a much craftier adversary than she'd first thought.

As she climbed into her vehicle, she warned herself to let it go. But that meant letting the painting go. She couldn't do that, she thought with a curse. And Laramie Cardwell was practically daring her to come steal it.

"WHAT IS GOING ON with you?" his brother Austin demanded when he showed up at Laramie's door later that afternoon.

He gave him a confused look. "I bought a house?" Motioning his brother in, he headed for the kitchen.

"*This* house?" Austin said from behind him as he closed the door and followed him. "The house where you saw what you believe was a cat burglar? I know what you're doing and I don't like it."

Laramie laughed. "You're the one who encouraged me to buy a house up here." He opened the refrigerator and offered his brother a beer.

Austin declined with a shake of his head. "I'm not talking about the house and you know it. Hud told me that someone ran you off the highway."

"Just some crazy driver," Laramie said, wondering how much Hud had told his brothers. Apparently nothing more than that since Austin didn't ask him about Taylor or Jade West.

"Is this just about the woman?" Austin asked instead.

"I didn't buy the house for that reason." *Well, not completely,* he thought as he closed the refrigerator. "Come take a look. You'll have to admit the house is perfect for me."

Austin stepped into the living room, still looking skeptical.

"Check out the view," he suggested as he walked to the front window in the living room area. "Open concept. Granite counters. State-of-the-art appliances. What's not to like?"

His brother looked out at Lone Mountain glowing in the afternoon light and seemed to relax a little. "It's nice."

"There are two more floors. The second floor is great for company, two bedrooms, another living area, another bath. The master is on the third floor."

"Where is the painting?" Austin asked.

Realizing there would be no getting rid of him without showing him the painting, Laramie led the way up to the third floor. "Check out the view from here."

"Impressive." But clearly he'd come to see the painting.

The painting was where it'd been when he moved in. And now the alleged original was hanging next to it.

"That's what all the fuss is about?" his brother asked, clearly not that impressed by the artwork.

"It's cowboy art."

Austin shot him a look. "I'm aware of that. What is the original worth?"

"Fifty K."

His brother's eyebrow shot up. "And you bought it with the house?"

"I got a deal on it."

"Not if it's the forgery," Austin pointed out. "Now you have *two* of them?"

"Unless Hud catches the cat burglar and needs them back for evidence."

Austin gave him a "knock off the bull" look. "You think she'll be back for it." Laramie said nothing. What would be the point since it was obvious Austin knew him too well? "Have you considered just how dangerous this might be?"

"I've already found the thief."

His brother's eyebrow shot up. *"What?"*

"I met her today at a cowboy art exhibit in Bozeman. We had coffee."

Austin shook his head as if trying to clear it. "You need to go to Hud and—"

"Without proof? Not a chance. Also I don't want to scare her away." Laramie headed down the stairs.

"So how do you plan to catch her? That is what you're doing, right?" his brother asked, catching up with him.

"I asked her to help me decorate the house."

"Why would you do that?" Austin let out a curse. "If you're right and this woman really is a criminal, then you are in over your head already. I'm serious. What has gotten into you?"

"Isn't it possible that I know what I'm doing? Just because I've always been the brains behind the business doesn't mean I can't do what you and Hayes have been doing for years."

Austin ignored the part about "the brains behind the business."

"Damn it, Laramie, you aren't trained for undercover work."

He leaned against his kitchen counter. "What about the times I've helped the two of you on cases? Give me a little credit."

"At least tell me what you're planning to do."

"I need to know what her game is. She's been seen leaving other houses, but nothing according to the owners was taken. Don't tell me that doesn't intrigue you."

Austin frowned. "I smell a scam, either with the artist, the owner of the painting and/or your cat burglar."

"I have no idea, but," Laramie said, smiling, "I hope to find out."

His brother seemed to run out of arguments. "What is this woman's name? I'll run a background check on her and see if she's had any arrests or convictions."

"Thanks, but I'd rather—"

"Your instincts aside, you need to know who you're dealing with. Unless you don't want to know the truth because... You haven't fallen for this woman, have you?"

"Of course not," he said and looked away, remembering the kiss.

"Laramie—"

"I just don't want you getting involved."

Austin sighed. "How did this woman get under your skin so quickly?"

Laramie shook his head. There was no denying it. Sid had gotten to him.

"If this is about proving something to yourself or to the rest of us—"

"Maybe it started out that way," Laramie admitted. "But if anyone can understand getting hooked on a case, it should be you."

His brother rubbed his neck for a moment before he smiled. "Apparently you are a lot more like me than I ever realized. Okay. All I'll do is run a background check on her. Just let me do that. Unless you're afraid of what I'm going to find out."

"Her name is Obsidian Forester. But I don't want you going to Hud with this yet."

"We'll keep it between us, for now. Obsidian Forester. With a name like that, I shouldn't have any trouble. In the meantime, be careful. You're sure she isn't the one who ran you off the road?"

"I can't imagine how she could be." That was at least true enough.

CHAPTER NINE

SID LOOKED AROUND her cabin at all the work she had
to do. Since coming back from the museum and her
encounter with Laramie Cardwell, she'd gotten little
done. Nor had she slept well last night. All her instincts
told her to forget about the painting Laramie Cardwell
now had in his possession.

If only she could. The painting was a loose end, one
she had to take care of, which meant she would have
to deal with Laramie Cardwell.

She kept rerunning their conversation in her head.
She wavered between, *he knows it was you* and *he
can't possibly know* and *even if he does suspect you,
he can't prove it*.

Still, getting closer to him—and the painting—felt
like a trap. She had no doubt that she could steal the
painting back. He would be spending some of the holidays with his family. It would be the perfect time to
take it.

But then he would know that, as well. Her head hurt
as she considered what he might be up to. If he suspected who she was, then he would try to get proof.
She couldn't shake the feeling that he was just waiting
for her to show up in the middle of the night to try to
retrieve the painting she'd dropped so he could catch
her red-handed.

Was Marshal Hud Savage in on it? She didn't think so. Since none of the paintings were missing, he wasn't apt to think that a crime had been committed.

So what was Laramie up to besides tempting her? The fact that he seemed to be tempting her for more than the painting unnerved her. During coffee a couple times she'd caught him looking at her as if…as if he was interested in her? Of course he was, but not because he was attracted to her. And yet, she had felt an electric spark between them. A stirring she hadn't felt in a very long time—if ever.

The thought made her laugh. If it wasn't complicated enough, she could never fall for a *businessman*. She bet that most of the time he wore a three-piece suit and spent his time behind a desk. Definitely not her type. And yet that image didn't quite seem to fit Laramie Cardwell.

No one who spent all his time behind a desk was in that great shape. No, when she closed her eyes, she saw him in boots, jeans and a Western shirt. He'd mentioned going horseback riding. Maybe she would take him up on it and see just how "Western" he really was.

The idea had too much appeal. If she were smart, she would keep her distance. But then how could she find out what he was up to, let alone get the painting back?

She picked up her keys before good sense could stop her and headed for her SUV. It was time to pay Laramie Cardwell a visit.

AUSTIN RAN THE name Obsidian Forester the moment he reached his computer at the small office he kept at his wife's gallery.

"You look awfully serious," Gillian said from the doorway.

"Laramie's met a woman."

She chuckled. "And that's bad?"

"It depends on whether or not she's a convicted felon or worse."

"There's something worse than a convicted felon?"

Austin watched as the information came up on the computer screen. He knew what he'd been expecting. A record that showed the woman was a thief, a forger... at the very least a con artist.

"Well?" Gillian asked as she came into the room.

"No record. Nothing."

"Why don't you sound relieved?"

Austin raked a hand through his hair. "He's my little brother."

"Maybe the woman is fine."

"Maybe she is just starting her criminal career and my little brother is her first victim."

"It sounds to me like you're just looking for trouble," Gillian said as she turned to leave.

LARAMIE HEARD THE sound of the vehicle coming up the road. Another of his brothers? They'd always been protective of him because he was the youngest. He hadn't minded, liking that they had watched his back. But this was different. This was something he wanted to handle himself.

He sighed as he looked out and was pleasantly and unexpectedly surprised to see Obsidian Forester's older-model blue SUV coming up the road. He hadn't expected her to take him up on his offer—let alone so soon.

Hurrying upstairs, he stashed the painting she'd dropped that night in the closet and then rushed back down. He would show it to her, but not right away.

As the blue SUV pulled in, his heart jumped in his chest with expectation. Even though he knew she was probably only here because of the painting, he still smiled to himself as he watched her get out of her vehicle from a window.

Laramie ran a hand through his thick dark hair and braced himself to see her again. Chimes filled the house as she rang the doorbell. He hoped that the reason Austin hadn't gotten back to him yet was because he hadn't found out anything worrisome about Sid. Bracing himself, he opened the door.

Sid looked out of a fur-trimmed hooded coat. Her face glowed from the cold and the afternoon light. Her breath came out in white puffs, her eyes clear blue like the ice on the river. Snowflakes danced in the air around her. She was a winter wonderland vision standing there.

"Did I catch you at a bad time?" she asked as a few moments passed without either of them speaking.

He mentally shook himself out of his reverie. "Sorry, you looked so…"

"Cold?" she suggested with a smile.

"Exactly, come on in." He stepped aside to let her enter.

"I probably should have called."

"Except you didn't take my number. But your timing couldn't have been more perfect. Let me take your coat. I have a fire going in the fireplace if you need to warm up, and I can make some coffee."

"Thank you," she said, shrugging out of the coat.

Her ginger hair was loose and now fell around her shoulders in a sunset wave of color. Her freckles seemed to stand out even more on her pale face. "It's Montana in late December." She shrugged as if being a little cold was expected.

"So you're used to winter," Laramie said as he hung up her coat in the closet by the front door. "I never asked you if you're from here or a newbie like me."

"New to this town. But I was raised in Montana not too far from here." She followed him into the kitchen.

"So where exactly are you from?" he asked as he poured her a mug.

"I grew up outside of Maudlow," she said with a laugh. "You've never heard of it, right? It's to the north. Not much of a town there anymore." She glanced around. "Nice house."

"Thanks. I didn't want anything too big, but by my condo standards, this place seems huge. It does make me want to stay here more, though."

"You aren't planning to stay long this time?" she asked as she wandered into the living room, then turned. "Do you mind?" she asked nodding toward the stairs.

"No, please. Take a look around. As you can see, the walls are all bare down here." He followed her up the stairs, again noting how fluidly she moved. Also how quietly.

On the second floor, she made a lap through the main room, then headed up the second set of stairs to the master bedroom. To the casual observer she didn't seem to know the house. But it was clear to him that she knew exactly what she was looking for.

On the third floor, she entered his bedroom slowly.

Fortunately, he'd made the bed this morning and he hadn't left any clothing lying around. Because he'd been expecting her. He was pleased that he'd been right. In fact, she'd shown up even sooner than he had hoped.

She stepped in, seeming to take in the view before she turned first to the right, then slowly to the left as if leaving the painting till the last.

Laramie had to smile to himself. This is what she'd come to see, he thought, as she took in the painting. Everything else had been pretense—he was sure of it.

"This is the painting you told me you bought from the owner?" she asked without looking at him.

"That's it. There was just something about it, if you know what I mean."

"No. Like I said, I'm not a fan of cowboy art, but as long as *you* like it…" She glanced around. Looking for the other painting?

"I'm not sure what I like, to tell you the truth."

"Isn't there art in your home in Houston?" she asked as if actually interested.

"I bought the condo new. It came decorated."

She shook her head as if she couldn't imagine doing something like that.

Her eyes were darker in his bedroom, a deeper blue. He wondered what color they would be when she opened her eyes in his bed in the morning. The thought shook him to his boots. Of course he was attracted her. What red-blooded Texas boy wouldn't be? But to think that there was a chance they might be lovers…

"What's funny about this painting," he said, drawing her back to it, "is that I have two of them."

That definitely got her attention. "Why would you buy two of them?"

"Good question, since, when I visited the artist, he told me he painted only one of them," Laramie said as he stepped past her to open the closet and pull out the second one. He hung it next to the first. "So which one is the original?"

SHE LOOKED AT THEM for a moment. "I have no idea."

Sid strangled back the cry that rose in her throat. Only moments before she had been looking at all the wonderful wall space he had in his house, thinking how fun it would be to fill it with art. She'd been excited about the ridiculous thought of helping him. How she would have loved it. She had tons of ideas. Not that it would ever happen, but it was fun to fantasize about a lot of things when it came to Laramie Cardwell.

Then he'd said he'd talked to Taylor West about the two paintings, and all the air had rushed out of her. The room suddenly felt too hot, too small, too bright.

She'd barely been able to get the words out. "You showed the work to the artist?" He nodded, hopefully unaware of how upset she'd become. "I would think he would know his own artwork," she said carefully.

"I thought the same thing. Apparently one of these is the original. The other, a forgery. A very good forgery."

"That's remarkable. Did he have any idea who might have been able to forge it?"

Laramie shook his head. "West said the only man good enough to have done the work was one H. F. Powell. Have you heard of him?"

She could only nod.

"But apparently he's dead. So it remains a mystery.

Just between you and me? What makes it all the more crazy is how I came to have both paintings."

Sid listened as he told her what she already knew. "That is quite the story," she said when he finished.

"It's a mystery."

"I'm sure you'll solve it," she said, hoping she was wrong.

"Maybe," he said meeting her gaze. "I'm sure hoping I do."

Sid reminded herself that the only reason she'd come over here was to get the painting back, which meant getting closer to Laramie Cardwell. But being here with him, standing this close to him, looking into those blue eyes…

She felt a small tremor move through her. *He knew.* It was time to quit kidding herself. He was just waiting for her to make a mistake. But that wasn't all she saw in his eyes or felt being this close to him. Some kind of chemistry was arcing between them and he felt it, too.

Sid tried to convince herself this was about nothing more than foreplay, flirtation. But the attraction was so strong between them that there was no denying it.

Worse, she *liked* him. Look at the interest he'd taken in Western art since the first night they'd met, she thought with a hidden smile. He'd become intrigued, just as she had become intrigued by him. She couldn't say that about most of the men she'd dated. Her last serious relationship had been in high school. Fortunately she'd been smart enough not to marry him.

But whatever feelings she might have when it came to Laramie Cardwell, the question now was how far she would go to get the painting back.

LARAMIE SAW THE WAY Sid was clutching the coffee mug in both hands. "Your coffee must be getting cold. Let's go back down. I want your opinion on that big wall in the living room."

He'd noticed the change in her. What he'd told her had upset her. But by the time they reached the kitchen, she seemed her cool, calm self again.

This woman would be the death of him. The thought surprised him as if it was a warning. But there was no denying whatever was going on between them under the surface. It wasn't his imagination. This woman did things to him. That alone made her dangerous—not to mention the fact that she was a criminal. A thief. Or worse.

He told himself he wouldn't be stupid enough to let her steal his heart.

"If I'm going to help find the right art for you, then I'll need to figure out what you like," Sid said after he'd warmed up her coffee and showed her the large, high-ceilinged wall in the living room.

"How do you suggest doing that since I don't know what I like?" he asked, inexplicably still intrigued and attracted by this woman. He really had to be careful. Austin was right. He had no idea what he was getting into.

She smiled as she looked up at him, her eyes locking with his. "I guess we'll have to spend more time together so I get to know you better."

He felt a dart of desire puncture his already weak reserve. *She was flirting with him.*

"I completely agree," he heard himself say, all the while reminding himself who he was dealing with. Austin was afraid this woman was dangerous. His brother had no idea given the mix of emotions Sid evoked in him.

She smiled. "Any suggestions?"

She *definitely* was flirting with him. Laying some sort of trap for him?

He decided to play along. "We could start by going horseback riding, but it's supposed to snow this afternoon."

Sid laughed. "I love riding in the snow, but if you—"

"No, I'm in. Just let me call my cousin Dana."

TAYLOR WEST TRIED his wife's cell phone number again. It went straight to voice mail—again. Only this time, the message said that her voice mail was full.

He slammed down the phone. Since seeing Jade's car in Rock Jackson's barn, he hadn't been able to sleep—except for the hours he'd drunk so much that he'd passed out.

"Don't do anything crazy," fellow artist Hank Ramsey had told him. Taylor hadn't wanted to tell anyone, but he was going out of his mind, so he'd called Hank for advice.

"Don't do anything *crazy*?" he'd demanded after hearing Hank's advice. "Rock has stolen my *wife*! And who knows what else he's done." He'd stopped short of telling Hank what else he suspected Rock Jackson of doing. Did he trust either Rock or Hank? Not anymore. Not since he'd seen the painting Laramie Cardwell had in his possession.

"You don't know for a fact that Jade is with Rock."

"Her car is parked in his barn," he'd said between clenched teeth. "And he has a room behind his studio with boarded-up windows and a padlock on the door.

"There could be another explanation than the one you've jumped to."

"What would that be if it was *your* wife?"

"Jade could be storing her car there. Didn't you say she was planning to go to Ohio to visit her sister for a while?"

"Indiana to visit her mother." He'd cursed under his breath, sorry he'd called Hank. "I thought that was where she would go. She never said—it doesn't matter where she went. *Her car is in Rock's barn.* Even if she flew to Mars, why would she leave her car with him?"

"Probably because she didn't want to pay the overnight fee at the airport. Gateway isn't that far from the airport. Rock probably gave her a ride."

He hadn't thought that Jade knew Rock that well. True, she'd been to enough cowboy artist conferences that maybe she'd come to know the artists better than he did. He spent most of his time at those things getting to know the bartender rather than listening to the bull the other artists were spouting.

"Also, I'd be careful about making any accusations since you have no proof about anything. You might want to watch the booze, too. The one thing we have to do is stick together."

Taylor had heard something in the man's voice. Was he warning him? "*I'm* not the problem."

"We don't even know there *is* a problem."

Hank wasn't talking about Jade any longer. "You didn't see the painting," Taylor'd said, trying to keep the anger and the fear out of his voice.

"I'll talk to Rock. I'm sure there is nothing to worry about."

Right, Taylor thought as he went to unlock his gun cabinet.

CHAPTER TEN

ON THE WAY to Cardwell Ranch to meet Sid and go horseback riding, Laramie's cell phone rang. It was his brother Austin.

He braced himself as he took the call. "So what did you find out about Sid?" he asked, just wanting to get it over with.

"*Sid?* You're using her nickname already?" Laramie could practically see his brother shaking his head.

"So did you find something or not?"

Austin sighed. "She appears to be squeaky clean. No arrests, no speeding tickets, nothing. She lives alone, owns a small, older cabin back in the woods outside of Big Sky and drives an older-model SUV." Not a large dark car. "No debt. Makes a modest living with her artwork."

Laramie wanted to laugh with relief. "So why don't you sound happy?"

"Because she's *too* squeaky clean."

"There is no satisfying you, Austin," he joked.

"You still think she's the woman you saw that night with the painting though, right?"

"I'm not sure." He knew he was hedging because he was starting to like Sid—and he *could* be wrong about her being the woman. It had been dark and she'd been wearing a ski mask. All he'd seen were her eyes, and there were a lot of women with blue eyes, right? But those lips... Not every woman had those.

"Just be careful. If you need my help..."

Laramie thanked his brother and drove on to Cardwell Ranch, where he and Sid had agreed to meet. Sid hadn't arrived yet, but his cousin Dana was waiting for him.

"So you've already met someone?" As they stood in her warm, ranch kitchen, Dana sounded too happy to hear that it would be a woman going riding with him.

"You're responsible for marrying off all my brothers, aren't you?" Laramie joked. "Well, this time you've met your match. Marriage is the last thing that is going to happen with this woman."

"I hope you don't have to eat your words," Dana said smiling.

"You'd *better* hope so."

She suddenly quit smiling. "This isn't the woman you caught with the painting?"

"That stopped your matchmaking cold," he said with a laugh.

"You're going horseback riding with *her*? Does Hud know?"

"We don't know for sure that it is even her. Also your husband is convinced this whole cat burglar thing is nothing more than a hoax."

"Well, *I'm* not convinced. What if the woman is dangerous?"

Laramie laughed. "You sound like Austin. Look, if I don't make it back from the horseback ride, you'll have your answer."

"I don't think that's funny."

"Dana, it's just a horseback ride. If you want to

worry…she's helping me purchase art for my new house."

His cousin looked aghast. "You be careful, Laramie Cardwell. I've been through enough with your brothers. I don't need you getting into trouble."

Outside, the ranch wrangler had saddled two horses. Laramie told his cousin he was more than capable of saddling his own horses, but Dana had insisted he come inside and visit with her while he waited for his "date" to arrive. Sid had said she needed to run some errands and would prefer to meet him at the ranch.

As a blue SUV pulled into the yard, he went out to greet her. Not surprisingly, Dana followed on his heels.

"Sid, this is my cousin Dana Cardwell Savage. Dana, Obsidian 'Sid' Forester."

Sid held out her hand. "It's a pleasure to meet you," she said. "Thank you for offering the use of your horses. I'm looking forward to it."

"You ride?" Dana asked.

"I grew up on a ranch and rode every day for years."

Laramie noticed that Dana seemed to soften toward the woman, ranch woman to ranch woman. "Then I am especially glad you're going to get to ride today," his cousin said. She turned to Laramie. "How far were you planning to ride?"

"Not far," he said. "We'll be back in a couple hours."

The wrangler handed each of them their reins. Laramie watched Sid swing up into the saddle. Clearly she was comfortable on a horse. He followed suit and they headed along a trail that followed the river. Fresh snow rose in the air around them as they rode.

The day was crisp and cold. Ice crystals hung in the air and the promise of snow rode on the breeze. But it felt good to be back in the saddle. Laramie had ridden often on his brother Jackson's place. He'd missed it since Jackson had sold his ranch in Texas and moved to Montana.

"Your cousin seems nice," Sid said as they rode.

"Dana? She's amazing. She's also responsible for getting us all to Montana."

Sid cut her eyes at him. "She seemed a little worried about you."

"She's overprotective when it comes to family. But I could tell she liked you. Wait until you get to know her. She's great."

WAIT UNTIL YOU get to know her. He made it sound as if they would be spending a lot of time together. Sid said nothing as they rode through snow-laden pines. Water rushed under the thick aquamarine-colored ice on the Gallatin River beside them. The air smelled of snow. She could see that it was already snowing on the top of Lone Mountain across the narrow river valley.

Was she wrong about Laramie's suspicions? Maybe he really was attracted to her and wanted nothing more than a date.

"I was surprised to hear you'd grown up on a ranch," he said.

"Why is that?"

"You don't like cowboy art."

She chuckled. "You think they go hand in hand?"

"I guess not."

"What about you? Where did you learn to ride?"

"We had relatives with horses when we were young. Then my brother Jackson bought a small ranch. I used to ride there almost every day. I've missed it. I've missed my brothers since they've all moved to Montana. Even my mother is here now."

"You're so lucky to have such a large, close family."

He looked over at her. "You don't?"

She shook her head. "My mother died when I was three. My father passed away some years ago. He taught me—" she hated the tremor she heard in her voice "—to ride."

"I'm so sorry for your loss. It sounds like you were close."

Sid just nodded, afraid to speak for fear she would cry. It surprised her, all this emotion. Let alone the fact that she had opened up to Laramie—the last person she should be letting her guard down with.

"You don't have any siblings?" he asked.

"An older sister who travels a lot."

"You must get lonely," he said, glancing over at her.

Catching a whiff of Laramie's fresh-from-the-shower scent, she felt a longing wash over her. But it was more than a desire to be in this man's arms. It was a need to trust someone other than herself. For just an instant, she wanted to tell him everything. What a weight that would be off her shoulders to confide in someone. To confide in this strong cowboy.

As if sensing the way she was feeling, Laramie reined in next to her. It happened so fast that she didn't have time to react. He reached over and she felt his thumb on her cheek. Until that moment, she hadn't realized she'd been crying as he smoothed away a tear.

His gaze locked with hers as he leaned into her, his mouth finding hers. She tasted the saltiness of her tears and the cold scent of the winter day on his lips. Her own lips parted as she leaned into the kiss. He cupped her face, the kiss sweet and soft, then more demanding. She felt heat run like hot water through her veins, warming her to the toes of her boots.

As if realizing what he was doing, he pulled back suddenly. "Sorry. I couldn't help myself."

She swallowed, desperately wanting to grab the collar of his winter coat and pull him into another kiss. His mouth, warm against hers, had kindled a flame in her like nothing she'd ever felt. She ached to lose herself in this man, which was so not like her that it terrified her. She was always careful. But at this moment, she wanted to throw caution to the wind and let her heart have what it wanted.

"I'm not sorry," she heard herself say, although she knew she should be. Did she have to remind herself how dangerous it was to get too close to Laramie Cardwell, of all men?

It was the second time they'd kissed, she realized with a start. Was that why he'd kissed her? If so, then did he now know she was his cat burglar?

Now what? she wondered as they rode back toward the ranch house. Was he setting her up for a fall? After that kiss, she feared she had a lot more to worry about than the painting.

ROCK JACKSON OPENED one eye to see the time on the clock beside the bed. He'd forgotten for a moment where he was. Then he remembered. He was hiding out in a friend's condo in Bozeman and he wasn't alone. He groaned pleasantly, surprised that he'd slept this late. Even more surprised that he could be this happy.

Rolling over, he looked into Jade West's young, beautiful face. He couldn't believe she was in his bed.

The hours they'd spent making love since she'd shown up at his door were a blur.

The moment he'd laid eyes on her the first time at an Old West Artists Conference, he'd been smitten. The worst part that first time was realizing that she was that old fart Taylor West's trophy wife. He'd said then that the marriage wouldn't last.

And he'd been right. But he never thought he had a chance with her. He was more than surprised when she'd shown up at his door and had fallen into his arms. The satisfaction that gave him was shameful, but he still enjoyed every moment of it. Jade was *his*.

Her lashes fluttered and a moment later her green eyes opened. She smiled, making him laugh with delight.

"What?" she asked as she rolled over onto her back. She had the best rack he'd ever seen and this morning she was displaying it for the world.

"I'm just happy." Happier than he had ever been. With two bad marriages and an imminent divorce, he'd had his share of heartbreak. Jade was his compensation for those hard times. It didn't hurt, either, that he'd stolen that smug SOB Taylor West's wife.

"I need to call Taylor."

Her words burst that moment of pure joy. Like a soap bubble, it popped right before his eyes. "Is that necessary?"

She turned onto her side to look at him again. "I need to *tell* him."

"You could let me do that."

Jade shook her head, her delightful lower lip protruding as she said, "I have to do it myself. It's the right thing to do. I don't want him thinking I'm coming back."

She was young, Rock thought. Barely legal to buy alcohol in Montana. What did she know about these things? "He isn't going to be happy. I'm sure he'll beg you to come back. Or threaten to kill us both."

"He wouldn't do that."

Rock wasn't so sure about that. Taylor could be a loose cannon when he was drinking—which was most of the time. Worse, there was bad blood between them and had been for years.

"You don't have to do it *right* now, do you?" he asked as he pulled her to him.

She purred in his arms and he felt his happiness level rise again. He had what he wanted. Well, almost. He was tired of feeling second rate because of Taylor West. Now that he had Jade, he told himself that nothing could stop him from getting what he deserved. He had Taylor's wife. Soon, she would have Taylor's money.

Life was perfect. Almost. After a quick shower, he checked his emails and found the message from Taylor about the painting.

DANA HAD A pot of chili and a pan of warm-from-the-oven corn bread ready for lunch when Laramie and Sid returned from their ride.

"You can't say no, Sid," Dana insisted as they handed over their reins to the wrangler. She stood on the porch wearing an apron, her hands on her hips. "Hud doesn't think he can make it home for lunch, the kids are with their aunt Stacy. I desperately need adult conversation."

Laramie glanced at Sid. She looked torn. He'd felt so close to her on their ride, but then he'd felt her pull away again as they'd neared the ranch house. Now she looked as if she wanted to run—and yet was tempted to stay. He might have wondered what she had to fear if he hadn't already known.

"Chili and corn bread," he said. "Did I mention that my cousin is a great cook?"

"I would love to," she said to him, "but I can't. Thank you so much. It sounds wonderful," she called to Dana on the porch. "But I have to go. Thank you again for the horseback ride. It was lovely."

Laramie watched her head for her SUV. The kiss had confirmed what he already knew. Obsidian "Sid" Forester was his cat burglar. There was no doubt now. "Maybe I'll see you later?" he called after her, wondering what would happen next. He knew what he wanted to happen.

She smiled and nodded. "Maybe."

"Well?" Dana demanded once the two of them were seated, chili and corn bread in front of them.

"I don't know what to tell you," he said honestly.

"You don't have to tell me anything. The look on your face says it all," Dana said with a grin. "The woman has gotten to you."

He wanted to deny it but didn't bother. "She told me she lost her father some years ago. I can tell that she is still hurting over that. Apparently, he was all the family she had other than an older sister who travels all the time."

"Oh, that's awful," Dana said, sounding close to tears. She knew what it was like to lose someone she loved. She'd lost her mother, Mary, a few years ago and then, because of a dispute over the ranch, nearly lost her sister and brothers. "I wish she'd stayed for lunch. You should invite her to the masquerade ball."

"I already mentioned it to her."

"And?" Dana asked hopefully.

"She wasn't interested."

"I'm sorry to hear that." He could tell that Sid's refusal had surprised her as much as it had him. "Well, *you* have to come. Don't even try to get out of it," Dana said. "We're all going, including all of your brothers. Everyone wears a costume and doesn't remove their masks until the stroke of midnight. It's the biggest event in the canyon."

He cringed inwardly just as he had the first time Dana had mentioned it. "Like I told you before, I'm not much on—"

Dana shook her head. "I'm not taking no for an answer. Believe me, you don't want to get on my bad side."

Hud laughed as he walked into the kitchen. "Trust me, she is so right about that," the marshal said as he bent to give his wife a kiss. "Whatever she wants you to do, just do it."

Dana slapped playfully at her husband as she said, "I thought you couldn't make lunch."

"I got to thinking about your chili and corn bread," he said with a shrug as he helped himself and joined them.

"I was just talking to Laramie about the masquerade ball. Now that he is going to own a house here…"

"You bought that house?" Hud asked he sat down at the table.

Laramie nodded.

"Did your brothers ever admit to playing that trick on you?" the marshal asked.

"Hayes swears they know nothing about a cat burglar. Any news on the vehicle?"

"What vehicle?" Dana said. "Did something happen?"

"Some fool ran Laramie off the highway yesterday," Hud said, keeping his head down as he ate.

"What? And this is the first I'm hearing about it?" Dana demanded.

"I didn't mention it because I thought you would overreact," Hud said. "Seems I was right."

"Are you all right?" Dana demanded of her cousin.

"You can see that he is all right," Hud said.

Dana shot him an impatient look. "Why would someone run you off the road?"

"The person must have been drinking," Laramie said. He felt Dana look from him to her husband as if sensing there was more to the story.

"As to the vehicle," Hud said to him. "Haven't found it yet." He took a bite of chili and chewed. "Ever see the woman again?" he asked after a moment.

Dana shot Laramie a conspiratorial look and gave him a slight shake of her head.

"You haven't had any more sightings?" Laramie asked, avoiding the question.

Hud shook his head. "Fortunately not. I have enough problems with whoever is behind the counterfeit twenties floating around. I got a call earlier from the gas station. Someone passed off another bogus twenty. Once they start circulating…"

They ate in silence for a few moments. "I can't wait to throw a housewarming party for you," Dana said.

"Give him a break, sweetheart," her husband said with a laugh. "You're going to scare him away with all this talk of parties."

"Well, be thinking about your costume for the ball—and a possible...date." She gave him a sly wink. "I promise you, you don't want to miss the masquerade party," she said, undeterred. "I'll write down the name of a local costume shop. You'll want to get yours soon."

Hud ate quickly and went back to work. Laramie stayed to help Dana with the dishes even though she protested.

"Why didn't you mention the horseback ride with my possible cat burglar to Hud?" he asked Dana.

She laughed. "Hud would have just turned into his marshal persona and started asking a lot of questions you clearly can't answer."

"Austin is already doing that."

"Exactly," she said, eyeing him thoughtfully. "Anyway, as far as we know she hasn't committed any crimes, right?"

He nodded.

"Also, I can tell that you're smitten with her. I liked her. Your brothers told me that you've dated a lot but haven't found *the one*. I guess time will tell with Sid, won't it? I hope she changes her mind about the ball."

"I don't see her doing that. She said she wouldn't be caught dead there."

Dana shuddered. "Those were the words she used?"

"It's just an expression," he said, seeing that Dana was now upset.

"Maybe it's for the best. Every year at the ball there's a silent art auction of several paintings to help continue funding the event," she said slowly. "Last year they were local watercolors. This year they are three works by cowboy artists."

"Who are the artists?" Laramie asked as his interest was piqued.

"Rock Jackson, Taylor West and H. F. Powell."

UPSET WITH HERSELF, Sid drove through Big Sky and turned on the road back to her cabin. She had let down her guard with Laramie. What was wrong with her? She knew what her best friend, Maisie, would say about it even before her friend answered her call.

"I kissed him again."

"You *what*?"

"Well, he kissed *me*, but I kissed him back."

"Sid. How did this happen?"

She told her about the horseback ride. "He caught me at a vulnerable moment. I was talking about…about my father dying and—"

"You went horseback riding with him and told him about your father? Have you lost your mind?"

"I only told him that my father had died." Sid sighed. "He could see that I'm clearly not over it."

"You need to be more careful. If you're right about him suspecting you…"

"I know, but there is something about him that makes me think I can trust him when I'm with him. And when he kissed me…"

"It didn't feel like a kiss from a man who was looking for an art thief?"

"No," Sid said with a groan. "It felt like kiss from a man whose reasons were strictly carnal. And I liked it," she cried.

Maisie laughed. "You know what you need, don't you?"

"If you are going to say a man—" As she pulled up beside her cabin she saw tracks in the snow where someone had walked along the back of the property. The tracks disappeared behind the house. "I have to go. If I don't call you back in five minutes…"

"I know what to do," her friend said solemnly.

Stuffing her cell phone into her pocket, she opened her glove box and pulled out the gun. Dropping it in her other coat pocket, she opened her car door and stepped out.

The snow crunched under her feet, a sign that the temperature was dropping as snow drifted down from a blinding white sky. She'd heard that another winter storm was coming in and was surprised it hadn't hit sooner.

Instead of going in the front, she walked along the side of the cabin to the back and looked toward the woods where the fresh boot prints in the snow had apparently come from. She saw a snowmobile parked some distance from the cabin. She could still smell the exhaust. Whoever was inside hadn't been here long.

Her hand in her coat pocket, her finger on the trigger, she opened the door and stepped in.

CHAPTER ELEVEN

LARAMIE HAD ALWAYS been the sensible one. He was the brother the others came to when they had financial questions. He was the one who tried to keep them out of trouble. He was the one—though the youngest—they all expected to be the rational, clear thinking one.

Given what had happened in the past few days, he shouldn't have been that surprised to see that all four of his brothers were waiting for him when he returned to his house. He suspected they hadn't come to see his new residence as he got out and walked toward the waiting vehicle—and his waiting brothers.

"I hope you brought me supper from the restaurant," Laramie said as his brothers all piled out of Austin's SUV. "And more beer." None of them even smiled. He braced himself for the lectures that he knew were coming as he opened the front door of the house.

"Why don't we all have a cold one?" he suggested as he walked into the kitchen. Behind him, they all trudged in, stopping to take their boots off at the door. He turned around to stare and then laugh.

"What's so damned funny?" Jackson demanded.

"All of you. You're all so well…trained now. Is that what marriage does to you? If so, I'll pass."

"Don't try to change the subject. You're in enough trouble," Hayes warned.

"I'll take that beer you offered," Tag said. The other three brothers shot him an annoyed look. "Hey, we can lay into him and still have a beer while we do it."

"If this is about Sid…" He opened the refrigerator and brought out five bottles of beer.

"We just heard about someone running you off the highway in the canyon," Hayes said. "You didn't even bother to tell us?"

"I'm fine," Laramie said. "But I appreciate your concern," he said as he handed them each a bottle.

"Where have you been?" Austin asked, sounding as though he was interrogating one of his suspects back when he was a deputy sheriff in Texas.

"At Cardwell Ranch having lunch with Dana and Hud," Laramie said, twisting off the cap from his beer. He took a drink, then added, "Before that I went on a horseback ride."

"Alone?" Austin asked, then sighed when Laramie said nothing. He wrenched the top off his bottle of beer. "I told you to be careful. A horseback ride?"

"You probably want to see the house," Laramie said. He was still too happy about his afternoon ride with Sid to want to argue with his brothers. Not that he didn't understand their concern. He was too smart not to realize he was playing with fire.

"I want to see these damned paintings," Tag said. He looked toward the stairs. "Are they up there?"

"They were when I left," Laramie said.

SID EASED HER FINGER off the trigger of the gun in her coat pocket. Her older sister stood over the painting on her easel—after having picked the lock on Sid's back door. Sid tried to tamp down her annoyance. Seeing her was like seeing a ghostly image of herself. People used to think the two of them were twins. They looked that much alike, especially when Zander had gone strawberry blonde.

The fact that they were half sisters wouldn't have surprised anyone to see them together—same father, different mothers. But few people knew they were even related because Zander was always gone and they were never seen together.

"Zander, what are you doing here?" Sid hated the edge to her voice. But from past experience, she feared a visit from her half sister didn't bode well.

Zander turned and smiled. "Merry Christmas!"

She slipped out of her coat and hung it on the hook by the back door. "You're here for *Christmas*?"

"Don't sound so surprised," her sister said, stepping to her to give her a hug. "We've missed too many holidays. I decided not to let another one go by without spending it with my little sis."

She caught a whiff of her sister's favorite perfume, a scent that transported her back to their teen years. It also reminded her that it was Zander who'd taught her about breaking and entering. And that was the least of Zander's crimes.

"So you just happened into the area, grabbed a snowmobile and decided to visit?" she asked as she stepped back from the hug.

Zander sighed. "You've always been so suspicious. I came by snowmobile because it had been too many years since I'd gotten to ride on one and I wanted to surprise you. Clearly, I did. Come on, we're all the family we have left."

"And you thought after several years of me not hearing from you that you'd just stop by and surprise me," she repeated.

Her sister laughed and shook her head. "Sid, in case no one has told you, it's *Christmas*. I've heard families get together, exchange presents, sit around the Christmas tree and drink eggnog. At least that's what they do in movies," she said, glancing around Sid's cabin. "But it certainly doesn't look like Christmas here. Where's the tree and the eggnog, the stockings hung with care?"

"If I'd known you were coming for a visit—"

"Not to worry. I'll take care of everything, including filling up your refrigerator. Sid, what do you eat...? Or do you?" She continued, not expecting an answer apparently. "You look thin. I hope it's because you're painting and not because of that crazy quest you've been on."

Sid didn't want to talk about either with her sister. "Where have you been this time?" Zander had taken after her mother, a model who'd disappeared a few years before Sid was born. Her sister had apparently picked up that wandering gene.

"I tend to follow the sun. You know me," Zander said noncommittally as she moved around the cabin. "Unless, of course, I get a hankering to spend Christmas in Big Sky with my sister."

Zander couldn't seem to let grass grow under her feet. According to their father, the photographs she'd seen of Zander's mother hadn't captured her wild spirit. Her father, who'd loved women to distraction, had moved on at fifty after Zander's mother had left, and had another child sans marriage. Even though Sid's mother was younger than he was, he'd managed to outlive her by twenty years.

"I don't have an extra bedroom," Sid said, unable to turn her sister away, "but you can take mine and I'll—"

"I already have a place to stay. I didn't come to move in. Or to keep you from your...work. But don't make any plans for Christmas Eve. I'll bring everything."

Sid looked at her sister and felt that old blood bond between them as well as the memories that would always link them. Her timing was questionable, but it *was* almost Christmas, wasn't it? It had been too long since she'd even seen her sister—Zander was right about that. Also, they were the last of their family and the last link to their father.

Sid hugged her again, harder this time while silently praying her sister was telling the truth about her reason for being here now. "I've missed you, Z."

"THE PAINTINGS ARE identical right down to the picture frame," Hayes said as he studied them. "I would swear they were painted by the same artist."

"I took the supposed forgery to an art expert. He offered me thirty thousand for it and offered to document it as the original," Laramie said. "Even the artist who painted it believed this was the original. At least at first."

"Are you sure the one you bought with the house isn't the forgery?" Jackson asked. "McKenzie says most forgeries are easy to spot. All you have to do is look at the colors, the brushstrokes, the canvas...but this one..." He shook his head.

"It is perplexing," he admitted. "But there is a certificate on the back claiming it is an original and one of a kind. That was good enough for its original owner."

"Something isn't right," Hayes said, looking worried. "Either the artist painted more than one of these and lied, or this is a masterful forger. What about the other houses where this...cat burglar was seen?"

"Hud said the owners checked their artwork," Austin said. "It hadn't been taken."

"That's why the marshal thinks the whole thing is a hoax," Laramie pointed out.

"Except you caught the woman and have a second painting that is identical or damned close," Austin said. "If she's switching the originals for forgeries, she has one profitable scam going, and so far she's gotten away with it. Which means she can't let you keep this painting." He glanced over at Laramie and swore. "That's what you're counting on, isn't it?"

"Or maybe the artist is in on it," Hayes said. "You said you talked to him?"

"Taylor West seemed as perplexed by it all as I was," he said. "But according to him, he's the top money-maker with his art. So if you were going to forge anyone's, it would seem smart to copy his."

"You were run off the road after you visited this Taylor West?" Austin asked, clearly knowing that was the case.

"Coincidence," Laramie said, shrugging. Austin mugged a face at him.

"Whoever is doing this is good, really good," Hayes said studying the artwork.

Laramie nodded. "I asked West who he would suspect of forging his work. The only artist he could think of who was that good was H. F. Powell."

"I've seen his work," Jackson said. "He was one of the originals like Charles M. Russell and Frederic

Remington. But didn't I hear that he's dead? Unless he forged this painting before he died…"

Laramie had thought of that. "What do you know about him?"

His brothers all shrugged.

"I just know that one of his paintings is going to be auctioned off at the ball," Hayes said. "McKenzie expects it to go for a lot of money because there aren't many of them around. Most of his work was lost in a house fire the night of his death. Apparently he was a character. I guess in his old age, he locked himself in his studio and no one saw him again. He died destitute with what would now be hundreds of thousands of dollars worth of his paintings going up in flames with him."

"The paintings all burned?" Laramie asked.

"McKenzie said the fire turned out to be arson. The old man apparently started the blaze himself."

"What about the one being auctioned off at the ball?" he asked.

"Apparently it was one that he'd sold before his death," Jackson said.

"I WAS HOPING you'd be glad to see me," Zander said, pretending to pout. "After all, I taught you everything you know."

"Not *everything*." Zander had taught her how to pick locks at a young age, how to break into houses through windows and not leave any evidence. She'd taught her how to steal—and how to get away with it. For that she owed her since that talent had certainly come in handy.

But fortunately, Sid had learned other things that had helped her in life that her sister could have benefited from. Everyone in Big Sky thought she had no siblings. She'd kept Zander a secret for reasons she didn't want to admit. Now she regretted that—and the times she'd wished it was true.

"So what have you been up to?" her sister said, studying her. "Is there a man in your life?"

Sid shook her head and turned away. "Why would you ask that?"

Zander laughed. "Because you're young, somewhat attractive," her sister joked since she was clearly aware how much they resembled each other, "and this place is crawling with rich men."

Sid groaned. "We're not all looking for a sugar daddy." She wondered now where her sister was staying. It would be just like Zander to have met some man who was letting her stay in his guesthouse—if not his master bedroom.

"Well, don't wait too long to find one," her sister said. "It gets harder as you get older."

Sid started to point out there was only seven years between them. But in the bright light reflecting off the snow outside, Zander looked as if the years they'd been apart had taken a toll on her. Her sister lived hard and fast as if that, too, was in her genes.

Zander walked around the cabin, picking up things and putting them back with no apparent real interest. "So are you almost finished with your diabolical plan?"

She sighed and gave her sister an impatient look. "Diabolical?"

Zander shrugged. "You are almost done, though, aren't you?" She turned to look at her. "You have all the paintings?"

"Not quite."

Her sister nodded. "Then what?"

"I really don't want to talk about this with you. Like you said, it's nearly Christmas. Let's not dig up the past."

Her sister looked angry for a moment, but then nodded. "You're right. We never agreed on much anyway, but we are still blood. Daddy would have wanted us to be friends."

The mention of their father brought tears to Sid's eyes. He was the one person in their lives they could agree on. They had both loved him in their own ways.

"I'm not here to keep you from your...work. But if I can help, you'll let me know. I might be a little rusty at the undercover stuff, but I doubt it would take much to bring it back." Zander grinned. "In fact, I'd welcome the diversion. Life has been too tame for too long."

Sid doubted that. "You didn't seem to have any trouble breaking into my cabin."

Her sister waved that off with a laugh. "Hardly a challenge. You really should consider getting better locks. You don't even have a security system," she said, looking around the small cabin and frowning. "Which means you don't keep anything you value here."

Sid had wondered how long it would take her sister to get to the heart of the matter. But she ignored it, determined not to discuss this with her. "If you're coming back Christmas Eve, I should tell you I don't like eggnog. But if you still remember how to make nachos like you did when we were kids..."

Zander's smile never reached her eyes. "Got the message."

Sid doubted she did. Before the holidays were over, her sister would return to her real reason for being in

Big Sky. In the meantime, she wondered what her sister might be up to and asked as much.

"I thought I'd do some skiing and maybe lay around in the hot tub at the place I'm staying."

Sid said nothing, but that didn't sound like the sister she'd known and loved. Since she was fourteen Sid had pretty much been on her own. Growing up with a father who worked all the time and a sister who was a thief, she had learned to take care of herself—any way she'd had to.

Unfortunately, Zander, the firstborn to the mother with the movie-star looks, had been pampered as a child—until her mother disappeared. After that, Zander had merely taken whatever she wanted—including any money she could steal from their father and, finally, the ranch itself.

"I have to run, but I'll be back Christmas Eve with bells on." Zander laughed as she left, her perfume lingering along with the good—and bad—memories she brought with her.

Sid listened to the sound of the snowmobile's motor as it died away in the distance. She couldn't let Zander jeopardize everything she'd worked so hard for. Sinking into a chair, she put her head in her hands and fought tears of anger and frustration. As much as she loved her sister, she couldn't trust her. That alone broke her heart.

She thought of Laramie Cardwell. This house of cards she'd built felt as if it was about to collapse around her. But she had no choice. She had to get that painting back from him. And, knowing her sister, she had to stop Zander from whatever she'd come back to Montana to do.

CHAPTER TWELVE

LATER THAT DAY, Sid stopped by the grocery store to pick up a few things. She couldn't be sure that she would ever see her sister again—that was until she got a call from someone that Zander was in trouble.

But she would buy a few groceries anyway, just in case. She couldn't depend on Zander not to show up Christmas Eve with only bells on.

Pulling a twenty from her purse, she handed it to the clerk. When the clerk hesitated and began to inspect the bill, Sid felt a chill race up her spine. In that instant, she realized that she couldn't be sure she'd had a twenty in her purse this morning.

With a groan, she also realized that she'd gotten out of the habit of checking her wallet when her sister was around. But it wasn't like Zander to take money and leave change.

"I'm sorry, but I can't take this bill," the clerk said as she motioned for her supervisor to come over.

Sid could feel her face heat with embarrassment as other customers began to stare at her. Her stomach roiled. "What is wrong with the bill?"

The clerk didn't answer. It wasn't until the marshal showed up that Sid learned she'd somehow picked up a counterfeit bill.

PARKED IN THE trees so he could see Rock Jackson's driveway, Taylor West checked to make sure the gun was loaded as he waited. He thought about his wife and took another pull on the bourbon bottle. Jade had called earlier.

"Where are you?" he'd asked as nice as he could the moment he answered.

"Bozeman," she'd said in a small, guilty voice.

He'd hoped Hank might be right about Jade leaving her car in Rock Jackson's barn so she wouldn't have to pay to leave it at the airport. Instead, she was still in the state? Only miles from home?

"What are you doing there?"

"Taylor, I have some news that might upset you," she'd said in that innocent voice she used when she needed money—or now wanted something much worse.

"You think?" he'd asked sarcastically. "I found your car in Rock Jackson's barn."

"What?"

"Don't tell me you didn't know it was there."

"Taylor—"

"Jade—"

"She's leaving you, Taylor," Rock had said after taking the phone. "I wouldn't try to fight her, if I were you. From what she's told me, she has more than enough grounds for a divorce. To avoid all the bad publicity, you would be smart to give her what she wants." With that, the bastard had ended the call.

What had Jade told Rock? The mere thought sent Taylor back to the quart of bourbon he'd picked up at the liquor store. The quick swig hit his stomach like a hot brick. He tried to remember the last time he'd eaten. He'd been a mess ever since Jade had left and now she was leaving him for good? Leaving him for Rock Jackson? Had she lost her mind?

On top of that, he'd heard that Rock Jackson had been spending money as if he had it. Taylor was familiar enough with Rock's art career to know that the money hadn't come from the sale of his paintings.

Taylor had a pretty good idea where the money had come from, the lying, cheating bastard. Rock hadn't just stolen his wife, he was jeopardizing everything.

He told himself to be patient as he waited for Rock and Jade to return. He turned on the car radio to keep him company. A holiday song began to play on the radio. With a groan, he realized Christmas was only days away. "Merry Christmas," he said bitterly as he turned off the radio.

Rock would have to come home at some point. He laid the gun in his lap, took another swig of bourbon and listened for the sound of an approaching vehicle.

When Taylor woke up, Rock still hadn't returned. Now almost sober, he started the engine and drove home, determined he would be back, though, tomorrow.

SID WAS ONLY a little surprised to find her sister waiting for her at the house. Zander had let herself in, of course, and was unloading into the refrigerator groceries that she'd apparently picked up in Bozeman.

"I was questioned by the marshal today," Sid said as she brought in what she'd purchased after the marshal had let her go.

Zander lifted a brow in alarm. "Does he know—?"

"No, not about that. Seems I picked up a counterfeit twenty-dollar bill somewhere. You wouldn't know anything about that, would you?"

"Me?" Zander slammed the refrigerator. "Why is it that no matter what happens, you are always suspicious of me?"

Sid laughed. "Yes, why is that? You haven't been in my purse?"

Zander turned to roll her eyes. "You know me so well, do you? Can you imagine me getting into your purse and *leaving* money? This…plot of yours has clearly destroyed your common sense."

"Stop trying to change the subject."

"Why? Don't you think it's time that we had a talk?" her sister said, coming back into the room and plopping down on the couch. "Come on, sit down and tell me what's going on. Remember when we used to talk for hours."

"About the boys you had crushes on," Sid said, going into the kitchen and putting away the perishables she'd purchased. As she finished she looked into the living room at her sister.

Zander smiled at her as she patted a spot beside her on the couch. "You can talk to me. Clearly something is bothering you." Her sister cocked her head at her. "You sure there isn't a man? I've never seen you so… off balance."

That her sister knew her so well bothered Sid more than she wanted to admit. She didn't think she was that easy to read. Clearly, she was wrong. Laramie threw her off balance. He made her heart beat too fast. He destroyed her common sense, because she'd actually been thinking of telling him the truth about the painting—and why she so desperately needed it back.

Sid sat down on the couch, curling her legs under her, remembering, not the times she'd had to save Zander, but the times her big sister had saved her. When had the tables turned? When they'd lost their father during those months before his death?

"What would you like for Christmas?" Sid asked, not wanting to confide in Zander about Laramie or anything to do with her so-called quest.

Zander shook her head, looking disappointed. "I didn't come back for presents."

"Why did you?"

Her sister rose to pace the cabin floor. "Isn't it possible I wanted to see you?" She turned to stare at her. "Isn't it possible I was worried about you?" Sid hoped that was the case. "You think you know me, Sid? Well, I know you."

That was what scared her.

"I wish I could trust you, Z," she said, speaking her innermost wish at that moment and then wishing she hadn't.

Zander smiled as she sat back down and took one of Sid's hands, squeezing it. "I guess I'm going to have to prove it to you."

"I'm sorry I thought you'd put the counterfeit twenty in my purse." She actually had thought Zander had switched it for a good twenty. "I probably picked it up somewhere without knowing it."

"See?" Her sister was all smiles. "So while you're in this trusting mood—"

She pulled her hand free. "Z, if this is about money—"

Her sister laughed. "I love it when you call me Z.

It's been too long. But I wasn't going to ask for money. I was going to offer my help on your…project."

Sid eyed her. "I thought you were against it."

"Not really. I thought it was dangerous, a waste of your talented time. I didn't see the point. And, while I'm being honest, I felt guilty for making things even harder for you before Dad died. But you've brought me over to your side. You're almost done, right?"

She nodded, studying her sister, wondering if she could trust this. But she felt herself weaken. She had adored Z growing up. She'd missed their connection in the years since.

As much as she didn't like to admit it, Laramie Cardwell *had* become a problem. Her own fault. She shouldn't have gotten this close to him. That had been foolhardy—and dangerous.

But she wasn't quite ready to ask for her sister's help in dealing with him.

WHEN ROCK AND JADE finally came up for air the next day, they left the condo where they'd been staying. Rock hadn't thought far enough ahead as to what they would do now. He'd been in a state of happy delirium, but now that he'd come out of it, he began to worry.

Since her talk with Taylor, Jade had seemed upset, making Rock all the more nervous. For a while he'd been able to forget about his soon-to-be-ex wife, Carla. She'd been looking for ammunition in the divorce. It was one reason he'd borrowed his friend's condo. He'd been so careful not to give her anything she could use against him—until Jade had turned up at his door.

All he could hope was that Carla didn't get wind of this until the divorce papers were signed. She knew he didn't have any money, but she wanted everything else, including his family ranch. He'd told her he would see her dead first.

But now that Jade would be able to take half of Taylor's money according to Montana law, he was willing to give Carla everything just to get his freedom. That would take care of that problem.

Unfortunately there were other things to be dealt with. He hadn't liked hearing that Taylor had been on his ranch and had found Jade's car in the barn. What else had he discovered? Had he been looking for Jade? Or something else?

He tried not to worry as he looked over at Jade and counted his blessings. She was every man's dream. Jade had modeled for lingerie catalogs, so maybe she wasn't a supermodel, but she was a beauty. He'd been jealous of Taylor from the first time he'd seen them together. Everyone knew the only reason she was with that old man was his money and fame, two things that had ruled Rock out from the get-go.

But then there she'd been, standing on his doorstep and then crying in his arms. It hadn't taken a lot to get her into his bed, once he'd assured her he would help her take Taylor to the cleaners in the divorce.

What he hadn't thought about was his own life. What was he going to do with Jade now? If only his divorce was already final. What if Carla was at the house waiting for him? She'd rented a house up Bear Canyon but she often stopped by the ranch without warning. How was he going to deal with her with Jade on his arm? It could get ugly fast.

Also, he realized belatedly, he needed some time to clear out a few things at his house. Now that he had

Jade and, soon, Taylor's money, he would be making some changes—more than just getting rid of Carla. But it would be better if Jade never found out how he'd been able to live the past six months.

He looked over at her, realizing he would have to drop her off somewhere. He couldn't take her home.

"I have an idea, a treat for you to make you feel better while I take care of some things," he said.

She looked at him expectantly. She'd been moody since talking to Taylor. She wouldn't be thinking about going back to the old fool, would she?

"I know of this great day spa."

That picked up her mood considerably. Jade liked the finer things in life. Nothing wrong with that, he thought.

"I don't have any money," she said in that little-girl voice he thought charming.

"My treat." He smiled over at her as he drove toward the day spa. "I'll pick you up later and we'll go see this lawyer I know."

"Don't you think I should talk to Taylor before I talk to a lawyer?" she asked. "Maybe he won't fight me on the divorce."

"Baby, trust me. He isn't going to let you go without a fight. That's why we need to beat him to the punch." He just hoped Taylor wasn't hitting the bottle. No telling what the man would do then. "Trust me, Jade. I'll take care of you." *And you'll take care of me*, he thought.

She leaned over to kiss him on the cheek. "I don't know what I would have done without you."

"You'll never have to find out."

Jade still had the body of a model. But sometimes,

he wondered about what went on in that pretty head of hers. The fact that she'd married Taylor to begin with had always bothered him. Was it just for the money or had she really cared about him?

"Just out of curiosity," he asked as he parked in front of the day spa, "why did you *marry* Taylor?"

She frowned. "I was in Mexico, drinking tequila at this cantina. He came in with a painting he'd just finished. I couldn't afford to buy it, but I really liked it."

"You married him for a painting?"

"That, and he told me he owned a ranch in Montana." She shrugged. "You know what's funny. Once I sobered up, I didn't even like the painting."

Rock laughed as he reached across to open her door. "Maybe half of everything Taylor has will make you feel better about it."

AFTER HER SISTER LEFT, Sid knew she had to end this before Christmas Eve if at all possible. Zander being in town added a new complication to her plan.

It didn't take Sid long to find out what new alarm systems Laramie had installed in his new house. She'd used different approaches to get past security systems in the past. But she'd found the best way was the most direct.

She'd gotten her old friend Maisie French to get a part-time job at the local security company. Almost all of the Big Sky residents used the same firm. She called her now to ask if Laramie Cardwell had contacted her office yet.

"He's sticking with the security system already in place but adding cameras around the house," Maisie said.

Sid laughed. He thought he could catch her on video?

"I can send you the location of the cameras," her friend offered. "Or, if I'm working that night, I can shut them down long enough to let you get in and out." Big Sky in winter was prone to power outages so if the system went out for no more than ten minutes, it wasn't anything anyone would question. Unless of course there was a burglary.

"I thought you had a rule about going back a second time?" her friend said after Sid told her that she now had no choice but to get the painting back from Laramie Cardwell.

"I know, but it can't be helped. I can't have that painting floating around out there."

"Can't you just offer to buy it?"

Sid laughed. "He's already suspicious—if not downright convinced I'm a thief."

"But right now he has no proof. If he catches you trying to get the painting back…"

"It's a chance I have to take. He mentioned that he has a family thing tomorrow night."

"And you don't think that sounds like a trap?" Maisie cried.

Sid had to laugh again. "It absolutely does. That's why I have to hit his house tonight." She sighed. "But there's another problem—Zander."

Her friend groaned. "Let me guess—she's broke, she needs help, she wants money." Maisie had known her and Zander since they were kids growing up.

"She says she's only in town to celebrate the holidays with me. She's coming over Christmas Eve. That is why I have to take care of this before then."

Maisie groaned. "You don't trust her, right?"

"She's my sister."

"Exactly."

"I have a plan."

"Of course you do." Her friend laughed, but quickly sobered. "Be careful. I don't like this. But since I am the new kid on the block, I'm working tonight. Just let me know what time. And watch Zander."

"I always do. This is almost over."

"And it's no coincidence that Zander shows up now. It's almost as if she…knows."

Sid had thought the same thing. She disconnected and looked across the room at the costume she'd rented along with the mask for the upcoming ball. She'd told Laramie she wouldn't be caught dead at the ball. She hoped she was right.

CHAPTER THIRTEEN

TAYLOR WAS GETTING sick of waiting again outside Rock Jackson's home. More than that, he'd run out of bourbon and found himself sobering up for the third day in a row. All of which wasn't good news. Today, he'd been determined to wait for Rock and Jade until the cows came home, if that's what it took.

But he decided a quick run into the packaged goods store to get another bottle wouldn't take that long. It took a little longer than he'd expected because he'd run into a couple of men he knew and they'd bought him drinks, trying to get a free painting out of him.

Sometimes it felt as if everyone wanted a piece of him. He thought of Jade and the first time he'd laid eyes on her. He'd had to have her, no matter the cost. He was no fool. He'd known why she'd agreed to marry him in Mexico. He'd talked up his ranch, his paintings, his fame and fortune. He hadn't had to look at her to see her disappointment when they'd gotten back to Montana. He'd felt it come rolling off her in waves.

Jade had expected a place like out of one of those fancy home magazines. His ranch house was newer but it wasn't as posh as she would have liked. Nor was his fame and fortune up to her standards. Not to mention how quickly she'd gotten bored living in the canyon.

She'd spent most of her days burning the rubber off his tires running back and forth to Bozeman.

Marrying Jade had been a mistake. He admitted that as he drove back toward Rock's place. Every bit of his common sense told him to let her go. Good riddance. He could afford to hire a housekeeper to cook and clean for him since Jade hadn't been good at doing either. He would be better off without her.

Except he didn't want Rock to have her.

LARAMIE HAD DONE his best to get Sid off his mind. He couldn't even explain it to himself, but there was something about her.

"What is your attraction to this woman other than the obvious?" Austin had said when he'd stopped by earlier.

"You mean that she's beautiful, intelligent, talented?"

"No, surely it hasn't skipped your attention that we Cardwell men have a weakness for women in trouble."

"She doesn't seem to be in trouble," Laramie had said.

Austin had chuckled. "You don't believe that for a minute and neither do I. Whatever she's up to, I'm betting it's dangerous. You've already been run off the road. Next time, it might be more than a warning."

After his brother had left, Laramie pulled out his phone. "Do you have plans for tonight?" Laramie asked when Sid answered. "I know it's kind of late, but the Cardwell family gets together to decorate cookies and drink hot chocolate, with marshmallows of course, and sing carols."

"Seriously? I can't even imagine such a family."

"It probably sounds awful to you, but I thought if you didn't have any plans…"

"I do have plans," Sid had said. She'd sounded surprised by the invitation. "Otherwise, I would love to."

"Really? I'm glad to hear that. Maybe next year."

"Next year?" She'd laughed. "You can plan ahead that far?"

"Can't you?"

She hadn't answered that.

"Dana also wanted me to tell you that we're having steaks."

"It sounds wonderful, but I can't," she'd said before she could weaken. "Thank you for the offer, though. Please give my regrets to Dana."

"I will. She'll be disappointed. Not as much as me, though," he'd added. "Well, enjoy your holidays if I don't see you before then. Maybe I'll see you after?"

"Maybe."

SID FELT A TIGHTENING in her throat and felt her eyes blur as she thought about his earlier call. She could envision the family in that large living room she'd only gotten a glimpse of through a window.

Steaks at Cardwell Ranch sounded wonderful. But to spend a holiday in that house with that family? There would be music and laughter. Knowing what little she did about Dana, there would be food and drinks. She could almost smell the evergreen tree, almost taste the gingerbread men fresh from the oven, almost hear the sound of Christmas carols being sung by the family.

Laughing at her foolishness, she pushed the vision away. She'd only seen family gatherings like that in movies and television soap operas. Did they really exist?

She thought of her own childhood and the goofy little tree she and Zander had dragged in one year. They'd made ornaments for it and bought presents to put under it. They hadn't been much. Those had been the lean years before things got really bad.

Swallowing the lump that had formed, she realized she was hugging herself. What would Laramie think if he knew the truth?

She shoved that thought away. For all she knew, the invitation was just him still trying to track down his elusive cat burglar. The invitation was just to let her know he wouldn't be home tonight. The trap was set.

Sid hated being this suspicious. Especially of a man she was developing feelings for. *Did* have feelings for, in spite of the circumstances. The thought made her laugh. She really needed to finish this and move on.

As ROCK DROVE into his ranch, he was glad to see that Taylor's SUV wasn't parked out front. He wouldn't have been surprised if it had been. Taylor could be a hothead. He drove straight to the back of the studio where his car would be out of sight just in case the fool came searching for his wife. He wasn't looking forward to a face-to-face with the artist, drunk or sober. There was too much history between them, not to mention the one big secret that had them locked in a death grip for life.

At the back of his studio, he was surprised to see where someone had beaten on his padlock trying to break in. Had it been Taylor when he'd found his wife's car in the barn? Or his not-ex-enough wife, Carla? He hadn't given her a key. He wasn't stupid.

Opening the lock with his key, he was glad to see that everything was as he'd left it. But the evidence couldn't stay here, not when he planned to bring Jade home with him. He popped open the back of the SUV. He had a storage shed rented in town that no one knew about, not even Carla, since he'd put it in his other ex-wife's name. He was damned glad of it right now.

With any luck, he would never need any of this again, he thought, as he loaded everything into the back of the vehicle. If things worked out with Jade, he wouldn't need to make extra money and could get rid of all the evidence soon. He still couldn't believe his luck.

He tried to relax, to be happy. Hell, he should be celebrating right now. He had it all. Or at least he would soon. But he'd never been one to count his chickens before that last egg hatched. His life had been too tough not to know that things could turn sour at a moment's notice. Especially when dealing with a woman like Jade…

It didn't take that long to load everything and drive down to the storage shed. On the way back, feeling confident he was in the clear now, he had a feeling he'd forgotten something. He swore as he remembered what it was, then he drove back toward the ranch. Glancing at his watch, he told himself to hurry. Jade would be getting antsy. He called her and, sure enough, she was finished and waiting for him.

"Go next door to the bar. I'll be there before you know it."

LARAMIE WAS DISAPPOINTED that Sid couldn't be here with him as he entered the Cardwell Ranch main house.

He wondered what her plans were as he made his way to the kitchen where Dana was at work.

"Sid's busy?" Dana asked as she slid warm cookies from a pan onto a cooling rack. "I'm sorry."

"Me, too." Would she take advantage of him being gone and take the painting tonight?

On the drive to the ranch he'd told himself he should cut this visit short after Christmas and return to the warmth of Houston—and the job he was getting paid to do. But watching over the Texas Boys Barbecue empire didn't take much watching. If he was being truthful, the company now had accountants and secretaries that did most of the work. He was more of an overseer. Maybe that was why he'd been getting a little bored with it.

Bored enough that he'd been looking forward to catching an art thief. The only thing worse would be falling for the thief.

His father, Angus, came into the kitchen and slapped Laramie on the shoulder, wishing him a merry Christmas. He hadn't seen his father yet on this trip to Montana. Dana was so excited that the whole family could be together, even Austin, who had been terrible about missing family get-togethers.

"The steaks are about ready," Angus said to Dana. "Hud wanted me to let you know." He took the huge platter Dana handed him and headed back outside.

"Everything else is ready," she called to Angus's retreating back, then turned to Laramie. "I'm sorry. But Sid probably has plans for the holidays, don't you think?"

He had no idea. In the time he'd spent with her, he had learned little about her. His gut told him, though, that she was in trouble, and that alone made him want to save her. It was a Cardwell trait that ran in his family, one he'd never felt so strongly before. Cardwell men were into helping women out of tight spots, he thought, as his brothers, father and uncle came in from the outside grill, followed by a flock of small laughing children.

Laramie had just never experienced what he was feeling for Sid. But now he understood its power. He realized he would do whatever it took to save Sid— even if it meant saving her from herself.

The smell of beef steaks filled the dining room as everyone began to take their seats, the kids all at a smaller table nearby. Laramie tried to enjoy himself, but he couldn't get his mind off Sid. What was she doing right now? He hated to think.

Earlier that day he'd found an article on a famous art forger who was so good that a lot of art experts would no longer authenticate paintings for fear of being wrong. Was there a cowboy artist that good here? Taylor had said the only person good enough was the deceased H. F. Powell.

Laramie barely heard the chatter around the table, the clink of glasses or the rattle of silverware. As the meal wound down, he looked out the window. It was already dark in the canyon even though it was still relatively early. Cardwell Ranch sat at the foot of the mountains alongside the Gallatin River. Earlier he'd driven over a wooden bridge to get here, the entire landscape shrouded in ice-cold white.

"Why do you keep looking at your watch?" Austin demanded from next to him at the huge dinner table in cousin Dana's dining room. A burst of giggles came from the children's table. Dana got up to see what was going on.

Laramie shook his head. He just had a feeling he couldn't shake. It wouldn't be enough to catch Sid on camera. He needed to catch her red-handed. He needed to see it for himself.

"You need to let it go," Austin said as they all rose to take their dishes into the kitchen. "You need to let *her* go."

Laramie looked at his brother. "What if I can't?"

His brother groaned and shook his head. Austin actually looked sorry for him.

"Tell Dana I had to go," Laramie said, realizing he had only one choice as he handed his brother his dirty plate. "She'll understand."

WHEN HE GOT BACK to Rock Jackson's ranch, Taylor was disappointed to see that they still hadn't returned even though it was getting dark. He settled in again with a new bottle. He'd gotten a quart since he was determined to stay until Rock returned and he'd realized that could take all night.

He kept the gun handy as he parked under some pines at the edge of the property where he could see any vehicle that pulled in, but where Rock wouldn't notice him.

Too much bourbon mixed with lack of sleep and food, and he found he couldn't keep his eyes open. Laying the seat back, he decided to take a nap, telling himself he'd hear Rock when he drove in.

The dream started out nice enough. A sunny, bright day in summer. He had been for a ride that morning after doing his chores. His father had gone to Fargo, North Dakota, to pick up a bull he'd bought. He'd wanted Taylor's older brother to go along, but Buzz didn't want to go.

"Then you're coming with me," his father had said.

Taylor couldn't think of anything worse than being trapped in a truck with the old man for two days. Not to mention, he'd been the old man's second choice. He knew his father would browbeat him the whole way. He'd always been a disappointment to his father.

On impulse, he had pretended to be sick to his stomach. His father had changed his mind about taking him and left alone. It was perfect. Buzz had some girl he planned to spend all his time with in town. Nothing could keep Taylor from doing what he loved.

He'd retrieved his paints and canvas from under the bed where he'd kept them hidden and went downstairs to the well-lit kitchen. A wave of nostalgia hit him now at the thought of the many hours he used to sit here with his mother when she was alive. She said she loved to watch him paint. She always protected him when his father caught him painting.

"You're making a sissy out of that boy," he would bellow. "I need a ranch hand, not some worthless, namby-pamby kid who likes to paint pretty pictures."

That day, with the sun coming in the kitchen window along with a warm breeze, he'd gotten lost in his art. He was so absorbed in what he was doing, he didn't hear his father return. He didn't hear his footfalls until the man was behind him and then it was too late.

All he felt was the first blow—the one that broke his arm. He never painted after that. Not until he'd escaped the ranch and his old man.

Taylor stirred, the dream making him moan with pain in his sleep. He blinked. Had he heard a vehicle?

CHAPTER FOURTEEN

SID HAD LITTLE to thank her sister Zander for, and yet tonight as she climbed on her snowmobile, pulling the ski mask down over her face, she was thankful for the part of Zander that loved breaking the rules. Her sister had acquired a talent for breaking and entering at a young age. A couple of times she'd dragged her unsuspecting little sister into her mischief. When Sid had gotten caught, she hadn't told on Zander.

Instead, Sid had used that leverage to force her sister to teach her the tricks. Since then, she'd picked up a few of her own thanks to the internet. That and making the right friends. Her childhood friend Maisie had been quick to help with Sid's plan by coming to Big Sky and getting the job at the security company.

Along with being able to shut off the power to a house for up to ten minutes, Maisie was also able to give Sid computer access to the cameras Laramie had installed. She could see him coming and going that way. Her computer beeped whenever the camera was activated.

Earlier, she'd watched on screen as Laramie came out of the house, all dressed up and carrying a bottle of wine as he got into his rental SUV and left. No doubt headed for Cardwell Ranch. She felt a pang of regret. If only she was going with him. She thought about the horseback ride and the kiss. There was something about this Texas cowboy that tugged at her heartstrings—the worst thing that could happen to her right now.

As she drove her snowmobile up the mountain, she told herself that Laramie Cardwell's only interest in her was as an art thief. If she thought it was more than that—which she wanted to be true—then she was setting herself up for a heartbreak.

Zander had called earlier asking about what kind of wine Sid preferred.

"Seriously?" Sid had said.

Zander had laughed. "So you're still a beer drinker. You're such a Montana girl. Okay. I can't wait for tomorrow night. Maybe I'll drop by a few things I've picked up later tonight. Would that be all right?"

She'd said she had to go out for a while. "But I trust you know how to let yourself in."

Her sister had chuckled. "See you later, then."

Sid hoped she had plenty of time to get this job done and return before her sister showed up. She didn't like the idea of Zander having too much time alone in her cabin.

Taking the back trails she knew so well, she put the Texas cowboy out of her mind. She was on a job. Just business—plain and simple. She would get in and out. And that would be the end of it. If Laramie suspected she was the one who'd taken the painting, well…let him prove it. Not even Laramie Cardwell could seduce the truth out of her. But she would like to see him try, she thought for only an errant moment.

If he was merely trying to catch a thief, then once she had the painting, he would lose interest in her. It would be over. She'd have the proof she needed about his feelings for her. That thought did little to warm the cold winter night.

She stopped a short distance from the house and killed the engine. Working her way through the snow up to the side of the house, she checked her watch and waited until the outside light behind the house blinked out.

A few moments later, she was climbing up the side of the house onto the roofline. She went in the same way she had the first time—through an upstairs window. She'd disabled the lock the first time she was there and doubted Laramie had noticed. Most windows this high above the ground were never locked anyway.

Lowering herself by the rope she'd attached to the chimney, she dropped down to the window, opened it and slipped inside. As long as she moved quickly, no one would be the wiser. In and out. Five minutes tops.

As she slipped into Laramie's master bedroom, she dropped to the floor and checked her watch. She waited a moment, listening, before she turned on her penlight.

"IT WAS GOOD to see you, son," Laramie's father said as he left. "I hope you think about spending even more time up here now." It was what Angus always said. It was no secret that he hoped all of his sons would return to Montana.

Once outside, Laramie breathed in the cold night air and headed for his SUV. He couldn't shake the feeling that Sid would hit his house tonight. The cameras he had installed would prove it. But he knew that what he needed more than anything was to catch her in the act.

Maybe then he could get some answers out of her. And then he could corral these feelings he had for her.

But it was still early. He told himself she wouldn't attempt the theft until later—just as she had done last time. Laramie knew he was hoping he was wrong about her. Maybe she really was busy tonight—doing something other than robbing him.

It had begun to snow again as Laramie drove toward Sid's cabin. Huge lacy flakes spiraled down from the darkness in a dizzying white. He told himself he was on a fool's errand. He would find her in her cabin wrapping presents, visiting with friends over a bottle of wine, possibly even spending a quiet evening with another man.

That thought jolted him hard. He hadn't even considered that there might be a man in her life. A woman who looked like her? Of course, there would be a man.

Or not, he thought. Wouldn't a man have to know what Sid did late at night? The man would either have to be in on it or…

He found her cabin from the directions the waitress who knew her at Texas Boys Barbecue had provided.

"You can't miss it. Small cabin, stuck back in the woods. It's the last place on that road."

As the cabin appeared in his headlights, he saw that there was no light behind the windows. He slowed, aware that he would now have to turn around. What if she was home…and sitting in the dark, waiting for him to drive by to check on her? He shook off that ridiculous idea.

She wasn't home, he told himself as he turned around. Probably out on a date. Or shopping for groceries. Or out on a date. Or finishing up her Christmas shopping. Mentally he kicked himself. What was wrong with him? He'd never acted like this with any other woman.

But when he stole a look in his rearview mirror as he pulled away, he knew that Obsidian "Sid" Forester was like no other woman he'd ever met. He also realized as the dark cabin disappeared from view, that it was probably no coincidence that she lived on such an isolated road. He couldn't see any other cabins near hers but it was dark and the pines were thick on the mountain behind her cabin. Maybe this place wasn't as isolated as he thought, but he wouldn't have bet on it.

The snow was falling harder now. It blew past horizontally on a gust of wind, shaking the SUV, shaking his thoughts. Sid wasn't out buying groceries or last-minute Christmas presents. Nor did he believe she was on a date.

No, if he was right about her, she was at his house right now stealing the painting like the thief she was.

JADE CALLED RIGHT AS Rock was pulling around the back of his studio. "I'm on my way."

"Are you trying to get me drunk?" she asked, sounding pouty. "I'm already on my third drink."

Just what he needed—her sloppy drunk before he rescued her. "I forgot to ask. How was the spa treatment?"

"Wonderful."

"Good. Sip that drink. I'll be there in ten minutes." He disconnected, pocketed his phone and got out. Even with darkness upon him, the temperature was in the forties. He loved a good holiday thaw when the snow disappeared at lower elevations and he didn't have to be bundled up as much. He was sick of winters. Maybe he and Jade should move south. They could get a place in Arizona. Jade might like that.

He unlocked the back door of the studio again and stepped in. The room smelled of chemicals and the odor hit him like a two-by-four in the face. He quickly moved to the windows and opened them even though this thaw couldn't last much longer.

Breathing a little easier, he looked around the room for what he might have forgotten. Maybe he was just being paranoid. No, he realized as he spotted it. He'd forgotten to clean up the garbage with the empty bottles of acetone and bleach, masks and gloves. He shook his head at how close he'd come to blowing it. Pulling out a garbage bag, he quickly filled it and spun around as a shadow filled the open doorway.

Alarmed, he dropped the bag. "Oh, you startled me there for a moment." He reached for the garbage bag, telling himself to play it cool. "I was just leaving, but maybe we can talk—" The rest died on his lips as he saw the gun. "Wait a minute." He held the full garbage bag in front of him as if it would stop a bullet, and he took a step back, his mind racing. "This is a mistake. You don't want to—"

The first shot caught him in the chest at heart level. He barely felt the second or third or even fourth shots as he fell to the concrete floor.

LARAMIE DROVE ONLY partway up the mountain to his house. He hadn't seen another soul on the road tonight once he'd left Meadow Village, other than the faint light of a snowmobile through the falling snow shortly after he'd turned around at Sid's cabin.

In a wide spot where the snowplow had turned around, he parked and got out. The walk up the mountain had him breathing fairly hard. Even though he was in good shape, he still wasn't used to the altitude.

As he reached the top of a rise, he slowed. Fortunately there was no moon tonight and clouds obscured even the stars. The darkness would have been complete if not for the blanket of reflective snow that covered the ground.

That gut feeling he'd had earlier at dinner had proved right, he thought as he looked toward the house. A tiny light bobbed in the master bedroom. *Sid was here.*

His heart began to pound with both excitement at finally catching her—and disappointment. He realized he'd been hoping he was wrong all this time. Or that there was a good explanation. Clearly he didn't know this woman. For that reason, he felt a sliver of concern that he might be walking into something more dangerous than he thought.

His plan on the way up the mountain had been to catch her in the act. Now that he was almost to the house, he realized she could be armed. He thought of the woman he'd kissed. She wouldn't shoot him, even if she was armed, he told himself.

You'd stake your life on a kiss? It was Austin's cynical voice in his head. He knew his brother had staked his life on even less.

Laramie reached the side door, unlocked it and stepped in. He had only a matter of seconds to disarm the silent security system. Or had she already disabled it? He couldn't take the chance that it might go off and alert her.

As quietly as possible, he stepped to it to punch in the code and saw that the system was off. He looked toward the stairs.

SID PICKED UP the painting and hesitated. Why had he left both of the paintings here together? Because he knew she would be back for one of them. She slid the light over the canvas of one and then the other until she found what she was looking for.

The difference between the two paintings was impossible for anyone else to discern. But she knew where to look. She picked up the forgery and, her penlight guiding the way, started toward the window with time to spare.

But still her footsteps faltered. Laramie would know she'd taken it. He'd been waiting for her to return. He'd had the cameras installed so he could catch her. She remembered his lips on hers, the taste and feel of him.

She shook off the memory. All the kiss had been was a ruse. Him making her doubt he was onto her. She mentally shook herself, telling herself she had known the score from the beginning. It wasn't as if she'd fallen for it. The irony didn't escape her. She was the thief, the liar, the one who wasn't being honest with *him*.

Sid wasn't sure if she heard or just sensed something.

Someone else was in the house.

She froze, listening. A faint sound two floors below. All houses had their own unique sounds, but this was human.

Her gaze shot up to the cameras. No light. They weren't on yet. She checked her watch. Time was running out. She had to move.

Hastily, she snapped off the penlight and slipped it into her pocket. As she started to step out the window into the falling snow, Sid belatedly realized the mistake she'd made in her hurry. The penlight, not all the way into her pocket, fell out, dropped to the floor and clattered on the hardwood.

LARAMIE LOOKED UP as he heard the sound. She was here, on the top floor. He felt his heart take off at a gallop at the thought of catching her red-handed. They could quit playing this game of cat and mouse.

The thought should have brought him more satisfaction. Wasn't this what he'd wanted since that first night? No, he thought as he turned toward the stairs. At first all he had wanted was to find the woman—not fall for her. Had he found her in Obsidian "Sid" Forester? He was about to find out.

He took a step toward the first stair, telling himself it would be over soon, one way or another. Behind him, he heard a floorboard creak and frowned in momentary confusion. Until that moment, he hadn't considered that there might be more than one of them.

As he spun around, he had only a moment to take in the person before him. "Sid?" The glare of the falling snow outside the window lit her face. Too late he caught the movement of her arm—and the weapon in her hand.

Instinctively, he tried to step back, bumping into the stairs. The blow to the side of his head staggered him. He fought to keep his balance, but his eyesight was dimming to nothing more than a pinpoint.

He felt himself falling, blackness filling his vision, filling his head. The last thing he saw was her standing over him with the weapon in her hand.

CHAPTER FIFTEEN

"YOU HIT HIM too hard," Sid said with a curse as she knelt down beside Laramie. She hadn't known what was going on downstairs and had been shocked to find her sister standing over him.

"I had no choice. He would have caught you."

Sid quickly felt for a pulse and then checked his pupils. "What are you doing here anyway?"

"I thought you might need my help. When I saw him come by the cabin…"

She shot her sister a look over her shoulder. The last thing she needed was help. In a few more seconds she would have been out the window and gone.

"He saw me," her sister said, raised her hands in surrender when Sid turned to glare at her in disbelief. "Don't worry, he thought I was you."

"Great. That's perfect."

"Maybe he won't remember anything," Zander offered.

Sid shook her head in exasperation as she turned back to Laramie. "Get me a cold cloth out of the kitchen."

Zander returned a few moments later. "Here." She thrust the cold wet cloth into Sid's hand. "So what are *you* doing here?" Her gaze went to the painting leaning against the wall where Sid had dropped it. "Is that one of them?" she asked in a hushed voice.

Sid didn't bother to answer as Laramie moaned, his eyelids fluttering.

"You should get out of here before he wakes up."

"We both should," Zander said, her eyes riveted to the painting. "And why all the concern over this guy? Is there more going on here than even I think?"

"Wait for me at my cabin. We can talk later." Zander still hesitated. Laramie moaned again. "Go! I don't want him catching both of us here."

Her sister finally moved, slipping out into the night. Laramie was coming to.

LARAMIE WOKE WITH a killer headache. He tried to get up from where he lay on the floor, but he settled for sitting on the lower step until his head cleared a little. He had a bump on his temple that throbbed and hurt like hell when he touched it.

At the sound of footfalls, he looked up, shocked to see he wasn't alone. "What did you hit me with?"

"I'm sorry about your headache."

"Are you?"

"How's your head?" she asked, ignoring the question.

"It hurts." He narrowed his eyes at her, trying to understand what she was still doing here. Why hadn't she just taken the painting and left? "I figured you'd be long gone."

She nodded. "So did I." She took a step toward him. "Here, I found these in your medicine cabinet. I'll get you a glass of water." She dropped two white pills into his open palm.

He stared at them.

"They're just aspirin," she said.

"Right."

"If I was going to drug you, don't you think I already would have?"

"Quite frankly, I never know what to expect with you," he said.

He took the two white pills she handed him and stared at them while she went into the kitchen. They looked like two over-the-counter pain pills.

She handed him a glass of water. He met her gaze, held it for a moment and downed the pills and the water.

"So are we going to be honest now?" he asked. When she didn't say anything, he added, "I hope you aren't going to tell me that the real cat burglar was the one who hit me."

"It's a long story."

"One I'm dying to hear."

"Maybe we'd better go into the living room where it is more comfortable, then," she said.

He got up from the step, still feeling woozy, but anxious to hear any explanation she had to give.

"I don't know where to begin," Sid said when they were seated across from each other.

"Why don't you start with why you need that painting so much," he said, pointing to it where she'd left it by the stairs.

She sighed and looked away for a moment. When she looked at him again, he saw that her beautiful eyes had filled with tears. "I need it to catch the men who murdered my father."

Laramie felt a start. Her father was *murdered*? "Who was your father?"

"H. F. Powell."

LARAMIE STARED AT HER. "You're his *daughter*? So Forester is your…married name?"

She shook her head. "My parents never married. I told you it was a long story."

His head ached. He rubbed his temples, trying to make sense of this. "You said your father was murdered? I hadn't heard anything about that."

"Because his death was ruled an accident. The investigators believed my father had started the fire that destroyed his studio and everything in it—including him."

"But you think it was murder?"

"I *know* it was murder, and I've been working to prove it."

He sat up a little straighter. While his brain probably wasn't functioning as well as it could have been under the circumstances, he couldn't help suspecting he was being conned.

"Excuse my skepticism, but I don't see how stealing paintings will help you solve his…alleged murder."

"At first, I thought that the investigators were right and that my father *had* started the fire," Sid said. "Until the forgeries started showing up."

"Maybe it's my headache, but I'm having trouble—"

She sighed again and got to her feet to pace. "You have to understand. My father was an eccentric genius and because of that he made enemies." Sid waved an arm through the air as if that was putting it mildly. "Admittedly, he was often his own worst enemy. He wasn't…conventional. He hated rules. Which is probably one reason he and my mother never married. He'd married once before and the woman had left him. My father also didn't make the best husband—or father, for that matter. He would lock himself in his studio for days on end until he was too exhausted to paint."

Laramie said nothing, just letting her talk, as he tried to make sense of what she was telling him.

"When the Old West Artists Coalition was started, my father just assumed they would invite him to join." She stopped pacing to let out a laugh. "He would have turned them down flat. He *hated* organizations. But instead, they shunned him, saying that while his paintings were all right, his character was lacking."

Laramie thought he could see how that might affect a man like the one she'd described. "He was angry?"

Sid barked out another laugh. "He was *furious*. He swore he would show them that he could paint so much better than any of them that they wouldn't be able to tell his forgeries from their own work." She nodded. "He became obsessed. He quit painting his own work, determined to show them up."

"They found out and tried to stop him," he guessed.

"He must have bragged to someone about what he was doing. He planned to expose them at their annual conference."

Laramie saw where she was headed with this. "The forgeries were in the studio the night of the fire?"

She nodded. "I've always questioned why he would go to all the trouble of painting the copies only to change his mind and destroy not just them, but also himself." Sid met his gaze. "That's just it. He wouldn't have."

"So whoever took the forgeries…"

"Killed my father."

Laramie blew out a breath of air as he leaned back. "And you think you know who took them. If you're right, then you do realize how dangerous this pursuit of yours is, don't you?"

She smiled at that.

"Right," he said, feeling foolish. This was a woman who ran along rooflines in the middle of the night, broke into houses, chancing everything to get these forgeries back. This was his cat burglar.

"So have you figured out who is responsible?"

"I suspected it was one of the four founders of OWAC, but now I'm thinking all four of them were behind it. They are the ones who kept my father out of organization, the ones he despised the most. They are the ones who had the most to lose by his plan to expose them and their organization. They'd been pulling some fast ones, using the organization to raise money for charities and pocketing most of it. They had reason to fear him. By then my father was being recognized as a great artist. Once he revealed the forgeries, there would have been a lot of bad publicity that would have hurt them and shone a light on their organization. They would have been lucky if they hadn't ended up in jail."

Laramie closed his eyes for a moment, glad that the aspirin seemed to be doing the job of relieving his headache a little. "What I don't understand is why did the person who killed your father take the forgeries? Why not leave them to burn?"

"I assume the killer was worried that the fire might be put out before all the evidence burned. Maybe they planned to destroy the copies. If I'm right and all four of them were in on it, then one of them must have been responsible for getting rid of the forgeries—but didn't."

Laramie nodded. "You're sure these are forgeries that your father painted?"

"Yes."

He thought about what Taylor West had told him. There was only one artist who was so good that he could make a forgery that even the artist believed was his painting—H. F. Powell. That explained why West got so upset once he realized the significance of the painting Laramie had brought to him. It was one of the forgeries.

"Still, it makes no sense," he argued. "Why would one of them take the chance of letting these forgeries get back on the market?"

Sid shrugged. "Money, would be my guess. Also, maybe he thought enough time had passed that the duplicate paintings wouldn't come to light."

He studied her beautiful face, realizing what she'd been doing. "So you're stealing back the forgeries."

She didn't deny it.

"So you have all of them?" Laramie asked.

"With the one you have, yes."

"And with them, you'll be able to prove who killed your father?"

She looked away. "I thought I would, but it isn't going to be as easy as I'd hoped. And now I have one more forgery that has turned up that I need to get. Unfortunately, I don't have an original to trade."

"WAS THAT HIM?" Zander asked as Sid came in the back door. Her sister was sprawled on the couch, a half-empty bottle of wine on the floor next to her.

She was already furious with her sister. "What?"

"The man you're falling for," Zander said, grinning as she sat up. "Don't try to deny it. I saw the way you were with him." She shook her head. "I can't see any way this is going to turn out well."

"Don't you have somewhere to be?"

"Not really. You never told me why you went there tonight."

She had no patience for this. "Guess."

"Another so-called forgery." Zander shook her head. "I was hoping you had turned into a real cat burglar. I guess it was too much to hope for. Seriously, when are you going to stop this?"

"When I'm finished with what I started. Thanks to you, I didn't get away clean tonight." She turned her back to her sister, too angry to deal with her right now. "I had to tell Laramie what I was doing."

Zander swore. "That was a mistake."

"Maybe." She trusted him, probably a mistake. But she'd had no choice, thanks to her sister.

"If you'd told me what you were doing, I could have helped you."

Sid turned. "*Helped me?* You could have helped by staying away."

"Isn't it possible that I want justice for our father, too?"

"I thought you didn't believe he was murdered?" Sid demanded. Then she saw her sister's expression. "You *do* believe it."

Zander's gaze met hers. "Does it matter? I still can't see how any of this is going to help. He's gone. Nothing you do can bring him back."

She didn't want to argue about this. It wasn't revenge. It was simple justice. But maybe it would end just as her sister had predicted and she wouldn't be able to prove who killed him—let alone see that the men responsible got what was coming to them.

"Just let me finish what I started."

Zander got up from the couch. "Tonight aside, you're pushing your luck. I don't even want to know what you told Laramie Cardwell after I left. If any of this gets out and the killer finds out you're after him… The way I see it, you *need* my help."

Sid would love to have argued that her sister was wrong. Unfortunately, if she had any hope of pulling off the next part, she could use Zander's expertise.

Seeing her weaken, her sister smiled. "You know I'm good because I taught you everything you know."

"Not *everything*. If I thought I could trust you…"

Her sister looked excited. "Whatever it is, I'm in."

"You might not be when I tell you my plan."

LARAMIE DIDN'T KNOW what to think after Sid left. She'd trusted him with her story. He'd believed her. And while he'd done his best to talk her into going to the marshal, she'd refused, telling him that while she had all the paintings, she didn't have any proof. Yet. She made him promise he wouldn't go to the authorities, either.

"I went to the police when the first forgery turned up," she'd said. "I saw it at a gallery in Bozeman. The police didn't believe me."

"How can you be so sure it was one of your father's?" he'd asked, hating how skeptical he sounded.

She'd gone to the painting she'd left leaning against the wall by the stairs and brought it over to him. "I know this looks identical to the original, but my father had too much ego to copy it exactly. He had to leave his mark on it." She'd cocked the painting so the over-head light fell across it. "It's very small but if you look closely," she'd said pointing to a spot.

"It looks like a wolf's face."

Sid laughed. "Like I said, my father's ego made him leave a little something of himself behind. The lone wolf. But it is camouflaged and easily goes unno-ticed—unless you know what to look for and where." She'd seen his still-skeptical expression and had left the painting to go upstairs to retrieve the original. "See for yourself."

He had.

Now he found himself pacing the floor as she had done. He couldn't help being worried about her. Like he'd told her, this was dangerous. It probably explained why someone had tried to run him off the road after his visit with Taylor West. He was reminded as well of Cody Kent's reaction to the painting as well as Taylor's. Had Taylor called Cody as soon as he'd left? He prob-ably called all of the others, if Sid was right and they were responsible for H. F. Powell's death.

"They know now that the forgeries were never de-stroyed," Laramie had told her. "They'll be running scared and who knows how far they'll go to keep this from ever coming out. It isn't just about ruining their reputations. We're talking murder."

Sid had smiled. "If I'm right, they'll start turning on each other—if they haven't already."

"Or they'll all come after you."

"They don't even know that I am H. F. Powell's daughter," she'd said with a shake of her head. "But I'll be careful."

He had seen that she was touched that he was worried about her. He had moved to her, cupping her cheek with his palm. "Let me help. Two of my brothers are private investigators and I—"

"No." She'd moved away before turning to look at him again. "I can't tell you how sorry I am that you are involved at all."

"Sid, can't you see that I... I care about you?"

She'd smiled and nodded. "But now I need you to trust me. Can you do that?"

He'd said he could. "But if you need me—"

Sid had stepped to him to give him a quick kiss. "I'm almost finished with this. Any interference now could destroy all the work I've done."

Against his better judgment, he'd agreed to stay out of it. What choice did he have? Go to Hud with what he knew? He couldn't do that to Sid. Nor did he know how to help her—other than letting her finish what she'd started.

Getting to his feet now, he walked into the kitchen and saw the wet cloth on the counter. Frowning, he picked it up as a flash of memory came rushing at him. Sid leaning over him, pressing the cold washcloth to his forehead.

More of the memory teased at him. Sid with something else in her hand, only...only something was wrong. He shook his head, regretting it as he felt his headache kick in again. The bottle of aspirin was also on the counter. She must have gotten it from the medicine cabinet upstairs.

A slice of memory wove its way in. He'd heard a sound upstairs, like someone dropping something on the hardwood floor. Or was it behind him? He remembered turning. The falling snow in the doorway. He'd seen a woman's face the instant before he'd felt the blow. Sid's? No.

His pulse jumped.

It hadn't been Sid who'd hit him.

CHAPTER SIXTEEN

LARAMIE HAD BELIEVED SID. But if there'd been someone else in his house last night, another woman who looked like Sid, then Sid had left out a key part of her story.

The problem was that this morning, in the light of day, he couldn't be sure of what he'd thought he'd seen before taking the blow. Wouldn't Sid have mentioned it if someone else had been there last night before he came to?

He'd quickly checked the security cameras he'd had installed. And hadn't been surprised to find the cameras had been turned off during the burglary. The woman knew how to cover her tracks. That should have given him some assurance that she knew what she was doing going after her father's killers.

His headache had subsided, but he still had a knot on his skull from where someone had nailed him. A mystery woman who looked enough like Sid to fool him? Or Sid herself?

He'd had trouble getting to sleep last night under the weight of what Sid had told him. He reached for his cell phone. Last night, he'd promised to stay out of it. But how could he? If he did and something happened to her—

Sid's number went straight to voice mail.

"It's just me. I was thinking about you this morning." He disconnected knowing there was no reason to ask her to call him. He doubted she would anyway. She'd been pretty clear last night.

Gingerly touching the bump on his head, he tried to remember what exactly he'd seen. He'd barely pocketed his phone when it rang again. He hoped it was Sid.

"It's Dana," his cousin said cheerfully. "I hope I'm not calling too early. I just wanted to remind you that the ball and auction is tonight." He groaned silently, having forgotten about it. "I took the liberty of having them hold three different costumes, but you need to let them know which one you want."

He swore silently. "Thank you," he said.

"I promise you will be glad you went to it," Dana said. "Everyone will be there."

Not everyone, he thought, thinking of Sid.

"I'll go and pick up my costume this morning," he told her.

"See you tonight. Let us know if you need a ride."

He had to smile as he pocketed his phone. There was no one quite like Dana. Whether or not he'd be glad he attended the ball was debatable, but he would go nonetheless because he adored her. Not because he thought for a moment he would enjoy it.

He couldn't get his mind off Sid and what she'd told him last night as he went to pick up his costume for tonight. She was so sure that the four founding members of the Old West Artists Coalition had been involved in her father's death.

They'd apparently stolen the forgeries and trusted one of them to destroy them. He hadn't. At least that was Sid's theory. Now she thought they would turn on each other. Laramie wished he believed that. They'd kept quiet about what they'd done, if Sid was right, for all these years.

It wasn't until later in the day, after running errands, that he turned on the television. He made up his mind that he couldn't sit back and do nothing. He would find out everything he could about the artists she thought were involved, he told himself, as he dressed for the ball.

That's why, when the local news came on, he couldn't have been more shocked. Maybe Sid was right after all.

ROCK JACKSON'S MURDER topped the news. Even more shocking was the arrest of Taylor West.

Laramie stood in front of the television, having a hard time believing what he was hearing. Taylor West had apparently been found passed out in his vehicle outside the Jackson residence, holding what was believed to be the murder weapon.

West had been intoxicated, resisted arrest and was now charged with multiple offenses, including homicide.

"The cowboy artist's death has now been linked to a counterfeit money operation," the broadcaster was saying. "It is uncertain if West was involved in the counterfeit operation with Jackson. But items found at the scene along with that found in a storage unit implicates artist Rock Jackson in the counterfeiting operation."

The broadcaster cut to an interview with Cody Kent and another man identified as cowboy artist Hank Ramsey. He recognized Cody and turned up the volume. Cody was saying he was shocked by the turn of events. He said he hadn't seen either man in some time.

"What a tragedy," Cody said. "Two such talented artists. They'll both be missed."

Hank Ramsey was as dark as Cody Kent was blond. Unlike Cody, he was clean-shaven with his dark hair cut short. He nervously turned the brim of his Stetson while he talked, his voice breaking at times.

"A tragedy. I only know what I heard on the news this morning. I talked to Taylor recently. I knew he was upset, but I never dreamed... Just a tragedy."

The television station cut back to the broadcaster, who moved on to other news. Laramie's phone rang.

"I assume you've seen the news," his brother Austin said.

"Do they know why Taylor West killed him?" Laramie had to ask. His head swam. Did this have something to do with the forgeries?

"I talked to Hud. Apparently Rock was having an affair with Taylor's wife. Taylor swears he didn't kill the man, but his gun appears to be the murder weapon, and he was in possession of it at the time of his arrest. Hud thinks it might also have something to do with the counterfeit money operation. Taylor swears he had nothing to do with that, either."

Laramie thought about telling his brother what had happened at his house last night. But apparently it had nothing to do with the murder or the counterfeit operation. At least he hoped to hell it didn't.

"Glad Hud caught the counterfeiter," he managed to say, wondering if anyone else was involved. And if Taylor West was telling the truth about not killing Rock, then who did?

He tried Sid's number again only to have it go

straight to voice mail. He didn't leave a message. As he pocketed the phone, he feared she might be up to her neck in all this.

THE HOLIDAY BALL and Art Auction was held each year at the Big Sky Pavilion. Laramie saw the lights from miles away. Valets parked cars in one of the huge snowy lots above it. Along with arranging for a costume, Dana had made sure that Laramie had his ticket.

She had a one-in-three chance of figuring out who he was, given that she had arranged the costumes. But he wasn't sure what she and Hud would be wearing. His brothers had been equally secretive.

Waiters moved through the crowd with bubbling champagne flutes and fancy hors d'oeuvres. The lobby was a roar of voices. Beyond it, Laramie could hear music playing. He asked one of the waiters about the art that would be auctioned off tonight and was pointed to a door off the ballroom.

The three paintings were displayed under spotlights along one wall. A dozen people milled around the room. A bored-looking older man wearing a jacket that read SECURITY stood in the corner.

Laramie moved in closer to look at the three cowboy paintings. One by Taylor West, one by Rock Jackson and the last by H. F. Powell. As he caught bits of conversation, it appeared that everyone had heard the news tonight. The expectation was that both the West and Jackson paintings' bids would go quite high.

But he realized the real prize in this room was the H. F. Powell painting—if the low murmurs he'd picked up were any indication. There was talk of the painting going for more than a couple hundred thousand, but that it could go even higher because it was one of the few works of the deceased artist anyone had seen in years.

"Excuse me." Laramie addressed a woman who was studying the Powell painting. "I take it H. F. Powell paintings are rare?" he asked, remembering what Sid had told him.

The woman lifted one fine shaped brow. "He was one of the most prolific artists of his time, but he stopped painting a few years before he died." She leaned in closer. "It was rumored that he had personal problems. It was such a tragedy. He was killed in a fire at his studio. A lot of his work was lost in the fire so any painting of his is even more valuable now. This is one I've never seen before."

Interesting, Laramie thought as he studied the Powell painting. It was of a beautiful woman on a galloping horse, a rock-and-pine landscape behind her. The colors were warm as if the day had been, as well. The woman's face was filled with joy. He got the feeling she was riding toward her lover.

He studied it, surprised that not only could he feel the warmth of the day, he could almost smell the dust being kicked up by the horse's hooves. Surprising himself, he also realized he was going to have to bid on the painting. He wanted it like he had never wanted anything before because, given the resemblance, he would swear the woman on the horse was Sid's mother.

He'd never cared that much about material things. But he had to have this painting—no matter what it cost. He just hoped that wasn't what everyone else in the room was thinking, as well.

SID SPOTTED THE MAN dressed as Zorro standing in front of the H. F. Powell painting. She had cheated, waiting outside until she'd seen Laramie Cardwell's SUV pull up. She hadn't wanted to take any chances, but the truth was she would have recognized him no matter his disguise.

She'd spent her life studying forms as an artist. Laramie's form was quite fine. As she slipped through the small crowd standing around the paintings, she realized she would love to paint him. The thought surprised her, since it had been so long since she'd gotten to paint what she really loved.

Sid could see that Laramie was taken with the H. F. Powell painting. The painting was one of her father's best compositions, she thought, as she admired it under the soft lights highlighting it. Then out of the corner of her eye, she watched Laramie.

He couldn't seem to take his eyes from the painting. She guessed he had seen the resemblance between her and her mother. Around her, she heard everyone talking about the painting, all of them wondering how high the bidding would go and ultimately, who would be taking it home.

It saddened her to think that most of her father's career, this kind of art hadn't been popular. With the influx of people like the ones in this room with money and a desire to rediscover the Old Wild West, paintings like this one were now coveted. Too bad he hadn't lived long enough to see how badly people wanted an H. F. Powell painting.

But then again, her father had never painted for the money. And he certainly wouldn't have been caught dead at an affair like this. She smiled to herself, remembering that she'd told Laramie the same thing about herself. She still hoped it was true.

As Laramie moved on to Rock Jackson's painting, Sid stepped closer to the H. F. Powell painting. She stared at it with a mix of emotions. The painting caught her mother's beauty as well as her wild spirit with brushstrokes that spoke of the love the artist had felt for this woman. Her mother had been caught with that excited look in her eyes, that unmasked joy in her face… Until that moment, Sid hadn't felt the emotion captured in the painting. Her mother had been a woman in love.

"It is beautiful, isn't it?" asked a woman on the other side of her. "It moves me to tears, as well." The woman pressed a tissue into Sid's hand as she moved away. Sid hadn't realized she was smiling through her tears.

LARAMIE CAUGHT A WHIFF of perfume in a room full of warring fragrances. But he couldn't be sure that light citrusy scent was what had made him aware of a woman standing in front of the H. F. Powell painting. Maybe he'd just sensed her.

When he looked over at the masked woman, he felt a start. She was dressed in all black, from the old-fashioned hooped-skirt dress to the large floppy hat that hid her hair. She turned her head. He caught only a glimpse of cool blue eyes framed by a dark mask— just as they had been the first time he'd ever laid eyes on her.

It couldn't be Sid. She'd said she wouldn't be caught dead here. And yet this woman was the right height and the right frame from what he could see of her. Her elaborate dress hid her figure and her face was obscured by the hat and mask along with the high neck of the dress.

But it was Obsidian "Sid" Forester. He moved closer, following the faint scent of her perfume. Why had she lied about coming here? Or had her plans changed since the time he'd ask her?

He was next to her now. All his senses told him it was her. But when she raised her lashes to meet his gaze, she gave no indication that she'd ever seen him before.

In the other room, someone announced that the ball was about to begin. Music soared and the crowd began to thin. As the woman in black began to move away, he grabbed her hand. Without looking at her, he whispered, "Dance with me."

He felt her freeze. When his gaze met hers, he saw both surprise and wariness in those beautiful eyes. He tried to hide his own shocked expression. This woman wasn't Sid, not the woman he'd kissed, not the woman he'd dreamed about every night since. But he was convinced that they'd met before. Last night, when she'd put the knot on his head.

He felt her hesitate and started to let go of her hand, when she nodded slowly and did an old-fashioned curtsy. As the crowd began to move toward the ballroom, she said, "If you will excuse me for just a moment…"

Before he could protest, she disappeared into the ladies' room. He waited patiently. A few moments later, she returned. He saw the change instantly and yet he questioned if he was losing his mind as he led her out of the art room, onto the dance floor and into his arms.

Her eyes met his briefly, almost shyly, before she lowered her lashes. He felt his heart cartwheel in his chest. This wasn't the same woman he'd asked to dance.

He glanced around for another woman in black, but didn't see one. What game were they playing with him? Sid moved gracefully in his arms. His cat burglar had been light on her feet. No wonder she was such a graceful dancer. But what was she doing here? Shouldn't she be burglarizing someone else's house right now?

"Enjoying the dance?" he whispered near her ear. He felt her shiver.

"I am," she replied in a whisper that had intrigued him the first time they'd met.

He breathed in the citrus scent of her, reveling in the feel of her in his arms. How badly he wanted to kiss her again, knowing that if he did, there would be no more hiding behind the mask. He would have to demand what she was doing here because all his instincts warned him that she was up to trouble.

But as they danced, he was so happy to have her in his arms that he didn't want it to end. Unfortunately, the song did end, though, and she stepped back. He reached for her, but she slipped from his grasp.

And with a slight shake of her head, she gave him another quick curtsy and disappeared into the crowd.

He thought about going after her, cornering her, unmasking her, but good sense kept him from it. He'd promised to stay out of her business. But what was she up to? He hated to think, as he glanced toward the art room. The door was closed, the older security guard standing in front of it.

When someone touched his shoulder, Laramie jumped.

"Is anything wrong?" his cousin Dana asked him.

Laramie shook his head, but he feared a lot of things were wrong.

"You're the only cousin I haven't danced with to-night," she said.

Laramie was happy to dance with Dana. He understood how she had become the matriarch of the family even at her young age. She'd brought them all together as a family because of her loving nature. Everyone loved Dana.

"Are you having fun?" she asked as they danced.

Fun didn't really describe it, but he nodded and smiled. "I'm glad I'm here," he said truthfully, which made her smile.

"I saw you dancing with a woman dressed all in black," Dana said.

"Did you recognize her?" he asked quickly.

"No." She frowned, looking surprised. "You didn't know who she was, either?" That seemed to amuse her. "That explains why you keep looking for her."

"I'm sorry," he apologized. He hadn't even realized he'd been doing that.

Dana laughed. "I'm just glad to see you enjoying yourself."

When the dance ended, she said, "There are some people I want you to meet." She led him back to the lobby.

For the next half hour, he tried to remember the names of the ranchers, business owners and neighbors Dana introduced him to. More champagne was forced on him as he nodded and smiled and thought about the woman he'd danced with.

It wasn't until someone announced it was almost time for the partygoers to reveal their identities that he escaped back into the ballroom. He had to find the woman.

He worked his way through the crowd, looking for her.

She'd left, he decided. And yet he'd been in the lobby. He hadn't been so distracted that he wouldn't have noticed if she'd passed him. Was there another way out of here? There would be emergency exits, but those would set off alarms.

Just when he thought he'd only imagined her—or she'd evaporated into thin air—he spotted her. She was coming out of the ladies' room. He hadn't thought that was where she might be. He hesitated, realizing also that she probably hadn't attended the ball alone.

He waited for her to make a beeline for some handsome man. The countdown began. Ten. Nine. Eight. The huge room went quiet as everyone anticipated the unmasking. Except his woman in black. Seven. Six. Five. She seemed to be making a beeline not for some handsome escort, but for the door.

Laramie stepped in front of her. Four. Three. Her gaze flew up to his. He saw the alarm as she tried to step around him. Two. One!

Masks started coming off all around the huge ballroom.

"Please," she said as she tried to get past him.

"It's time to unmask," he said and peeled off his own.

She met his eyes with a steely look. Her eyes had gone from cool blue to silver steel. With an arrogant lift of her head, she reached for her mask.

A blood-curdling scream filled the ballroom, followed by the sound of several people running. Laramie turned to see that the door to the art room was open.

Even from where he was standing, he could see that the H. F. Powell painting was gone.

As he turned back, he saw that the painting wasn't the only thing missing. His woman in black was also gone.

CHAPTER SEVENTEEN

LARAMIE SAW THE marshal and his brothers Austin and
Hayes heading for the art room and quickly followed.
Hud barked out orders to the pavilion guards to have
all the doors blocked. No one was to leave. Then he
motioned them and the guard in and closed the door.

"This door was locked?" Hud asked the guard the
moment they were all in the room.

"I locked it myself."

"And there was no one in the room?"

"No." The guard glanced around the space. "Where
would they have hidden?"

It was a good question. The room had been bare except for the paintings. Not a stick of furniture was in
the room. Laramie looked toward the windows as Hud
walked over to them.

"The windows don't open. Nor are there any foot-
prints in the snow outside them," the marshal said as
he turned back to the room. "No other doors in or out."

It must have dawned on them all at the same time,
because they all looked up. Hud swore. A piece of the
dropped ceiling had been left ajar.

"Seal the room," he said as he reached for his cell
phone and barked, "Make sure no one leaves."

"Are you going to detain and question everyone outside this room?" Austin asked. They would be here all night and then some if that was the case.

Hud shook his head irritably. "But I need some men at the door to make sure no one walks out of here with that painting in case the burglar left that ceiling tile like that to misdirect us." He looked from Austin to Hayes and then Laramie. "Mind helping until I can get deputies and a crime-scene team over here?"

Laramie joined his brothers at the pavilion's main entrance. The Powell painting was large enough that it wouldn't fit under most costumes, so screening people as they left went fairly fast.

The whole time, he found himself looking for the woman in black. She didn't come through the lines. Which meant she'd left right after the missing painting was discovered? But Hud had asked that all the doors be covered. Maybe she slipped out before the guards could get to the doors. He thought of her hooped skirt and swore. The Powell painting could have fit under it.

Then he saw her. She had taken off her mask, but still wore the wide-brimmed hat that hid most of her face. Only when she glanced up did he catch the glint of her silvery-blue eyes. Eyes like a wolf, he thought.

She had started toward his line, then looked up and seen him. Hesitating, he saw her look to the other lines.

Something shone in those eyes for a moment. Defiance? Challenge? It must have been, because she stepped into his line. As he checked one after another ball goer through, she moved closer and closer. It wouldn't be long before she was standing directly in front of him.

Laramie could hear people complaining. Some were threatening to call their lawyers.

He let two more people out and turned to find himself face-to-face with the woman of his nightly dreams and his growing obsession. Her head was down, the hat shadowing her face.

He hoped to hell she didn't think he would let her get out of here with the painting. "I'm going to have one of the women check under your hoop skirt," he said.

"That isn't necessary," she said and lifted the framework of the skirt. She wore black yoga pants beneath the skirt. No painting. When he glanced up at her, he saw the smile and the amusement in her eyes before he jerked back in surprise.

This woman looked like Obsidian "Sid" Forester. They would have been twins...

"Let's keep the lines moving," Hud ordered as the grumbling increased among the waiting guests.

"If that's all..." the woman said. She even sounded like Sid, he thought as he watched the woman who'd coldcocked him last night walk away.

TAYLOR WEST NEEDED a drink like he'd never needed one before. He'd awakened with a killer headache and the worst taste in his mouth. When he'd sat up, it took him a few moments to realize where he was. In jail. For murder.

Stumbling to his feet, he lurched toward the bars. "Hey!" he yelled and listened for someone to come. No one did. "Hey!"

When a deputy finally did show his face, Taylor said, "I'll pay you to get me a drink."

The deputy shook his head and started to close the door.

"Wait! Do you know who I am? I'm Taylor West.

I'll give you any painting you want. Just between you and me."

"You need to quiet down. Try to get some rest." He closed the door and even when Taylor yelled obscenities at his departing form, the deputy didn't return.

He banged on the bars of his cell and yelled, "I didn't murder anyone!"

"Didn't your lawyer tell you not to talk about your case?" asked a voice. Taylor couldn't see the man because they were in separate cells divided by a wall instead of bars.

"What's it to you?" he demanded.

"You should listen to your lawyer."

Taylor scoffed at that. "You know what they say about lawyers? Once you need one, you're already screwed." He wandered over to his bunk and sat down, his head in his hands. He would kill for a drink.

"Who didn't you murder?" the man asked.

"The two-bit artist Rock Jackson."

"I know who Rock is," the voice said. "Why *didn't* you kill him?"

Taylor wasn't about to get into it with a stranger. "He was running around with my wife."

"That can get a man killed, all right."

"I planned to kill him. I was waiting outside his house."

"So what happened?"

Taylor thought of the crime shows he'd seen on television. The incarcerated killer always had a big mouth and talked too much to a jailhouse snitch. "What's it to you?"

"I can't sleep, either."

"What are you in for?"

"Writing hot checks."

"*Hot* checks?"

"Checks you can't make good on because you don't have any money."

"At least I don't have that problem," Taylor said, and they both laughed. "When the cops found me I was passed out in my truck with an empty quart bourbon bottle in one hand and my gun in the other. The last thing I remember before that was closing my eyes to wait for my cheating wife and Rock to return."

"Sounds to me like you were framed."

Framed? He lay back on the bunk, staring up at the stained ceiling. "Who would want to frame me?"

"Good question," the man said. "Have you made anyone mad lately?"

"Who *haven't* I made mad?" Taylor said to himself and closed his eyes. But the list of the people who might want to frame him for murder was short and he'd confided in them about the forged painting.

SID WASN'T SURPRISED when she heard the knock at her door. She glanced at the clock. Almost two in the morning. She'd known she wouldn't be able to sleep, so she hadn't even tried. Instead, she'd been painting. It was what she did when she was upset.

"Your light was on," Laramie said by way of explanation when she opened the door. He glanced past her to the costume from the ball that had been tossed onto a chair. Sid now wore jeans and a T-shirt.

Opening the door wider, she motioned him in with a wave of her hand. After seeing him at the ball, she'd suspected it was only a matter of time before he showed up. What surprised her was that the marshal and a couple of deputies weren't with him.

"I thought you said you wouldn't be caught dead at the ball," he said as she closed the door and turned to look at him. He had stopped in the middle of her living room.

She could tell he was angry. But she suspected he was also scared. "Fortunately I wasn't."

He stepped toward her. "Where is the Powell painting?"

"You don't understand."

"Don't I?" He took another step. "You've been playing some kind of game with me since the first night we met. You're lucky I'm here instead of with the marshal."

"Why isn't the marshal here?"

Another step toward her. The room seemed to be closing in, getting smaller and smaller. She could smell the cold night air on him and remembered the way he'd pulled her close earlier when they'd danced. He was almost that close again.

"Because I wanted to give you the opportunity to level with me. For starters, I know you're in more trouble than you're telling me."

She smiled, holding her ground. "You think you know me?"

He was just inches away now. "I know how you feel in my arms. I know how you taste."

She felt something give in her chest as he reached out and cupped her cheek. She'd tried to forget how his mouth had felt and tasted on hers, how safe she'd felt in his arms, how her heart raced when he was this close.

"You weren't alone at my house last night," Laramie said, his voice little more than a whisper. He was so close she could smell his warm scent. "It was your twin."

"My twin? I don't have—"

"You don't have a sister or cousin or some relative who looks enough like you that you used her tonight to pull off the heist? You want to keep pretending you don't know what I'm talking about?"

She started to step away, needing to put space between them, afraid of what she would do if she didn't.

He grabbed her arm and pulled her into him. His voice was rough, his hands strong. "Tell me what's going on. All that stuff you told me last night? Was it just a crock of crap to keep me out of your hair tonight? Come on, Sid. You're too good at what you do," he said as his gaze swept over the painting on her easel.

She'd known he would figure it out. She'd let him get too close. Her mistake.

Laramie looked from the painting to her. His eyes widened as if the truth had just struck him. "You're not just a master thief. *You're* an art forger."

SID WRENCHED FREE of his grasp and stepped past him and, for a moment, Laramie thought she might be going for a weapon. His head still ached from last night. If he could help it, he wasn't going to let that happen again. He turned to watch her step into the kitchen and open the refrigerator.

"I'll take that as a compliment," she said as she grabbed two bottles of beer. She held one out to him. When he didn't reach for it, she said, "You came here for the truth, right? Now you're not sure you want to hear it."

"Try me. Or we can just call the marshal."

"Which makes me wonder why you haven't called him." She squinted, studying him openly. "Maybe because you have no proof. You cried wolf once, the first night we met. You don't want to do it again with the marshal. Am I right?"

She was. It didn't surprise him that she knew he'd gone to the marshal the first night when he'd caught her coming out of his future house with the painting.

The truth. That was why he'd come here tonight. At least in part. He took one of the beers that she offered. Twisting off the top with both anger and frustration, he took a drink, watching her over the bottle. "What you told me last night—"

"Was all true."

"But you didn't tell me everything."

Sid met his gaze. "I wasn't sure I could trust you."

"Trust *me*?" He laughed as he watched her twist off the bottle cap and toss it into the trash before taking a long drink.

She motioned toward a place for him to sit, but he was too restless. She was right. He wasn't sure he wanted to hear the truth. He'd fallen for this woman— a thief, an apparent forger, a cat burglar.

He stepped into her studio off the living room. The room was small with large windows. Because of the lack of wall space, paintings were stacked against the walls. "You painted all of these?" he asked turning to find her standing in the doorway, holding her beer. She nodded.

"I thought you didn't like cowboy art?"

She said nothing as she took another swig of her beer. In one corner of the room was a stack of old logging crosscut handsaws. The rusted metal between the handles had Montana scenes painted on them. He noticed at once that they weren't half as good as the paintings. That wasn't all he noticed. Her cowboy art wasn't just good, it was masterful and yet she wasn't in the Old West Artists Coalition—just like her father. Nor had he seen her work in any of the galleries he'd visited.

He stared at one of the paintings for a long moment, something stirring inside him. He could feel her watching him. It came to him like another knock to his head.

Turning quickly, he stared at her. "Tell me I'm wrong about you."

"I wish I could."

"I don't get you."

"I think you do."

He smiled at that and shook his head. "I *want* to. You're obviously talented. *Very* talented. So I ask myself what is she doing painting old saw blades? What is it she's hiding other than her obvious talent?"

She lifted her chin. He'd seen that defiant look on her before. "Now you think you have me all figured out."

"Nope, I suspect it could take a lifetime to do that." He put down his beer and closed the distance between them in two long strides. He took her bottle from her and set it aside as he drew her to him. "The H. F. Powell painting that was stolen tonight? I wanted it more than I have wanted anything. Except," he drawled, "*you*. It was because, on some level, I knew. You painted it. But what about the auction?"

"I couldn't let it be auctioned off as one of my father's paintings. It was stolen from his art studio the night he was killed. One of the members of the OWAC donated it anonymously. The killer knows I'm coming for him. Don't worry. I'll make it right with the charity."

"If you're still alive. Sid, we have to go to the marshal."

"Are you sure we have to go right now?" She looked up at him, her blue eyes bright as diamonds, her lips parting. He dropped his mouth to hers.

Then he swung her up into his arms and carried her to the bedroom just off the studio.

SID LOOKED INTO his eyes as he gently laid her on the bed. His expression made her weak inside. His touch was so tender as he crawled onto the bed next to her and drew her close again. He dropped his mouth to hers, exploring her intimately as if there was still so much he wanted to know about her.

She felt the same way. As he drew back from the passionate kiss, he traced his thumb over her lower lip.

"I fell in love with your mouth that night," he said quietly. As he lifted his gaze, he said, "And your eyes. You have the most incredible eyes. I feel as if I can look into your soul."

Sid shivered. "Don't look too closely."

He shook his head. "You're not as bad as you want me to believe," he said just as quietly. "What do you see when you look into my eyes?"

"Kindness, compassion…" She halted seeing something that tied her tongue in a knot for a moment. "Caring."

He smiled. "Caring? Look deeper."

She let out a nervous laugh even as she was filled with pure joy. "Love?"

Laramie nodded. "I've fallen for you, Obsidian Forester. Fallen hard."

Sid couldn't speak, which was just as well because in the next moment he stole her breath away as he cupped her face in his big hands and kissed her again.

She felt wrapped in wisps of soft, warm clouds as he began to unbutton her shirt. His fingers brushed over the tops of her breasts, hardened her nipples to aching pebbles. He followed his fingers with his mouth, suckling at her until she cried out with a desire that burned to the heart of her.

With fumbling fingers, she helped him remove her own and his clothing. She sighed at the feel of his naked skin, the taut muscles of his chest and arms and stomach. Wrapping her arms around him, she pulled him to her.

When they came together it was as if they had been missing pieces of a puzzle that finally had found each other. They moved with the ancient rhythm of passion and love.

Sid arched against him, crying out when he brought her to the peak of desire, and she shuddered in his arms as she collapsed on the bed. The cool night air moved over her perspiring bare skin like a caress.

They might have stayed like that the rest of the night—if it hadn't been for the back door banging open.

CHAPTER EIGHTEEN

LARAMIE SAT UP with a start, grabbing for his jeans as heavy footfalls could be heard from the other room. He glanced at Sid, her face pale and worried in the soft glow coming through the window. From her expression, she had no idea who had just broken into her cabin.

She was reaching for her robe and he'd only managed to drag on his jeans and button all but the top button when a figure filled the doorway, a second larger figure behind it.

The overhead light came on, momentarily blinding him.

"Sorry, it wasn't my idea to come barging in," a woman said. Laramie did a double take at her—and the armed masked man holding the gun to the woman's head.

"What have you done now, Zander?" Sid demanded as she pulled on her robe and tied the sash tight around her middle.

The woman who was the spitting image of Sid shrugged. "You know me, sis. Trouble just seems to find me. But this time I have a feeling this is more about you than me."

"She *is* your sister," Laramie said as he realized this

had been the woman who'd knocked him out the previous night at his house.

"*Half* sister," Zander said and smiled. "The bad half, if you ask Sid."

"Enough. Give me the paintings," the man said. "All of them, including the one you stole tonight, or I kill her."

"I don't think so," Sid said.

Laramie recognized the man's voice. Cody Kent. "You'd better listen to him, Sid. If you're right, he's already killed once. Isn't that right, Cody? You killed H. F. Powell the night you stole the paintings."

"What?" the artist was clearly taken aback. "I didn't kill Powell." He ripped off the ski mask as he shoved Zander into the room. Waving the gun, he said, "Just give me the paintings and no one gets hurt."

"Is that what you told our father?" Sid demanded.

"Your father?" Cody asked in confusion. "I didn't think H.F. had any family."

"He didn't have much regard for marriage," Zander said with a sigh. "But, like his daughters, he believed in justice. He planned to nail you and the others to the wall. He would have shown you all up and you knew it."

Cody waved the gun at them. "Look, we just went to his studio to talk to the crazy old coot. No one was supposed to get hurt. But H.F. was determined to ruin us all and destroy everything we'd built with the coalition. We didn't even believe he'd forged our paintings until we entered the studio and saw them."

Sid made a disparaging sound. "But once you did, you couldn't let the public see them. Were you afraid that if you just took them, he would only repaint them? He wasn't a man easily persuaded."

Cody swore. "I saw that we were getting nowhere with him, I wanted to leave. But we weren't leaving without the forgeries. H.F. put up a fight, but finally he gave in. We carried the paintings to the car."

"Including the one that was up for auction tonight," Laramie said.

"That was Rock. He had to have it. We tried to talk him out of it, but he wouldn't listen," Cody said.

"So how did you end up with all of the paintings?" Sid asked.

The artist looked surprised. "What makes you think—"

"You're the one standing here with the gun," she said.

Cody chuckled. "Rock promised to get rid of the forgeries, but I didn't trust him. I was right. I discovered where he'd hidden them. That's why he couldn't tell anyone when he discovered they were missing."

Laramie wanted to rush the man, but he couldn't take the chance that Cody wouldn't get off a shot. In the small cabin, it would be too easy to wound or kill one of them.

"Why didn't *you* destroy them?" Laramie asked.

Cody shook his head. "They were beautiful." He looked at Sid. "Your father was the most talented artist I've ever met. He was brilliant. Crazy as a loon, but a real genius. I knew I should destroy them, but I couldn't. After a few years, I sold them. They were worth a lot more by then because our careers were going better. I figured the chances were good no one would ever find out."

"It wasn't easy, but I found them," Sid said.

He didn't seem to hear her. "Once I saw the one you brought to the gallery, I pretended to be as upset as Taylor was," he said to Laramie. "We were all trying to get ahold of Rock. I knew he'd admit that they'd been stolen from him, but no one would believe him. But I had bigger problems. There was talk of a cat burglar in Big Sky. Only this cat burglar didn't take anything. I paid a couple of houses a visit and realized quickly what was going on when I saw some of the originals H.F. had used to make his forgeries."

"Is that when you panicked and anonymously donated what you thought was an H. F. Powell painting to the auction? That painting was a new one still on the easel in his studio the night he was killed."

"You have no idea how hard it was to part with it," Cody said. "That painting is worth a small fortune."

Sid shook her head. "It would be—if my father had painted it. During the last years of his life, H.F. quit painting his own art to make forgeries of all your work. To keep the creditors at bay and the three of us fed, I painted in my father's style."

"It was a *forgery*?" Cody let out a bitter curse. "You're just a family of forgers."

"Exactly," Zander said. "Our family was all smoke and mirrors."

Cody looked sick. "I knew someone was switching the real paintings and collecting the forgeries once I heard about the so-called cat burglar. I just didn't know who until tonight. I thought you would try to steal the painting. But I didn't know how you would do it. Imagine my shock when I saw you in that black dress jumping down off the roof with it. I planned to follow you, but you got away. I thought I'd blown it, then low and behold, I spotted your double and she led me right to you."

"Hank Ramsey was in on it, too, right?" Laramie asked. "Why isn't he here?"

"I stopped by his place tonight." Cody sighed. "I found him hanging from a beam in his kitchen."

"You might as well put down the gun," Laramie said. "It's all going to come out now."

Cody shook his head. He looked broken, like a man who had nothing to lose. "My art is all I have. Destroy that and I have nothing." He leveled the gun at Sid. "No matter what happens to me, those forgeries have to be destroyed." He pulled a bottle from his coat pocket. Laramie recognized it for what it was. A homemade firebomb—probably like the one he had used the night of H. F. Powell's studio fire.

SID HAD BEEN watching everything play out in front of her, feeling a little dazed. Since her father's death, she'd been grieving for all that had been lost. Once the first forgery had turned up, she'd been on a mission to catch her father's killer.

Cody Kent. She'd known it would be one of the original cowboy artists who started the coalition—or all four of them. She'd just never guessed it would be Cody who showed up at her door.

Laramie took a step toward Cody. She could tell he was trying to gauge his chances. He had to know that there was no one more dangerous than a man backed into a corner.

Sid stepped in front of Laramie. Her heart broke at the thought that she might get him killed over all this.

If only she hadn't gotten him involved. Zander, as well. She was going to get them all killed, and for what? Some artist's ego? Or the price of an artist's reputation?

"I didn't want it to be you," Sid said to Cody. "I guess we all wanted to believe it was Rock Jackson. But when I heard the news, I wondered why Rock would be making counterfeit money if he was the one who'd been selling the paintings he'd stolen from my father that night."

Cody nodded, a bitter smile coming to his lips. "I realized that something like this could happen. That some fool might take H.F.'s copy of one of the paintings to an expert. I wasn't stupid."

"So why sell them?" Laramie asked.

Cody shrugged. "In retrospect, I should have destroyed them."

Sid shook her head. "If Rock had already taken the forgeries that night…you didn't have to go back and kill my father. H.F. was old and tired. He wouldn't have redone the forgeries. But you couldn't let him show you up. It was more about your pride, your ego, than the paintings or even what the organization had been doing. By then, I'm sure your group had covered up the charity scam." She glanced at the glass jar clutched in his hand. "You went there to end it once and for all."

"I thought I could talk some sense into the old fool." Cody shook his head. "It's all water under the bridge now, though. There won't be anyone left who will be able to say differently and the forgeries will be destroyed for good."

"What about Taylor?" Laramie demanded, moving up beside Sid, determined to protect her. How she loved this gallant man. "Taylor's going to sing like a canary. He'll tell everything he knows."

"Even if anyone believed a word he said now that he's facing a murder charge, Taylor doesn't know anything," Cody said.

"That's too bad because I'm betting he didn't kill Rock," Laramie said. "Or that Hank Ramsey didn't hang himself, either."

"If you're expecting a confession…" Cody said as he took a step back.

"You toss that in here and you'll never get out in time to save yourself," Sid said, seeing him look toward a candle that still burned next to the bed. "I don't think you've thought this through. Also you will destroy some of my father's paintings. Thanks to you, they're worth more now than when he was alive." He hadn't been able to destroy the forgeries. He wouldn't be able to burn her father's originals. "Not to mention…" She looked toward the bank of windows in the studio.

Cody looked angry and upset as he followed her gaze. He realized as she had that the windows were large enough that at least one of them might be able to get out before the fire killed them.

"Thank you for pointing that out," he said. At gunpoint, he forced them all into a windowless storage room at the back of the cabin where Sid kept the old saws and milk cans she'd collected for her crafts.

"I'm sorry you have to die," Cody said. "You have your father's talent. But you also don't follow the rules. You could never be a member of the Old West Artists Coalition."

Laramie balled up his fist and took a step forward,

but Sid caught his arm as Cody retreated from the room, slamming the door behind him and pitching them into darkness. Sid heard him lock the door and shove what sounded like her heavy buffet in front of it.

CHAPTER NINETEEN

LARAMIE SNAPPED ON the switch he'd seen by the door. The small storage room was suddenly illuminated by a dim bulb hanging from the ceiling. He turned to Sid. "Tell me there is a reason you wanted him to trap us in here."

"Other than my sister is as crazy as our father and is determined to get us all killed?" Zander asked.

Sid stepped to the door, putting her ear against it. "Just as I thought, he's looking for the forgeries and stealing some of my paintings. I'm just thankful Cody appreciates good art. Now that he knows I'm H.F.'s daughter…he probably figures they'll be worth a lot of money once I'm dead." Her lips turned up in a knowing yet bitter smile. Then she quickly turned toward the old metal milk cans stacked in a corner. "Help me move these as quietly as we can."

"See what I mean? Crazy, just like our father," Zander said. Laramie thought the last thing Sid had done was lose her mind, so he hurried to help her and saw what had been hidden under the milk cans—a hatch in the floor.

He moved quickly to lift it. A blast of freezing cold air rose with the door. He looked down at the steps that disappeared into the darkness. "An escape tunnel?"

Zander laughed as her sister handed her a flashlight. "So this is where you hid the forgeries."

"Quickly," Laramie said as Zander snapped on the light and began to climb down. "We have to get out of here before he sets the place on fire." He looked at Sid. "If he burns the cabin, your work will go up in flames."

She smiled almost sadly and descended the stairs.

Laramie followed on her heels. They moved through a long tunnel that ended with a set of crude steps that went up.

"This is that other cabin in the woods," Zander said as they climbed up into a small laundry room lit with daylight coming through the windows.

The moment they stepped out of that room into a larger one, Laramie saw the paintings. Along with the forgeries, he saw dozens of Sid's. Still, he couldn't imagine letting Cody Kent destroy even one of her works.

"Alert the authorities," he said as he headed for the door.

"It's already been done," Sid said. "The moment the hatch was opened an alarm was set off. I have a friend who works at the security company. Wait, where are you going?"

"I can't let him destroy your paintings, let alone get away."

"They aren't worth dying over. I can paint more," she said, grabbing at his sleeve. "Neither is catching Cody."

Laramie heard sirens in the distance. "Stay here with your sister." With that, he rushed out the door into the snowy morning.

CHAPTER TWENTY

SID QUICKLY CHANGED into the clothing she also kept in the second cabin. She'd tried to be prepared for anything that might happen. What she hadn't seen coming was Laramie Cardwell.

"Stay here," she said to Zander as she opened the door to follow Laramie.

"Like that is going to happen," Zander said, right behind her.

Sid couldn't see Laramie as she rushed down the steps and started through the snow-laden pines toward her cabin. One of the reasons she'd bought the property was the tunnel between the two cabins. The owner had told her the tunnel had been dug back in the fifties as a bomb shelter when nuclear war had seemed imminent. The owner had kept the tunnel maintained.

It had saved them temporarily and given her a place to stash the forgeries as well as the bulk of her paintings.

Snow began to fall. At first it was only a few flakes drifting past on the breeze. Then a flurry of them whirled around them as they hurried toward the cabin obscured by trees and snow. Sid could hear sirens coming up the mountain, but feared they would never get there in time. Laramie had the advantage, she told herself. Cody would be busy trying to make his escape.

But he was greedy. He would also try to pack up as many of the paintings as he could before he realized the forgeries weren't there and burned the cabin.

The cabin was old. It would burn quickly. Had they still been locked in the storage room, she doubted any of them would have survived.

Ahead, she could see the cabin. Cody had come by snowmobile, forcing Zander along. It was still sitting out front. There was no sign of either Cody or Laramie through the pines.

"Shouldn't one of us have a plan?" Zander said behind her.

She saw that her sister had picked up a limb from the snow. It was thick enough that it could make a pretty good dent in Cody's head—if Zander got the chance to use it.

They slowed as they approached the cabin. "I have a gun just inside the back door in the wicker basket with my scarves and gloves," Sid whispered. "It's loaded. So if something happens—"

"I've got you covered, sis."

LARAMIE SPOTTED THE snowmobile sitting outside the cabin with a half dozen paintings leaning against it. Sid had been right. The bastard couldn't pass up stealing even more paintings. He treasured them more than the lives he'd planned to snuff out in the storage room.

Laramie moved cautiously along the side of the cabin. He could hear Cody inside ransacking the place, no doubt looking for the forgeries. Which meant that he'd have had to put down the firebomb he'd made.

As he neared the open doorway of the cabin, Laramie peered inside. He couldn't see Cody, but he could hear him. Stepping in, he made his way to the fireplace where the poker leaned against the stone chimney.

"What the hell?" Cody swore as he came out of Sid's studio. He held a painting in both hands. "How did you…?" The rest of his words were lost as he realized that the tables had turned. He threw the painting he'd been holding at Laramie and reached into his pocket for the gun.

From the confused look on his face, Laramie realized that Cody must have laid down the gun somewhere—just as he had the firebomb.

As Cody looked around wildly for both weapons, Laramie spotted the gun lying on the kitchen table about the same time that Cody did. Cody dived for it. Laramie charged. He caught the artist in the back with the poker. Cody let out a loud grunt and staggered, but he didn't go down. Instead, he lurched toward the gun, his fingers within inches of it when Laramie again swung the poker.

This time it caught him in the side of the head. The sound of sirens filled the air as Cody dropped to his knees. Laramie quickly stepped around him and pushed the gun out of the artist's reach.

"You don't understand. That crazy old fool was going to ruin me," Cody said.

Laramie spotted the homemade turpentine firebomb on the kitchen counter where Cody had left it as Sid and Zander rushed in, with Marshal Hud Savage and his deputies on their heels.

THE NEWS HIT the canyon as if it were Cody's firebomb. Cody Kent had been arrested. The homemade turpentine firebomb and Cody's gun had been taken as evidence. Trapped, Cody had broken down and told the authorities everything. He confessed to killing H. F. Powell after the man had tried to destroy his career. After that, he'd confessed to killing Rock and trying to frame Taylor and making Hank Ramsey's death look like a suicide.

The broadcaster was saying, "H. F. Powell's story is one of madness and genius. When he was denied membership in the organization, Old West Artists Coalition, he swore retribution, which ultimately led to his murder. And Cody Kent would have gotten away with it if not for Powell's daughter Obsidian Forester."

Sid got up to turn off the news as, on screen, Cody was being led into the courthouse. "You don't understand," he told reporters. "All I have is my art."

"Maybe he'll teach an art class in prison," Zander said as Sid turned off the television.

"Maybe," she agreed and looked at Laramie who was frowning at the television. "Is something wrong?" she asked him.

"Just a little confused," he admitted. "If all the paintings but the ones that were stolen burned in the fire…"

"The originals my father copied from were in a safe at the house," Sid said. "He planned to expose the artists at their annual conference, which was to be held here in Big Sky a few days after his death. More than likely our father bragged to someone about what he was going to do."

"Not all of the originals were in the safe," Zander said, shooting a look at her sister. "What Sid isn't telling you is that her sister stole several of the paintings from the safe and she had to buy them back before she could replace the forgeries." Zander smiled sheepishly at Sid. "I'm sorry I made things harder for you. Because of me, we lost the family ranch."

Sid shook her head. "Dad was so in debt by the time he died, there wouldn't have been a way to save it anyway. You were right. This…quest I've been on… I should have let it go, but I wanted justice and I hated the idea of everyone believing he was so crazy he would kill himself."

"He *was* crazy," Zander said and laughed. "We should know. We're his daughters and the apple doesn't fall far from the tree."

"Well, your father has justice now," Laramie said. "And his daughters have found their way back to each other. I'd say you accomplished more than you set out to." He rose to leave. "The invitation is still open for Christmas Eve at Cardwell Ranch. Open to both of you," he said to Zander.

"So what now?" Zander asked after Laramie left. "You don't have a murderer to catch, no houses to break into… What will my little sis do to keep herself busy?"

"Wipe that grin off your face, Z," she said playfully.

"He's in love with you, you know."

Sid said nothing. She still couldn't believe it. She loved Laramie as well, but their lives were in different states. "He's going back to Houston after the holidays."

Zander lifted a brow. "So go with him."

She shook her head. "My life is here."

"Painting cowboy art." Her sister shook her head and laughed. "I thought Dad messed *me* up, but he really did a number on you."

"We can't spend the rest of our lives blaming H.F. for our choices," Sid said.

"Maybe you can't," Zander said with a laugh. "But I can. I'm just like him. I'll never settle down."

"Don't say never. Who knows what the future holds."

Her sister seemed to study her for a long moment. "This is the most contented I've ever seen you. Those years when you worked so hard to keep a roof over our heads when Dad had locked himself in his studio and refused to paint his own work and support us… You always did what you had to do."

Sid wished she could believe that. "I forged his work while he was forging others'. You're right. We really *are* messed up, huh?"

Zander smiled. "The ironic thing about all of it? You're a better artist than even the great H. F. Powell." She held up her hand to keep Sid from arguing the point. "It's true, sis. That painting…" She pointed to the one of Sid's mother on horseback that Cody had stolen from her father's studio. "It's a masterpiece. It would have sold for a fortune."

She heard the wistfulness as well as the larceny in her sister's voice.

"We could have both retired on that money," Zander continued. "Instead, you had to give up one of the real H. F. Powells you managed to keep me from stealing to keep us from going to prison."

Sid chuckled. "I don't want to retire. I want to paint. What about you? You have our father's gift, as well."

"Gift? More like a curse." Zander shook her head. "No, you couldn't make me paint even at gunpoint. I've always hated it. Maybe because it takes practice and I don't care enough to hone my skills. I'll leave art to you. Anyway, look what Cody's artist talent did for him." She stood and reached for her bag. "The difference is that you have more than your art. You have a chance for real happiness with Laramie Cardwell."

"Wait a minute, where are you going? It's Christmas Eve. You said we were going to—"

"We're going to Cardwell Ranch."

"I already told Laramie that we were spending Christmas Eve here," Sid said.

"Well, there's been a change of plans. He invited us both to a real Christmas celebration," Zander said. "It sounds incredibly cheesy, but I'm not about to let you miss that. Come on."

"Are you sure, Z? Hot chocolate, tree trimming, carols around the fire?"

Zander put her arm around her sister. "I can stand it for one night. There will be presents, though, right?"

Sid shook her head at her sister. "I really am glad you came here for Christmas."

LARAMIE HADN'T REALIZED he'd been watching for her until he saw the SUV pull up out front of the ranch house.

Dana grinned at him as he headed out to the porch. It had been a crazy time after the ball, but his cousin was determined that they would have their Christmas Eve come hell or high water.

"Invite Sid and her sister," she'd insisted. "The more the merrier."

"She's having Christmas with her sister at the cabin," he'd told his cousin. "It's just as well. I don't see how anything can come of this. I live in Houston. Sid has her own life here."

"You can't see any way to overcome that obstacle?" Dana had asked in exasperation.

"It's more than the fact that our lives are thousands of miles apart," he'd said. "We don't really know each other."

His cousin had given him an impatient look. "You don't believe that any more than I do. And even if it is the case, surely there is some way you can rectify it. Is Houston really calling you back? Or are you just like your brothers were and afraid of giving away your heart?"

Laramie had smiled at Dana. "You just can't stand one of your cousins making a clean getaway."

She'd looked as if she might cry. "No, I can't. Nor do I want Sid to get away. Look what she did to try to bring her father's killer to justice. She risked her life and her reputation and prison."

Fortunately, once the Holiday Masquerade Ball and Auction committee members had learned how it was that the H. F. Powell painting was a forgery and Sid had offered them a real Powell to replace it, they'd dropped any legal charges. Also, Sid had promised to donate one of her paintings for the auction next year. Her paintings were now sought after as much as her father's had been.

"Hello," Laramie called from the porch as Sid and her sister climbed out of the SUV. "Glad to see you changed your mind."

"I changed it for her," Zander said.

He smiled. "That was nice of you." As the two climbed the steps, Zander went on past, letting him pull Sid in for quick kiss. "Merry Christmas."

SID STEPPED INTO his arms as if it was the most natural thing. She parted her lips for his warm, sweet kiss and could have stayed in that very spot forever.

At the door, Zander cleared her throat and said, "The kids are watching you two."

They turned, laughing, to see all of the Cardwell brood at the window, hands cupped around their eyes, making faces and laughing.

"Must be time to go in," Sid said, straightening her coat and bracing herself to meet the rest of the family.

Later, Sid sat listening to the sound of a family at play. It was loud and unruly and wonderful.

"Are you doing all right?" Laramie whispered next to her.

She nodded and smiled. "This is normal?"

He laughed. "As normal as the Cardwells get."

"I love it." She'd met his brothers, their wives, Dana's sister and two brothers and their mates, along with Dana's father, Laramie and his brothers' father and mother and his mother's new husband and all the children. There was also Dana's best friend, Hilde, and her husband, a local deputy.

It was insane. The air was filled with noise and the smells of holiday food. There'd been eggnog and hot chocolate and gingerbread men just as she'd predicted…and homemade fudge.

When it got late, the children were put to bed. The finishing touches were put on the tree. Sid had expected a huge, beautiful pine. Instead, it was a large ungainly tree.

"Dana can't stand the idea of an ugly tree not getting to be a Christmas tree," her husband the marshal explained with a shake of his head. "We do what we can for it."

When the lights came on, the tree was transformed. As the fire crackled they gathered to sing "Silent Night." Laramie put his arm around her shoulders and pulled her close. She stared at the sparkling lights of the tree and reached for her sister's hand.

"This is the best Christmas I've ever had," she whispered when the song ended.

"It's only the first of many if I have anything to say about it," Laramie told her as he drew her into his arms. "I'm not letting you get away from me again."

From the opposite side of the room, Dana gave him a wink.

* * * * *

THE MASKED MAN

This book is for Travis Ness,
who came into our lives on a prayer—and now
believes in love at first sight. Montana born, he
loves our annual summer weekend at Flathead Lake.
He also loves my daughter, and we love him.

PROLOGUE

HE PICKED HER up in his headlights as he came around the curve. She stood beside the narrow lake road, thumb out. He slowed to make sure before he stopped, but his blood was already pounding.

Yes. Long blond hair, sun-kissed bare limbs, sixteen, seventeen tops. She wore a pink T-shirt that hugged her small breasts and navy shorts that exposed slim, coltish legs and, as he stopped the car beside her, he saw that she had The Look.

He was a sucker for The Look. That cool, confident conviction that her life was only just beginning, that she would live forever, that nothing would harm *her*. It was a look that came only with youth.

"Hey," he said as he rolled down the passenger-side window and leaned over to smile at her. "Where ya headed?"

She stepped closer, bending at the waist to look in at him. "Bigfork?"

Her sweet scent rushed in with the warm summer night. Raspberry, he thought, one of his favorites. She hooked a hand over the open window frame. Her fingernails were painted a pale pink. He really liked that. On her slim, tanned wrist a tiny silver charm bracelet with a perfect little silver heart tinkled softly.

He could hardly contain himself. "Hop in, I'm going

that way. You must be in Bigfork working for the summer." He didn't want to make the mistake of trying to pick up a local girl again.

She nodded, stepped closer.

It always came down to a few crucial seconds.

She glanced at his car, then at him again.

In her blue eyes he saw that instant of uncertainty that could save—or destroy—her.

Seconds. Life or death. He loved this part.

"Thanks," she said and reached for the door handle. *Ain't no big, bad wolf here.*

He smiled. All teeth.

CHAPTER ONE

J<small>ILL</small> L<small>AWSON</small> <small>COULDN'T</small> believe it.

Trevor had stood her up *again*. Only this time it was for his parents' anniversary masquerade party. This time she was dressed as Scarlett O'Hara and feeling foolish as she waited in a far wing of the house, alone. This time was going to be the last time.

"I can't marry this man. I'm breaking off the engagement." The words echoed in the dark, empty room. *"Tonight."*

She watched the approaching thunderstorm move across the lake and waited for the aftershock of her decision. She had expected to feel something other than… relief. Certainly more regret.

She didn't.

This far down the east wing of the Foresters' massive lake house the sounds of the ongoing party were muted. That was one of the reasons she had come down here. To get away from all the merriment and the reminder that she was alone, the engagement ring on her finger feeling suddenly too tight. The ache in her heart too familiar.

She ached for something she wasn't even sure existed except maybe in the movies.

"You act like you expect fireworks, maybe the earth to move? Really, Jill, you are such a fool," Trevor had said when she'd tried to voice her concerns the last time she'd seen him.

Well, she certainly felt like a fool tonight, she thought. She had hardly seen Trevor since he'd asked her to marry him, but when he'd called, he'd promised that tonight would be different. After all, it was his parents' thirty-fifth anniversary, and summer was almost over, another season gone.

Heddy and Alistair threw a costume party to celebrate the event at the end of August every year at their house on the east shore of Flathead Lake. This year the theme was famous lovers, and Trevor had insisted Jill come as Scarlett so he could be Rhett Butler. And he'd stood her up.

"Quite frankly, Rhett, I don't give a damn," she said to the dark room. A lie. She did give a damn. She had wanted Trevor Forester to be The One. And at first, he'd made her believe he was.

She looked down at the silver charm bracelet on her wrist, the tiny heart dangling from the chain, and remembered the night he'd given it to her. On her birthday two months ago. It was right after that when he'd asked her to marry him and had given her the antique engagement ring now on her finger.

Her instincts warned her that everything between her and Trevor had happened too fast. She'd let him bowl her over, not giving her time to think. Or hardly react. And suddenly she was engaged to a man she didn't really know.

He'd been involved in his construction project, an upscale resort he called Inspiration Island south of Bigfork, Montana, in the middle of Flathead Lake, almost since they'd started dating.

Admittedly, he *had* been working a lot. A week ago he'd stopped by her bakery and she'd barely recognized him. He was tanned, leaner, more muscular.

She felt herself weaken a little at the memory of how good he'd looked and quickly was reminded that he had only made love to her once, soon after the engagement. In the weeks since, he always had an excuse—he was too tired or had to meet one of the investors or had to get back to the island.

"Everything will be different once we're married," he'd promised.

"Right," she said to the dark. She didn't believe that. Didn't believe anything Trevor told her anymore. "We're never going to know if things will be different because I'm not marrying you, Trevor Forester." She spun around in surprise. Someone had come into the dark room without her realizing it. How long had he or she been there, listening?

A small table lamp came on, blinding her for an instant. She thought at first the other person was Trevor and she would get this over with quickly. This quiet wing of the house would serve her purpose well.

But it wasn't Trevor. "I heard you mention my son's name," Heddy Forester said. She was dressed as Cleopatra. Her Anthony, Alistair Forester, didn't seem to be with her.

Obviously Heddy had heard her. But Jill didn't want to spoil Heddy's anniversary party. The older woman would hear soon enough about the broken engagement. Then again, maybe Heddy wouldn't be that disappointed by the news.

"I'm just upset because Trevor is so late," Jill said.

"I'm sure he has a good reason." Heddy always defended her only offspring. "He's been working such long hours on the island."

"Yes, but I thought he'd call," Jill said, trying not to show just how upset she really was. Heddy Forester didn't miss much, though.

"Maybe he can't get to a phone," Heddy offered, studying her. The sound of music, chattering guests and fireworks going off drifted in from the patio. There must have been at least a hundred people at the party.

Jill thought about mentioning that Trevor had a cell phone with him all the time, but didn't. "I'm sure he'll be along soon," she said diplomatically. In the distance thunder rumbled, the horizon over the lake dark and ominous.

"Or maybe he's trapped on the island and can't get back," Heddy suggested, looking anxiously out the window at the storm brewing over the water. "I'll bet his cell phone won't work in a storm like this."

"I thought Trevor wasn't going to the island today."

Heddy didn't seem to hear. "I'd better get my guests in before the storm hits. Send Trevor to find me when he arrives."

Jill nodded. Heddy was right. Trevor wouldn't miss his parents' anniversary party. He had to have a good reason for being this late. For standing Jill up. Again.

After Heddy left, Jill turned the light back off, preferring to watch the approaching storm in the dark, preferring to let Trevor find her. She loved thunderstorms, the dramatic light, the awesome power, the smell of the rain-washed summer evening afterward.

She didn't know how long she stood there, watching all the guests rush in as the storm moved across the water toward them, the darkness complete. Down the slope from the house, the wind tore leaves from the trees and sent waves splashing over the docks. Jill caught the flicker of boat lights on the other side of the Foresters' small guest cottage at the edge of the lake and wondered what fool would go out in a storm like this.

Speaking of fools… She glanced at her watch. Eight-fifteen. Trevor was almost two hours late. Thunder rumbled in the distance. The red-white-and-blue flags snapped in the wind out on the patio under a flapping striped canopy. The patio was empty, everyone now inside as lightning flashed and thunder rumbled. She should go home before it started to rain.

She could break off the engagement tomorrow. To-morrow, when she was less angry. Tomorrow, when she wasn't dressed in a hoop skirt and green-velvet curtain material. Why had Trevor insisted they come to the party as Rhett Butler and Scarlett O'Hara, any-way? Hadn't Scarlett ended up alone?

Then again, maybe this was the perfect costume.

"Say good-night, Scarlett," she said to the room and started to turn from the window. A jagged bolt of light-ning flashed, spiking down into the water, illuminating the patio and the curve of rock steps that swept down the grassy slope to the lake cottage. And in that flash of light she saw him.

Rhett Butler. He ducked into the cottage just an in-stant before thunder rumbled overhead. The first rain-drops spattered the window. Trevor must have been on the boat she'd seen and now he'd gone into the cottage to wait out the storm.

When the lights didn't come on inside the cottage, she realized the shutters were closed. Trevor was alone down there, offering her the perfect opportunity to talk to him. This couldn't wait. She suspected he'd been avoiding her because he, too, thought their engagement was a mistake. He couldn't avoid her now.

She braced herself, then opened the patio door, lifted the hoop skirt with one hand and, holding on to her hat with the other, raced across the patio to the rock steps that descended to the cottage.

Behind her, the wind moaned through the trees, sending leaves scurrying. Snatches of the music from the party chased after her but were quickly drowned out by the crash of waves. Lightning struck so close it raised the tiny hairs on the back of her neck. As she ran toward the cottage, rain slashed down, hard as hail and just as cold. Thunder boomed, deafening.

She was close enough to the water now that she could feel the spray from the waves. Her hand was on the doorknob when lightning electrified the sky overhead once more. This time the thunderclap reverberated in her chest.

The lights on the patio blinked out and behind her the main house went dark. She opened the cottage door, the room inside as black as the bottom of a bucket. Chilled, wet and a little disoriented by the darkness, she stepped in and quickly closed the door behind her.

Her lips parted as she started to say Trevor's name, sensing, rather than hearing, him near her.

Before she could get his name out, his arm snaked around her waist and he dragged her to him, his mouth unerringly dropping to hers.

She gasped in surprise and pushed with both palms against his broad chest, the darkness so intense she couldn't see his features, could only feel him, the unfamiliar Rhett Butler costume mustache, the unfamiliar hardness of his body. Had he seen her coming down from the house and thought he could make things up to her by taking her to bed? Fat chance.

She tried to push him away, but he only deepened the kiss, holding her to him as if he never wanted to let her go, as if he'd been waiting for her, needing her.

This wasn't why she'd come down here. Or was it? Had she secretly hoped Trevor could change her mind?

He groaned against her mouth and she felt herself weaken in his arms. He'd never kissed her like this before. His body was so muscular, so solid, harder than it had been the last time they'd made love.

If this was his way of saying he was sorry… She lost herself in his kiss, in the warmth of his body molded to hers, stirred in a way she'd never been before by this unexpected ardor.

Her hat fell to the floor as he buried his fingers in her hair and pressed her against the wall with his body, his mouth exploring hers as his hand moved up her waist and over her rib cage to cup her breast in his warm palm. Heat shot through her.

She had never wanted him so badly. Her body felt on fire as he moved his hands over her, exploring her flesh with his fingertips in the blind darkness. She arched against him, strangely uninhibited. There was something exciting about not being able to see each other, only feel. It was as if they'd never touched before as his fingers explored beneath the confines of her costume.

His touch sure and strong, he swiftly and efficiently relieved her of her clothing, the hoop skirt, the entire dress, leaving only her skimpy silk panties and bra.

Outside the warm cottage the storm raged. She

sighed with pleasure against his mouth, his lips never leaving hers as if he'd feared what she might have said if he hadn't kissed her the moment she came into the cottage. Had he realized how abandoned and alone she'd been feeling? How afraid she was that they were about to make a mistake by marrying?

She'd never felt more naked as his fingers skimmed over her skin, stopping to fondle her through the thin silk of her underthings. Hadn't she, in fact, worn the sexy lingerie hoping things would be different between them tonight, just as Trevor had promised?

She worked feverishly at the buttons of his costume, his kisses growing more ardent, more demanding, her need becoming more frantic as she worked with wanton abandon to free him of his clothing. His need matched hers as he relieved her of her bra and panties and helped discard his own clothing, and all the time, never stopped kissing her.

She shuddered at the first touch of his naked skin against hers, heard his soft groan as he dragged her down to the floor, their lovemaking as wild and frenzied as the storm outside.

He took her higher than she'd ever been, a rarefied place depleted of oxygen, where stars blinded her vision and each breath seemed her last until the final crescendo of storm and passion and release, sending her reeling into a dark, infinite universe of pleasure.

She felt tears come to her eyes as he curled her to him on the floor, spooning her into his warmth, spent and seemingly as awed as she.

She snuggled close, content for the first time in her life. She knew there was no going back. She'd just committed to this man in a way more binding than any engagement ring or pronouncement of love. She'd been so wrong about him. So wrong about *them*.

She closed her eyes, her skin still tingling, her heart still hammering like the rain on the roof. She didn't hear the door open.

A chill wind blew in, rippling over her skin. At the same moment she opened her eyes, a flash of lightning lit the outside world, illuminating the driving rain— and the dark figure silhouetted in the doorway.

So content, so sated, so happy was Jill that it took her a moment to recognize the familiar silhouette in the doorway. The hat, the hair, the hoop skirt. Another Scarlett. It took even longer for the words the other Scarlett spoke to register. "Trevor, darling, I'm sorry I'm late but I—"

In that instant Jill saw the other Scarlett take in the hurriedly discarded costumes on the floor, her head coming up to look where Jill lay on the floor in Trevor's arms in that instant before the lightning flash blinked out, pitching everything back into blackness.

"You bastard!" the woman shrieked. "You lousy—" A boom of thunder drowned out the rest as she whirled away.

For just an instant Jill didn't move. Then the truth hit her. A cry caught in her throat as she jerked free of Trevor's arms, recoiling in shame. She stumbled to her feet and grabbed at the pile of clothing she'd seen in that flash of light, that flash of understanding—Trevor had thought he was making love to someone else! The other Scarlett. No wonder it had been so passionate! So amazingly tender and loving and filled with desire!

Behind her, he still hadn't said a word. But she could

feel him watching her. Wasn't he even going to bother to try to talk himself out of this?

It was too dark inside the cottage to find her skimpy underwear. With her back to him, she dressed with only one thing in mind—getting out of there as quickly as possible. She pulled on the hoop, frantically tied it and slipped the damp dress over her head, then felt around for her shoes in the dark, wanting nothing more than to flee before he tried to apologize, which would make it all so much worse.

On the way to the door she tripped on her hat, which she then swept up from the floor. Fighting tears of humiliation and anger, she tugged off the engagement ring.

She was grateful for the darkness in the cottage. From the doorway she didn't have to see his face, only the dark shape of him on the floor. He hadn't moved. Hadn't said a word. But then, what could he say?

"You *are* a lousy bastard, Trevor Forester," she said, and flung the engagement ring at him before rushing out.

Fool that she was, she expected to hear him call after her. She thought she heard him groan, but it could have been the wind.

She lifted the wet velvet hem of the dress and, her shoes still in her hand, ran up the hillside, avoiding the main house, afraid to look back for fear she would see Trevor standing in the doorway of the cottage—and feel something other than hatred for him.

She didn't let herself cry until she was in her van driving back to her apartment over the bakery. Tears scalded her eyes, blurring her vision as the windshield wipers clacked back and forth against the pounding rain.

She could still smell him on her, still feel his touch as if it was imprinted on her skin, still taste his kisses. Damn Trevor Forester. Damn him to hell.

Rain fell in a torrent. Jill barely recognized the little red Saturn sedan that almost ran her off the road as it came up from behind and whizzed past, going too fast for the narrow, winding road along the lakeshore. But in her headlights she read the personalized license plate: JILLS. It was her car, the car Trevor had borrowed the last time she'd seen him, saying his Audi Quatro sports car was in the shop. Since then, Jill had been driving her bakery delivery van with The Best Buns In Town painted on the side.

The driver went by so fast that Jill hadn't seen who was behind the wheel. Trevor? Or had he loaned her car to his girlfriend? Or were they both in the car?

And Jill thought she was angry with Trevor before!

She pushed the van's gas pedal of the van to the floor, trying to close the distance between her and the red Saturn. Was Trevor hoping to beat her back to her apartment? Beg her forgiveness? Or trying to get away? He had to have recognized the van. It was darned hard to miss.

Jill kept the Saturn's taillights in sight as she raced after it, the van forced to take the curves more slowly. The narrow road was cut into the side of the mountain. In some places, the land beneath the road dropped in rocky cliffs to the water. In others, cherry orchards clung to the steep hillside for miles, broken only by tall dense pines and rock.

On the outskirts of Bigfork, Montana, the Saturn turned right into a new complex, where Trevor had rented a condo until he and Jill were married. At least that had been the plan. He had said he was going to buy her a house on the lake. He didn't want them living in some dinky condo.

As Jill parked the van behind her car in front of the condo, she told herself she should just take the car and leave. As angry as she was, this wouldn't be a good time for a confrontation—with Trevor or his girlfriend.

But then, how would she get the van back to the bakery? She'd need it early in the morning to make deliveries.

Also, she would never know who'd been driving her car. And suddenly she had a whole lot she wanted to say to Trevor. Or his girlfriend. Or both.

She got out of the van in the cumbersome costume. The front door of the condo stood open, a faint light on inside. Whoever had gone in must have been in a big hurry.

It was dark inside the condo. She could hear what sounded like someone rummaging around in the bedroom. The only light spilled from the partially opened bedroom doorway. From this angle, Jill could see nothing but shadowed movement on one wall and the flicker of what had to be a flashlight beam.

Her heart caught in her throat. Why hadn't the person in the bedroom turned on the lights? And why would Trevor be searching for something in his own bedroom in the dark?

The other Scarlett?

Jill moved through the dark living room following the path of light coming from the bedroom and caught the scent of the woman's perfume. She realized she'd smelled it earlier—that moment when the other Scarlett had been framed in the lake cottage doorway. A heavy, cloying scent that made her sick to her stomach.

Trevor had never been much of a housekeeper, but this place looked as if it had been ransacked. As she tried to step around the mess on the floor, the hem of her dress caught on a pile of books dumped on the floor. One of the books tumbled off the top of the heap and thumped to the floor.

The sound of rummaging in the bedroom stopped. The flashlight beam blinked out.

In the blinding darkness, Jill felt on the wall for the light switch and flipped it on. Nothing happened. Had Trevor forgotten to pay his light bill or—

A figure came barreling out of the bedroom. Jill tried to get out of the way, hearing the movement rather than seeing the person in the dark. She felt an object strike her hard on the head. Her knees buckled.

As she dropped to the floor, she heard the retreating footfalls, then the sound of her car engine and the squeal of rubber tires on the wet pavement.

Dazed, she stumbled to her feet and moved to the open doorway. Her car was gone. So was the driver. She turned toward the bedroom and the scent of the woman's perfume that still hung in the air.

What had the woman been looking for? And had she found it?

Jill felt her way in the dark to the bedroom door, remembering the candle she'd bought Trevor as a housewarming present. She stumbled through the mess on the floor to the nightstand beside his bed and felt around for the candle. The light from an outside yard lamp shone through the thin bedroom curtains. She could make out something large and looming on the bed.

She found the candle and matches. Striking a match, she touched it to the wick. The light flickered, illuminating the small room.

An open suitcase lay on the bed, piled high with Trevor's clothing. The closet doors stood open, the hangers empty. The same with the dresser drawers.

Like the living room, the bedroom appeared to have been ransacked. Or Trevor had obviously packed in a hurry. His clothes in the suitcase were a jumble. It was obvious that the other Scarlet had been looking for something in the suitcase.

Holding the candle up for better illumination, Jill took a step toward the suitcase. Her shoe kicked a balled-up sheet of paper on the floor at her feet. She bent down and picked it up. Smoothing the paper, she held it to the candlelight. It was an eviction notice. Trevor was four months behind in his rent? How was that possible? Even if he'd put all his money into the island development, his parents were wealthy. She realized that if he hadn't paid his rent, he probably hadn't paid his electricity bill, either.

Head aching, she looked into the suitcase, still wondering what the woman had been searching for. Jill picked up one of Trevor's shirts. An airline-ticket folder fell to the bed.

She lifted it carefully, afraid of what she was going to find. Inside was Trevor's passport and a one-way ticket on a flight out of Kalispell *tonight,* final destination: Rio de Janeiro, Brazil.

Brazil? Trevor hadn't just been planning to run out on his rent and his electricity bill. He'd been running out on her, as well. When had he planned to tell her? At the party? And what about the other Scarlett?

Jill leafed through the folder until she found the receipt from the travel agent. Her hand began to tremble. Trevor had purchased *two* tickets on a credit card. One for himself. The other for his wife. The name on the other ticket was Rachel Forester.

The other Scarlett? Is that what she'd taken from the suitcase—her ticket?

Jill leaned against the bed frame, feeling dizzy and sick. Trevor had been planning to marry someone named Rachel *tonight* and run off with her to Brazil? It was unbelievable. She thought she couldn't despise him more than she already did. She was wrong.

As she started to put the ticket back into the suitcase, she noticed the credit-card number on the receipt for the tickets. "Trevor, you really are a lousy bastard." He'd used Jill's credit card to buy the tickets for himself and his secret new bride.

Reeling, Jill stumbled out of the condo. Her head throbbed, and when she touched the bump on her forehead, her fingers came away sticky with blood.

All she wanted to do was go home and forget this day had ever happened. Forget Trevor. Too bad she couldn't forget what had happened between them in the cottage—before the other Scarlett had shown up.

As she drove downtown to her apartment over the bakery she owned, she told herself this night couldn't get any worse. But as she passed the bakery, she saw the sheriff's deputy car parked across the street. Two deputies got out as she parked the van out front rather than continue on around to the back entrance to the upstairs apartment.

She stood paralyzed with worry on the sidewalk as they approached, afraid it had something to do with her father. Gary Lawson hadn't been well enough to attend the party tonight. He'd said it was only the flu—

"Jill Lawson?" the taller of the deputies asked, the one whose name tag read James Samuelson. "Sorry to bother you so late. May we come in and have a word with you?"

She nodded dumbly and swallowed, her throat constricting, as she shakily unlocked the door to the bakery and let them in.

"We're here about Trevor Forester," the shorter, stouter of the two said. He introduced himself as Rex Duncan. He took out a small notebook and pen.

She stared at the deputy. "Is Trevor in some kind of trouble?" Understatement of the year.

She could feel Samuelson studying her face. Past him, she caught her reflection in the front window. Her eyes were red and puffy from crying, and the bump on her forehead was now bruised and caked with blood around the small cut where she'd been hit.

"When was the last time you saw him?" Samuelson asked.

"Tonight. At the party." She saw the deputies exchange a look.

"Tonight? What time was that?" Duncan asked.

"About eight-fifteen."

"You're sure you saw him?" Samuelson said.

"I was with him until about…nine-thirty, then I left. Has something happened?"

The deputies exchanged another look.

"Please tell me what this is about," she said. "You're scaring me."

"Ms. Lawson, you couldn't have been with Trevor Forester tonight at the party," Samuelson said. "Mr.

Forester was murdered during the time you say you were with him at another location. I think you'd better tell us why you'd make up such a story."

CHAPTER TWO

AS THE WOMAN stormed out of the lake cottage, Mackenzie Cooper pushed himself up from the floor on one elbow and groaned.

"Who the hell was that?" he asked the darkness, still stunned by what had happened between them.

Silently he cursed himself. When she'd come into the cottage while he was spying on the boat just off the shore, he'd kissed her, only planning to shut her up and keep her from giving him away. But one thing had led to another so quickly...

Damn. What had he been thinking? That was just it. He hadn't been thinking.

He felt dazed as he checked his watch. Nine-forty. He'd completely lost track of the time. Completely lost track of everything. Especially his senses.

He quickly dressed, changing enough of the costume so that he wouldn't be recognized as Rhett Butler. The last thing he wanted to do was run into either of the Scarlett O'Haras again tonight. In the mood they were in it could be dangerous. Another reason to hightail it out of here as fast as possible.

It was obvious the man he was supposed to meet here had stood him up. Which, all things considered, was just as well.

But first, Mac had to know what the woman had

thrown at him. Using the penlight he'd brought with him, he shone it around on the floor.

Something in the corner glittered in the light and he bent to pick it up. A diamond ring. The stone was a nice size, the setting obviously old. He pocketed the ring and started to leave, but spotted something else on the floor in the beam of the penlight.

It appeared to be a scrap of black fabric. He picked up the skimpy, sexy panties. Silk. Her scent filled his nostrils, momentarily paralyzing him with total recall of the woman he'd had in his arms tonight.

Suddenly he wished he could have seen her in these. But his tactile memory flashed on an image of her that was now branded on his mouth, his hands, his body and his brain.

It seemed the woman had thought he was Trevor Forester—her fiancé. At least he *had* been her fiancé until the other Scarlett O'Hara had shown up.

He swore again, realizing the magnitude of what he'd done. He'd just made love to the last woman on earth he should have!

Not wanting to leave any evidence, he pocketed the panties along with the ring, then moved to the cottage door to make sure the coast was clear. It was time to get out of here. He'd gotten more than he'd come for. And then some.

TREVOR DEAD? MURDERED? Jill staggered, her legs suddenly unable to hold her.

Deputy Rex Duncan pulled out a chair for her at one of the small round serving tables at the front of her bakery and helped her into it. He then drew up seats across from her for him and Samuelson, who pulled a small tape recorder from his pocket, set it on the table and clicked it on.

"There must be some mistake," she said, looking from one to the other of them.

"There is no mistake," Samuelson said. "That's why we're confused. Why would you say you were with Trevor Forester tonight at the party? Unless for some reason you think you need an alibi."

She stared at him, stunned. "An alibi? I was with Trevor in the lake cottage during the time I told you." She looked from Samuelson to Duncan.

Duncan shook his head.

She felt the blood leave her head. If she hadn't been in the cottage with Trevor... Oh, my God.

"Why don't you start at the beginning?" Duncan suggested as he handed her a napkin from the dispenser on the table. "You arrived at the party at what time?"

She took the napkin and wiped her eyes, panic making her hands shake. "About seven-thirty."

"Alone?" Duncan asked.

She nodded. "I thought Trevor would meet me at the party since he was running so late."

"Trevor Forester was your fiancé?" Deputy Samuelson asked.

She nodded, then glanced down at her ringless finger, the white mark on her lightly tanned skin where the diamond engagement ring had been. The deputies followed her gaze. She quickly covered her hand.

"I think you'd better tell us what happened tonight," Samuelson said. "It's obvious you've been crying. How did you get that bump on your head?"

She looked up at him, then at Deputy Duncan, and fought to swallow back the dam of tears that threatened to break loose. Trevor dead. Murdered. And the man in the cottage who'd been dressed like Rhett Butler…?

"The truth, Ms. Lawson. You weren't with Trevor Forester tonight at the party. So where were you?" Samuelson asked impatiently.

"I thought I *was* with Trevor," she cried, and saw them exchange another look. "I know this will sound crazy…"

"Believe me, we've heard it all," Duncan said, not unkindly. "Just tell us what happened."

She took a breath. "Trevor was supposed to pick me up for the party at six-thirty," she began. "We were going as Rhett Butler and Scarlett O'Hara." Jill told them how she'd gone alone to the Foresters at seven-thirty, waited for him in a room off the far wing until she'd seen the man she believed to be Trevor dressed as Rhett Butler duck into the lake cottage at eight-fifteen. She'd just looked at her watch—that was why she remembered the time. "It was just before the electricity went out."

Duncan nodded. "A transformer blew on that side of the lake about then. The man you saw, he had on a mask?"

She nodded and realized she'd only gotten a glimpse as he'd gone into the cottage. Just an impression of Rhett Butler.

"So you went down to the cottage in a downpour to see him?" Samuelson asked. "Why not wait until the storm let up? Or he came up to the party?"

"I wanted to speak with Trevor alone first."

Samuelson raised an eyebrow. "About what? I see you aren't wearing your engagement ring."

"The truth is, I had planned to break off our engagement," she admitted, wondering if they'd already found her engagement ring in the cottage. She assumed they'd already talked with Heddy and Alistair. Had Heddy told the deputies how upset Jill had been? That she'd planned to break the engagement?

"Why break up?" Samuelson asked, eyeing her closely.

She shook her head, not knowing where to begin. "I had hardly seen Trevor lately, and I just felt that we shouldn't be getting married."

"You said *had* planned to break off your engagement. Did something change your mind?" Duncan asked.

"Actually, Trevor did—at first. Or at least the man I thought was Trevor." She could see the deputies' skepticism. She hurriedly told them how the electricity had gone out, how in the darkness the man she thought was Trevor had grabbed her, kissed her, seduced her—all without a word spoken between them.

She dropped her gaze to her hands, clasped in her lap, for a moment, the shame and humiliation almost getting the better of her as she thought of what she'd done with a stranger. She had opened herself up to him. At the time she'd thought it was the darkness that had let her put all her inhibitions aside and make love as she'd never made love before—completely.

When she looked up, she saw they didn't believe a word she'd said. "It's true! I can prove it. Someone saw us together. A woman." She groaned silently, mortified to have to tell them.

"What woman?" Duncan asked.

Jill looked at him and realized she didn't have a clue who the woman was. Reluctantly she explained how it seemed Trevor had planned to meet, not her, but the other Scarlett in the cottage. "The woman saw us, became angry and left."

"I thought it was dark inside the cottage?" Samuelson said.

"It was, but there was a flash of lightning as she opened the door," Jill said.

"You didn't see the man in this flash of lightning?" he asked incredulously.

She shook her head, remembering how he'd spooned her against him, the gentle way he'd nuzzled the nape of her neck, his breath on her bare, hot skin... "I was facing the door and he was...behind me."

"What did you do after this woman interrupted the two of you?" Duncan asked.

"I realized Trevor—" she heard her voice break "—I mean, the man I thought was Trevor...had just made love to the wrong woman. I hurriedly dressed, threw the engagement ring at him and left."

"You never saw his face?" Duncan asked.

She shook her head.

"You must have been furious," Samuelson said.

"I was hurt." She dropped her gaze, remembering the depth of that hurt because of what they had just shared.

"Did you tell anyone about this?" Duncan asked.

"No. I left by the side yard. I was upset. I certainly didn't want to talk about it." She saw the way they were both looking at her and added, "I think the woman's name might be Rachel, but you'll have to catch her tonight before she gets on a plane for Brazil."

Samuelson raised a brow. "Why would you think that?"

Jill told them about almost being run off the road by her own red Saturn and how she'd followed it, thinking at first that Trevor was driving the car, since he was the one who'd borrowed it the last time she saw him.

"The front door was open. Someone was in the bedroom, rummaging around, using a flashlight," she continued. She told them how the person had come flying out, hit her and left in her car. "I caught a whiff of the same perfume I had smelled when the woman opened the door to the cottage."

"So you think it was the same woman," Duncan said.

"Was she still wearing her costume?" Samuelson asked.

Now that Jill thought about it… "No. She must have had a change of clothing with her." Maybe her traveling wedding suit since, if she was Rachel, she and Trevor were headed for a justice of the peace and a plane, it seemed. "If you've been to his condo, you know that Trevor was running away tonight with a woman named Rachel." Their poker faces told her nothing.

"We'll try to find your car," Duncan offered. "And this woman." His tone implied, *If she exists.*

"Thank you."

Samuelson was shaking his head. "Come on, Ms. Lawson, how could you have made love with a man and not realized he wasn't your fiancé?"

Her face flamed with embarrassment. "Trevor and I had only been…intimate once." She thought of the differences, not just in the lovemaking but in the man's body. She'd believed it was because Trevor had been doing manual labor for the past few months. He was so much more muscular. Stronger. More…forceful. He'd lost some weight and was leaner—just like when she'd seen him recently. And he'd promised her that tonight would be different. Oh, and it had been, she thought, fiddling nervously with the silver charm bracelet at her wrist.

"Heddy Forester says when she saw you at about seven-forty-five, you were very upset with Trevor," Samuelson said. "She says she thought you left right after that. You have keys to the Foresters' boats, right?"

"Yes, but—"

"In a ski boat, it takes how long—ten, fifteen minutes?—to get down the lake to the island," he asked.

She stared at him. "Trevor was killed on the island?" What was he saying? That she would have had plenty of time to get to the island, kill Trevor and return to the party—and the cottage. "I told you—"

"Yes, you told us," Samuelson interrupted. "You were in the cottage. Then how do you explain the fact that Heddy Forester saw you get out of a boat at the dock just a little before nine-thirty?"

"It wasn't me. It must have been the woman I told you about, the one who was also dressed as Scarlett O'Hara."

It was clear Samuelson didn't believe her.

"Was there anything about her you can remember other than the costume?" Duncan asked.

"All I saw was her silhouette in the doorway. But I think I'd recognize her voice if I heard it again." A strident, high-pitched voice.

Duncan shifted in his chair. "When was the last time you were on Inspiration Island?"

"I've never been on the island. Trevor didn't want me seeing it until everything was finished. He said he didn't allow anyone but crews on the island during construction, not even investors, if he could help it." She realized how stupid she'd been. Trevor had probably used the island as a place to spend time with the other Scarlett. Not that Jill cared to go out there, given the island's history. Maybe that was why she'd never pushed the subject.

"Do you know anyone who might have wanted to harm Trevor Forester?" Duncan asked.

She shook her head. "I would have said Trevor had no enemies. But I realized tonight that I didn't know Trevor at all."

"I think that will be enough for now." Duncan turned off the tape recorder. Both deputies pushed to their feet. "We'll check out your story, Ms. Lawson. You might want to have someone take a look at that cut on your forehead."

"It's fine." She told herself there was no reason to worry about anything. The man she was with in the cottage would come forward once he heard about the murder. Also the other Scarlett. Once the deputies found her car...

"When you search the cottage, you'll find my engagement ring I threw at the man as I was leaving." She cringed as she remembered what else she'd left behind. "You'll also find some black silk...underthings of mine that I didn't take the time to collect." She was mortified that her risqué panties and bra would now be... evidence in a murder investigation. Her face burned. "All of which prove I'm telling the truth."

Duncan looked sympathetic, but doubtful. "They prove you were in the cottage. Not that you were with anyone. We'll get back to you. Please don't leave town."

"I have no intention of going anywhere," she snapped. "I have a bakery to run. I also have no reason to leave. I want to know who killed Trevor as much as you do. More so, since you seem to think I'm a suspect."

"If you think of anything else, please give me a call." Deputy Duncan handed her his card.

She watched them both leave, feeling heartsick. The events of the night seemed surreal, a bad dream. Trevor murdered? Herself a suspect? A chill skittered over her skin. Was it possible that she'd found the passion she'd always longed for—in the arms of a total stranger?

MACKENZIE COOPER LEFT the Foresters' and walked down the road in the pouring rain to his pickup. He'd had to park a half mile back up the lane because of all the cars. Those cars were gone now, and when he turned to look back, he saw something that sent his heart pounding. The sheriff's car was parked near the rear entrance of the house.

Getting into his Chevy truck, the camper on the back, he drove north down the narrow, winding lake road toward Bandit's Bay Marina, where he kept his houseboat. What had happened to cause the sheriff to go up to the house? He had a feeling he didn't want to know.

At the Beach Bar at the end of the pier at the marina, he ordered a beer. "What's all the excitement?" he asked the bartender.

"Trevor Forester was murdered tonight," the bartender said.

Mac felt as if he'd been kicked in the gut. Trevor was dead and Mac had just slept with his fiancée. Talk about bad karma.

He drank his beer, hardly tasting it, and listened to some of the locals talking about how Forester's boat was found floating about a half mile off Inspiration Island. A fisherman found Trevor lying in a pool of blood in the bottom of the boat. He'd been shot twice in the heart.

Murder was rare enough in this part of Montana. The last one was back in 1997 when some guy was killed on Hawk Island. What made this murder more tantalizing was that the victim was a local and that he was developing Inspiration Island, an island the men at the bar said should have been left alone. They hinted that the island was haunted, which was a good reason not to develop it.

Mac didn't buy into any of that mumbo jumbo. What interested him was that the locals hadn't liked Trevor. Partially because of the resentment they harbored for him and the Forester family money. Partially because Trevor was a jackass who also hadn't been paying his bills of late.

Mac sipped his beer, unable to shake the anxiety he'd felt the moment he'd seen the sheriff's car at the Foresters' lake house. It was just a matter of time before the sheriff found out about Trevor's call to Mac.

"I think someone's trying to kill me," Trevor had said on the phone yesterday, sounding scared. "I heard you're a private investigator. I need you to find out who it is before it's too late."

It had been Trevor's plan for them to meet at the party to discuss the job. Trevor had sent Mac a costume: Rhett Butler. They were to meet at the lake cottage at eight-fifteen tonight. Trevor would be arriving by boat.

Except Trevor never made it. Another boat pulled up. And Mac had recognized the man's voice as he came onto shore with a woman on his arm. Nathaniel Pierce. He and Mac had gone to university together. Mac had forgotten that Pierce had bought a place up this way.

He'd been watching Pierce from the window when the cottage door opened and the woman came in. The last thing Mac wanted to do was see Pierce, so Mac had kissed the woman to keep her quiet.

According to the discussion at the bar, Trevor's fiancée was a woman named Jill Lawson. While locals had little regard for Trevor, they had nothing but praise for Jill, although, like Mac, they couldn't understand what she saw in Trevor Forester. Jill owned a bakery in town called The Best Buns in Town.

A name that had more than a little truth to it, he thought. According to the locals at the bar, Jill was a hard worker, a fine-looking, intelligent young woman who baked the best cinnamon rolls in four states, not just in town.

If the locals knew about Trevor's other woman, they weren't talking. Mac listened to everyone speculate on who might have killed Trevor. It was clear no one had a clue. Mac finished his beer and walked down the dock to his boat, thinking of Jill Lawson. Worrying about her and wondering how she was going to take the murder of her fiancé, given what had happened tonight.

His houseboat was basically a box on pontoons, containing just the basics for living. He had it docked at the farthest slip at the end of an older section of the marina. The cheap seats.

The boat wasn't much, but it was home. It had a flat

roof, with a railing around both the bottom and top decks, a retractable diving board and a slide that he'd used more for escape in the past than for swimming.

He entered the houseboat cabin without a key—he never bothered to keep the place locked—and was instantly aware that someone was inside waiting for him. He heard the telltale squeak of his favorite chair, but he'd also developed a sixth sense for unwelcome company. It had saved his life on more than one occasion.

Drawing his weapon from his ankle holster, he moved soundlessly through to the living area at the center of the cabin. He aimed the gun at the person sitting in the dark in his chair and turned on a light.

"I do like a cautious man," Nathaniel Pierce said as he looked up from the recliner where he was lounging, a bottle of Mac's beer in his hand.

"Pierce," Mac said.

The man was tanned, his body lean, his hair blond, his eyes blue, and even dressed down in jeans, a polo shirt and deck shoes, Nathaniel Pierce reeked of money. Old money.

Mac put the weapon away, walked to the small kitchen, pulled a bottle of beer from the fridge and twisted off the cap, pretty sure he was going to need a drink.

It wasn't every day he came home to find Nathaniel Pierce sitting in his living room in the dark waiting for him. Mac thanked his lucky stars for that. He and Pierce had been roommates at university—actually at several Ivy League universities, which they'd attended during a troubled period in both of their lives. They hadn't been friends for years.

Finding Pierce here made him nervous—and wary. "Slumming?" Mac asked.

Pierce laughed with only mild amusement.

"I'm sure you've heard that Trevor Forester was murdered tonight," Pierce said.

So much for small talk. "Trevor Forester?"

Pierce smiled. "I saw your truck at the party, but I never did see you."

Mac took a sip of his beer, wondering what Pierce was doing here. More importantly, what his interest in Forester was, or in himself, for that matter. "You hanging out with people like the Foresters?" Pierce had always been an old-money snob. Sure, the Foresters had money, but it was new and not nearly as much as the Pierces'. It was like the difference between a hot dog and beluga caviar.

"It's a small community," Pierce said in answer.

Not that small.

"I'm curious what you were doing there." Pierce took a swig of beer and smiled as if enjoying the taste. Not likely.

"I had an invitation." Mac put his feet up on the coffee table and downed half his beer, telling himself he was nothing like the man sitting in his recliner. True, they looked alike and were both thirty-six. At six-four, Pierce was a couple of inches taller, carried a little more weight and his hair was blonder, his eyes bluer.

And they came from the same backgrounds. Mac had tried to overcome his. He'd chosen the worst possible career and lived on his houseboat on one lake or another or in the camper on the back of his truck. He kept a small office in Whitefish, Montana, where his sister lived, and he checked in every week or so, taking only the jobs that interested him.

He drank beer, dressed in old blue jeans, ragged T-shirts and Mexican sandals. Most days he was as close to happy as he could get, all things considered.

Clearly Pierce found all of that amusing, as if he thought Mac tried too hard to disguise who he was. A rich kid from old money. Just not as rich as Pierce.

Nathaniel Pierce loved being rich and flaunted it—when he wasn't slumming, like tonight. He believed it was the privileged's duty to acquire more wealth.

Mac, on the other hand, liked working for a living. He didn't require much. What he did require was a purpose in life. He thrived on challenging himself, both mentally and physically. That was why he'd gotten into private investigation.

"What is it you really want, Pierce?" he asked, deciding to cut to the chase.

"I told you, I want to know your interest in the Foresters. I wasn't aware you even knew them."

Mac smiled as he got to his feet. "It's late. I'm tired. I've had a big night."

Pierce didn't move. "I have a job for you, Mac."

"I already have a job."

His old friend lifted an eyebrow. "I'll pay you double what you're getting from your current client."

Mac smiled at that. His current client was dead. "You know waving money at me is a waste of time."

Pierce nodded, smiled and slowly pushed himself to his feet. "I do know that about you, Mac." He said it as if he found that to be a flaw in Mac's character. "Why don't you come out to my ranch, say in the morning about nine? I have a little place down the lake where I raise a few buffalo."

Little. Right. Mac sighed impatiently. "I told you—"

"You're already on another job. Yes, you told me." Pierce picked up a plain black videotape from beside the recliner. Mac hadn't noticed that Pierce had put it there. "Take a look at this. If you still aren't interested…" Pierce shrugged and tossed Mac the tape.

Mac caught it and watched Pierce leave. He stood there, listening to Pierce retreat down the old wooden dock until the footfalls became too faint to hear. Then he looked down with apprehension at the videotape in his hand.

What the hell was on this? Something that Nathaniel Pierce was confident would change Mac's mind about the job offer.

That alone was enough to make Mac nervous as hell. But to find Pierce sitting in the dark on the houseboat drinking beer, waiting…

Mac walked over to the VCR, turned on the TV, popped in the tape and hit Play. The images were blurred, everything a grainy black-and-white. The tape appeared to be a security surveillance video.

In the soundless recording were three people. Two wore ski masks, one of whom carried a sledgehammer. A third stood just out of the camera's view, but part of that person's shadow could be seen against the side wall.

Mac watched as the one with the sledgehammer worked to break through some expensive-looking wood. The other man in the ski mask had his back to the camera. The third appeared to be just watching, but the other two would glance back at him from time to time and say something Mac couldn't make out.

After a few minutes the hammer had made a large hole in what appeared to be a hidden compartment in the wall. The other masked man pushed the one with the sledgehammer out of the way and took a metal box from inside the compartment. The box looked to be about eight inches square and three or four inches deep. There didn't seem to be anything else in the hole in the wall because the men turned and left, disappearing from the camera's lens.

The videotape flickered, and the setting changed to outdoors. An old Ford van, dark in color, sat with the engine running, and the driver's face was captured on film. He was watching out the windshield, looking very young and very nervous. He was the only one not wearing a mask.

An instant later the two men in ski masks emerged from the house and ran toward the van. As they ran, they ripped off their masks. Mac's heart stopped.

One of the men was Mac's nineteen-year-old nephew, Shane Ramsey, who was supposed to be in Whitefish with Mac's sister.

The other man running toward the getaway van was Trevor Forester.

CHAPTER THREE

MAC COULDN'T SLEEP. He lay sprawled on his back in the bed, staring up at the ceiling, afraid to close his eyes. When he'd closed them, his thoughts closed in on him, an unsettling mix of pleasure and pain.

Even the pleasure was painful. He'd promised himself in his youth that he wasn't going to be one of those men who had regrets. Not like his father. Or his father before him. That was why he lived the life he did. On his own terms.

What a joke. He knew regret as keenly as he knew sorrow. And tonight would be a night he knew he would live to regret.

He gave up on sleep, got up, pulled on his jeans and, taking a cold beer from the fridge, wandered out on the deck to sit in the cool darkness.

The marina was dead quiet. The lake was calm under a limitless sky of dark blue velvet and glittering stars. He closed his eyes and tilted the mouth of the bottle to his lips. The glass was cool and wet, the beer icy cold as it ran down his throat.

He opened his eyes. It was the darkness, he realized. The blackness behind his eyelids that stole any chance of sleep. The same kind of blind darkness that would always remind him of the intimate inkiness inside the cottage—and her.

He smiled to himself wryly, remembering. He'd been lost the moment his lips touched hers. She'd stolen his breath, taken his pounding pulse hostage and carried him away to a place he'd sworn to never go again. Never find again even if he'd been tempted to look.

And what surprised him was that she'd seemed as blown away by the experience as he'd been. Something had happened tonight in the cottage, something that scared the hell out of him, because it made him feel as if he'd boarded a runaway freight train that couldn't be stopped. And now all he could do was wait for the inevitable train wreck.

He'd known that in one split second, one moment of weakness, life could irrevocably change. Mac had seen his father go from wealthy to piss poor in one of those seconds. The man's reputation ruined. His life destroyed. How many times had his father wanted to take back that instant in time?

Mac had always sworn he wouldn't end up like his father. He'd live his life, take on little baggage and never care too much about anything. He'd screwed up once and it had cost him more than he could bear. He wouldn't let it happen again.

He'd slipped up tonight in the cottage. He just hoped to hell he could weather the storm he feared was coming because of it. Every action had a consequence. The moment he'd kissed her. The moment he saw his nephew and Trevor Forester on that videotape. Both life altering in ways he didn't even want to think about.

And now he was working for Pierce. He swore. Mac had few ways he could be coerced. His sister and nephew were the only family he had.

Mac swore as he looked out over the dark lake and

thought about his nephew, a spoiled kid who'd hated his grandfather for losing the family fortune. Thanks to previous Cooper generations, though, both Mac and his sister had substantial trust funds. Just enough, it seemed, to make Shane crave real wealth. Apparently the kind Nathaniel Pierce had.

Mac took another long drink of his beer, dreading what Pierce would tell him in the morning. There was a reason Pierce hadn't called the sheriff when he'd been robbed. Mac knew Pierce hadn't done it out of some loyalty to either Mac or his nephew. Not Pierce. No, Pierce didn't want the cops knowing about the metal box. Now why was that?

Not that it mattered. There was no way Mac couldn't take the job. Not if he hoped to save his nephew— although it might already be too late for that. Someone had murdered Trevor Forester tonight. What were the chances it wasn't connected to the robbery?

Mac also suspected that Pierce wanted him in on this for reasons of his own that had nothing to do with Shane. Shane was just a means to an end. And that made Mac worry he was already in over his head.

Leaning back, he stared up at the stars and knew this restlessness he felt had little to do with Pierce or Shane. As a breeze washed over the bare skin of his chest, he found himself drowning in memories of the woman from the cottage. He breathed in the night, the cool, damp scent of the lake. Closing his eyes, he was engulfed by the darkness and the feel of her. Jill Lawson.

Seeing her was out of the question. But he could no more forget her than he could the image of his nephew and Trevor Forester in ski masks on a grainy black-and-white videotape.

Pleasure and pain. He opened his eyes. A moment of weakness, he thought with a curse as he went inside the houseboat for his shirt, shoes and weapon. There was no turning back now.

AFTER THE DEPUTIES LEFT, Jill locked up the front door and walked through the bakery to the rear of the building and the inside stairs that led up to the apartment.

With her father's encouragement and some money her grandmother had left her, she'd bought the two-story brick building right out of college and started her bakery, The Best Buns in Town. Gram Lawson was the one who got Jill hooked on baking in the first place. Grandpa had always said Gram made the best cinnamon buns in town.

From the time Jill was a child, she remembered Gram's house smelling of flour and yeast. She loved that smell. Especially tonight as she walked past the now-silent equipment, the sparkling kitchen. The mere sight grounded her and gave her strength.

As she started up the narrow back stairs, she felt a draft and looked up. Her breath caught. The door to her apartment was standing open. She always kept that door closed and locked when she was gone.

She froze, heart pounding, and strained to listen. She heard nothing but silence overhead. Maybe she'd left the door open earlier. She'd been so upset about Trevor not picking her up on time...

Slowly, she climbed the stairs, all the horror of the night making her jumpy. Her head still ached from where she'd been hit and she felt sick to her stomach when she thought about Trevor. He'd been her first.

The only man she'd ever been intimate with—until tonight. Dead. Murdered.

At the top of the stairs she stopped and listened again. Silence. Cautiously, she reached through the open doorway and flicked on the light, illuminating the small kitchen and breakfast nook. Beyond it to the left was the living room.

She blinked in disbelief and horror, a small cry of alarm escaping her lips. Her apartment had been ransacked—just as Trevor's had.

She heard a floorboard groan in the direction of the pantry. She started to turn, and then she saw him. A man wearing a black ski mask. She screamed as he grabbed her, but the sound was cut off by his gloved hand clamping over her mouth.

He slammed her against the wall, knocking her breath from her lungs, and struggled to pull a wadded-up rag from his pocket. She fought him, but he was too strong for her.

"Where is it?" he demanded, removing his hand from her mouth.

She tried to scream, but he quickly stuffed the nasty-tasting rag in her mouth, pinned her hands to her sides and flattened her body against the wall with his own. She couldn't breathe! Couldn't scream! He was going to kill her. Or worse.

"Where is it, bitch?" the hoarse voice demanded. "Where's the damned ring?"

The ring? She felt him pull hard on the silver charm bracelet at her wrist, felt pain tear down her arm. She struggled to get one leg free of his body and brought it up hard into his groin.

He let out a howl of pain, then reared back and hit

her in the side of the face. As she slid to the floor, she heard him stumbling down the stairs and out of the building.

"As far as you can tell nothing seems to be missing?" Deputy Rex Duncan inquired. Duncan had done a thorough search of the apartment while Samuelson had gone down to the bakery to make sure no one was in the building.

Jill felt numb as she shook her head. She sat in one of her overstuffed chairs watching the deputy as he looked around the room. The paramedics had left, after telling her how lucky she was. She just had a cut on her forehead, a small abrasion on her cheek where she'd been hit and a scrape on her wrist. Neither blow tonight had been life-threatening. Nor was anything broken. No concussion. Just a headache from the first blow and a bruise to go with the other one.

"No signs of forced entry," Samuelson said as he came up the steps and joined them in the living room.

Jill saw the two exchange a look. "What does that mean?"

"Is it possible you forgot to lock a door?" Duncan asked.

"No. They were all locked when I left for the party."

Samuelson was eyeing her again as if she was lying. "Unless you left the door open or the guy had a key."

"Who has a key to your apartment?" Duncan asked.

"My father and…Trevor had one."

"There were no keys on him other than the boat key when he was found," Duncan said.

Her blood went cold. "You mean the person who was in my apartment had Trevor's key?"

"We don't know that," Samuelson said.

Jill shook her head. "Trevor's key to my apartment was on the same ring as the one to my car. It stands to reason that whoever has my car has a key to this apartment."

"But you said you thought the person at the condo earlier who'd been driving your car was a woman," Samuelson pointed out.

She nodded, her head aching. "I smelled the perfume, but I never saw her. I can't be sure."

"You're sure the person in your apartment tonight was a man, though?" Duncan asked.

"Yes."

"Well, you said nothing seems to be missing." Duncan glanced around. "The place has been tossed pretty good."

"He must have been up here waiting for you while we were downstairs in the bakery," Samuelson said. "It seems like we would have heard him." He turned to Duncan. "Make some noise," he said, and went downstairs again.

Duncan walked around, opened and closed drawers, moved furniture. Jill watched him, knowing what Samuelson was trying to prove. That maybe she herself had torn up this place, hit herself in the head, pretended she was attacked. And for what possible reason? To somehow cover up killing Trevor? She groaned and closed her eyes as she heard Samuelson come back up the stairs.

"Well?" Duncan asked.

"I didn't hear anything," the other deputy said, sounding disappointed. "The apartment is over the kitchen, not the coffee shop, and the building must be pretty well insulated."

"It appears he was looking for something in particular," Duncan said. "He didn't take the stereo or the TV or that expensive camera sitting right there on his way out. It has the same MO as the others."

The Bigfork area had been hit by dozens of burglaries over the past year, all believed to have been executed by someone local who knew exactly what he was after because of the items he didn't take.

With a start, Jill opened her eyes. "He asked me where my ring was."

"Your ring?" Duncan asked.

"I assume he meant my engagement ring since it's the only one I wear—wore." She frowned and looked down at her bare wrist. "He broke off my bracelet." Her skin was raw where the chain had scraped her.

"What kind of bracelet was it?" Samuelson asked.

"A silver charm bracelet with a small silver heart with my name engraved on it," she said. "It was a present from Trevor." She could feel Samuelson staring at her again, wondering no doubt why the thief would take something like a cheap charm bracelet and not her camera.

"Is there someone you could stay with the rest of the night?" Duncan asked.

Her eyes felt as if they had sand in them. She was bone tired. Her head pounded. And she was sore and scared and angry and as vulnerable as she'd ever been. She just wanted the deputies to leave.

She wasn't waking up her father at this time of the night. Not when he'd been too sick earlier to attend the party. Nor was she going to a friend's. She just wanted to go to sleep in her own bed and pretend none of this had happened.

"I'm staying here. I'll lock the doors from the inside with the slide bolt. The windows are locked. I doubt he'll come back tonight, anyway." She saw the deputies exchange a look, but she didn't give a fig what they thought at this point.

"I suggest you get your locks changed," Duncan said. "In the meantime we'll see if Trevor's keys turn up. You have my number."

She nodded and followed them downstairs to lock and bolt the door, then she checked the entry to the bakery. Double locked and bolted.

Back upstairs, she headed for her bedroom. She would straighten up the mess in the morning. Tonight all she wanted was to get out of this ridiculous costume, take a hot shower and go to bed.

By the time she finished, she was so exhausted she crawled between the clean sheets and fell into a comalike sleep haunted by men with ski masks—one masked man in particular.

JILL AWOKE TO POUNDING. Without opening her eyes, she reached for the man next to her in the bed, the memory of their lovemaking so fresh—

Her eyes flew open, and her hand jerked back from the empty space next to her, the memories coming in nauseating waves. Trevor. Murdered. Trevor, the man who had betrayed her.

She sat up, remembering the other Scarlet silhouetted in the doorway, the woman's words echoing in her head. A woman who called Trevor "darling" and had planned to run away with him last night.

Jill groaned as she recalled that last night she, the woman who'd made love only once before, and that with her fiancé, had made love—an amazing and passionate and wonderful experience—with a complete stranger. And now she was a suspect in Trevor's murder.

She wanted to bury her head under the covers and stay there, but the pounding wouldn't stop and she realized someone was downstairs banging at the outside door. She glanced at the clock, shocked to find she'd overslept. It was almost three-thirty in the morning.

Hurriedly, she pulled on a pair of jeans, a sweater and her slippers. As she opened her bedroom door, she saw her ransacked apartment and remembered the man in the ski mask. A shiver of fear skittered up her spine.

In the wall mirror she caught a glimpse of herself. She looked as if she'd gone ten rounds in a boxing ring—and lost.

At the bottom of the stairs she turned on the outside light and was relieved to see Zoe Grosfield, her baking assistant. Zoe mimed that she'd forgotten her key, then mimed a heartfelt apology.

Oh, why hadn't Jill thought to call Zoe to tell her not to come in today?

"Hey," Zoe said as Jill unlocked and opened the door. "Sorry. You know me, airhead extraordinaire." She pretended to refill her head with air as she breezed in, bringing the fresh, cold morning with her.

Just the sight of Zoe cheered Jill immensely, and she realized that she needed to bake today, needed that normalcy and the comfort her work afforded her. She could lose herself in baking, and today that was exactly what she needed.

"So you want me to start the breads?" Zoe asked with her usual exuberance as she headed for the kitchen.

Zoe's hair was green today, spiked with a stiff gel that made her head look like an unkempt lawn. She'd filled her many piercings with silver and wore makeup that gave her a straight-from-the-grave look. Frightening. Especially at this hour of the morning.

Jill had thought twice about hiring Zoe. For one thing, she was young—only seventeen, not even out of high school. Cute as a pixie, but her makeup was heinous, her many piercings painful-looking and her neonbright, short spiked hair changed color with frightening regularity. Jill had been afraid the girl would scare the older customers.

Plus, Zoe had an ever-changing string of boyfriends whose appearance rivaled her own. And it was no secret that the girl loved to party. Almost every T-shirt Zoe owned proclaimed it. Everything about Zoe screamed "unreliable bakery assistant."

But from the first day, Zoe had seemed fascinated by the workings of the bakery, so Jill had weakened and given her the job.

Zoe had proved to be a good worker, prompt and dependable. And Jill had felt guilty for judging the girl by her appearance.

Also of late, Zoe had fallen in love. Which wasn't rare. But this one had lasted for more than a week. Which *was*.

"Breads. That would be great," Jill said. "If you want to get started, I'll be right down."

"Rough night?" Zoe asked, eyeing her.

Had she heard about Trevor's murder? Jill knew from her glance in the mirror that she looked bad.

"Just a late night," she said. "That stupid costume I was wearing." She raised her hand to the knot on her head. It was tender. So was the spot beneath her left eye. "I kept running into things." So true.

Zoe nodded knowingly. "One of those hoop-skirt things, right? Man, can you imagine dressing like that all the time? Too weird. And in your case, too dangerous!"

Jill laughed. Yes, Zoe was exactly what she needed.

"I'll get some coffee going first," Zoe said. "You look like you could use a cup."

"Thanks, I really could." She was grateful that she wouldn't have to discuss last night—or Trevor. If Zoe knew about Trevor's murder she'd be asking a dozen questions. "I'll be down in just a few minutes to get going on the cinnamon buns."

"Cool," Zoe said, and headed for the bakery's kitchen. Beyond it, Jill could see the dark shapes of the tables and chairs of the small coffee shop. And beyond that the dark street. What caught her eye was a car parked across the intersection. A shiny black sports car. Was there someone sitting in it behind the tinted windows? Someone watching the bakery?

"Jill? Are you sure you're all right?"

She blinked and focused on Zoe, who'd turned to look back at her in concern.

Jill nodded. "Just tired." She hurried back upstairs to her apartment, ran a brush through her long brown hair and plaited it into one long braid down her back. After she brushed her teeth, she put on makeup, something she seldom wore, to cover the worst of the scrapes and bruises. Not great, but definitely better.

She tidied the apartment a little and returned to the kitchen to find Zoe hard at work getting the bread doughs started.

"How was *your* night?" she asked the girl, who was sifting flour into a large metal bowl. It was the way they started their days. With Zoe's stories about her dates, her parents, her friends and the latest love of her life, a guy known only as Spider. "Did you see Spider?"

"Finally." Zoe measured flour into the large floor mixer and sighed. "He promised to take me to a party, but he didn't show up in time."

Jill knew the feeling. "I'm sorry."

"He came around later, said he'd been working."

Working. Jill had heard that one before, too.

"But we went out on the beach, parked and talked." Zoe shrugged shyly. "He's the coolest guy I know. Older, you know. And he likes me." She grinned. "A lot. But I'm taking it slow. You know, kinda playing hard to get."

"Good idea," Jill agreed, curious about this Spider. Older. That was the first time Zoe had revealed that. "How much older?"

Zoe shrugged. "He drives a great car."

"Really?" Jill glanced out the front window thinking it might be a black sports car. But the car was gone.

"It doesn't happen to be black, something sleek and sporty, does it?" Jill asked.

Zoe laughed. "Not likely. It's old. You know, one of those cars from, like, the sixties that's been made cool again."

"Cool." Jill felt relieved Spider's cool car wasn't a

black sports car. She knew she was just being paranoid, but then, she had a right to be, all things considered. She lost herself in making the cinnamon-roll dough.

It was hard not to worry about Zoe. The girl was too trusting, especially in light of the disappearances there'd been in the area over the years. Most were girls about Zoe's age who'd come to the lake for summer jobs. As far as Jill knew, none of them had ever been found.

Jill felt sick remembering the year she was sixteen and the close call she'd had. It had been the only time she'd hitchhiked. Her first and last time.

Carefully, she dumped the flour and yeast into the large mixer and turned it on low as she added the warm water. Work was exactly what she needed. Work that she'd loved since those early days in her grandmother's kitchen. Jill had always turned to work to help her get through the rough times, like four years ago when her mother died, or like the past few weeks when she'd known something was wrong between her and Trevor. This morning was no different.

What annoyed her was how naive she'd been. Why hadn't she suspected it was another woman? It seemed so obvious in retrospect. Was it possible there'd been more than one?

She assumed the other Scarlett and Rachel were the same woman. Unless Trevor had three women he was taking for fools. *That* could definitely get a man killed.

What amazed her was that whoever the other Scarlett had been, it appeared she'd planned to take Jill's place at the party—after Trevor broke his engagement. The sheer nerve of the woman! And the cowardice of Trevor! The only reason he'd have broken their engagement at the party was that Jill wouldn't have made a scene with other people around. What a jerk he'd been.

Jill tried to concentrate on the baking, but as hard as she tried, she couldn't stop thinking about last night and the man she'd made love with.

Each breath she took seemed to remind her of his kisses, each movement reminded her of his body, each sound reminded her of his soft groans as his hands and mouth explored her.

She felt herself blushing, followed by a drowning wave of guilt. Her fiancé had just been murdered. What was wrong with her? But her feelings toward Trevor had never been as strong as those she'd had toward a total stranger last night in the cottage. And to think that she'd "saved herself" for Trevor!

Why *had* Trevor asked her to marry him? And why had she accepted? They'd hardly spoken throughout high school. Even after college when she'd first opened the bakery, she seldom saw him. They ran in different social circles.

Then one day out of the blue, he'd asked her to a party at his parents' house. She'd been flattered. And over the next couple of weeks, he'd romanced her, pulling out all the stops with flowers, dinners at fancy restaurants, cards, phone calls and gifts, like the charm bracelet.

It had been the first gift he'd given her. But looking back, Jill had never felt as if his heart was in it. Even the one time they'd made love…

All the signs had been there. She'd ignored them. Because she'd wanted to.

But no matter her feelings for Trevor, her heart went

out to his parents. Heddy and Alistair must be devastated. Their only child. Their precious son.

Had they even an inkling that Trevor was planning to run off last night? One-way tickets to Brazil didn't make it look as if Trevor and his new wife had any plans of coming back. Heddy must be crushed.

It just didn't make any sense, though. Trevor had had such plans for the island development. In fact, she remembered that when Alistair had the chance to buy the island, Trevor had practically begged his father to give it to him.

"Someone else will develop it otherwise," Trevor had said. He'd been in a frenzy the day Alistair was to sign the papers, afraid something might go wrong and the island might end up in someone else's hands.

What had happened out on the island the past two months? She'd heard rumors that there had been problems. Setbacks, delays, accidents on the island, which of course only added to the stories of the island's being cursed, haunted. When she'd asked Trevor, he'd said someone had been sabotaging some of the equipment. Kids.

She shook her head, shocked that the deputies thought she might have had something to do with Trevor's death. With a start, she reminded herself that she needed an alibi, as crazy as that was. If either her mystery lover or the other Scarlett didn't come forward soon, she'd have to find them.

Trevor's girlfriend might be easier to locate, Jill realized. At least, Jill thought she'd be able to recognize the woman's voice if she ever heard it again.

Recognizing the mystery lover was a whole different story. She wouldn't know him with his clothes on!

Not even naked unless it was by touch. Her memory of him was all tactile, sensual, physical. He'd smelled like the storm. No aftershave or cologne. His body had resembled Trevor's enough to fool her. Only more muscular, more solid.

She fanned herself at the memory and suddenly had a horrible thought. Why had the man been dressed as Rhett Butler? Had he known what Trevor would be wearing last night? Had he purposely tried to take Trevor's place? Or—

The large empty bun pan slipped from her fingers and crashed to the floor. Oh, my God. Was it possible she'd made love with the killer?

CHAPTER FOUR

NATHANIEL PIERCE SMILED as he opened his front door to Mac just before nine the next morning.

"Mac," Pierce said cheerfully, and motioned him inside the massive ranch house, which was set back in the pines on the mountainside overlooking the lake. The interior decor was a combination of antlers and leather, rock and wood, antiques and Americana.

Pierce led the way through the huge living room, past a wall-size black-and-white photograph of a pasture running as far as the eye could see. In the foreground stood a massive herd of buffalo.

"Buffalo—it's the new beef," Pierce said when he saw Mac looking at the mural. "That was taken on part of my ranch," he said proudly. "Come out to the sunroom."

Mac followed him through the house to the screened-in room. Snowcapped peaks poked up from the horizon. In between was the blue-green of the lake. Mac took a look through the high-powered telescope aimed at the north end of the lake. He wasn't surprised to see that it was sited on the marina where his houseboat was docked.

He swung the telescope slowly southward, down the wooded lakefront. The view of the Foresters' home on the water, including the cottage, was damned good. A little farther south, Inspiration Island. Even the bay where Trevor Forester's boat and body had been found could be seen from here through the high-powered lens.

Was it possible Pierce had witnessed the murder?

"So what do you think?" Pierce asked.

Mac wasn't sure if they were talking about the ranch or the view, the burglary or the videotape, or the telescope and what could be seen through it from here.

"Amazing," Mac said, pretty much covering it all as he stepped away from the telescope to stand at the window.

Pierce smiled. "Quite the view, huh?"

The view was incredible. From here, the lake gleamed like a crystal ball. Mac stared at the water, afraid he could see the future in all the blue. "That was an interesting videotape you gave me. I'm surprised the sheriff hasn't already nailed the men responsible."

Pierce laughed. "You know I didn't call the authorities. Juice or coffee?"

Yes, Mac knew. He turned to find Pierce standing next to a table, holding a pottery pitcher in his hand, waiting expectantly.

"I had this juice flown in from Hawaii," he said. "There's nothing like fresh pineapple juice, don't you think?"

"Yes, it's amazing what money can buy," Mac said. "Or there's always blackmail. And what can't be bought or blackmailed can always be stolen, right?"

Pierce smiled. "You have such a wonderful grasp of life's finer points."

"It must be annoying, though, to have your already stolen property be stolen," Mac said. "In fact, it must really piss you off. I'll bet that's why you don't seem at all broken up over Trevor Forester's death."

"Trevor was a...thief."

Among other things, Mac thought. "Isn't calling him a thief a little like the pot calling the kettle black?"

"There's a difference between someone who steals for money or revenge and someone who appropriates because they appreciate the value of what they're stealing."

"Right. So which was it?"

"I beg your pardon?" Pierce said.

"Was it money or revenge that Trevor Forester stole for?"

"Who knows and why does it matter?" Pierce filled both glasses on the table with juice. "You must try this."

"It matters," Mac said, taking the glass Pierce offered him, "especially if you killed him."

His former classmate feigned shock. "You think I could kill someone?"

"No," Mac said, glancing at the telescope. "But you would hire someone to."

Pierce smiled. "I'm trying to hire *you* and I know you don't kill people—except in the line of duty. Now why would I bother to hire you if I'd already taken care of the problem?" He shook his head. "I just want my property back. If the men were all to die before I got it, now, that would be unfortunate." He waved a manicured hand through the air. "What do you think of the juice?"

Mac downed the pineapple juice and licked his lips. "Delicious. What was in the metal box?"

Pierce took a small sip of his own juice, obviously

not wanting to be rushed. Either that, or he was hesitant to tell him. But then, Pierce had little choice if he hoped to get the contents back. "Some rather rare coins."

"How rare?"

Pierce lifted a brow. "Rare enough that I'm going to the trouble of hiring you to get them back."

Mac cocked an eyebrow. "That rare."

"They're priceless, all right? They're a set of Double Eagle twenty-dollar gold pieces. There is a Liberty figure on the front and an eagle on the back. Since I know you don't collect coins, why be more specific than that?"

Mac didn't know anything about rare coins, but he had seen an article in the paper the previous year about the world's rarest coin. A 1933 Double Eagle that fetched $7.59 million at auction. Back in 1933 President Roosevelt had decided to take the nation off the gold standard, so he'd ordered that all the newly minted twenty-dollar gold pieces be melted down. Someone had illegally smuggled the coin out, and it had ended up in the collection of Egypt's King Farouk. The coin disappeared again and finally turned up when a British coin dealer had tried to sell it to an undercover secret service agent.

Mac wondered what the history of Pierce's coin set was and was glad he didn't know. "How do you know the thieves haven't already fenced the coins?"

Pierce shook his head. "The burglary was two months ago. The coins would have turned up by now."

"Two months ago?" Mac couldn't have been more shocked. "And you're just now getting around to hiring me?"

"I'd hoped Trevor would try to sell the coins," Pierce

said. "I have a few…contacts. The coins are worth much more as a set. I would have heard about it. The coins were the only thing Trevor took, so he knew what he was getting. He wouldn't have split up the set. You do realize that Trevor's the one who's been burglarizing all the houses in the area, don't you?"

"What makes you think that?" Mac had to ask.

Pierce gave him a pitying look. "It stands to reason. Trevor knew all the people who were robbed because he attended the same parties they did, he could never have enough money and he thought he was above the law."

"You just described yourself," Mac noted.

Pierce laughed. "Yes, well, my grandfather and Trevor's were…acquaintances, but my grandfather had more money."

"I've always wondered," Mac said, "why your father sold the island to the Foresters."

"To make a profit," Pierce snapped, and turned his back to pour himself more juice.

"Really? I didn't know he needed the money."

"My father won the island years ago in a poker game," Pierce said.

"Really?" Mac hadn't known that. He'd just assumed the island had been part of the land that Pierce's grandfather had bought up around the lake years ago. But he could see why Pierce's father had wanted to unload it. Even if half the stories about the island were true…

"Yes, really. Anyway, the island's always had questionable value and the potential for lawsuits if anyone got hurt on it. Trevor seemed to think he could make money by turning it into an upscale resort. What a fool. Now the island is worth even less."

"How did Trevor know about the coins—or where in your house they were hidden?"

Pierce turned away from Mac and faced the view for a moment. Then he turned back. "I hate to admit this, but a stupid indiscretion on my part."

"A woman." Mac shook his head. "Showing her the ranch wasn't enough? You had to show her the coins? Did you tell her the house's security code, as well?"

Anger flickered in Pierce's gaze, but it was brief. Pierce hid it with a smile. "I like to think it was the alcohol I'd drunk that night."

It didn't take a rocket scientist to figure this one out. "She had some connection to Trevor Forester."

"I guess so." Pierce shrugged. "As you would say, I was slumming."

"Who was she?" Mac asked, afraid of the answer. He didn't even want to consider that he and Pierce had more in common than money and the universities they'd attended.

"You really don't think I remember her name, do you? She was just some shapely brunette with long legs and amazingly large breasts. I think her name was Rainie or Rita, something like that."

Not Jill Lawson. One of Trevor's other women. Mac knew if he had any sense at all, he'd walk away from this. No, he'd run.

"You let her watch you deactivate the security system?" Mac asked in disbelief.

"I guess the woman was less of an airhead than I thought and a whole lot less drunk than she acted."

Pierce must have been very drunk. Also it wasn't

like him just to let this woman get away with what she'd done without some sort of retribution. "What are you going to do about her?"

"All I want is the metal box and its contents back and to forget this ever happened. I'll just chalk it up to experience."

Why don't I believe that? Mac thought. "I'm going to need to know who the players are."

"They're all on the videotape," Pierce said.

Mac shook his head. "Not the one standing behind Trevor."

"What?"

"The shadow on the wall. Someone was standing behind Trevor, maybe giving the orders," Mac said. "Or maybe just along for the ride."

"I guess I didn't notice more than three people, counting the driver, in the video," Pierce said, still frowning. "Not that it matters. Like I said, I just want my...collection back. In fact, because of the history of the coins—"

"You mean because they're stolen."

"—I'd prefer that you simply locate the box and let me take it from there. That way you never have to actually have the coins in your possession. Does that make you a little more comfortable with this?"

Not really. "The coins are probably long gone by now."

"I'm sure once you locate your nephew, he'll prove to be a valuable resource in finding them."

Shane Ramsey's value was debatable right now. Mac looked toward the lake again, the mirror-slick water reflecting the wisps of clouds floating overhead.

Under other circumstances, he would have bailed

out on this job in a heartbeat. He'd learned early on to avoid jobs that made him uneasy. Usually his uneasiness was for a damned good reason. A reason that could get a man killed—and it almost had happened on more than one occasion.

"Trevor's death will make it harder to find the coins," Mac said, turning back to Pierce.

"If I didn't know you better, I'd think you were trying to get more money out of me for your fee."

Mac studied the other man. "Everything about this one feels off somehow."

Pierce nodded, his blue eyes hard as ice chips. "Yes, Trevor getting himself killed after stealing my coins does make it a little…unpleasant." Pierce shook his head. "With a killer out there, you must be worried that the same thing could happen to your nephew. Especially if he has my coins."

"ARE YOU ALL RIGHT?" Zoe cried, picking up the pan Jill had dropped.

Jill felt her eyes well up with tears. Suddenly she couldn't quit shaking. The cinnamon rolls were in the oven and several kinds of additional buns and breads were about to go in when the cinnamon rolls came out. Hours had passed, and she was exhausted from trying to act like everything was fine and nothing had happened last night.

"I just remembered a phone call I need to make," she said. "Can you handle everything for a while?"

Zoe nodded, still looking concerned.

Jill dusted her hands on her apron and headed for the small office off the kitchen. She closed the door behind her and looked up the number for Guises and Disguises.

"Hello," she said, her heart in her throat. "I need to find out about the Rhett Butler costume I rented for Trevor Forester. I need to know when he picked it up yesterday. Are you the manager?"

"Yes, Tony Burns. Remember, we talked when you came in to reserve the costumes," he said. "As a matter of fact, I was going to call you this morning."

"Really?"

"Mr. Forester didn't pick up his costume."

Had someone else picked it up for him? The other Scarlett?

"The costume you had me hold for Mr. Forester is still right here. I just wanted to let you know that I will have to charge the deposit to your card."

If Mr. Burns had been in the room, she would have kissed him. Trevor didn't pick up his costume! That meant the man she'd made love to hadn't been wearing *Trevor's* costume. She dropped into the chair next to the desk with relief.

Then she reminded herself that it didn't necessarily rule out the man being the killer. He'd arrived by boat about the time Trevor had been killed. The deputies could be off fifteen or twenty minutes in their estimation of the time of death. Nor did it explain why he was dressed in the same costume Trevor Forester was supposed to have been wearing.

"Mr. Burns, how many Rhett Butler costumes do you carry?" Guises and Disguises was the only costume rental shop around.

"Two." He sounded suspicious as if she was trying to get out of paying the deposit.

"Who rented the other Rhett Butler costume?" she asked, and held her breath.

"If you're thinking we gave Mr. Forester the wrong costume…"

She was hoping that wasn't the case. Otherwise, she was back to the man she'd made love to wearing Trevor's costume—and that was the last place she wanted to be. "You would have a record of who rented it, right?" she said, praying that was true. Unless Trevor had picked up the wrong costume, Mr. Burns would have the name of her mystery lover.

"Let me check." He sighed and laid down the phone. She waited. He finally came back on the line, his voice sounding not quite as confident. "There might be a problem."

She held her breath.

"The other Rhett Butler and Scarlett O'Hara costumes were rented by Trevor Forester."

Jill slumped in the chair. "You're sure?"

"Yes. I'm sorry. I guess Mr. Forester picked up the wrong costume."

Not necessarily. He'd just planned to go with a different Scarlett. Whoever the woman was, she'd planned to meet Trevor at the party. Jill wondered whose idea that had been. Trevor's? Or the other Scarlett's?

Jill suspected the latter, given that Trevor tended to avoid conflict at all costs. Two Scarletts at his parents' anniversary party spelled conflict with a capital *C*. But the other Scarlett had probably planned to meet Trevor in the lake cottage after he'd broken his engagement.

Could she despise Trevor more? She didn't think so, but she was reserving final judgment until all the facts were in. She suspected she might have just uncovered the tip of the iceberg when it came to how rotten he'd been.

"Of course I won't charge you for the deposit, since there seems to have been some mistake," the manager said.

"No, the mistake was on my part," Jill assured him. "Please, I insist you charge me for the deposit." Why not? Trevor had charged two tickets to Brazil to her.

Mr. Burns sounded relieved. "You are most kind for being so understanding."

That was her. Understanding. Her hand was shaking as she hung up the phone. Her mystery lover had been dressed in the only other Rhett Butler costume. Trevor's costume. She felt sick.

After a moment she picked up the phone and called her best friend, Brenna Margaret Boyd. Her family owned the Bandit's Bay Marina, but Brenna had gone into journalism and worked for the *Lake Courier,* helping out at the marina in her spare time.

"Brenna, it's Jill."

"Jill! I just tried to call you, but the line was busy. I just heard. How are you?"

Over the past few months, Jill had shared her concerns about Trevor with her friend. At least, the problems she'd had *before* last night. "Still in shock. I need your help."

"Name it."

With Brenna everything said between them was off the record, and Brenna had the resources to find out most anything. "The deputies seem to think I killed Trevor."

"No! That's crazy."

"That's why I need to know everything you've got on the murder," Jill said. "Even the gossip."

"I'll call you back from the coffee shop up the block. Two minutes?"

"Thanks." Jill hung up and waited. The newspaper was rumor-mill central. Brenna would have heard a lot more than could be printed in the paper.

The phone rang not two minutes later.

"Okay, you want the basics?" Brenna asked. "This is what will be coming out in the newspaper this afternoon. Trevor's boat was found floating northwest of the island at 8:45 p.m. His body was lying on the floor of the boat. He'd been shot twice through the heart at close range, making the sheriff believe Trevor knew his killer."

Jill felt sick. "What was he wearing?"

"Work clothes. Jeans, T-shirt, work boots. He and the clothing were dirty."

"So they think he'd been working on the island?" Jill asked in surprise, given that Trevor had told her he didn't have to go to Inspiration Island yesterday.

"He'd been working somewhere," Brenna said. "But since it was a Saturday, there wasn't anyone else working on the island. So it's unclear where he'd been. Still, the proximity to the island makes them think that someone followed him when he left to get gas and killed him out on the water."

"They didn't find anything that would indicate he'd had his costume with him?" Jill asked.

"No costume."

Okay, he hadn't been wearing the costume. It wasn't in the boat. The killer hadn't taken it off Trevor's body and dressed him in work clothing.

It stood to reason that Trevor would have left his costume back at the condo. Obviously he'd planned to take his boat back to the marina at the condo and shower and change before the party. Unless he'd chickened out and decided to skip the party, given that two Scarletts would be waiting for him.

"No weapon's been found," Brenna continued. "No sign of a struggle, either. They haven't released the caliber of gun used."

"What about time of death?" Jill asked.

"Trevor bought gas at Heaven's Gate Marina at the south end of the lake just a few minutes before eight. The deputies found a receipt in his pocket with the time on it. The dock boy didn't notice which way Trevor went, but the sheriff's speculating he went to the island for some reason, then might have been on his way to his parents' house when he was shot."

"They're sure he was killed in the boat—not on the island?"

"Yes. And the dock boy remembers Trevor seeming nervous, upset. He kept looking at his watch. Trevor told the boy to hurry because he had to meet someone and it was about to storm."

Jill thought about the boat she'd seen just offshore about eight-fifteen, only minutes before she saw the man wearing the Rhett Butler costume and thought it was Trevor. Did the man have time to kill Trevor and get to the party? But that didn't explain the costume or why the man was in the lake cottage.

"Are you sure you don't want to come stay with me for a while?" Brenna asked.

"Thanks, but I need to keep the bakery open. I need to work right now to keep my mind off everything."

She filled Brenna in on all that had happened, including the mystery lover in the cottage.

"You have no idea who the man could have been?" Brenna cried.

"Not a clue. Except he was built kind of like Trevor," Jill said, realizing how lame that sounded. "I need to find him or the other Scarlett—who might be the Rachel that Trevor was planning to run off with."

"Well, if Trevor and Rachel really were going to get married before they flew to Brazil, then they would need blood tests and a marriage license. They would have filled out a marriage-license application. Give me the name of the travel agent. Maybe he set it up for Trevor."

"I hadn't thought of that," Jill said, and gave her friend the information.

"I'll see what I can find. If you need anything else, just let me know. I'll call when I hear something."

"Thanks." She'd barely hung up the phone when it rang again. "Hello?"

"It's Alistair, Jill." Trevor's father sounded desolate.

"I'm so sorry about Trevor," she said. "I was going to call you this morning, once it was a decent time. You must be in shock."

"Yes," he agreed. "The sheriff was here all night. It's beyond comprehension. How are you, dear?"

"Just sick. Who would want to hurt Trevor?"

"I wish I knew," Alistair said, then fell silent for a moment. "Could you come out here later? I really need to talk to you."

"Of course." They agreed on two o'clock. She wondered what he wanted to talk to her about. No doubt her relationship with his son. "How is Heddy?"

"Not good." He hung up, unable to say much more.

Zoe was icing a huge tray of cinnamon rolls when Jill came out of the office. "Was that about me?" she asked, looking worried.

Her question took Jill by surprise. "Why would it be about you?"

Zoe shook her head. "You know me, always in trouble of some sort." She sounded almost scared.

"Not this time," Jill assured her as the back door banged open as it did every morning at this time and Jill turned to see her father. Since Jill's mother had passed away four years ago, Gary Lawson stopped by in the morning for a warm cinnamon roll, a cup of coffee and a chat.

Jill loved the early-morning chats with her father, but this morning when she saw his face, she knew he'd heard about Trevor's murder. Her father had wanted Jill to have the kind of marriage he'd had with her mother, and for a while, it had looked as though Trevor Forester would give her everything she could ever want.

"Hi, honey," her dad said.

Just looking at him, she felt the tears she'd fought so hard fill her eyes.

"I'm so sorry, Jill," her dad said, pulling her into his arms. "You must be devastated. I cannot believe it myself. Who would want to murder Trevor?"

They both turned at the shriek and crash behind them. Zoe stood with a rubber spatula in her hand, icing dripping from it onto the floor, an almost empty pan of cinnamon rolls on the floor where it had fallen.

Zoe's black-rimmed eyes were round as plates, and she looked even paler than usual. "Someone murdered Trevor?" she asked in a hoarse whisper. "Oh, God. I'm going to be sick." She dropped the spatula on the counter and ran out the back door.

Jill stared after her, surprised by her reaction. Zoe and Trevor had never been close. In fact, Trevor thought Jill irresponsible and stupid for hiring the girl and hadn't hidden his attitude from Zoe. The two had never said more than two words to each other.

"Is she all right?" Gary Lawson asked.

"I'd better go see if she—" Jill stopped at the sound of Zoe's VW Beetle roaring away. "Oh, no! She was supposed to make deliveries this morning."

"Don't worry, I'll make them for you," her father said. "Why don't you plan on closing early today?"

She hugged her dad. "You are the greatest. Are you sure you feel up to this?"

"No problem."

MAC STARED AT PIERCE. "I didn't just hear you threaten my nephew, did I?"

"No, I was just saying… Look, I came to you so you could protect Shane," Pierce said quickly. "I'm willing to bet that one of the thieves killed Trevor for the coins. If Shane has them—" he held up his hands "—the same thing could happen to him. As far as Shane stealing from me goes, I have no hard feelings against him."

"That's right, you just want the coins," Mac said. "Retribution would be the last thing on your mind."

"Not my style."

Right. Mac recalled a time in college when Pierce had beaten another student within an inch of his life— over some girl.

Mac turned to leave, a curse on his lips. Why did his nephew have to steal from Nathaniel Pierce, of all people? And how had Shane gotten involved in the first place? It made no sense. Shane lived in White-fish with his mother. What the hell had he been doing down here? And how stupid was that, getting caught on videotape?

"I'll let you know when I find your coins," Mac said as he left. It was all he could do if he hoped to save Shane. But if his nephew had anything to do with Trevor Forester's death, nothing could save him. If Trevor had graduated from burglary to murder, he was on his own.

Mac didn't look back as he walked to his pickup. It was a newer Chevy with a camper, his home when a case took him away from the houseboat.

As he pulled onto the road, he wondered where to start looking for Shane. Maybe Shane had taken off after the heist with his share of the loot. But Mac had a feeling the boy hadn't.

He took out his cell phone and speed-dialed his sister's number in Whitefish.

She answered on the first ring. "Shane?"

"No, Carrie, it's Mac." He groaned silently at the worry he heard in his older sister's voice. "What's wrong?"

"Nothing, I was just hoping it was Shane," she said, sounding close to tears.

"You haven't heard from him?"

"Not for over two months," she said. "He was talking about taking a trip with some friends, so maybe he just—"

"Some friends?" Mac interrupted. "What friends?"

"I'm not sure. I called Oz and Bongo and Skidder, those are the guys he usually hangs out with. No one has seen him, but Oz's girlfriend, Mountain Woman, said she saw him with some guy called Buffalo Boy."

Didn't any of Shane's friends have real names? "She have any idea what Buffalo Boy's real name is?"

"No one's ever heard him called anything but Buffalo Boy." She was crying now. "I'm worried sick about Shane. I just have this awful feeling." Awful feelings ran in the family.

Carrie had probably done as well as she could raising Shane alone after her husband drowned in Flathead Lake a dozen years ago when Shane was seven. So far most of Shane's scrapes with the law had been relatively minor: shoplifting, vandalism, driving under the influence and disorderly conduct.

Now, at nineteen, it seemed Shane had graduated to a higher level of criminal.

"I'll see what I can find out," Mac told his sister, keeping what he knew to himself for now.

"You're the best, little brother."

Yeah. He made a few calls on the way back to the marina, talked to some of Shane's former friends, guys his nephew had dumped when he'd moved on to less-desirable types.

A guy nicknamed Raker told Mac that all he knew about Buffalo Boy was that he'd worked on a big ranch that raised buffalo. "Never said what ranch," Raker said, anxious to get back to flipping his burgers. "But Buffalo Boy and Shane were talking about going down there and maybe working for the summer."

Mac had a pretty good idea whose ranch it was. He called Pierce and asked if Shane had been on the payroll and wasn't surprised that his old friend didn't have a clue.

"I have people who run the ranch," Pierce said.

"Ask those people and get back to me."

"I can't see that it matters—"

"It matters." Mac hung up, wondering how much.

As he drove through Bigfork, he noticed the sign on a two-story brick building: The Best Buns In Town.

It was foolish. Dangerous. His worst plan yet. But he had to see the woman he'd made love with in the cottage last night. Trevor Forester's former fiancée.

Mac knew he was taking a hell of a chance. He told himself it was nothing more than curiosity. The truth was, she'd been haunting his thoughts ever since last night and that damned first kiss. Too much was at stake to have any woman on his mind—especially this one.

The bakery was busy, all but one table occupied as he pushed open the door. A little bell tinkled over his head, and he was immediately assaulted by the warm sweet buttery scent of cinnamon rolls—and the knock-him-to-his-knees sight of Jill Lawson.

CHAPTER FIVE

JILL LOOKED UP as the bell over the door jangled and she saw the man come in. She gave him only a quick glance. The place was hopping, just as it was every morning at this time. Zoe hadn't come back. Jill had tried to reach her at home, but there was no answer. She was worried. Worried about Zoe's reaction to Trevor's murder.

Now Jill wished she'd had the sense to close the shop, but she'd needed to bake this morning to try to keep her mind off what had happened. Not that it had done much good.

"Can I help you?" Jill asked as the man walked up to the counter. At first glance he looked like a lot of summer people—thirtysomething, tanned, blond, dressed in cutoffs, T-shirt and Mexican sandals.

That was why she was surprised by the tiny shock of awareness that made her skin tingle and her gaze dart up to his. His eyes were hidden behind sunglasses, the mirrored kind, so all she saw was her own reflection and the startled, flushed look on her face before he pushed them up and rested them on his head.

He was boy-next-door handsome, yes. But with an edge. And he was obviously fit, his shoulders broad, arms muscular and matted with blond hair, legs long, tan and strong-looking.

That still didn't explain her reaction. Or his.

A lock of blond hair hung over his forehead. He looked like a man who was comfortable with himself, with his surroundings. So why did he seem surprised by her reaction to him? Startled by it? He was probably used to women falling all over him.

"I'd really like one of those cinnamon rolls," he said. "They smell incredible." He smiled then, almost tentatively, as if afraid of her reaction.

She returned the smile, hoping he didn't notice just how flustered he made her. "Would you like coffee with that?"

He glanced toward the empty table by the window. "Please. I could use the caffeine. Black."

She rang up his order and took the money he'd set on the counter. "I'll bring it over to you if you'd like to grab that seat."

Her hand trembled as she scooped a cinnamon roll from the pan and slid it onto a plate for him. It was just nerves. A delayed reaction to Trevor's murder. To everything that had happened.

But she knew what had her shaken was her reaction to the man in the cottage last night. Surely she wasn't now reacting like that to *all* men, was she?

She added a fork to the plate, poured a mug of coffee and headed to his table, aware he'd been watching her intently the whole time. Probably wondering what her problem was.

"Thanks," he said as she put the coffee down in front of him. "This is a great place you have here. I wish I'd known about it sooner." He was studying her, frowning a little as his gaze skimmed over her bruised cheek and forehead.

"Are you here for the summer?" she asked, trying to make her usual conversation as his long, tanned fingers curled around the mug to move it out of the way so she could put down the plate with the cinnamon roll on it.

His fingers brushed hers.

The shock wave arced from her fingers through her body. She jerked back, dropping the plate the last couple of inches. It rattled down on the tabletop.

"Oh, I'm so sorry," she said, feeling foolish for jumping the way she had. Her fingers still tingled where he'd touched them, and her heart was pounding.

"My fault. Static electricity," he said. "It's the dry heat."

She nodded, momentarily distracted by his mouth, a generous mouth, the lips almost…familiar. "Have we met before?" She couldn't believe she'd said that as she raised her gaze to his. "I'm sorry, that sounds like a line. I didn't mean—"

"It happens to me all the time," he said easily. "I guess I have a generic look."

Generic? No. Like Trevor? Yes. His body was about average height. Muscular. A lot like Trevor's had been the last time she'd seen him. Except this man was stronger-looking, harder—

The bell over the door jangled, and she swung around to see Deputies Duncan and Samuelson enter the bakery.

"I'm not usually…" Words failed her as she looked again at the man at the table.

"You're swamped," he said. He seemed to study her. "It looks like you have everything under control."

She smiled at that because it was so far off base.

Without another word, she hurried to the counter, the air thick with the scent of warm, cinnamony baked buns.

She couldn't believe the way she'd embarrassed herself. She shot a glance at the man she'd just served. He was watching the deputies with interest. Again she felt an odd jolt of…something familiar.

"We'll take a couple cups of coffee, black, and—" Deputy Duncan looked at Samuelson, who shook his head "—just one of your cinnamon rolls." Duncan smiled.

But Jill knew they hadn't come here for her coffee or cinnamon rolls. She rang up their order and took the cash Duncan handed her.

"Keep the change," he said. "When you have a minute, we'd like to talk to you." He and Samuelson headed for a table that had just been vacated.

Jill heard the kitchen door swing open and wondered how her father had gotten back so soon from making deliveries.

But it was Zoe. "I'm sorry," the girl said quickly, looking contrite. "I didn't mean to run out like that. It's just that…"

Yes, it was just what? Jill waited.

"…I've never known anyone who was murdered before." Zoe's eyes were wide with genuine fear.

"It's all right," Jill said, and reached for Zoe. The girl stepped into her hug and held on to Jill with a force that surprised her. She'd always thought that nothing could scare Zoe. "We're all upset. Can you help finish up here? I think we'll close early."

Zoe nodded wordlessly. "I can stay as long as you need me."

"Great. Bus the tables and then start on the kitchen."

Jill filled two mugs with black coffee and scooped a cinnamon roll onto a plate, added a fork and, taking a breath, walked toward the deputies. She didn't know how much more of this she could take. She felt as if she was losing her mind.

Coffee breaks over, the bakery started to clear out. Except for the man at the table by the window—and the deputies sitting in a back corner.

She glanced toward the window, still surprised by her reaction to him. Hadn't she known she wouldn't be the same after making love to that man last night in the cottage?

She returned her attention to the deputies as she neared their table. Why were they here? Maybe they'd brought some good news. She was tired of running scared, waiting for them to arrest her for Trevor's murder. She was tired of feeling helpless.

And if it was bad news? Well, then, she'd find her mystery lover or the other Scarlett. Or both. And if that wasn't possible, she'd have to find Trevor's murderer. Whatever it took to prove her innocence.

She wondered if she should get a lawyer, then vetoed the idea. She had nothing to hide. Not anymore. She'd bared her soul to the deputies after baring everything else last night to a total stranger.

She put the two black coffees on the table, then the cinnamon roll, and sat down, aware of the only other customer watching her. "You wanted to ask me something?"

MAC FINALLY GOT his heart to settle back down. He couldn't believe her reaction. Or his. Coming here had been beyond stupid. It was almost as if she'd known on some level who he was.

He took a bite of the cinnamon roll. It was amazing. So was Jill Lawson. He knew he should just leave. He'd found out what he'd come for.

She was bruised, but all right. Better than all right. He'd been worried last night when he'd parked on a street by her apartment and seen lights on and the sheriff's department cars parked right outside.

There was no doubt that she was under a hell of a strain, but she seemed to be holding up all right. He picked up a newspaper from one of the other tables and pretended to read it as he picked up what he could of the deputies' conversation with her. Just as he'd suspected, her apartment had been broken into the night before.

But he was shocked to hear that the burglar had still been on the premises when she'd returned and that she'd fought him off. That explained the bruises. He swore under his breath. The burglar must have been after Pierce's damned coins and thought Trevor had hidden them in Jill's apartment. Until the coins were found, Jill Lawson was in danger, just as he'd suspected last night. The reason he'd spent the night in his truck outside her apartment.

He glanced at her. She was adorable, no doubt about that. Slim but nicely rounded in all the right places, a body he knew intimately and a face that reminded him of angels, as corny as that was. She had dark-lashed, intelligent brown eyes that complemented her apparent strength of character.

He watched her, impressed. He'd already found out that she'd started the bakery right out of college and had made a real success of it. He could understand why.

This cinnamon roll was like none he'd ever tasted. But she also had to be a damned good businesswoman.

The emotions she evoked in him, however, came from some deeper place. It wasn't just her looks or her success. This woman had touched him.

He closed his eyes, letting the bite of cinnamon roll melt in his mouth, shocked at the sensory effect it had on him. Just as Jill did. What was it about this woman? She had captivated him in the cottage last night with a single kiss, but her cinnamon rolls could bewitch a man in ways he hadn't even dreamed.

He opened his eyes with a silent curse. What was he going to do about Jill Lawson? This mess had him between a rock and a hard place. He couldn't very well tell Jill about the coins without jeopardizing his nephew, let alone taking the chance that the sheriff would find out that Pierce had stolen the coins to start with.

Damn, what *was* he going to do?

"Ms. LAWSON, WE spoke with several of Trevor Forester's neighbors," Deputy Duncan said quietly. "They told us about an argument you and Mr. Forester had a week ago Sunday."

She stared at the deputy. "I didn't see Trevor a week ago Sunday."

"Ms. Lawson, the neighbors saw you leaving after the argument with Mr. Forester," Samuelson said.

She tried to contain her anger. "No, what they saw was a woman driving my red Saturn. Obviously Trevor's *other* fiancée. The same one he rented the Scarlett O'Hara costume for at Guises and Disguises."

"Yes, we know that Trevor rented a Rhett Butler and

a Scarlett O'Hara costume—and so did you," Samuelson said. "Trevor didn't pick his up."

"But someone picked up the other set," she said.

"Yes. The clerk recalls you picking up the costumes and discussing who was going to pick up the other Rhett Butler," the deputy said.

She shook her head in disbelief. "I only picked up the one costume. The clerk is mistaken."

"That is possible," Duncan acknowledged. "She admits she was busy with all the costume rentals because of the Foresters' big party."

"We searched the cottage," Duncan continued. "There was no ring or anything else of yours that we could find. Nothing that would indicate you had a liaison there last night. The bedsheets and cover weren't even wrinkled."

"We never made it to the bed," she said, her voice falling. "Someone took my ring and my underwear. That should tell you something." But what? Had her mystery lover taken the items? Why would he do that except to cover up what had happened there? She felt heartsick and changed the subject. "What about my car?"

Duncan shook his head.

"When you find it, you'll find this other woman." Right now it was the only lead Jill had to the other Scarlett. That and the woman's voice.

"We have deputies looking for your car," Samuelson said. "If it's out there, we'll find it." He leaned toward her. "Come on, Ms. Lawson, stop wasting our time. You weren't in the lake cottage making love with some complete stranger last night. You went to the island to see Trevor, didn't you? What happened? You had a fight? You'd found out about this other woman."

Jill tried to keep her voice down. "If I had killed Trevor, do you think I would be stupid enough to say I was making love to a stranger in the lake cottage right after?"

"People tend to not think things through when they're under a lot of stress," Duncan said. He sighed. "The problem we're having here is that you seem to think you need an alibi, and quite frankly, you came up with one that only makes you look even guiltier."

MAC TOOK THE last bite of his cinnamon roll, mentally kicking himself for coming here. Out of the corner of his eye, he watched the discussion between Jill and the deputies heating up and caught enough of it to deduce that the deputies thought Jill murdered Trevor Forester.

It hadn't dawned on Mac that she might need an alibi. He swore under his breath. He was her only alibi? Great. The problem was, he couldn't tell the deputies the truth for several good reasons.

Which meant Jill Lawson was on her own with the authorities. At least for the time being. It also meant he had to stay out of her sight. He didn't think it would take much for her to realize he was the man from the cottage last night. Little more than another accidental touch could trigger it.

But Mac was more worried that if he spent any time around her, he wouldn't be able to help himself. He'd do something stupid like confess all. Or worse, kiss her again, and he feared where that would lead.

He stole a glance at her, jolted again by just the sight of her, let alone the memory of the two of them last night in the cottage. He felt like a schoolboy. What the hell was wrong with him?

Worse, he found himself wishing Trevor Forester was still alive so he could kick his sorry ass. For cheating on Jill. For ever being her fiancé in the first place. For putting her in this position—and Mac, as well.

He couldn't believe what a jackass Trevor Forester had been. This morning Mac had checked out the engagement ring Jill Lawson had thrown at him. He'd found faint initials on the inside of the band. They appeared to have been filed down, making him even more suspicious about where Trevor had gotten the ring. Mac remembered what Pierce had said about suspecting Trevor Forester was the burglar who'd been robbing area houses.

He suspected, like Pierce's coins, Trevor had stolen the ring.

Mac had sent a description of the ring to an old friend of his, Charley Johnson, at the Kalispell Police Department, to see if the ring came up on any stolen-property list. From what Mac had learned at the bar last night, Jill and Trevor hadn't been engaged long and there'd been no recent burglaries. If the ring was stolen, then it could mean that Trevor Forester had been a thief for some time.

Not that any of that helped Mac figure out what Trevor might have done with the stolen coins. If the burglary was more than two months ago, the coins could be anywhere.

What bothered Mac was that it appeared someone thought the coins were still in Bigfork. Why else had Jill's apartment been hit last night?

"Everyone knows you and Trevor weren't getting

along," one of the deputies said, his voice carrying. "You said yourself you were going to break off the engagement."

Jill had planned to break her engagement to Trevor *before* she'd come to the cottage?

Mac tried not to take too much pleasure in that. He kept reminding himself that what happened last night could never happen again.

He watched her worry her lower lip with her teeth, making him unable not to recall her mouth on his. Jill Lawson was a dangerous woman. Smart, pretty, competent, sexy, independent—the kind of woman a man could fall in love with, the kind who made a man think about settling down, something Mac had no intention of ever doing. Not again. Jill Lawson was the ever-after kind, and Mac hated Trevor Forester for having somehow gotten this woman to love him.

"Can I get you more coffee?"

Mac looked up to see a girl with green hair holding a coffeepot.

"No, I have to get going, but thank you," he said, aware that the girl had seen him watching Jill and the deputies. "This is the best cinnamon roll I've ever eaten. Please give my compliments to the baker."

"You got it," the girl said.

Mac slipped a generous tip under his cup, feeling the girl's gaze on him. He couldn't come back here again. It was too dangerous.

But he hated like hell to leave the deputies badgering Jill. He hated like hell to leave her alone. He feared that the man who'd searched her apartment last night hadn't gotten what he'd been looking for. That meant he'd be back, and that meant Mac would be spending his nights watching her apartment.

In the meantime he had to concentrate on finding the coins and Shane during the daylight hours. Once Pierce had the coins again, Jill would be safe. Then if Jill still needed that alibi... Mac told himself he wouldn't let her go to jail—if it came to that. Damn, but he hoped it wouldn't.

As he rose from his chair to leave, the bell over the door jangled. A thirtysomething, dark-haired man burst into the bakery and made a beeline for Jill Lawson.

"I heard you think Jill killed Trevor Forester," the man said loudly. He was about Mac's height and size, his tanned arms corded with muscle, his face lined with squint lines from the sun. A man who worked outdoors.

"Excuse me, but this is sheriff's department business," the larger of the deputies said, getting to his feet.

"Oh, yeah? Well, I'm here to tell you Jill couldn't have killed Trevor," the man said. "She was with me last night. In the lake cottage." The man looked at Jill and added, "Making love."

CHAPTER SIX

J ILL SCRAMBLED TO her feet. She was shaking her head, staring at Arnie Evans, telling herself it wasn't possible. "Arnie, don't make things any worse by lying."

"Could we discuss this in private in your apartment?" Duncan suggested. "Mr. Evans, if you'd please hold down your voice until we can go upstairs."

Jill glanced up. The man who'd been sitting by the window was standing next to his table, staring at them as if in shock. She couldn't blame him, given what he'd just overheard. "Yes, my apartment." She glanced at Zoe, who also looked stunned.

"Take care of closing up?" Jill said.

Zoe nodded. "Should I call…someone?"

"I'll be fine." Not if Arnie had been her mystery lover.

Zoe nodded, big-eyed as they left for Jill's upstairs apartment.

Once upstairs Arnie sat in one of her overstuffed chairs, looking bashful and shy as he glanced around. Duncan put the cushions back on the couch and sat down. Samuelson leaned in the doorway to the kitchen, watching them all.

Jill didn't want to sit. She wanted to pace. But she made herself take the other chair, the one farthest from

Arnie, as if that could somehow distance her from his…story.

"Are you telling me that this isn't the man from the cottage?" Duncan asked her.

Oh, God, I hope not. "It can't be."

"She didn't know it was me," Arnie said sheepishly. "She thought it was Trevor. Okay, maybe I let her think that. When I came up with the idea to dress in the same costume as Trevor, I thought it would be fun. I didn't mean for it to hurt anyone."

Jill wanted to pull the floor over her head. Arnie Evans. Since kindergarten, Arnie had been Trevor's shadow and her tormentor. Whatever Trevor did, Arnie tried, usually failing badly. When he hadn't been emulating Trevor as a boy, he'd been throwing worms at Jill or putting gum in her hair or pushing her down in the playground.

Jill had learned to avoid Arnie.

As they grew older, Arnie had done poorly in school, not gone to college, ended up in construction and now had to work for a living with his hands—all just the opposite of Trevor.

What had always amazed her was that Arnie and Trevor had been such good friends. She suspected, knowing what she now knew about her former fiancé, that the reason was because Trevor loved being idolized. Trevor used to say that every man should have a friend like Arnie—and then he'd laugh.

While Arnie hadn't taunted or teased Jill as an adult, she'd felt that he was jealous of her relationship with Trevor. And when she was around the two of them, she had felt like a third wheel. She knew that Arnie would do anything for Trevor. Anything.

"He's lying," she said. *Oh, please, let him be lying.* She could never have been seduced by Arnie Evans. And yet, physically, he could have been the man. He was about Trevor's height, but then, so were a lot of men. He'd worked construction since he was young and he was strong, lean and solid, just like the man from the cottage.

Even Arnie's stupid explanation for why he was wearing the same costume as Trevor made sense, if you knew Arnie.

Why was Arnie doing this? "He *has* to be lying."

The deputies questioned him about the time, the storm, power outage, everything. Arnie, to her horror, seemed to have all the answers.

"What name did you rent the costume under?" Duncan asked.

Arnie shrugged. "Trevor rented it. I knew he had an extra Rhett Butler costume on his hands. That's how I came up with the idea."

"Arnie was Trevor's best friend!" Jill cried. "That's how he knew about the extra costume. I'm telling you, he's lying. How did he even know I needed an alibi? Don't you see? He must have heard all this from his cousin who works at city hall, right next to the sheriff's department."

Duncan looked at Jill as if she'd lost her mind. Here was a man ready to provide her with an alibi, and she was doing everything in her power to challenge it.

"Is there any way you can prove you were the man with Ms. Lawson in the cottage last night?" Duncan asked.

Arnie nodded and pulled the silk bra she'd been wearing last night from his pocket, dangling it before them.

Jill was going to be sick. And just when she thought things couldn't get any worse.

No way! Mac couldn't believe what he'd overhead just before the deputies went upstairs with Jill and the man she'd called Arnie. Arnie Evans, the deputy had said.

Mac's first instinct was to step forward and take credit where credit was due. But as much as he wanted to for more reasons than he cared to admit, he couldn't. He told himself there was no way Jill would believe that this Arnie was the man, would she?

He drove back to the houseboat. Who the hell was Arnie Evans, anyway? Mac had seen Jill's adverse reaction to the man—and his story. More importantly, why was the man lying? To save Jill? Or himself?

It didn't take Mac long at the Beach Bar to find out that Arnie Evans had supposedly been Trevor Forester's best friend. And that he had not only invested in the Inspiration Island development, he worked out there.

After a phone call to his cop buddy Charley Johnson, Mac found out that Arnie had run into some trouble with the law when he was younger. Twice he'd been picked up for having sex with underage girls. Both times he'd gotten off, supposedly because Trevor had paid off the parents of the girls.

Arnie had been one of the people the local sheriff had looked at in the cases of the missing teens. But they'd never been able to get anything on him.

Mac could feel himself getting deeper and deeper into Trevor Forester's murder. He started beating the bushes, looking for Shane, in a race against the clock. Come dark, he would be camped outside Jill Lawson's apartment—a dangerous place for him to be in more ways than one.

JILL COULDN'T RECALL a worse day.

Both Deputies Duncan and Samuelson seemed satisfied that Arnie Evans was her mystery lover—and her alibi for the time of the murder. As crazy as it seemed, she preferred being a suspect in Trevor Forester's murder than this.

After Arnie promised to go to the sheriff's department and make a statement, the deputies left. Duncan gave her an apologetic nod. Samuelson merely looked from Arnie to her and back, obviously disgusted that she'd made love with Trevor's best friend on the night her fiancé was murdered.

Samuelson didn't know the half of it. If Arnie was telling the truth, she'd made love with a man she couldn't stand the sight of.

Her face burned with embarrassment as she watched the deputies leave. Finally she made herself look at Arnie. It was difficult. "Maybe they believe your story, but I don't."

"You sure hold a grudge a long time," Arnie said. "I think the reason I bugged you so much when were kids is that I just wanted you to notice me."

"Oh, I noticed you all right."

"I always liked you. It really ticked me off the way Trevor treated you." He sounded sincere. Then he got to his feet. "I should get going. I'm sorry if you're disappointed I was the man with you. I didn't mean to embarrass you. I had a feeling you wouldn't be happy about…us. I just couldn't let them hassle you anymore. And you were right, I did hear about that through my cousin. You know how news travels in this town."

Jill groaned. The whole town knew about her tryst

in the lake cottage last night—and now they'd hear it was with Arnie.

"It'll blow over," he said as if reading her mind. "And don't worry. I won't bother you, considering how you feel about things…now."

She'd never seen this side of Arnie before. He was being much nicer than she ever would have guessed. Was it possible he really had been the man in the cottage?

It was that first kiss, she realized. The moment their lips had touched. That kiss had melted all her anger, resentment, fears about Trevor. She'd been seduced by a kiss. A kiss from Arnie Evans?

She cringed at the thought, even with him acting almost human. She just couldn't imagine him being the generous, loving man who'd transported her to another world and introduced her to passion. It had been more than sex. She had bonded with that man and now missed him, ached for him. And her heart and soul told her he wasn't Arnie Evans.

Arnie walked to the door and stopped. "I know Trevor could be a real jackass, but he was my best friend."

"Is that why you decided to give me an alibi?" she asked.

He shook his head, his dark gaze meeting hers. He really did seem shy around her without Trevor here. "I told the truth, Jill. I'm sorry, but it was me last night." He turned and started toward the door.

"Arnie?"

He stopped, his back to her.

"Did you know about the woman Trevor was seeing, Rachel?"

He didn't turn around. "I knew there was someone. I saw her driving your car once."

"Do you know her name?"

"Rachel. That's all I knew. But she never really mattered to Trevor. He was just stringing her along like he did all women."

He was planning to marry this one. "I appreciate you trying to help me," she said, feeling a little guilty. She swore she'd never have sex again.

Moments later she glanced out the window and saw Arnie getting into a new black sports car—the same one that had been parked in front of the bakery this morning.

Why would Arnie be sitting across the street in his car at three-thirty in the morning watching her bakery? Was it possible he'd been considering telling her he was the man? Could she be wrong about him?

AFTER ARNIE LEFT, Jill called to get her locks replaced, remembering that someone had Trevor's key to her apartment. Brenna called just as she was getting ready to leave.

"Trevor never applied for a marriage license or got any blood tests and—are you ready for this?—he cashed in the second ticket, the one for Rachel Forester, the day *before* the party," Brenna said. "Either he changed his mind about marrying her, or he never planned to."

Maybe Arnie had been right about Trevor not caring about Rachel.

"I would say she had a great motive for murder if she found out," Brenna noted.

"No kidding." But what had she been looking for at the condo if not the ticket?

After they hung up, Jill changed clothes and drove out to meet with Alistair Forester, all the time thinking about motives for murder—and the other Scarlett. Was she Rachel?

The road to the Forester house was narrow and winding, providing glimpses of the lake through the cherry trees, some still heavy with fruit. Flathead cherries were famous and only grew on this side of the lake.

This early in the afternoon, the water was glassy smooth and green. The leaves of the cherry trees shimmered in the summer heat.

As the road narrowed even more along the rocky cliffs, Jill was reminded of the previous night when she'd been chasing her red Saturn. She'd thought it was Trevor driving her car. Instead, it must have been the other Scarlett.

As she parked the van, she caught sight of the cottage through the pine trees and felt a rush of emotion that had nothing to do with Arnie Evans. He couldn't have been the man, no matter what he said or how he acted or what evidence he was able to provide, she thought, remembering how she'd felt in the man's arms, the feelings he'd elicited from her.

The cottage seemed to pull her. She walked down to it and opened the door, peering inside. The deputies had already searched it. But still she had to look. Not that she knew what she was looking for.

The cottage was small. Just room enough for a bed, two club chairs, a small table and a bathroom. How had Arnie gotten the bra, she wondered, if he hadn't been the man? And what about the ring and her panties? Who had them?

She stood in the middle of the room. She could almost feel the man's presence, his touch such a clear memory her skin tingled and her body ached. She closed her eyes, sensing something of the man still there in the room, an intangible essence that assured her everything she believed about last night was true. Her lover was still masked, still a mystery, waiting to be found, wanting her as badly as she wanted him.

She opened her eyes. "Right. If he wants you so badly, where is he? Why hasn't he come looking for you? Why hasn't he come to your rescue?"

The only thing she could be sure of was that whoever the man had been last night, he'd stirred a desire in her she feared no other man could satisfy.

She started to leave, closing the door behind her, wishing she could close the door on last night as easily. The soles of her sandals scraped on something gritty on the floor. She looked down and saw what appeared to be mustard-colored dried mud on the threshold.

She bent and picked up a piece of it, surprised since she knew of no place around here that had mud that color. Crumbling it in her fingers, she had a flash of memory. She'd seen this kind of dried mud before. On Trevor's boots the last time he'd come into the bakery from the island!

ALISTAIR OPENED THE door at Jill's knock. He looked ten years older, his face gray and drawn. Without a word, he hugged her.

"I am so sorry," Jill whispered.

He nodded wordlessly, his eyes shining with fresh

tears as he led her to his den. "I had the maid make us some lemonade."

She wasn't thirsty but took the drink he offered her and sat down beside him on the sofa, wondering where Heddy was.

He seemed nervous, unsure, something totally alien for a man like him. "I know things weren't…good between you and my son."

She nodded. "I hadn't really seen Trevor lately. I had the feeling he'd been avoiding me. I wanted to believe it was just his work, but I think I knew better. I was going to break off the engagement last night, even before I found out there was someone else."

"Another woman," Alistair said.

"Yes. Did you know about her?"

He shook his head. "I'm sorry. You know how delighted I was that you were going to be part of our family. Trevor knew my sentiments, as well." His eyes filled with more tears. He squeezed her hand. "I am deeply saddened that you won't be my daughter-in-law."

She smiled. "Thank you."

"If there is anything you need, anything at all, please let me know," he said. "The funeral is tomorrow. Heddy insisted we open it up to the entire town. I think she needs to see a big turnout."

Jill nodded in understanding.

"We thought it was best to have it as soon as the coroner released the…body." His voice broke. "What did Trevor do that made someone want to kill him?"

Jill took Alistair's hand, knowing how hard this must be on him. How many women had Trevor been stringing along? Had one of them killed him?

"I hadn't seen Trevor much myself lately," Alistair said, composing himself. "Not since I cut him off financially." He nodded at Jill's surprise. "I know Trevor had planned to leave town last night. The sheriff said he'd purchased a second plane ticket. For a Mrs. Forester. A Rachel Forester. I told myself there must be some mistake."

Jill shook her head. There was no mistake. "There was a woman at the party dressed in the same costume I had on. It seems she planned to take my place once Trevor broke the news to me."

Alistair shook his head. "Despicable behavior. I am so ashamed." He closed his eyes as if he was in pain. "I'm so sorry."

"It's not your fault," she said.

He shook his head. "Yes, it is," he said, opening his eyes again. "Heddy and I spoiled Trevor, and kept right on spoiling him. We gave him everything he ever asked for. Including that awful island. He wanted it so badly. As much as I disliked the idea, I thought he might make something of it. I thought it might…change him. Unfortunately his intent seems to have only been to swindle the people who trusted him, myself and the other investors. Inspiration Island indeed. I guess it was Trevor's little joke on us all."

"Who were the other investors?" Jill asked, suddenly wondering if one of the investors had found out about the swindle and killed Trevor.

Alistair named four people: Wesley Morgan, a local landowner; J. P. Davies, a retired computer whiz with a summer home on the lake—J.P. never spent more than a few weeks at the lake each year; and Arnie and Burt Evans.

Arnie's father invested in Inspiration Island? Burt Evans had owned a gas station in Polson, at the south end of the lake. He'd died in May from a heart attack, but Jill doubted he'd had much to invest. She'd always gotten the impression he'd barely scraped by.

"Trevor was much deeper in debt than I suspected," Alistair said. "Even if he had completed the island project, he couldn't have made enough to get himself out of debt and pay back the investors. Finishing the project is out of the question."

"What will happen to the island?" Jill asked.

"No one wanted that island before because of its history. Now its value is diminished because of the mess Trevor made out there," Alistair said.

How had Trevor made such a mess of things? She felt so sorry for Alistair. And Heddy. The woman must be beside herself. Trevor was her baby boy. He could do no wrong. "How is Heddy? This must be devastating for her on top of everything else."

"Your concern is touching," Heddy said sarcastically from the doorway, making them both turn in surprise.

Jill wondered how long Heddy had been standing there listening. Jill hurriedly stood and started toward the woman, but Heddy stopped her short.

"What are you doing here?" Heddy demanded.

Jill was taken aback. "Alistair asked me to—"

"I needed to talk to her about Trevor," Alistair said, pushing himself up from the couch.

"She never loved our son," Heddy accused, her eyes hard as stones as she glared at Jill. "I heard you say you weren't going to marry him. For all I know you killed him!"

"Heddy! Don't be ridiculous!" Alistair cried.

Heddy ignored him, her eyes like daggers. "This is all your fault, Jill. I told Alistair not to force Trevor into marrying you. 'Get yourself a nice girl. A girl like that Jill Lawson,'" Heddy mimicked. "'Otherwise, you're not going to get a red cent of my money!' Isn't that what you told him, Alistair?"

"Heddy, for God's sake—"

"If you'd been half the woman Trevor needed, he wouldn't have gotten involved with that other woman and he'd be alive today," Heddy said angrily.

"No," Alistair said, taking his wife by the shoulders and turning her to face him. "Don't you dare blame this poor girl for our son's behavior. Don't you dare."

Heddy crumpled against him, sobbing in horrible gasps. Alistair held his wife to him, his eyes brimming with tears as he looked over Heddy's silver-blond head at Jill.

"I'm so sorry," Jill whispered.

Alistair closed his eyes.

Jill quietly slipped out, mortified by what she'd learned. Trevor had only asked her to marry him to please his father—and get the Forester money. Amazing that Trevor could still humiliate her even in death.

As she left, she wondered what Heddy had meant about Trevor being alive today if he hadn't gotten involved with that woman. The other Scarlett?

CHAPTER SEVEN

JILL'S FATHER'S FISHING boat was gone when she reached his house. She left him a note saying she had borrowed the ski boat and would be back soon.

The lake was a mirror, the late-afternoon sun hot as she hit the throttle and sped down the lake to the roar of the engine and the spray of the cool water.

She got her love of lakes from her father. He'd moved to Flathead Lake from Billings, bought the modest house on the lake and started an auto-parts business near Yellow Bay. He'd been successful and now, in his sixties, spent his days fishing on the lake. As the story went, her parents had both given up any hope of having children after years of trying when Jill had come along.

"It must have been the lake water," her father always joked. "Or maybe the good fishing. But your mother flourished here," he would say, and look at the lake with a kind of devotion. "We were blessed here. We got you."

So it was no wonder Jill loved the lake as much as her father. She'd grown up here and knew the lake well.

Except for what Trevor had named Inspiration Island. The island had always been off-limits. In the early days it had been owned by a wealthy recluse family.

After the tragedies there, the island had been fenced and posted.

She'd heard rumors about there being deadly quick-sand in places. Those rumors ran as rampant as the ones about the screams heard coming from the island some summer nights. Locals swore the place was haunted and avoided it.

Even her father, who was the most down-to-earth man she knew, always warned her to keep away from the island. He said that something about it frightened him. He never fished near it.

Given all that, she'd been surprised that, when the island had come up for sale, Trevor had talked Alistair into buying it and letting him develop it into an island resort.

The boat trip to the island took about thirty minutes from her father's place at the other end of the lake. Last night from the Foresters', which was closer, it would have taken more like ten, maybe fifteen minutes in the right boat.

Had that been Arnie who she thought got out of the boat at the Foresters' dock last night at eight-fifteen? Or had the man dressed as Rhett Butler been on the boat at all? She couldn't be sure. Once she'd seen the man go into the cottage, she hadn't noticed anyone else.

As she neared the island, she slowed the boat, a chill creeping over her at the sight of the old mansion sitting high on the cliffs at the island's north end. Weathered and dark, the stark frame of the empty structure could barely be seen through the pines, but there was just enough of it to disturb her.

While the other islands were dotted with cabins and expensive houses, boat docks and water toys strewn across the beaches, this island was just as it had been for decades.

She always avoided the island just as her father had and not because of the signs warning trespassers of prosecution.

It was the stories. Stories of a crazed young woman who'd been kept a prisoner there. According to local legend, Aria Hillinger had been the only daughter of Claude Hillinger and he'd treated her like a princess. But when she was in her teens, she realized she was a captive princess and she went mad.

She escaped once. When her father brought her back to the island, she was pregnant, according to the stories. Claude had delivered the baby himself so his daughter would never have to leave again.

At night Aria would stand on the fourth-floor balcony and cry for help. She was not even eighteen the day her father found her hanging from a rafter on the fourth-floor balcony overlooking the lake. Her child would have been five.

Claude killed himself when he found his daughter hanging there. He jumped from the balcony to the cliffs below. It was weeks before anyone found the two of them. By then, Aria's child was missing. Everyone speculated the child had either starved to death or drowned. Of course, some people said Aria had never escaped the island, not even once, and her baby had been Claude's, which was why she'd killed herself.

Some people still swore that on some still summer nights they could hear the woman's cries miles away.

Jill shivered and wondered why Trevor had thought anyone would want to live on this island again. As she glanced up at the weathered mansion, she also wondered why he hadn't torn down the old structure first thing.

She feared Trevor had planned to capitalize on the tragedies of this island. Why else would he leave that awful monstrosity standing? She could still see the old No Trespassing signs along the shore and pushed away thoughts of Claude Hillinger. If evil could survive, it did so here, she thought.

The largest cove on the east side sheltered a dock where two boats were moored. She slowed, pulled along one side of the dock and cut the engine. Grabbing the rope, she jumped out to tie it to a cleat, ignoring the large sign on the shore end of the dock: No Trespassing. Authorized Personnel Only.

She didn't recognize either of the boats, but she recognized the face that appeared at the construction-office window and quickly disappeared from view. Wesley Morgan, one of the investors.

She questioned why someone like Wesley would have invested in this island and then immediately knew the answer. Fast money. The only island left undeveloped in a beautiful Montana lake. Maybe it could have overcome its creepy past. Out-of-staters wouldn't know the history. All they would see was the beauty of the area.

As she neared the office, she thought about Trevor's big plans. High-end summerhouses. A marina. A four-star hotel and restaurant.

From what she could see, none of those plans had materialized. The small office was little more than a shed at the edge of the shore overlooking the dock. She could see no other buildings through the trees.

"Jill?" The voice behind her sounded surprised,

maybe a little apprehensive. She turned, glad to see it was Wesley Morgan who came out of the office, not whoever owned the other boat.

Wesley was fiftysomething, slim, prematurely gray with a fatherly face. She watched him glance behind him as if he'd expected to see someone else come out of the office.

"What are you doing here?" Wesley asked, softening the words with a smile and, "Not that it isn't always nice to see you."

Uh-huh. "I wanted a look at the island."

He frowned. "There really isn't much to see."

She could believe that as she glanced toward several pieces of heavy equipment that had obviously been brought out by barge. A narrow dirt road snaked through the pines and disappeared, possibly the same road Claude Hillinger had once used to get to his mansion.

This did seem like a waste of time now that she was here. What had she hoped to find? Some yellow mud. But what would that prove? That the man she'd made love to had been on the island last night? Or at least someone who'd gone into the cottage since last night had been on the island.

She glanced at the office, not ready to give up. "I'd love a tour," she said, and flashed him a smile.

Wesley looked more than surprised. "A tour? I'm not sure—"

"I really need to see this place." She glanced away. "I need to know why Trevor... I just need to see the island for myself."

Wesley looked as if he had better things to do, but finally he nodded and motioned toward a Jeep parked next to the office. "Hop in. Like I said, there isn't much to see."

As she walked along the side of the office, a shadow passed the window. She saw Wesley glance in that direction.

"Who's manning the office?" she asked as she climbed into the passenger side of the Jeep.

Wesley looked uncomfortable as he started the Jeep and backed out. "Nathaniel Pierce. Do you know him?"

She shook her head. But she knew him by reputation.

Wesley seemed to not want to say any more, but must have felt compelled to, given that she'd caught them both out here. "He might be interested in buying the island, but at this point, I don't want to jinx the deal—and he doesn't really want that made public."

She could understand now why Wesley was acting so secretive. Jill knew that if Nathaniel Pierce bought the island the investors would get at least some of their money back. It was no secret Pierce came from old family money.

"Why would he want the island?" she asked, really wondering more why Trevor had wanted it.

Wesley shook his head. "He says he wouldn't develop it. Just let it go back to the way it's been for years. I think he's worried about his view." He shrugged at the whims of the rich. "His house overlooks the island."

Wesley drove south along what was obviously a newer narrow dirt road cut through the trees. The island was only about a mile long and maybe half a mile wide. Through the pines she would get glimpses of the lake. The sun seemed to beat down mercilessly on the island, and the air was eerily still and dry. She yearned to be back in the boat on the cool water and far from here.

"I'm surprised Trevor didn't get more done," she said. Especially as he'd told her he'd been working day and night for the past few months. Uh-huh.

Wesley didn't look away from his driving. "Bet you're not as surprised as the investors."

"Trevor didn't let you come out here, either?"

Wesley shook his head. "He said he wanted to surprise us. Even scheduled a Labor Day grand opening to start selling lots for the next summer season." Wesley's voice was laced with bitterness. "Oh, he surprised us all right."

The road ended abruptly at a gate with a sign that read Restricted. No Admittance.

Wesley stopped and shifted down as he started to turn onto an even narrower road that ran along the west side of the island.

To the south, through a tall, steel-mesh fence, Jill could see pines giving way to cattails, ferns and reeds. With a start, she noticed the tracks going through the gate. The road was rutted and muddy—the same odd mustard-colored mud she'd found in the cottage. The same mud she'd seen on Trevor's boots the last time she'd seen him.

"What's through there?" she asked, pointing at the gate.

"Swamp. The whole south end of the island is worthless, completely uninhabitable, and the north end is high cliffs and not much better. The engineering report that I saw…well, it glossed over some of the island's obvious problems as far as development went."

It sounded more and more like Trevor's only big plans for the island were to bilk the investors and skip town.

"That's a strange-colored mud," she commented. "I've never seen it anywhere else around the lake, have you?"

"No," he said. "Awful stuff. Like quicksand, it's so sticky and deep." Wesley released the clutch. The Jeep lurched up the west-side road.

Jill turned to look back through the fence. Quicksand? That must be why Trevor had gone to the trouble of fencing off the swamp. Seemed like a waste of money, though.

A man's face suddenly materialized out of the trees just beyond the fence.

"Wait!" she cried. "That man—"

Wesley hit the brakes and turned to look in the direction she indicated. "What man?"

She stared at the spot where she'd just seen the blond man from the bakery this morning. He was gone! How was that possible? He'd just been standing there. Where had he gone?

She kept looking. He had to still be there. He couldn't have moved that quickly. Unless he'd realized that she'd seen him and had some reason to hide.

"Didn't you say there wasn't anyone else on the island but Nathaniel Pierce and us?" she asked.

"There isn't. Who did you think you saw?"

She caught Wesley's pitying expression. Did he think she thought she saw Trevor? "I guess it was nothing."

"This must be hell for you," he said kindly.

She nodded. Trevor was definitely one reason she'd come out here today, but that wasn't the man she'd seen. She told herself she hadn't imagined him. But then again, she couldn't forget her reaction to him in the bakery this morning. It was so…odd.

Wesley got the Jeep going again.

She pretended to stare at the passing landscape. Wesley passed an area of scraped rocky earth that might have been cleared for a house. Who knew what Trevor had planned? A few stakes with small red flags on them fluttered in the breeze around the perimeter of the spot.

Why had Trevor bothered if he'd always planned to run out on the investors—and her? Maybe he really had been serious about Inspiration Island at some point. Maybe before the other Scarlett came along. Is that what his mother had meant?

Near the shoreline she spotted more wooden stakes, more red flags moving restlessly in the breeze.

Wesley drove over a rise near the north end of the island and the rear of the mansion appeared out of the pines. The heat pressed down on her and for a moment she couldn't breathe.

"That's where they found Trevor's boat," Wesley said, pointing off to the west.

She could feel Wesley watching her, expecting what reaction? she wondered.

"Who found him?" she asked even though Brenna had already told her.

"A fisherman noticed the boat as he was passing the island but didn't see anyone inside, so he went over to check."

It seemed strange that Trevor had been killed within view of the island. Within view of the mansion people around the area swore was haunted.

She felt a chill as Wesley drove on past the mansion, back through the pines to the office.

"Anything else?" he asked as he parked in the patch of shade beside the small wooden office.

"Do you know anyone named Rachel?" She watched his face. "She was a friend of Trevor's."

He frowned. "Rachel? No, sorry."

She nodded. "Thanks for showing me around," she said, climbing out of the Jeep. He followed her around to the front of the office.

"Can I ask you one more thing?" she said before he went back inside. She could see that only Wesley's boat remained at the dock. Nathaniel Pierce must have decided not to wait. She hoped her showing up here hadn't made him rush off or change his mind about buying the island. "Did you lose a lot of money in this project?"

Wesley looked toward the lake. "Just my life's savings."

"I'm sorry. I suppose you heard that Trevor was planning to leave the country?"

He raked a hand through his hair, his features taut with anger. "No. When was he leaving?"

"The night of the party."

Wesley looked over at her. "You weren't going with him?"

She shook her head. "Thanks again for the tour." As she started down the slope to the dock, she thought about the three investors. She doubted J.P. was worried about any money he'd put into the project, since the last she'd heard he was worth billions. And Arnie's father, Burt, couldn't have invested much since he didn't have much to begin with.

That left Wesley Morgan. He had the most to lose—

and that gave him a motive for Trevor's murder, she realized with a start.

She found herself hurrying, but not because she feared Wesley. She just wanted off this island. It felt cursed. And Trevor's murder seemed to prove it.

But as she got into the boat, started the engine and pulled away from the island, she thought about the man she'd seen in the trees at the south end of the island. The blond man from the bakery that morning.

Instead of turning her boat home, she motored slowly toward the southern, marshy end of the island, staying close to the shore. This end of the lake was shallow and full of weeds.

An enormous flock of pelicans floated overhead, and she could see ducks and geese in pockets of water in the marshy area before the bushes and trees began. She cut the engine and let the boat drift as she neared the far-south end of the island.

A flash of silver caught her eye. A small fishing boat was tied up under some bushes. She picked up the emergency paddle her father kept on board and maneuvered her boat under the limbs of a clump of bushes in a small cove—a spot just far enough away that when whoever owned the fishing boat returned, neither she nor her boat could be seen. But she could see him.

She didn't have to wait long.

The man she'd seen earlier behind the restricted area, the same one who'd come into the bakery that morning, appeared from behind the bushes. He was carrying a small navy duffel bag. The bottom of the bag, which was thick with the mustard-yellow mud from behind the restricted area, sagged under the weight of whatever was inside.

He put the bag carefully down in the bow, then untied the bow rope from a branch, shoved out the craft and jumped in. His boat motor spurted to life an instant later.

She watched him angle away, heading west. He was going along the far side of the island, the side opposite from the office. So no one would see him?

She waited, then eased her boat out of the cove with the paddle, moving along the edge of the bushes until she could see him again. A little farther up the lake in the shallows was a favorite spot for lake-trout fishing. He headed for that as if it had been his destination all along. But he didn't stop to fish. He kept going until he was past the island. Past the spot where Trevor's boat had been found with his body inside.

The man turned once to look back at the island, then he hit the throttle and headed north up the lake.

What was in the bag he'd brought out of the restricted area of the island? And who was he?

She remembered her reaction to him in the bakery that morning. That instant when she'd seen him in the trees. And his shock of recognition just before he'd ducked out of sight.

The sun had dropped behind the mountains, leaving the lake's surface bathed in gold.

Jill waited, hanging back, then she followed him.

CHAPTER EIGHT

JILL WATCHED FROM a distance as the man tied up the fishing boat to the stern of a houseboat docked at the far end of the marina and disappeared inside it. He'd left the duffel bag in the fishing boat, but she knew there was no way to get a look at the contents until after dark.

In the long, cool shadows of the pines stretching out over the water, she pulled her boat up on shore and walked toward the Bandit's Bay Marina office. The fading sunset streaked the lake's surface like oil. She could hear music coming from the jukebox at the Beach Bar, the sound of children splashing in the swimming area, the drone of a motorboat crossing the lake.

As she stepped into the marina office, she kept her eye on the houseboat, afraid he would come out and see her and know she'd followed him.

"Well, hello!"

Jill turned to see Brenna behind the marina-office counter.

"Mom bribed me with dinner if I'd come by and help," Brenna said, coming around the counter to give Jill a hug. "She's making her famous barbecued pork ribs. She would love it if you could stay for dinner."

"Thanks, but I really can't." Especially tonight. She smiled at her friend. Brenna was as sweet as she was pretty and smart. She could have been anything, but she'd opted to go into journalism, got a job at the local paper and stuck around Bigfork to help her family at the marina in her spare time.

"How are you doing?" Brenna asked, studying Jill.

"Okay."

"I'm still trying to find out more about this Rachel person for you," Brenna said. "It would help if we had a last name."

Jill nodded, hating to ask. "I have another favor."

"Sure."

"I need to know who owns that houseboat tied up at the far end of the docks," she said.

"The one down in the old slips?"

Jill nodded.

"Does this have anything to do with Trevor's murder?"

"Possibly."

Brenna flipped through the file and pulled out a card. "Mackenzie Cooper. Listed a post-office box in Whitefish as permanent address."

"I wonder what he's doing here?"

She looked up from the card. "Fishing, I would imagine. Speaking of fishing—"

"I saw him out on the island earlier and I got the impression he didn't want to be seen."

"You went out to the island? Oh, you couldn't get me near that place. I can't believe you went out there by yourself."

"Wesley was there." She didn't mention Nathaniel Pierce. Not even to Brenna. "The place is way creepy. Especially the south end where I saw this Mackenzie Cooper guy."

"Jill, if you think he knows something about Trevor's murder, you should call the sheriff."

"All the man's done so far is trespass. I want to do some checking on him first."

"I can put him in the computer as soon as I get home," Brenna promised. "Want me to call you if I come up with anything, if it isn't too late?"

"Even if it's late. You don't know anything about him?"

Brenna shook her head. "He really keeps to himself. Except I have seen him go to the Beach Bar. Usually in the evening just before dark. He doesn't stay long. Has a beer and walks back to his boat. I'd say he was lonely, except he doesn't look like the lonely type."

Jill nodded. Mackenzie Cooper had no reason to be lonely—unless he chose to be.

"He's really good-looking."

"I suppose so." Jill felt her cheeks flush. "You wouldn't be interested in having a beer later, after dinner, at the Beach Bar, would you?"

Brenna smiled. "I'd love to have a beer with you— Oh, no, you don't."

"I just need you to detain him as long as you can," Jill said quickly. "Buy him a beer. He can't say no, right?"

"Wrong. What are you planning to do?"

"It's probably better if you don't know."

Brenna groaned. "Tell me you aren't going aboard his boat."

"Okay, I'm not going aboard." She quickly hugged her friend. "I really appreciate this."

"What if I can't keep him in the bar long enough?" Brenna asked, sounding scared. "We need some kind of signal so you'll know he's coming back to his boat. I could ring the bell down at the gas docks. It isn't very loud, though."

"That's perfect." Jill smiled. "You're the best."

"Just be careful. I'd feel a lot better if Trevor's killer was behind bars and we knew more about this Mackenzie Cooper."

Wouldn't they all? Jill thought as she returned the ski boat to her father's dock. His car was in the driveway, but his fishing boat was still gone. Gary fished most days until dark. She wondered if he was alone. She'd heard he'd been playing a lot of bingo lately with one of the ladies from the seniors center and that the woman liked to fish.

On the drive to her apartment, Jill thought about the idea of her father remarrying. It had been four years since her mother had died. Still, it seemed too soon for her father to have found someone else. Jill knew she was being selfish, but she couldn't help it.

Didn't she want to see her father find love again? As if it was that easy to find it even once, let alone twice in a lifetime.

A cool breeze stirred the large poplar tree next to her bakery as she parked the van and got out. She had enough time to get something to eat and change clothes.

She glanced down the street and saw Arnie's black sports car. Her stomach clenched at the sight. He was the last person she wanted to see. It had been a long day, and she was tired and hungry and in no mood for him.

But the car appeared to be empty. Maybe he was at the video store down the block or one of the restaurants along the main drag.

She climbed the back steps to her apartment, her thoughts returning to the island and the man she'd seen. Mackenzie Cooper. What had he carried off the island in that duffel bag?

As she started to open the apartment door with her key, she stopped, momentarily confused to find the door already slightly ajar. Beyond it, she could hear someone inside her apartment. Not again!

She started to turn back down the stairs, intending to go out to her van and call the sheriff's department from her cell phone, when she heard Arnie's voice.

Cautiously she pushed open the door and peered in. The bedroom door was open and she could see Arnie digging through one of her kitchen drawers as if looking for something. He was talking to himself, although she couldn't make out the words.

"What are you doing?" she demanded, stepping into the apartment.

He looked up, startled to see her, his eyes narrowing for a moment before he grinned sheepishly. "You caught me," he said, and closed the drawer. "I was looking for a pen to leave you a note."

It was an obvious lie. He'd been searching the back of the drawer as if looking for something other than a pen. "How did you get in here?"

"I just changed all of your locks," he said. "Oh, you didn't know I moonlight for Doug's Key and Safe?"

No, she hadn't known that when she'd called them. But then, Doug's was the only locksmith in town.

Arnie held out her new keys. "That's why I was leaving you the note. The larger key fits the front door of the bakery, the smaller one the back door. You get two keys each, but you should probably make at least one spare."

She took the keys he handed her. "How many spares did you make?"

He looked insulted. "You really don't trust me, do you."

"Should I?"

"Yes. I'm sorry I was such a jerk when we were kids. But you've never made the effort to get to know me since we've been adults."

"Can you blame me?"

He seemed to consider that. "No, I guess not." He smiled. "Sorry if I scared you. I wanted to make sure you had new locks before tonight."

"Thanks." He was making her feel like a real bitch.

He started toward the door, then stopped. "Do you have any idea who might have killed Trevor?"

The question took her by surprise. "No. Do you?"

He shook his head.

"Did you know it was Alistair's idea that Trevor marry me?" she asked, not realizing she was going to.

Arnie looked away.

"So you did know." Everyone had known but her.

"Trevor was…" He waved a hand, looked at the floor, then at her. "I know how he was, but I miss him." He shrugged. "He and I were close, you know?"

She nodded, feeling the need to say something. "He always said you were his best friend."

Arnie smiled. "Thanks."

Maybe Arnie Evans was right. Maybe she didn't know him. And maybe he wasn't such a bad guy, after all.

"There is one more thing," Arnie said slowly. He

looked embarrassed, unsure. "Trevor had something of mine. An IOU from an old gambling debt. If you run across it…"

So that was what he'd been looking for.

"I'll call you and let you know, but I haven't seen it," she said. How like Trevor to hold Arnie to a gambling debt.

"I knew you'd give it to me if you found it." Arnie stepped toward her until he was only an arm's length away. His dark eyes bored into hers as he looked down at her. "I wish I could change the past," he said, his voice little more than a whisper.

Then, before she could react, he grabbed her upper arms, pulled her to him and kissed her. His kiss was hard and wet, his tongue forcing her lips apart, plundering her surprised mouth.

Then just as suddenly, he let go of her and stepped back, seeming surprised and embarrassed by his impetuousness. "I'm sorry. I just…" He stumbled backward to the door and then was gone.

Jill stared after him for a moment before she hurried to the door, closed and locked it. Leaning against it, she wiped her mouth with her hand, wanting to scrub the taste of him from her and at the same time wanting to rejoice.

Arnie Evans had not been the man in the cottage last night! She wanted to shout it from the rooftop.

Her buoyant mood fell like a lead balloon. When she told the deputies, she'd destroy her alibi.

Not just hers, but Arnie's. So why had he lied? Was he just trying to help her—or was he the one who really needed the alibi?

She closed her eyes and rubbed her temples. She

needed to shower and brush her teeth to banish every trace of Arnie Evans. The fact that he hadn't been her lover still cheered her to no end. She'd known in her heart he wasn't the man. She'd known!

But what had he really been looking for when she'd come into the apartment? An IOU? Or something else?

She opened her eyes and pushed away from the door when something crunched under the sole of her shoe. Looking down, she spotted the dried yellow mud on her floor. It must have come from Arnie's work boots, because she'd cleaned the apartment this morning after it had been ransacked last night.

Arnie had been in the restricted area of the island!

What was behind that steel fence that had recently attracted so many people there?

She had no idea, but she was going to find out. The sun was down and soon she'd find out what Mackenzie Cooper had brought out of the restricted area in his duffel bag.

JILL WAITED IN the cool shadows of the pines at the edge of the water until she saw Mackenzie Cooper leave his houseboat and walk up to the Beach Bar, just as Brenna said he did every evening.

The Beach Bar was a classic Montana bar with silver dollars, elk antlers and stuffed lake trout on the walls. Brenna's family had built the bar at the end of the pier on pilings so that it overlooked the marina resort. One whole side was open to the air with stools and a few tables.

It was where both locals and tourists hung out, one of the few bars on the water and definitely blue-collar and fishermen friendly. Country-and-western music throbbed from the jukebox, blending with the sound of voices and the lap of water against the docks.

Jill waited until Mackenzie Cooper was well on his way to the bar before she slipped out of the pines and headed for the houseboat tied at the farthest dock from the marina, about thirty yards offshore.

She'd known she wouldn't be able to just walk down the dock to the boat without being seen. That left only one way out to the houseboat with any hope of going undetected. Swim.

No light glowed inside the houseboat as she waded into the dark water. She couldn't be sure that Brenna would be able to keep him at the bar. Jill couldn't even be sure that tonight he wouldn't change his routine, cut the evening short and return before she'd had time to search the houseboat and get away again.

She took a deep breath. She'd worn a shortie wet suit and a waterproof bag clipped to her waist with what she could find for tools to break into the boat. The water chilled her exposed skin as she dived under the surface. The small dry bag at her waist slowed her as she began to swim underwater through the open area to the docks.

She needed to stay under to keep from being seen for as long as she could. Once she reached the docks, she could swim alongside them to the houseboat.

Her pulse pounded in her ears, beating faster at just the thought of what she'd find in the duffel bag.

She tried to gauge her distance. If she surfaced too soon, she could be spotted from the bar. If she didn't surface soon enough, she'd come up under the docks.

Her pulse spiked when she thought of being caught under a dock again. When she was nine, she and a neighbor boy had been playing and decided to hide under the dock at her house. She'd gotten her suit caught on a nail.

She released a little of her held breath now, swimming through the cold darkness, calculating in her head how far she'd come, how much farther she had to go and trying not to remember that day so many years ago when she was trapped under the dock.

She was already running out of air, her growing panic stealing too much oxygen, stealing too much of the time she would be able to stay underwater. Something brushed her bare leg. Just weeds, she knew, but her panic, her fear fueled by the memory of almost drowning all those years ago, took over.

She surfaced in a rush, gasping for air, surprised by how far she still was from the docks and the houseboat. She shot a look toward the bar. She could see Mackenzie Cooper sitting on a stool, boot heels hooked on the rung, a beer bottle in his hand, a lazy look on his face, all his focus on the woman before him. Brenna. Thank heaven for Brenna.

Diving beneath the surface again, Jill swam toward the docks, more aware of the distance yet spurred on by a need to see what the man had found on the island today.

At last, she reached the docks and surfaced, then swam alongside to the houseboat and climbed the short ladder onto the deck. She stood dripping and trying to catch her breath as she heard the distinct sound of footsteps on the dock headed her way. Was it possible he was already coming back? That Brenna had rung the bell while Jill was underwater?

Jill placed a hand over her thumping heart as she

realized there was more than one person coming down
the dock. She could hear the voices, the clink of ice in
glasses and the sound of laughter.

Peeking around the bow of the houseboat, Jill saw
four people headed for a sailboat in a slip about fifty
yards away. Mackenzie Cooper's boat was isolated
from any of the other boats. She suspected that was
the way he wanted it, which made her all the more
suspicious.

The people boarded the sailboat, laughing and talking loudly, and Jill pulled the penlight from the dry bag
at her waist and crept back to the stern of the houseboat
where the small fishing boat had been tied.

Shining the light into the bottom of the fishing boat,
she saw that the duffel bag wasn't still there. But then,
she hadn't expected it to be. She'd noticed the way he'd
carried the duffel, the way he'd laid it carefully in the
bow of his fishing boat. Whatever he'd found in the
restricted area of the island, it was something valuable,
something too valuable to leave out in the fishing boat.

Keeping to the shadow of the houseboat, she moved
across the stern to the back entrance. To her surprise
the door wasn't locked. He must have figured he could
see the boat from the bar and wasn't worried anyone
would bother with it.

Carefully she slid open the screen door and slipped
in, glad she wouldn't have to use the makeshift break-
ing-and-entering tools she'd brought from the bakery.
Technically, then, she wasn't breaking and entering,
right? She didn't close the screen. Just in case she
needed to make a fast getaway.

It was dark in the houseboat, the curtains on the
windows drawn. She swept the beam of the penlight

across the cabin. The inside of the boat was modestly furnished, clean and uncluttered.

Was there a Mrs. Cooper? Jill didn't think so. No feminine touches anywhere that she could see. She quickly went through the boat. It didn't take long. One bedroom. Bed made. Bedding in the storage compartment under it. Bureau drawers, neat. Not a lot of clothing. Nothing fancy.

Lots of books, worn classics. A man who read. In the living area, she found more books, stereo, TV, VCR. Some storage.

She still hadn't found the duffel bag. She went into the small kitchen-dining room and looked in the cupboards. He had a lot of spices and staples, well-worn cookbooks, a well-stocked pantry and fridge. He must like to cook. That, of course, appealed to her.

No navy duffel. Could he have gotten rid of it between the time she'd left and returned?

She saw something through the bedroom doorway that made her heart jump. The closet door stood open. She'd been so busy looking for the duffel that she'd given the clothes hanging in his closet only a cursory glance, her attention more on the floor under them.

But now her gaze settled on something dark, something familiar.

She moved toward the open closet like a sleepwalker. Even before she touched the fabric, she caught the faint hint of her perfume still in the weave. As she stared at the Rhett Butler costume, her pulse pounded so hard she almost didn't hear the bell ring down at the gas dock.

Now more than ever she needed to find the duffel

bag. She had to know what this man was doing on the island. What he was doing in the cottage last night.

Her hands were shaking as she looked around the boat, frantically trying to see if there was some hiding place she'd overlooked. She glanced at her watch. She had a few minutes. Three at the most before he reached the boat.

The duffel wasn't in the boat. She'd looked everywhere. As she moved toward the open doorway at the stern, she spotted a storage compartment she hadn't noticed before. She rushed to it, unlatched the door and shone the penlight inside.

It was deep, so deep she realized it must have another opening out on the deck. All she could see from this vantage point was the side of an orange plastic crate.

She hurried out the door to find she'd been right. There was another opening to the compartment. She lifted the hatch.

Her heart leaped at the sight of the navy duffel bag. Any moment now she would hear his footfalls on the old wooden dock.

Her pulse pounded as she reached for the duffel, then stopped. The bag sat on top of the plastic crate, and under it she could see an old anchor, some worn rubber boots, an assortment of old gloves. The zipper on the bag was open a few inches.

Maybe she'd been wrong about the value of the contents, she thought as she stared at the mud-encrusted duffel bag. She glanced at her watch. Time was up!

Hurriedly, she unzipped the bag fully, now expecting to find rocks or driftwood, and shone the beam of the penlight inside. Her chest tightened as the beam skittered over what appeared to be a volleyball-size clod of that distinctive mustard mud from the restricted area of the island.

The beam stilled on a dark place in the dried mud. A hole. No, not a hole—she moved the light—two eye sockets! A skull! A human skull! The scream caught in her throat as she heard the creak of a heavy step on the deck behind her.

CHAPTER NINE

M AC HAD HOPED for news of Shane at the bar. Instead, the daughter of the owner of the marina had bought him a beer. She was attractive and nice, but had seemed nervous in her attempt to make small talk.

He'd downed the beer quickly, not sure exactly what she'd been hoping for. Whatever it was, it wasn't happening.

He'd left a lot of messages around town, but still nothing from Shane. Now he was just anxious to grab what he needed and head for Jill's apartment, where he would spend the night making sure she was safe.

It was his own fault for getting involved with her. Once he found Shane and returned the coins to Pierce, he told himself, she would be safe. Then he would pack up and leave Flathead Lake earlier than he'd planned, even though summer wasn't quite over.

Change of plans. Thanks to that one instant in time when he'd kissed Jill Lawson.

As he neared the houseboat, he heard a scuffling sound and tensed. It was growing dark now, but he could see movement in the shadows by his houseboat. His pace quickened.

He was within yards of the boat when he saw what appeared to be two figures fighting. A man in a black ski mask and a woman in a wet suit. The man struck the woman and she slumped in his arms just an instant before the man spotted Mac running down the docks toward him.

Mac saw at once what the man was about to do and knew there was nothing he could do to stop him. In one swift movement, the man threw the unconscious woman over the side of the boat. She hit the water with a splash and went under. Then the man ran the length of the dock and dived into the lake, disappearing into the darkness and water as Mac raced toward the spot where he'd seen the woman go under.

He dived in. The water was shockingly cold, as well as dark and murky, but fortunately not deep. He brushed her arm and quickly made contact with her rubber-clad body and dragged her to the surface and up onto the dock.

As he laid her down on the dock and brushed her long dark hair from her face, he let out a curse. Jill Lawson. Quickly he leaned down to see if she was still breathing. What the hell had she been doing on his boat?

He started to give her mouth-to-mouth resuscitation, but the moment his mouth touched hers, she let out a gasp, her eyes flying open. She looked surprised, scared, confused, all at once. Then she coughed and tried to sit up.

"Are you all right?" he asked as he helped her into a sitting position.

She coughed a few more times, then looked around as if she wasn't sure where she was. She was shaking either from fear or the cold. Or both.

He lifted her into his arms and carried her into the houseboat. Her teeth chattered as he took her into the bathroom, sat her on the closed lid of the toilet and reached in to get the shower going.

"Wh-what are you d-doing?" she stammered.

"Getting you warmed up."

Something flickered in her gaze.

"Can you get out of that wet suit by yourself?"

She made a determined try, but she was shaking too hard. He turned her around and unzipped the back, revealing a strong, bare tanned back and a small, red string bikini. This woman was going to be the death of him.

The moment she felt the zipper stop, she was working at the sleeves, trying to pull them from her arms, struggling without much success as she said, "I can get it."

"Uh-huh. Here." He slipped the sleeve from her arm. She clutched the neoprene to her chest with a modesty that made him smile. He knew every wonderful inch of that body. "Let me help you. I'll close my eyes."

He dragged the wet-suit sleeve from her other arm, then—closing his eyes more for his protection than hers—pulled the neoprene down her slim body. The wet suit fit like a glove and sucked down over her contours like a second skin. He peeled the rubbery material down her legs to her feet.

She rested a hand on his shoulder for balance as he tugged the wet suit off her feet.

Then, the wet suit in hand and his eyes still closed, he rose slowly to a standing position. "Will you be all right in the shower alone?"

"I'll be fine," she said, sounding a little breathless, her teeth still chattering.

"Okay. I'll be just outside the door if you need me."

He turned his back to her, opened his eyes and left with the dripping wet suit. He went out on the deck, needing the cool air, and sucked in several breaths. He hung the suit over the railing to dry and listened for her. He could hear the shower running.

He worried she might pass out and fall. But he heard no alarming thumps, just the water running. He was still shaken from how close she'd come to getting killed.

He swore, angry with himself. Angry with her— what was she doing here, anyway? Angry that he'd let the bad guy get away. He told himself that protecting Jill Lawson wasn't his job. His job was finding Pierce's coins. But he knew he was only telling himself that because he'd failed at both.

He had to get this woman out of his hair, out of his mind, and soon. The shower stopped.

He started to go back inside, but spotted something on the deck. A penlight and a small, dark dry bag. He picked up both. In the dry bag, he found bakery tools and smiled in spite of himself. It appeared Jill Lawson had intended to break into his houseboat with a spatula.

He stepped back inside and looked up as she came out of the bedroom, her face flushed from the shower. She was wearing one of his shirts, a pale-blue chambray. Behind her he could see the wet string bikini on his towel bar.

She stopped when she saw him and looked ill at ease even though his shirt hung down to her knees, more than covering her. She plucked the fabric away from her breasts with her right hand, making him keenly aware that she wore nothing under the shirt. Her other hand was down at her side, hidden behind the folds of the shirt, but all he could think about was the body he knew so well beneath those folds.

Her long, golden-brown hair was pulled up off her neck, wet tendrils curling at her temples and framing her lightly freckled face.

His chest constricted. God, she was something! She smelled of his soap and a heat that wasn't all from the shower. He'd never wanted a woman more than he wanted her right now.

She raised her chin and met his gaze. His knees almost buckled. He stepped to her, lost in those big brown eyes and the chemistry shooting like sparks between them. His hand cupped the nape of her neck. Gently, he pulled her to him. His gaze dropped to her full mouth, the lips slightly parted. Lost. He was completely lost.

He breathed her in as he dropped his mouth to hers. She tasted just as he remembered. Sweet, warm, wet—

He froze when he felt cold steel jab into his ribs. His pistol. He'd left it beside the bed before he went to the bar.

"Who are you?" she asked, sounding scared.

"My name's Mackenzie Cooper." Carefully he removed his hand from her neck and stepped back, concerned in her current state she just might shoot him. From the way she held the gun, she'd used one before. Just his luck. If she pulled the trigger, it wouldn't be an accident.

"I know your name," she said. "Who *are* you?"

"I'm a private investigator. Want to tell me what you were doing on my boat?"

"I followed you from the island. I know you were

behind the restricted area. I know there was a human skull in the duffel bag you brought out of there."

He tried not to show his surprise. "I see." He glanced toward the compartment where he'd put the duffel earlier. The door was closed and the man who'd attacked her hadn't taken it—he'd had nothing in his hands when he'd dived into the water.

"How's your head?" he asked. "I think I have some aspirin."

"My head's fine. So you're a private investigator." She frowned. "Were you investigating last night at the Forester party?"

He glanced toward the closet. The door was open and that damned costume was right where he'd hung it. He should have burned it, but he hadn't been able to. So much for sentimental value. "Why don't you put the gun down and we can talk about this."

She kept the weapon trained on him. "Were you investigating in the cottage last night?"

He flinched. She'd finally gotten to the heart of it. "I found the Rhett Butler costume in your closet," she said, "with these in the right-hand pocket." She pulled out her black panties and dangled them before him.

He swore under his breath. She'd think he was some kind of pervert.

"I'd like my engagement ring back," she said. "I assume you picked it up, too."

He met her gaze. "I don't have it."

She lifted a brow. "Then maybe Arnie has it. Maybe he's the one I remember from the cottage, after all."

Ouch, that hurt. "One of us was definitely a lucky man," he said, then wished he'd bitten his tongue.

Anger flashed in her eyes. "You're lucky I don't

shoot you. When you were in the bakery this morning, you could have told me who you were. You saw the deputies there. I know you overheard what was being said, and you knew I needed an alibi for the time of Trevor's murder."

He nodded. He might be a lot of things, but he wasn't a liar. At least not about this.

"They didn't believe my lame excuse about a man in the cottage seducing me."

Who had seduced whom? He wasn't sure.

Her voice rose with her anger. "Or you could have said something when Arnie Evans came in and announced that he had been my mystery lover."

"Did you believe him?" Mac had to ask.

"No."

He knew he shouldn't have taken so much satisfaction in that. "I wouldn't have let you go to jail."

She shook her head, obviously disgusted with him, but not as disgusted as he was with himself.

"I'm sorry," he added, "but I had my reasons."

Her eyes narrowed and he could see that if she had even an ounce of killer's instinct in her, she would have pulled the trigger. He watched her reach for his cell phone on the coffee table where he'd tossed it earlier.

"I'm sure you also have a good reason why you were at the Foresters' party last night dressed in the same costume Trevor was planning to wear," she said. "And an even better reason why you haven't told the sheriff you were with me in the cottage."

She picked up the phone and hit three numbers. He put his money on 911. "Not to mention the human skull you have in your duffel bag."

"Hang up."

She put the phone to her ear.

"*Hang up.* Please."

She glared at him for a moment, then hit the off button, but still kept the weapon trained on him. He considered taking it away from her, but decided it would only make matters worse. Somehow he had to convince her to stay out of this.

"I do have a good reason for being at the party last night," he said. As for what had happened in the cottage…well, he could explain gravity better than he could that.

He turned his back on her and walked into the small galley kitchen. He knew Jill Lawson wasn't the kind of woman to shoot a man in the back—even if she didn't. "I need a beer. You want one?" She didn't answer, so he pulled two long-necks out of the fridge, walked back into the living room, twisted off the top of one and held it out to her.

When she didn't take it, he set the beer on the coffee table next to where she stood, then sat down in a chair facing her and twisted the cap off his own beer. He took a swig, studying her, trying to decide the best way to handle her. And handle her, literally, was exactly what he wanted to do. But then, that was what had gotten him into this mess.

"Trevor Forester called me the day before the party," he said after a moment. "He'd heard I was a private investigator and wanted to hire me."

"Hire *you?*" she said, suspicion in her tone as she glanced around the houseboat.

"There aren't many private investigators in Bigfork. I actually have an office in Whitefish." He didn't know why he was explaining himself. Maybe because he wanted her to know he was legit. "Trevor said he feared his life was in danger."

Her eyes widened and she lowered herself into the chair next to the coffee table. She rested the weapon on her thigh and reached for the beer with her free hand. She took a sip, watching him over the bottle.

"Trevor said he needed to talk to me in person, but couldn't until the next evening," Mac continued. "I was to meet him at the party, or more precisely, in the lake cottage at eight-fifteen. He had a costume delivered to the marina for me with instructions that I was to go straight to the cottage via the shore and be inconspicuous."

"Inconspicuous as Rhett Butler?"

"I had no idea he planned to show up in the same costume. Or that you would mistake me for him."

Her eyes narrowed. "You were the one who kissed *me* the instant I stepped into the cottage."

"I did it to shut you up. I saw a boat approaching. I wasn't sure who was on board." A small lie, but he didn't want to bring up Nathaniel Pierce. "I figured Trevor had his reasons for such a clandestine meeting—and his reasons for believing his life was in danger. I didn't want you giving me away."

"So that was all there was to it," she said.

He knew she was waiting for him to tell her that there was a hell of a lot more to the part where they'd made love.

He looked her in the eye, knowing how important it was that he make her believe him. "We just got a little carried away, I guess. Pretty hot sex. Must have been the intrigue of it. I'm sure we'd be disappointed if we tried it again."

The hurt in her eyes was almost his undoing. He feared, though, that he was right. They would be disappointed. Last night had been…amazing. He also feared the reverse—that making love to her would be even better the second time—and that he'd be tempted to love. Again.

He cursed himself for hurting her, but it would be much worse to let her think anything was going to come out of last night's lovemaking. It would serve no purpose to tell her he'd never felt anything like what they'd shared. Even if they'd ended up making love again a few minutes ago before she pulled the gun on him, it wouldn't have changed the final outcome—which was him leaving. Soon.

He was a loner, a guy who never stayed in one place long, and he liked it that way. Jill Lawson was a woman with deep roots, a woman who, until a couple of days ago, was engaged to be married.

"Now you know my reasons for not telling the deputies I was with you in the cottage. I didn't want to get involved in Trevor's murder."

OH, SHE UNDERSTOOD all right. He didn't want to get involved with the authorities—or with her. It was just a one-night stand.

So why didn't she believe him? Not his supposed nonchalance about their lovemaking last night or his refusal to become involved in Trevor's murder.

"If you didn't want to get involved, then what were you doing out on the island today, Mackenzie?"

He took a swallow of beer. "I was curious. And you can call me Mac."

Mac. "I saw the skull in the duffel bag, Mac," she reminded him.

He shrugged. "There's an old cemetery on the island. Probably early pioneers. That's not that unusual."

"And it interests you because…?"

He shrugged. "I was just curious what was behind that restricted fence. Weren't you?"

"I still am. I know Trevor and Arnie Evans have been in there working. I've seen the mud on their boots."

Mac nodded. "They were probably trying to get rid of the bodies before anyone found out. If there are any relatives of those pioneers still around, they could make a stink about the bodies being moved. Even shut down construction, possibly."

She stared at him, wishing she could find a flaw in his logic. He seemed to have all the answers.

She couldn't help being disappointed the skull hadn't meant more. And angry with him for making it sound as if their lovemaking had been…what? Great sex but a fluke?

"Where is the skull?" he asked.

"Still in the duffel, unless whoever jumped me took it."

He shook his head. "He didn't have it when he dived into the water."

"I wonder what he was after," she said, watching Mac, curious how he would explain this away.

"You."

"Me?"

"I imagine he followed you here."

She couldn't believe this. "Why?"

"Trevor owed a lot of people, people who might

think that because you were his fiancée, you were in on scamming them."

She hadn't thought of that. "I think the man was the same one who was in my apartment last night. He demanded my engagement ring and was upset when I told him I didn't have it." She noticed Mac's surprise. "He tore the silver bracelet that Trevor gave me from my wrist."

"Did he take any of your other jewelry?"

She shook her head. "You think it was someone who knew Trevor had given me the ring and the bracelet? The bracelet was just a trinket, not worth anything."

Mac took another swallow of beer. "The word around the area is that Trevor hadn't been paying his bills. It sounds like whoever took your bracelet was just trying to get even. That's why I think you should stop snooping around, stay some place other than your apartment until things blow over. At least until Trevor's killer is caught. And try to keep a low profile."

"I have a business to run."

"Hard to run dead."

She got to her feet, put the gun on the coffee table and turned to him again. "I took the bullets out before I came out of the bedroom."

"I know." He shrugged. "Otherwise, I would have taken the weapon away from you."

He was an impossible man. She went back into the bathroom. Her bikini was still wet, but she closed the door and put it on, anyway. It helped cool her anger. "Where's my wet suit?"

"Just take the shirt," he called through the closed door. "It's an old one."

She put the shirt back on. The cloth was worn and

soft and smelled a little like him. She'd get it back to him tomorrow.

When she came out, he was sitting where she'd left him, drinking his beer.

"Are you going to try to find out who killed Trevor?"

He shook his head. "I stay clear of ongoing murder investigations. It keeps me out of trouble."

She studied him for a long moment, feeling that electric excitement in the air between them. She didn't believe for a moment that if they made love again it would be anything but amazing. Maybe even more amazing than last night.

She ached for him to take her in his arms again, ached to feel his touch once more on her skin. But more than that, to feel that connection she'd felt between them. More than sex. Much more.

"About last night in the cottage—"

"Do me a favor," he said interrupting her. "Don't make me have to rescue you again. Tonight makes us even, okay?"

Even? She glared at him. "You're scared, aren't you."

He looked surprised.

"You're afraid of what would happen if we made love again." She couldn't believe the brazen words coming out of her mouth.

He couldn't seem to, either. He laughed and shook his head as he got up from his chair. She watched him go out onto the deck and pull her wet suit off the railing. He stayed there in the shadowy darkness, holding her wet suit out to her. "I think you better get going before I prove you wrong and disappoint us both. Let's just keep last night a memory, okay?"

She walked to him, snatched the wet suit from his fingers and crossed the deck to the opening in the railing. Once on the dock, she started the long walk to her van.

The dock felt warm under her bare feet as she left. A quiet darkness had settled over the marina. A light fog had moved in off the lake. The marina lights cast an eerie glow over the water.

She didn't look back at the houseboat until she reached the stand of pines where she'd left her van. Mackenzie Cooper was leaning against the boat railing, looking out into the darkness.

Just the sight of him made her ache. But Mackenzie Cooper had made it clear that last night was a mistake. One he didn't plan to repeat. Unfortunately it didn't make her want him any less.

What was it about last night and her that seemed to scare him? He didn't seem like a man who scared easily.

And she didn't believe for a moment that he wasn't looking for Trevor's killer. Which meant they'd be seeing each other again. Soon.

CHAPTER TEN

AFTER A SLEEPLESS night watching Jill's apartment, Mac returned to the houseboat, took a cold shower and was getting dressed when his cell phone rang. He hoped it was Shane, who, Mac worried, was hiding, trying to figure out how to turn twelve gold coins into cash.

"Hello?" His hope was dashed at the sound of Pierce's voice.

"Well?" Pierce said.

"Well, what? You didn't really expect me to find your…merchandise this soon, did you?" Mac snapped back.

The silence on the other end of the line made it clear that Pierce had.

"I checked with my ranch foreman," Pierce said, sounding put out. "Shane did work on the ranch. For a week. He quit. So did his buddy who was hired with him, some guy who called himself Buffalo Boy."

Buffalo Boy. "I assume he has a real name," Mac said.

"Marvin. Marvin Dodd. You realize how important it is that the contents of that box don't just start turning up, don't you?"

Mac groaned to himself. "I have another call coming in. I'll let you know as soon as I have something."

He clicked off. *What a pompous ass,* he thought, as he took the other call.

"Mackenzie? It's Charley Johnson." Charles was one of the few people on earth Mac let call him Mackenzie.

The tone of his cop friend's voice scared him. Had Shane been found?

"I just got a report on that ring you called me about," Charley said. "You're right. It was stolen. Are you sitting down?"

He wasn't.

"A seventeen-year-old girl by the name of Tara French was wearing that ring the night she disappeared from Bigfork seven years ago," Charley said. "The ring had belonged to her grandmother. It was made especially for her, so it's very distinctive—and valuable. Mackenzie, Tara French was one of eleven young women who've disappeared in that area over the past twenty years. Where the hell did you get this ring?"

Mac dropped into a chair, all the ramifications knocking the wind out of him. "I've got a human skull that might go with it. But I need this kept under wraps until we're sure. If I get the skull to you—"

Charley let out a curse. "We can't sit on this with a serial killer out there running loose and you with important evidence."

"If I'm right, the killer is dead, Charley," Mac said. "Just give me forty-eight hours. I'll get the skull to you this morning. How long do you think it will take for an ID?"

Silence. "It will probably take me that long to get dental records on the eleven victims. Damn, I hope you're right about the killer being dead."

When Mac hung up, he thought about Jill and how

she would take the news, if he was right about Trevor. Trevor had given her a ring that had belonged to a girl who'd been missing for seven years.

Mac uttered a vicious curse. To think that Jill had been engaged to a serial killer! Was it possible the other bodies were buried out there? Is that why Trevor had been "developing" Inspiration Island?

So what had he been doing out there? Reburying the bodies? Or moving them? But moving them where?

To the south end of the island, Mac thought with a start. To the swampy part where the mud was like quicksand.

The cell phone rang again, making him jump. "Hello?"

"I heard you were looking for a guy named Shane?" a young male voice asked.

Mac's pulse took off. "Yes, I am."

"You a cop?"

"No. A relative." Sometimes that was worse.

"He was living at Curtis Lakeview Apartments with a bunch of guys. Unit number seven. Does that help?"

"Thanks. I'll leave something for you at the Beach Bar. Just tell the bartender you're a friend of mine." He hung up. Curtis Lakeview Apartments. He felt as if the clock was ticking faster as he got into his pickup and drove north.

Curtis Lakeview Apartments had no view of the lake. Had no view at all. It was seven units stuck back in the pines, hastily thrown up and now quickly coming down.

The place was dead quiet. Either everyone was still asleep at this time of the morning, or some actually had jobs. Mac guessed that more than likely most of the units were empty. The building looked as if it could be condemned at any moment.

He wasn't expecting to find Shane here. By now Shane would have heard about Trevor Forester's murder. His nephew might not have the good sense to skip town, but he would be smart enough to change his address.

At least Mac hoped so. If Pierce was right about the collection being more valuable as a set than split up, then Trevor would have been trying to find a buyer. It made sense, given what he'd heard about Trevor Forester—that Trevor needed money and would even steal for it. Trevor must have been planning to skip town for some time now.

But now he was dead, and Mac feared Shane had the coins. It was how the kid had come to have the coins that worried him, since someone else was frantically looking for them. The shadowy figure on the videotape?

Mac groaned, wondering what plan Shane had to sell the coins. Shane wouldn't have the contacts or the patience to try to sell the coins as a set. He would try to dump the coins quickly, any way he could, and he'd leave a trail the other thief could follow. Shane was going to get himself killed, sure as hell.

The only hope Mac had of saving his nephew was to find him before he got rid of the coins.

Mac tried the door to the apartment. It was locked. He pulled out a credit card, inserted it between the door and jamb, and heard the click as the lock opened. Cautiously, he turned the knob. The door swung inward.

It was a studio apartment with only two pieces of furniture: a lawn chair and a card table.

It appeared his nephew had left in a hurry. There were stinky fast-food containers on the table, the chair was overturned and dirty clothing lay on the floor, along with a couple of magazines and newspapers and some junk mail.

Shane was definitely not getting his cleaning deposit back.

One small pale-green square of paper on the floor caught Mac's eye. He stooped to pick it up. It was a paycheck stub with Shane's name on it and Inspiration Island Enterprises. Made sense. Shane had worked for Trevor Forester on the island.

Mac pocketed the stub and checked his watch. He had a funeral to go to. Maybe he'd get lucky. Maybe Shane would show up at Trevor's funeral. It was something the kid was dumb enough to do.

DRESSED IN A plain black dress and a hat with a veil that had belonged to her mother, Jill slipped quietly into the back of the church at Trevor's funeral. She didn't want her presence to upset Heddy.

Alistair was right. Heddy had opened the service to the entire town. The church was packed. Jill didn't have to worry about being seen.

From behind the veil, she looked for the other Scarlett and Mackenzie Cooper. Jill wasn't sure how much of what he'd told her the previous night she could believe. One thing she was sure of: there was a lot more going on with him—and Trevor's murder.

Heddy had insinuated that the murder of her son was somehow related to the other Scarlett. Jill knew she wouldn't feel safe until Trevor's murderer was caught. Maybe Mac was right. Maybe these attacks on her had to do with Trevor's misdeeds. But she suspected it was more complicated than that. She had a feeling that Mackenzie Cooper knew what was going on, and that was why he'd tried to warn her off.

If the other Scarlett was the same woman Trevor had supposedly been going to marry and run away with, then the woman would be here at the funeral, if for no other reason than to spit on his grave—assuming she'd found out that Trevor had cashed in her plane ticket.

Or maybe the woman had really loved Trevor and was here sobbing her eyes out. Uh-huh. Or maybe she'd just been after the Forester money to start with.

In any case, there was no way Jill was going to find her here. Too many people. And too quiet. Jill's only hope was to recognize the woman's voice.

She spotted her father and Zoe in the crowd and dozens of other people she knew. But she didn't see Mac.

Jill half listened to the service, thinking about Trevor. He had only dated her to please his father—and for the money. She almost felt sorry for him. Almost. What bothered her most was her own culpability. She'd wanted to believe Trevor. She'd been so busy going to college, getting her business going, making it successful, that she hadn't had time for romance—but her heart must have yearned for it more than she'd known, a discovery she'd made that night in the lake cottage with Mackenzie Cooper. As she stood at the back of the church, she didn't see him, but that didn't mean he wasn't here.

Maybe he'd been telling the truth. Maybe he couldn't care less who killed Trevor. Just like he couldn't care less about her? Or ever making love with her again?

The service, thankfully, was short, since the day

was already hot even this early in the morning. She followed all the other cars out to the cemetery. By the time she reached the burial site, cars lined both sides of the narrow cemetery roads. She knew the cemetery well, because she came here weekly to put flowers on her mother's grave, so she parked the bakery delivery van well away from all the other cars and cut across to where the crowd was already twelve deep and others were coming in behind her.

She searched from behind her veil for the other Scarlett, a foolish endeavor since she had no idea what the woman looked like. She sensed someone moving through the crowd toward her and turned to see Arnie. He stood next to her.

"I wanted to apologize," he said quietly without looking at her. "That was really stupid what I did last night."

Yes, she thought, it was. "Let's just forget about it. Just like the night in the cottage," she whispered back.

He glanced at her as if surprised. Had he thought he'd blown it by kissing her? He had, of course, but she'd decided to keep it from him until she found out why he'd lied.

She felt a chill at the notion that the killer could be any of the people surrounding the grave—or standing next to her. Her gaze stopped on one man standing off by a tree a few yards away. Mackenzie Cooper. He'd been watching her, and he didn't look the least bit happy to see Arnie with her. That cheered her.

When her gaze met Mac's, her heart took off like a speedboat. She felt a small thrill and knew he'd felt it, too, as she watched him drag his gaze away first. He seemed to be looking for someone in the crowd.

She looked around, as well. When she couldn't help herself and glanced in his direction again, Mac was gone. But she felt some satisfaction in the fact that he'd attended the funeral. She was more certain than before that he was investigating Trevor's murder. What she didn't understand was why. Unless he felt bad that he hadn't been able to save Trevor.

The pastor finished speaking. Jill caught sight of Heddy through a break in the crowd. She was crying, hanging on to Alistair for support. It was a sight Jill would never forget, the two of them standing beside their only son's grave, both devastated.

With the service over, a murmur of voices moved like a wave through the crowd. One voice carried on the morning air. Jill jerked around as she tried to locate the woman she'd heard speaking behind her. She'd know that voice anywhere. The other Scarlett.

Jill could catch only snatches of the woman's voice. "Trevor…blame…awful."

Nor could she see the woman's face, only the woman's hat, as the voice moved away from the gravesite and along the row of parked cars.

Jill followed the hat, a floppy black disk of a hat with a red rose on the crown, and the strident voice.

"Heartless…cold…bitch."

Jill wondered who the woman was talking about. The black hat stopped beside one of the cars, then moved toward the other side of the cemetery. Jill spotted the red Saturn parked behind a stand of trees at the far side. The woman had the nerve to drive Jill's car to the funeral!

Jill tried to move through the dispersing crowd of

people and cars, but saw that it was going to be impossible to reach the woman before she drove off.

Determined not to let the other Scarlett get away, Jill cut back across the cemetery, hurrying for her van, knowing she'd never be able to catch the woman on foot.

As Jill started the engine of The Best Buns in Town van, the other Scarlett looked back, saw her and rushed to the Saturn. A moment later the Saturn roared toward one of the less-used exits away from the line of cars leaving the cemetery.

Jill raced after the other Scarlett, taking several of the service roads, all the time keeping the red Saturn in sight through the trees and gravestones.

She couldn't let the woman get away. Not this time, she thought, remembering two nights ago at Trevor's condo when the person driving the car had struck her in the head and taken off.

Jill was dying to know what the woman had been doing in Trevor's condo, what she'd been looking for in the bedroom and if she'd found it.

The red Saturn sped toward the exit, traveling at a right angle to Jill's van. Jill floored the van as she raced down the narrow cemetery road that with luck would connect with the road the other Scarlett was on—before the woman got there.

Jill reached the road, hit the brakes and skidded to a stop in the middle—blocking the exit with the van just seconds before the Saturn got there. Jill braced herself, half expecting the other Scarlett to broadside her.

The woman seemed to consider that option. But at the last minute, hit the brakes, bringing the Saturn to a dust-boiling stop in the middle of the road.

Jill leaped from the van and jerked the Saturn's door open before the other Scarlett had a chance to shift into reverse. Jill grabbed the car keys from the ignition, killing the engine.

"What are you doing?"

"This is my car!" Jill yelled. "Get out."

The woman had taken off her black hat, and Jill noted that the length of their hair was their only resemblance to one another. The woman's hair was a dingy brown and straight as string. Her nose was too big for her face. So was her mouth and her voice—

"Trevor gave me this car."

"He borrowed it from me," Jill snapped. "Check the registration and title."

"He *paid* for it," the woman shot back defiantly.

"He did not!" Jill wanted to drag the woman bodily from the car, but she restrained herself. "He didn't even pay for your airline ticket himself." The woman's surprised reaction confirmed what Jill suspected. "You're Rachel, aren't you. Were you looking for your ticket night before last in his bedroom? I suppose by now you know that he cashed it in."

Once again, the woman's expression confirmed it. "He did it because of you! He told me that you said you'd rather see him dead than with me."

"I didn't even know you existed," Jill said. "Haven't you figured out by now that Trevor lied to us both?"

"None of that matters," Rachel said, looking around nervously as if afraid someone might be listening. But the other mourners were too far away to hear. "Please, just leave me alone. If someone sees us together—"

"Who would care if they saw us together?" Jill asked, remembering that Heddy said she'd seen Scarlett O'Hara get off a boat at the dock a little after nine-thirty—just before Rachel had opened the cottage door. Rachel must have known about Trevor's meeting with Mac.

"That scene at the cottage was just a ruse to make it look as if you *thought* I was in there with Trevor, when all the time you knew better, didn't you?" Jill said in surprise. "You knew Trevor was dead."

"Stop asking questions about Trevor's murder, or you'll wish you had," Rachel spat.

The woman's words startled Jill. "I couldn't care less about you or who killed Trevor. I just want my car—and you to tell the sheriff you saw me in the cottage that night. Unless there's a reason you don't want to come forward?" The same reason she was far back in the crowd at the funeral hiding under a large black hat. Unless…she not only knew that Trevor was dead that night, she knew who did it—because she herself had put those two slugs in his heart.

The woman glanced around again. "Is that all you want? You can have the car. As for the sheriff—" she dug in her purse on the seat beside her and pulled out her cell phone "—I'll tell them right now. Then I want you to leave me alone. Trevor told me all about you," she said as she dialed 911. "He said you were a cold fish in bed and dangerous. I want nothing to do with you."

A cold fish, indeed. Jill felt her blood boil. It was all she could do not to drag the woman bodily from her car.

She looked down at the key ring in her hand. It was the one she'd given Trevor with her car key and her apartment key on it. Now there was only one key. So who had the old key to her apartment? The man in the black ski mask who'd gotten in the night before last?

"You're the one who sent that man over to take back the gifts Trevor had given me, aren't you."

"I don't know what you're talking about," Rachel said as she waited for the line to ring.

The emergency number should have answered by now, Jill thought. She started to reach for the phone when the woman said into the phone that she needed help. Her car was being hijacked by a crazy woman.

"Here, he wants to speak with you, Ice Princess," the other Scarlett said, holding out the cell phone.

Jill took it and said, "Hello, this is Jill Lawson and—"

In that instant Rachel gave Jill a shove away from the car and slammed the door, locking it. The engine roared to life a moment later, then the tires threw up gravel as the car lurched backward.

Jill jumped clear as Rachel tore up the road in reverse for a few dozen yards to a side road, turned and took off in a cloud of dust.

The woman apparently had a spare key, and she must have taken it from her purse when she'd gotten out the cell phone.

"She's stealing my car!" Jill yelled into the phone before realizing there was no one on the other end of the line. The other Scarlett hadn't called 911.

Jill scrambled to the van, backed it up and turned down the road, hoping to catch up with the Saturn and Rachel. But by the time she reached the cemetery exit, the woman was gone.

Braking hard, Jill slammed her fist down on the

steering wheel, then picked up Rachel's cell phone and dialed 911.

"We've already got an all points bulletin out for the car and driver," Deputy Duncan told her after she explained what had happened. "Give me her cell-phone number."

She did and Duncan said, "That's Trevor's cell phone."

"He always had it with him," Jill told the deputy. "How did she get it?"

"Well, she doesn't have it anymore," he said quietly. "You do."

Jill hung up, angry and frustrated. Who knew how long it would take the sheriff's department to find the Saturn and the other woman? And now she had Trevor's cell phone and only her word that she'd taken if from the other Scarlett.

She looked up to see Mackenzie Cooper's pickup in the line of funeral cars leaving the cemetery. Like the rest of Bigfork, he'd witnessed her confrontation with the other Scarlett from a distance—just too great a distance to prove anything.

As she shifted the van into gear, she watched his pickup head down the lake road and wondered again why he had come to the funeral of a man he'd never met.

In his rearview mirror, Mac saw The Best Buns in Town van tailing him. He took a quick right, a left, then another right. When he looked back again, the van was still there. He couldn't outrun her in the pickup, not with the camper on the back.

He cursed and pulled over to the curb, waiting until

she pulled in behind him before getting out and walking back to the van.

She rolled down her window.

"What the hell do you think you're doing?" he asked.

"Following you." She had the same determined set to her jaw that he'd seen last night. No gun, though, which was a plus. "You lied."

He stared at her. "What?"

"You felt something the other night."

"Is that what this is about?" Her look dared him to lie again. "All right, I felt something. Happy?"

"Something amazing. Something more than great sex."

He smiled in spite of himself. "Something amazing. Something more than great sex. Okay? Now that we have that settled, don't follow me." He turned to walk away.

"I know where you can find Marvin Dodd," she said. "You are looking for him, right?" she said when he was standing at her driver's-side window again.

That was the trouble with a small town like Bigfork. But he knew his trouble ran much deeper. "Just because it felt like more than great sex the other night—"

"This has nothing to do with that," she said.

He gave her a give-me-a-break look.

"Do you want to find Marvin or not?"

He waited for her to ask him why he was looking for Marvin, but she didn't. "What's the catch?"

"No catch. Marvin worked for Trevor on the island. That's why you're looking for him. You're trying to find Trevor's murderer."

It was news to him that Marvin had also worked for Trevor, but he shouldn't have been surprised. She looked so pleased with herself he hated to bust her bubble.

"Wrong. I'm looking for my nephew."

"Whatever," she said. "I guess I'll just have to find Trevor's killer on my own." Her brown eyes flashed, reminding him of another fire he'd seen burning in all that amber when he'd kissed her last night on his houseboat.

"Have a death wish, do you?"

"No, just the opposite. I guess because I was Trevor's fiancée—well one of them, anyway—I'm involved. Up to my neck, and I think you are, too. If you won't tell me what's going on, I'll just follow you and find out for myself. And I should warn you, I've had a really bad day so far."

He cursed under his breath and turned on his heel. "Get in the truck," he said over his shoulder.

She scrambled from the van, catching up with him at the pickup.

He didn't look at her as she climbed into the passenger side. Couldn't. He was too angry with her. "I'm trying to protect you."

"Well, stop," she said, looking out the windshield, waiting for him to start the engine.

What the hell was he going to do with her? "You are an incredibly stubborn woman."

"Thank you."

"That wasn't a compliment."

She smiled and looked over at him. "Why is it so hard for you to be honest with me?"

"You have heard of privileged information, haven't you? I'm on a case." He put the truck into gear.

"Trevor's dead," she said.

"It's another case." He could feel her gaze on him.

"Turn right up here and head down the lake toward Polson," she ordered.

"Why were you chasing that woman in the red Saturn?" he asked as he pressed the accelerator.

"That woman was the other Scarlett and she was driving *my* car!"

"Seems she's still driving your car."

She shot him a warning look. "You could have helped me."

"I didn't realize you needed help. Did you get her name?"

"No, I only know her first name—Rachel. She got away before I could get anything but mad," Jill said. "She's driving *my* car and she says Trevor gave it to her."

"He probably did." Mac watched her tug at her lower lip with her teeth. "I take it the two of you had words?" He was surprised to see tears in her eyes.

"She told me I was a cold fish, and that's why Trevor—"

"Bull," Mac snapped. "Trevor was a fool and obviously not much of a lover." He handed her his handkerchief. "Trevor was out of his league with a woman like you."

Jill looked over at him and smiled through her tears. "You can be pretty nice when you want to be."

He focused his attention on his driving, warning himself that being too nice to Jill was trouble. Too easily he could find her in his arms—and they both knew where that would lead.

"Turn up here on the right," she said, all business again. "Marvin lives in a trailer out on Finley Point."

She smiled. "I grew up in Bigfork. News travels fast. Especially if you know who to ask."

"You've been asking questions about me?" He wasn't happy to hear this. "Who told you I was looking for Marvin?"

She smiled. "You're actually looking for a nineteen-year-old named Shane Ramsey. Marvin Dodd used to be his roommate. Well?"

"Nice work. You really are determined to get yourself killed, aren't you."

"I thought your investigation had nothing to do with Trevor's death."

"Did you ever think that just being around me might be dangerous?" he asked, shooting her a look.

Her smile broadened. "After the other night in the cottage, I know just how dangerous you can be."

He growled under his breath and tried to change the subject. "So you've lived here your whole life?"

"You sound aghast at the thought. I'm content here. It's a great place to live."

"I don't doubt it." He remembered the last time he was content somewhere.

"I'm sure you've heard gossip about me around town," she said. "How bad is it? What's everyone saying? What a fool I was to think Trevor wanted to marry me?"

"Everything I heard about you was glowing," he said. "True, people wondered what you saw in Trevor… What *did* you see in him?"

She stared out at the passing green blur of pines for a long moment, so long he didn't think she was going to answer. "Trevor could be quite charming. I think he was an actor—he would play whatever role he thought you wanted." She shrugged. "And he paid attention to the small things." She looked away.

"Like what?" he asked, needing to know what she'd seen in the man. Now more than ever.

"I had this horrible experience when I was sixteen," she said. "I never hitchhiked, but this one night I was at a party and my ride's car broke down and I was frantic to get home on time, so I did something really stupid. I took off by myself, walking down the lake road. It was really late, one of those dark cloudy nights, and this car stopped for me."

Mac felt his chest constrict. Dear God.

"I never saw his face. It was just a voice in the darkness of the car. He asked if I needed a ride. I didn't even pay any attention to the car. It was just large and black and I started to get in. Then, I don't know why, I changed my mind. I guess somehow I…knew." She looked out her side window, away from him. He saw her chin quiver, and it was all he could do not to reach for her. "The driver grabbed my wrist, but I was wearing this bracelet my aunt had given me for my birthday. The bracelet saved me. It came off and I was able to pull free and run. I ran into the trees. He got out of the car and started to follow me, but must have changed his mind. I heard the car leave. I'd never been so scared in my life."

Mac reached over and took the hand resting on her thigh. It was cold as ice. She was shaking. But so was he. "You must have been terrified." She nodded. "And you told Trevor about this?" He took his hand back to steer the pickup down the narrow, twisting road to Finley Point. In places, as it wound through cherry orchards and pines, the road was like a tunnel.

"The day after I told Trevor, he brought me a present," she said. "A silver charm bracelet with my name on it like the one I'd lost. Trevor said the bracelet had brought me luck once before—and would again." She looked over at Mac, tears in her eyes. "That's the kind of thing Trevor did." She rubbed her bare wrist.

Mac felt as if he'd been kicked in the chest as he thought about the charm bracelet Trevor had given her. The same one the burglar had taken the other night. A bracelet like the one she'd lost when she was sixteen? Or the exact same bracelet? If Mac was right about Trevor Forester...

He pulled over to the side of the road. He could see the lake stretching clear blue to a horizon, broken only by a single white sail in the distance. "There's something I have to tell you."

He'd been worried before, but now he was terrified for her. He told himself that Trevor was dead. Jill was safe. But her apartment had been burglarized. Worse, the burglar had attacked her, taken the bracelet—and asked about the engagement ring.

Mac couldn't pretend it had been someone Trevor owed money to. Not anymore. Nor could he keep the truth from Jill anymore.

"My nephew was involved in a robbery—with Trevor Forester," Mac said. "They stole some coins. Trevor's now dead and the coins are missing. But there's more." He looked into her eyes. Deep and brown. The flecks of gold shimmering in the summer sunlight.

"I picked up your engagement ring that night in the cottage, along with your panties. The ring appeared to have been old and the inscription filed down. I called a friend of mine who's a cop in Kalispell. I had a feeling that the job Trevor pulled off with my nephew probably wasn't his first."

"You aren't telling me that the engagement ring Trevor gave me was stolen?"

"Jill, the ring belonged to a teenaged girl who disappeared from Bigfork seven years ago," Mac said. "She was never found."

CHAPTER ELEVEN

JILL FELT THE blood drain from her head. "No." She remembered the stories in the papers over the years. Teenaged girls who'd come to the area to work for the summer just disappearing without a trace.

"I sent the skull I found on the island to Kalispell this morning," Mac said, his voice sounding far away. "I know I told you it was probably an old gravesite, but I'm afraid that skull hasn't been in the ground very long."

Jill shook her head, feeling the sting of tears in her eyes. "You think Trevor…"

"I think whoever killed those girls kept a piece of their jewelry as a souvenir," Mac said softly. "I also think there is a good possibility that the killer buried the girls on the island."

A chill quaked through her as she recalled the skull she'd seen in Mac's duffel bag. "Tell me Trevor couldn't do something so horrible." But she thought of how he'd lied and stolen and cheated. How he'd planned to leave the country.

"He gave you the ring," Mac said.

Yes, he'd given her the ring. The ring he'd said was an old family heirloom. A lie. But could it really have been Trevor Forester in the car that stopped for her on the lake road that night fourteen years ago? She'd been sixteen. Trevor would have been twenty. Old-sounding to a sixteen-year-old.

She closed her eyes, remembering the headlights as the car came up the road and stopped. She squeezed her eyes shut more tightly, trying to remember, to see into the darkness inside the car. A large, dark car. His father's car? The whir of the electric window on the passenger side coming down. A voice from the blackness inside as she leaned down and took hold of the door handle, thinking only about getting home on time.

Her eyes flew open, the taste of fear in her mouth, the sound of her heart hammering in her ears as he grabbed her wrist, and then her pulling free, running, running for her life.

She warned herself not to cry. The last thing Mac needed was a bawling woman on his hands. Actually, he didn't seem to need any woman at all, especially her.

He handed her a tissue from the glove box.

She didn't cry. She balled up the tissue in her hand. She wasn't a sixteen-year-old girl anymore. No, she was a strong, independent woman. And the past few days had made her stronger, more resilient, definitely more outspoken—almost brazen and, surprisingly, less afraid of her feelings. "It could have been him."

"I know. That's what scares me." His words sent a shaft of heat through her.

She looked at him and their eyes locked.

After Trevor, she knew she should have been gun-shy when it came to men. But Mackenzie Cooper was a different breed of male. She was intimately aware of that, she thought as she gazed into the deep blue of his eyes. He hadn't forgotten the other night in the cottage any more than she had.

He reached for her, cupped the nape of her neck just as he'd done last night on the boat and pulled her toward him as if he needed to feel her in his arms as badly as she needed to be there. "This is just lust," he whispered against her hair.

"Mmm-hmm."

"We'd both regret it if we make love again."

"Mmm."

He kissed her hair, her temple, her cheek, angling toward her mouth. Her breath caught in her throat as his lips hovered over hers. In his eyes, she saw the fear. Did he really believe they would be disappointed, regretful? She didn't think so.

His mouth lowered slowly, painfully to hers. He brushed a kiss over her lips. She sighed and leaned into him. His body was warm and hard. He groaned against her mouth. Her lips parted and his mouth met hers fully. The kiss deepened. The tip of his tongue slid slowly across her upper lip, and she thought she would die with wanting him.

"Oh, Jill," he said with a sigh as he pulled back to look at her, cupping her face in his hands.

What was he so afraid of?

His gaze moved over her face like a caress, then he pulled away, groaning. As he leaned back in his seat, he ran a hand over his face, then gripped the steering wheel with both hands as he looked out the windshield—not at her.

Disappointment made her eyes well up with tears. She felt weak, the ache in her crying out for him. She wanted to touch his broad shoulders, feel the warmth of his shirt. To lean her face into his chest and breathe in the clean, masculine scent of him.

"I'm sorry." He cleared his throat. "Where did Trevor say he got the engagement ring?"

She sat back, her heart pounding, the ache inside making her want desperately to cry. She took a breath. Let it out.

He looked at her. His look was a plea. *Just tell me about the ring.*

She took another breath and said, "Trevor told me the ring belonged to his favorite great-aunt, but I remember Heddy's surprise when she first saw the ring." Jill's voice didn't betray the unbearable need inside her. "I thought it was because Heddy didn't think he should have given me such a valuable family heirloom."

"He obviously lied about where he'd gotten the ring," Mac said, "and his mother covered for him."

"Yes, that would be like Heddy." Jill couldn't bear to look at Mac. She glanced out at the lake and remembered something. "The day he found out the island was for sale, Trevor was beside himself. We were at his parents' house and he was practically begging his father to buy the island for him. I remember him saying, 'If I don't develop it, someone else will.'" She shivered. "Alistair said he'd never seen his son so excited or anxious. At the time we all thought Trevor wanted to prove himself to his father, and Inspiration Island was going to be the means." She looked over at Mac now. "But Trevor's had the island for months. I would think if his purpose was to move the bodies, he would have done it by now."

"I suspect he'd forgotten where all the bodies were buried. Plus, animals have gotten into the remains. I suspect he was moving the bodies to the south end of the island, thinking he could hide them behind the restricted area. Or maybe that was where he'd buried them to start with and was just reburying them. I think the bodies were floating up in the mud. The skull I found was sticking up out of some weeds."

She thought she might throw up. "We have to tell the sheriff."

"I asked my cop friend for forty-eight hours," Mac said. "It will take that long to try to get an ID on the skull through dental records. Give me the same amount of time. Let me find my nephew. We still don't know who killed Trevor. Or why. And my client's coins are still missing. I'm afraid any one of those factors could get Shane killed if the authorities became involved."

"You can't tell me who your client is?"

"Sorry. He's a victim of Trevor Forester, too. Just like us, it seems," Mac said, meeting her gaze. "I still don't know why Trevor sent me a Rhett Butler costume and told me to meet him in the lake cottage. That concerns me."

"Yes." She had to agree. "I also wish I knew what Trevor had planned for *me* the night of the party." When she thought of what the man might have been capable of…

"Can you hold off going to the sheriff for forty-eight hours?" Mac asked.

"Maybe we can make a deal."

He groaned.

"I help you find your nephew and you help me find the other Scarlett. What do you say?" He started to argue, but she stopped him. "Please, don't try to warn me about the dangers, okay?" She gently touched her bruised forehead, remembering the man in the black ski mask.

Mac sighed, then nodded with obvious reluctance.

She gave him a smile, as much as it hurt. "Marvin lives just up the road."

"Wait here," Mac said as he pulled up in front of the blue-and-white striped trailer Marvin rented. Jill didn't argue about staying in the pickup as he climbed out.

He wore jeans, a pale-blue cotton shirt and a dark suede jacket, his idea of funeral attire. Under his jacket, the weapon in his shoulder holster fit snuggly against his ribs, not that he expected he would have to use it. At least he hoped not.

He could feel Jill watching him as he knocked on the side of the trailer and then tried the door.

Unlocked. Almost like an invitation. He opened the door and stepped in, drawing the weapon from the shoulder holster. The place looked and smelled like a summer-kid rental. It was cluttered with clothes, the counters covered in beer bottles and empty fast-food boxes, and the air smelled of stale beer and pepperoni pizza.

He found Marvin passed out in a back bedroom of the trailer. He appeared to be the only one home this late morning. Either he didn't have to go to work yet or he didn't have a job. Likely the latter. Mac called his name. Loudly.

Marvin squinted up from the crumpled covers of the twin bed stuffed in a corner of the otherwise packed-with-junk bedroom.

"Who the hell are you?" Marvin looked about fifteen, but according to the driver's license Mac took from the wallet lying on the bedside table, the kid was nineteen—the same age as Shane. His greasy brown hair hung in strings about his acne-covered face, and he looked as if he had the hangover from hell, but there was no doubt he was the kid who'd been driving the getaway van the night of the coin theft at Pierce's.

Mac grimaced just looking at him. "Get up."

"If this is about the rent, you gotta talk to my roommate," the kid said, and covered his head with the blanket.

"It's about the robbery. The one you pulled off with Trevor Forester." Mac opened the back door, needing a little fresh air.

Marvin's head came out from under the covers. "I don't know what you're talking out."

"Sure you do. Get dressed." He turned and saw Jill standing in the trailer's kitchen. He started down the hall toward her, angry. Damn, why couldn't she just run her bakery and let him do his job?

"What do you think you're—" The rest of the words were cut off by the look on her face. She was holding a paper bag in one hand and a bakery roll in the other, her eyes large, her face white as snow.

She held the roll out to him.

He stared down at the perfect impression of a double-eagle, twenty-dollar gold piece in the baked dough. "Where did you find this?"

She pointed to the trash.

That was when he noticed the bag in her hand and the name on it: The Best Buns In Town.

Just then he heard Marvin go out the back door of the trailer.

Mac swore and went after him. He caught the punk kid a few yards from the trailer and took him down with a football tackle that knocked the wind out of them both.

He jerked Marvin to his feet and dragged him back toward the trailer. "Are you a cop or something?" the skinny kid whined.

Mac pushed Marvin in through the front door of the trailer and pointed to the kitchen table. "Sit."

He looked at Jill. She was right. She was up to her neck in this. He took the roll from her and showed Marvin the impression of a coin that had been baked in the dough. "Where are the coins?"

"I swear I don't know." He was dressed in thong sandals, basketball shorts and a once-white T-shirt that hung on his scrawny frame.

"I know you were driving the van the night of the robbery," Mac said to Marvin. "It's all on videotape."

"Mr. Forester, Trevor, he said he needed some help. This guy owed him money and wouldn't pay, so we helped him. But I got the impression it had something to do with a woman."

Didn't it always? Mac shoved the roll with the coin impression in front of the kid's face. "The coins?"

Marvin swallowed, eyes wide. "My roommate is the one who had them, and he's gone."

"Who's your roommate?"

"Just some guy I worked with. He called himself Spider. That's all I know."

Mac heard Jill gasp. He shot her a look. Damn, it appeared she knew this Spider. "How exactly did your roommate end up with the coins?"

"I don't know. Really. He gave me one of the rolls, all right. The coin was baked inside it. It was my payment for the job."

This Spider had paid Marvin with one of the coins. "Tell me you still have the coin."

Marvin seemed to hesitate, but only for a second. He hurried to a closet and dug around in the back, pulled out an old boot and upended it. A gold coin fell out and clinked on the worn linoleum floor.

Mac picked it up. It still had dough on it. "Did Spider kill Trevor for these?"

"I don't know anything about that, I swear. I didn't ask him. I wanted nothing to do with it. I just worked for Mr. Forester, okay?"

"And felony burglary was part of the job?"

"He offered me five hundred bucks to drive a van one night. It was a hell of a lot better than digging up bones on the island."

Mac shot Jill a look. Her skin had paled even more. "Who was the other guy involved in the burglary?"

"Mr. Forester and Spider. That's all."

"You didn't see anyone else in the house?" Mac asked, remembering the shadow he'd seen on the video.

"I just drove the van, man."

That meant the fourth man was either already inside the house or had met them after they got out of the van. That man must have known about the surveillance cameras or just lucked out and stayed out of the picture. Except for his shadow.

"One more question. Who is Buffalo Boy?"

Marvin reddened. "It's just this name I picked up."

Mac nodded. "And you met Spider in Whitefish, right?"

Buffalo Boy nodded.

"You need to clean this place up, Marvin."

"No, man, somebody trashed it yesterday," the kid said. "At least they didn't take my stereo or anything."

"Let me guess—Spider hadn't dropped off your share yet?" Mac asked, holding up the half roll.

Marvin paled. "You think they were looking for the coins?"

Mac felt protective, probably because Marvin reminded him of Shane. "You might consider lying low for a while."

Taking the roll and the coin, he and Jill returned to the pickup. Some of the color had come back into her face. "Any idea how that coin ended up inside the baked roll?" he asked her after they were in the truck and pulling away.

"I'm afraid so," she said.

"And Spider? You know him?"

"I know just the person to ask about him," Jill said, sounding awful. "My baking assistant, Zoe."

JILL COULDN'T BELIEVE IT. But then again, she could. Zoe was head over heels for this Spider guy. She was young and had an excuse for being naive and falling for a man's line.

But Jill was almost thirty, and look how she'd been conned by Trevor, a man who was a liar, a thief and maybe even a killer.

"The coins were baked into the rolls," she said, and realized Mac had figured that much out on his own.

Jill thought back to the morning of the party. Zoe had been excited because her boyfriend was going to stop by the bakery. Jill's father had called, saying he wouldn't be by because he had the flu, doubted he'd be going to the party, either, sorry. She'd left Zoe with the unbaked rolls while she'd run to the drugstore to get her father a few things.

"I let Zoe finish up the rolls the morning of the party. I should have known something was up, but she's been so anxious to learn and do things on her own... And her boyfriend was stopping by..."

"Spider, right?"

Jill nodded.

"The morning of the party?" Mac said, sounding surprised. "That means Spider had the coins *before* Trevor was killed. Where do we find this baking assistant of yours?"

"Summer school. Algebra II. Head back toward Bigfork."

"Let's hope they still have the coins," Mac said.

Jill was worried about Zoe. She'd trusted the girl. And now all she could think about was Zoe's reaction when she heard about Trevor's murder. How deep was the girl in all this?

As THE SMALL summer-school class let out, the students and teacher left quickly. Jill stepped into the classroom and watched Zoe finish an algebra problem, then fold several papers and stuff them into her algebra book before she rose to her feet. Her hair was blue today like everything she wore, including her fingernail polish.

When she saw Jill, Zoe froze, fear in her eyes. She clutched her algebra book to her chest and looked from Jill to Mac and back again.

"We need to talk to you," Jill said. "This is Mackenzie Cooper. He's a private investigator looking for the coins you hid in the rolls you baked the morning of the party."

Zoe's face crumpled as she dropped back into the seat at her desk. Mac closed the classroom door.

"I had to help Spider!" Zoe cried. "He would have killed him if he found out."

"Who would have killed him?" Mac asked.

"Trevor," the girl said, close to tears.

"Is this Spider?" Mac asked as he walked over to her, opened his wallet and showed her a photo of a young man with blond hair, blue eyes and an angular face.

"Yes, that's him." Zoe looked up in confusion.

"His name is Shane Ramsey," Mac said. "He's my nephew and I have to find him. His life is in danger because of the coins, the ones you put into the rolls."

"I don't know where he is," she wailed. "He swears he didn't know Trevor was going to rob anyone that night."

"You'd think he'd get suspicious when Trevor told him to put on the ski mask," Mac said.

"I know it looks bad..." Zoe's eyes teared up.

Jill shot Mac a pleading look.

"He was afraid of Trevor," the girl said. "He didn't say it, but I knew. Trevor had hired him to do some work on the island."

"Do you know what work precisely?" Mac asked.

Zoe shook her head, then frowned. "One night though, when he picked me up, he said he'd been digging in muck all day and that he was going to quit, but the next time I saw him, he said Trevor wasn't going to let him quit. I got the impression that maybe Trevor had threatened him, you know?"

Digging in muck. "Yeah, I can see where Trevor might have changed Spider's mind." Was that how

Shane had gotten involved in the robbery? Had Trevor forced him? Or had Shane gone along willingly?

"Where are the coins now?"

Zoe shook her head. "I don't know. Honestly."

"How is it Spider ended up with them?" Mac persisted.

Zoe hesitated. "Trevor changed his mind. Said it was a big mistake taking the coins and that Spider had to return them. Trevor was acting all weird—like the guy they stole the coins from was going to kill him. There was no way Spider was going back there with those coins."

Mac groaned. "So my nephew decided to sell the coins, instead?"

"No," Zoe said indignantly. "He had to come up with some way to return them without actually going there, you know?"

Jill nodded. "So he hid the coins in the dough, then you baked them."

"Spider called, left a message that the rolls were on their way and to look inside them," Zoe said.

"Not a bad idea. When were they delivered?" Mac asked.

"The day of the party."

Jill shot a look at Mac. The coins had been returned? Then why was Mac still looking for them?

"How many did Shane return?" he asked.

Zoe smiled. "You know, I kinda like the name Shane."

"How many coins did he return?" Jill prodded her.

The girl blinked. "Oh, we returned all but two. Shane gave one to…someone because he thought that was only fair that he be paid—" Marvin, Jill surmised

"—and he kept one. So I guess we sent ten rolls in the delivery."

"Tell me you didn't send the rolls in one of The Best Buns in Town bags," Jill said, almost adding, *like you did the one for Marvin*.

"Of course not," Zoe said. "We used a plain white bag. We didn't want him knowing where the rolls came from."

Thank goodness for that. Jill looked at Mac. "Where were these rolls delivered?" She figured to the home of the man Mac was working for.

"To Inspiration Island," Zoe said, making them both stare at her. Zoe nodded. "When Shane called back a second time to see if the guy got the first message, he said to deliver them to the island and leave them at some cove."

"Shane took them out by boat?"

Zoe shook her head. "He hired some kids to take them out. You know, just in case it was a trap."

Mac groaned. "How do you know the kids actually took the rolls to the island like they were told to?"

"Shane called him back the next morning. He got the rolls."

"But?" Jill said, hearing the *but* in Zoe's voice.

"But he wants the rest," she said, and sighed.

"The coins are part of a twelve-piece set," Mac said. "I imagine the owner wants all twelve back. Shane never told you the man's name?"

She shook her head. "Shane's in trouble, isn't he."

"That's putting it mildly," Mac said. "There's a killer out there who seems willing to do anything to get these coins. You have to tell me where I can find Shane."

"I don't know, honest. He can't stay in one place. So he calls me at night from a pay phone."

"When he calls, I want you to talk him into calling me." Mac handed her his card. "If you care anything about him—"

"I love him." Zoe began to cry in earnest. "Please help him."

Jill put her arm around Zoe and looked beseechingly at Mac, who groaned.

CHAPTER TWELVE

AFTER JILL ASSURED a teary-eyed Zoe that she wasn't going to fire her, Zoe promised to go home and stay there.

"What do we do now?" Jill asked Mac once they were back in his pickup.

"I wait to hear from Shane." And try to keep his distance from Jill. Her baking assistant had been a real surprise. He couldn't see anyone as straitlaced as Jill hiring a girl who looked like Zoe. And yet Jill had. He liked this woman more all the time—which wasn't the plan.

He glanced over at her. There were so many layers to this woman he knew he'd never see them all in a lifetime.

"While we wait, we find Rachel and complete our deal," he said. The sooner Jill went back to baking the better.

"And how do you propose we do that?"

"I'm a trained professional, remember? We consider where Trevor could have met her. I take it he spent a lot of time on the island, right? She probably doesn't live in his condo complex." Jill nodded. "So what does that leave?"

"Meals."

He smiled. "Oh, you're good." He had a pretty complete picture of Trevor Forester from everything he'd learned. "I doubt he spent much time in the kitchen cooking for himself, right?" Or much time alone. Nor did he probably have much trouble picking up women.

"Trevor? He couldn't boil water. And I didn't see much of him so..."

"Where did he eat?"

She thought about that for a moment. "I know of a couple of places."

The first one, a sandwich shop along the highway south of Bigfork, was a bust. No Rachel worked there or hung out there. They tried several fast-food places near Trevor's condo and finally stopped at a burger joint along the lake that also served alcohol.

"I don't know about you, but I'm hungry," Mac said, grinning as he pointed to one of the Employee of the Month photos on the wall.

"That's her!" Jill whispered. Rachel Wells, the name under the photo read. January's Employee of the Month. "I'm starved!"

Mac led them to a booth by the window so they could catch the last of the sunset—and keep an eye out for Rachel. He sat across from Jill and flipped open the plastic-covered menu, trying to concentrate on food rather than the woman across from him. "How does a cheeseburger deluxe sound to you?"

"Wonderful," she said, and seemed to relax.

But Rachel Wells, it appeared, wasn't working today. At least they didn't see her.

They talked about lakes and what they loved about them and how they couldn't imagine living away from water, then laughed that they had that in common, both pretty convinced they only had one thing in common and that was the night they'd shared in the cottage.

But Mac was learning just how much they shared. It made what happened between them the night in the cottage make more sense. He also noted that Jill was beautiful when she laughed. Her whole face lit up, her brown eyes dancing.

When the burgers arrived, Jill dug right in.

They had that in common, too, it seemed, he thought. They loved to eat. They ate in a comfortable, contented silence, appreciating their burgers and fries and each other. He felt as if he'd known this woman always. The closeness was almost painful for him.

When he'd finished eating, he pushed back his plate, sighed and looked at her. "That's the nicest meal I've had with a woman since…I can't remember when," he said as he watched her dunk the last of her fries in ketchup and take a bite.

She smiled and licked her lips. "What made it so nice? The fries? The burger?"

"You," he said truthfully.

She raised a brow. "Honesty becomes you. I feel comfortable with you, too. Maybe it's because of the other night in the cottage or maybe we would have felt this way, anyway."

"We'll never know," he said, and dug out his wallet to pay the check. What he did know was that they wouldn't be together now if it hadn't been for what happened in the cottage. He went out of his way to avoid attachments. He would have avoided Jill Lawson like the plague.

How could Trevor Forester not have seen what a kind, loving woman Jill was? Maybe Trevor wasn't looking for that kind of woman any more than he himself was, Mac thought.

She was watching him with her big doe eyes, studying him as if she could read his mind and found it amusing that he was fighting this spark—hell, forest fire—between them. How could she not see how hard he was struggling to keep his distance from her?

"It wouldn't work, you and me," he said, not sure who he was trying to convince. "I go wherever the wind blows me. You—"

"I own a bakery, an apartment, a building," she said, her gaze meeting his and holding it. "Definitely not compatible."

He knew she was making fun of him. And he couldn't blame her. What a fool he was, trying to convince her that their problem was location. Or that the air between them wasn't charged with current, or that he didn't want to take her in his arms and kiss her every time he looked at her, or that what they'd shared the other night wasn't incredible.

All powerful stuff. All wrong at this point in their lives. At any point in his. But damned if he didn't want to see where this chemistry took them—just as she did. Except…he knew exactly where it would take them. And he couldn't go there.

Jill had been hurt enough by Trevor Forester. Mac didn't want to cause her more pain. He knew that she'd be far more hurt if they became lovers again before he left. And he *would* leave.

The young blond waitress with the ponytail and bright red lipstick brought their bill. "Excuse me," Mac said. "I was hoping Rachel was working today. I promised a friend I'd tell her hello."

"Rachel?" The girl looked toward the kitchen and the cook. She lowered her voice. "I wouldn't mention Rachel if I were you. She hasn't shown up for work. Bud gave her the morning off for the funeral—Trevor Forester's funeral, you know. But she was supposed to work this afternoon."

Obviously Rachel hadn't been planning to give two weeks' notice before running off with Trevor. Or maybe she'd never planned to go because she'd planned to kill Trevor, instead.

"Are you a good friend of hers?" Jill asked.

The waitress made a so-so motion with her hand. "Rachel's all right. Not exactly friendly to other women, if you know what I mean. Prefers men."

Men? Plural? "I thought she and Trevor Forester were pretty serious," Jill said.

The waitress shrugged. "I never thought Trevor was serious about her. And it wasn't like Rachel didn't keep her options open—and so did Trevor." She bent down a little and whispered, "He asked me out just last week."

Jill found R. Wells in the phone directory in the telephone booth outside the burger joint and read off the address to Mac. It was dark now. Still no call from Shane, and Mac was getting more worried all the time. He didn't think going over to Rachel's house was a good idea, but he knew Jill would go alone if they didn't.

"Why don't you call the sheriff's department and let them handle this?" he suggested.

"Come on, it doesn't appear they've made any effort to find her. I don't think they even believe she exists."

Mac couldn't argue that.

"I also don't want her to get away again," Jill said.

"Arnie has a cousin who works next door to the sheriff's department. Arnie has known too much not to have been getting inside information. And if Trevor knew Rachel, then so did Arnie. Arnie was his shadow."

Rachel Wells lived in a small apartment north of Bigfork. Jill's red Saturn was nowhere to be seen.

"She doesn't know me. Why don't you let me go to the door? If she spots you, she might bolt."

"All right. Just don't let her get away."

He smiled. "I'll tackle her if she makes a run for it."

"You used to play football, didn't you?"

"A long time ago."

"I'll bet you were good. High school? College?"

"Both." This kind of talk was making him uncomfortable. He didn't tell anyone about his past. "Sit tight."

Mac knocked. No answer. He tried several more times, then peered in the windows. The place looked as if it'd been ransacked. Impossible to tell if it had happened before or after Rachel Wells had packed up and cleared out. There was a photo on the floor, the frame and glass broken. It was the same woman as in the Employee of the Month photo.

He checked the back, then returned to the pickup and Jill. "It looks like she's taken off. The place has been ransacked."

Jill groaned. "I just know she's involved in Trevor's murder somehow. She warned me at the funeral that it was dangerous to be asking questions about the murder."

"I believe I told you the same thing," Mac said. "Call the sheriff's department. Maybe she left a clue in the apartment about where she went, and they can go in and find it."

He listened while Jill placed the call on her cell. Deputy Duncan wasn't in, so she left a message for him with Rachel Wells's name and address.

When she hung up she looked over at Mac. "Well, I guess that's it. I helped you find Marvin and you helped me find Rachel."

He looked out at the darkness, not wanting to leave her any more than he suspected she wanted him to. "Technically, we didn't find Rachel."

"True, and we might not," Jill said. "I'm sure she's skipped town. And to add insult to injury, probably in my car."

This was crazy. And dangerous. "I don't think you should be alone right now."

She shot him a look. "What are you suggesting?"

He had trouble saying the words. "I think I should stay with you, on your couch, at least for a while."

"I just got new locks—"

"Look," he said, turning to face her, "your couch has to be better than sleeping in the front of this truck every night."

She smiled at him. "You've been watching my apartment?"

"You didn't give me much choice," he said.

"Why?"

"So you wouldn't get killed."

"No," she said. "I mean why do you feel you have to protect me? What makes it your job?"

"After the other night..."

She started laughing. "Do you protect every woman you sleep with?"

"Of course not," he said, wishing he hadn't told her about the night vigils.

She raised a brow. "Then why me?"

"You know the answer to that. I made love with Trevor Forester's fiancée while he was being murdered just before he was going to hire me to find his killer."

She shook her head. "Nice try. But that isn't it."

He swore under his breath. "Are you going to let me stay on your couch or not?"

"Of course. I appreciate your wanting to protect me, although I don't think it's necessary."

"Let me be the judge of that." He started the truck and drove back to where they'd left her van earlier. "I'll follow you to your apartment."

THE MOON FLIRTED with the clouds as Jill drove her van back to her apartment. She rolled down the windows in the van and let the warm, pine-scented night air blow in. She turned up the radio. She couldn't remember ever being this happy. Not even the day Trevor asked her to marry him.

When she parked, she saw that she had company. Brenna was waiting anxiously on her doorstep.

"I'm so glad to see you," Brenna said. "I have to tell you—" She stopped abruptly when she saw Mac pull up behind the van and get out of his truck.

Jill figured whatever her friend had found out must be about him.

"Mac, this is my friend Brenna Margaret Boyd. Brenna, Mackenzie Cooper."

Mac's smile had an edge to it. "Mac. But we've met. Last night at the Beach Bar." He shot Jill a look that said he had only suspected he'd been set up the night before—but was well aware of it now. He shook

Brenna's hand, then glanced at Jill. "Let's go up to your apartment, and then I'll have a look around."

Brenna looked as if she was bursting to tell Jill something, but asked first, when Mac left the room, "What happened last night on the boat?"

Jill filled her in, skipping the part about the skull. Nor did she tell Brenna about the ring Trevor had given her. Both stories were too big for a reporter to sit on, and Jill didn't want to put her friend in that position. When Mac found out from his friend whether or not the skull was that of one of the missing teenaged girls, then Jill would tell Brenna and let her go after the story.

"*He* was your mystery lover?" Brenna cried.

Jill shushed her. "I've never felt like this."

"You do look flushed and a little wild-eyed," her friend said. "Jill, you know nothing about this man!"

"I know everything I need to know." Jill saw Brenna look uncomfortable. "Don't I?"

Mac rejoined them. "I've checked all the locks and windows in both the apartment and bakery—"

His cell phone rang. He held Jill's gaze for a moment, then answered it.

"Uncle Mac?"

"Shane." Mac took a relieved breath, fighting the urge to yell at his nephew. "Where are you?"

"I'm in trouble."

As if Mac didn't know that.

"I need your help." The fear he heard in Shane's voice scared him. "I think someone's trying to kill me." Shane sounded close to tears.

"Tell me where you are," Mac ordered. He looked up to see Jill watching him, looking concerned.

"I'm at the gas station phone booth at Yellow Bay, but I can't stay here," Shane said.

"All right. Just tell me where to meet you."

"Do you know where that abandoned cherry-packing plant is near Finley Point?"

Mac remembered passing it earlier that day on the way out to Marvin Dodd's. "Yes. I'll be there in just a few minutes. Shane?"

"Yes?"

"Be careful."

He hung up and looked at Jill.

"Go," she said. "I'll be fine."

"I'll stay with her," Brenna said.

Mac couldn't take his eyes off Jill. He didn't want to leave her, but she was much safer here than where he was headed. "Lock up behind me. I'll be back as soon as I can."

She nodded and followed him down the stairs.

"She seems like a good friend," he said, knowing Brenna was waiting for Jill upstairs and, from the looks of her, dying to talk to Jill alone.

"She is a good friend."

He nodded, wanting to pull Jill into his arms, wanting to kiss her. "You have a good life here." Kissing her would mess up that life.

She looked as if she might cry. "Be careful?"

He touched her cheek, then turned and left before he said something he couldn't take back. Something that could change his life. Forever.

JILL WATCHED MAC LEAVE. He'd looked worried. About his nephew? Or was he worried about what Brenna might tell her? She wanted to believe it was because he cared more than he wanted to admit.

She'd wanted him to kiss her. For a moment at the door, she thought he might. But she knew if he did, she'd only want more.

When she got back upstairs, Brenna was pacing. "Okay, what is it you're dying to tell me?"

"He was married."

"Mac?"

"They met his last year in college."

"And?"

"And she died. Cancer."

Jill sat down. "Oh, how awful. She must have been very young."

Brenna nodded. "They'd been living in Denver, but he left right after that. The people he worked with at a private-investigations office there said he was devastated by his wife's death. His whole personality changed. He started keeping to himself, moving a lot and became bitter and cynical. I guess he avoids relationships big time."

"That explains why he seems so…afraid of what happened between us. So determined it won't happen again."

"Maybe it shouldn't," Brenna said.

Jill sighed. "I don't know. I just know that what happened between us wasn't just great sex. Something clicked, something…big. And I'm afraid this sort of thing only comes along once in a lifetime. I don't want to pass it up. I want to see where it takes me."

"What about Mac?" Brenna asked.

"He's determined to keep me at arm's length." The

phone rang, making Jill jump. She went to answer it, worried about Mac and Shane.

It was her father. "I'm fine," she told him. "Brenna is here with me. Catch any fish?"

"We got a few."

We? "Who went with you?" she asked.

Silence. "Darlene. I've been wanting the two of you to meet." Silence.

Jill felt tears burn her eyes. She'd caught the sound of happiness in her father's voice. "I would love to meet her." She could almost feel his relief over the phone line.

"Oh, Jill, I can't tell you how glad that makes me."

She was crying softly. "Dad, I like it that you've found someone. I don't want you to be sad anymore."

"I'll see you in the morning, then," he said. "Sleep tight, sweetheart."

"You too, Dad."

As Jill hung up, she dried her tears and noticed the answering machine blinking. She pushed Play and was startled to hear the other Scarlett's voice. Only, there was another layer to it. Fear.

"It's Rachel. I have to talk to you." She was whispering as if she thought someone might be listening in. "Call me. It's urgent." She left a cell-phone number.

When Jill looked up, Brenna was standing in the doorway. "Our missing Rachel? She sounds scared."

Jill nodded. According to the answering machine, Rachel had called shortly after the funeral this morning. Jill dialed the number, her fingers shaking. As horrible as the woman had been to her after the funeral, what could she possibly want to talk to her about?

The phone rang and rang. Jill was about to hang up

when someone picked up. She could hear breathing on the line and held the phone so Brenna could listen, too.

"Rachel? It's Jill."

Silence. Then, Rachel crying, her voice breaking. "He's going to kill me. Oh, God. I need money to get out of town. You have to help me. No cops."

"Who?"

No answer.

"I lost him, but he knows the cops are looking for me. If they find me, he'll know." She was crying harder now.

"Where are you?"

"Waterside. Hurry." The line disconnected.

The old Waterside Campground was down the lake road about twenty miles. It hadn't been open in years. Jill looked at her watch, then at Brenna.

"You told Mac you wouldn't leave," her friend reminded her.

"I have to go. You heard her. She seems to think whoever is after her has some connection to the police," Jill said, remembering how Arnie had found out about her mystery lover through his cousin at city hall. "The killer might have a scanner."

Brenna nodded. "I still don't like this."

"I don't, either, but you heard her. She's scared and in trouble. If I send the sheriff's deputies, the killer could get to her first."

"Well, I'm going with you," Brenna said. "Better leave a note for Mac."

Jill and Brenna climbed into The Best Buns in Town van and started down the lake road. Only occasionally did the moon peek through the clouds. A cold, damp blackness had settled in and the air smelled of rain.

They left Bigfork behind. There was little traffic this time of the night and this late in the summer. The pines gave way to cherry orchards and long stretches of nothing but trees and darkness.

Just past an abandoned orchard, the right front tire on the van blew.

CHAPTER THIRTEEN

JILL GRIPPED THE steering wheel, fighting to keep the van on the narrow road as she braked to a stop. Fortunately she hadn't been going fast, but then, she couldn't on this stretch of the highway.

At a wide spot she pulled off the road, the tire thumping, the van listing forward and to the right.

"I can't believe we have a blowout now," Brenna said as she climbed out with the flashlight from the glove compartment.

Jill got out, glanced at the flat, right-front tire and went around to the back of the van to get the jack. She was digging it out when she heard Brenna say, "That's funny. The tire has a hole in it. Almost looks like a bullet hole."

"A bullet hole? Like someone shot it?" Jill hauled the jack to the front of the van but didn't see her friend. The flashlight lay on the ground by the tire. "Brenna?" A cold wind blew off the water. The dark pines swayed, the limbs moaning softly.

Where had she gone? Jill looked down at the flat tire, saw the perfect hole in the sidewall and felt a chill. "Brenna?" She stared up and down the road and saw nothing but darkness. On either side of the pavement the bare limbs of the abandoned orchard were etched black against the night. "Brenna!" Her voice was lost in the wind.

Jill put down the jack and walked around to the driver's side of the van, fighting the urge to run. Brenna wouldn't just walk off. Someone had shot out the tire. Someone had taken Brenna. Someone was still out there.

Her hands shaking, she hurriedly climbed in and reached for her purse with her cell phone inside. It wasn't between the seats where she'd left it.

Get out of here! Fear made her limbs numb, useless, her movements slow. She could still drive on a flat. To get help she would do whatever she had to. She reached to turn on the ignition.

The keys were gone!

Her pulse pounded. Behind her, she heard the whisper of a sound and for just an instant thought it might be Brenna. Her gaze flew to the rearview mirror. She saw a pair of eyes glittering from a black ski mask as a man lunged at her.

A gloved hand brushed her arm, but didn't find purchase as she threw open the van door and jumped out.

The moment her feet hit the pavement, she took off at a run, remembering another night long ago when she'd done the same on this very road.

She heard her assailant come crashing out of the back of the van. She ran down the middle of the road, knowing she didn't stand a chance of disappearing into the stark trees of the old cherry orchard, nor could she run down the steep mountainside.

She didn't dare look back as she ran up the long incline, praying a car would come along. Her side ached and her legs felt numb. On one side tall pines made a dark wall along the edge of the narrow road. On the opposite side the land fell away, dropping radically the half mile down to the lake.

In the distance she thought she heard the sound of a car engine. Suddenly the glare of headlights blinded her as a vehicle came up over the rise in the road, answering her prayers. She could hear the roar of the engine. She waved her arms frantically. "Stop! Please help me!"

THE OLD CHERRY-PACKING plant loomed up from the road, dark and massive against the night sky. Mac cut the lights and engine, coasting to a stop fifty yards away.

He waited for a moment, letting his eyes adjust to the dark, then he quietly opened his door and stepped out, pulling his weapon from his ankle holster as he headed toward the building.

He hadn't gone far when he saw movement. Shane stepped out of the shadows.

"Uncle Mac, man, he's trying to kill me."

Mac motioned for Shane to be quiet until they reached the truck. The kid loped along beside him, looking over his shoulder, obviously scared.

Once back in the pickup, Mac holstered his weapon, started the engine and headed back to town, keeping an eye on his rearview mirror. "Okay, let's hear it."

"It wasn't my fault."

"It never is." Mac was glad he was driving or he might have torn the kid limb from limb. "Tell me about the coins."

"Trevor ordered Marvin and me to be ready one night. We didn't know we were going to *rob* someone. I'm telling you the truth. And I think there was something else in that metal box beside those coins."

"Like what?" Mac asked.

"I don't know, man. Something that got Trevor killed."

"Did you have anything to do with Trevor's death?" Mac asked, shooting a look at his nephew. "Don't lie to me, Shane."

"No way, man! No way!"

Mac let out a sigh. "There was a surveillance camera that caught you on tape. You, Trevor and Marvin. Who was the other guy? The one who was inside during the burglary?"

Shane looked scared. "I think that's the dude that's been trying to kill me."

"What's his name?" Mac said, losing patience.

"Arnie. Arnie Evans. He was Trevor's best friend, but I gotta tell you, I think he killed Trevor." Shane was nodding. "I know it sounds crazy, them being best friends and all, but I think the dude killed him, man."

As JILL WAVED her arms, the car came to a screeching halt just feet from her in the middle of the lake road. She shielded her eyes, trying to see past the bright headlights. "Please, help me!" she cried again, hearing the hysteria in her voice.

"Jill?"

Arnie? She rushed to the driver's side of the car. "Oh, thank God, Arnie. There's someone…" She looked back down the road toward the van. No one was behind her. "Brenna. I can't find Brenna. And there was this man—"

"Get in," Arnie said, turning his headlights to bright. The van, back down the road a short distance, was visible in the light, its right-front tire flat. There was no movement around it. Just darkness. "Hurry," Arnie said.

She ran around the front of the car to the passenger side. Arnie already had the door open. She leaped in and slammed the door after her. She heard the click of the automatic lock.

"We…we had a flat. Brenna got out to look and then…" Jill was gasping for air, her heart hammering and her body shaking so hard she was having trouble speaking. "Someone shot out the tire and now Brenna is gone and there was this man in the back of the van…"

"Easy," Arnie said.

"He was wearing a black ski mask. We have to look for Brenna. Where's your cell phone? We have to call for help."

"I don't have a cell phone." He let the black sports car coast slowly down the hill past the van, his expression grim. "You're sure you saw a man in a black ski mask?"

"Yes." Why wasn't he asking about Brenna? Why wasn't he racing into town for help? "Arnie, we have to get to town. We have to get help." She started to cry. "I'm so afraid something terrible has happened to Brenna."

As they passed the van, she saw that both its back doors were open, the dome light was on and it was empty.

Arnie looked down the road and suddenly spun the sports car around highway-patrol style and started back up the hill he'd just come down.

"Where are you going?" she cried. "Town's the other way."

He glanced in his rearview mirror and swore. "There was someone waiting for us down the road."

"I don't see anyone," she said, looking back.

"Someone's following us with his headlights turned off." Arnie sounded scared as he sped up.

She swiveled around in the seat to look back, but saw nothing but darkness.

"We have to try to lose him," Arnie said. "Hang on."

She buckled up her seat belt. "Arnie, I don't see anyone back there. Please, turn around. Let's go back to town to the sheriff's department. If there really is someone following us—"

"We'd never reach town," he said as he pushed the gas pedal to the floor. The sports car took off, pressing her back against the seat. The car shot down the road, the tires squealing as he took the curves of the narrow, steep road, driving farther and farther away from town—and help.

Arnie glanced in the rearview mirror again and swore. "He's staying right with us." In the dash lights, she could see beads of sweat on his forehead, his knuckles white on the steering wheel, his eyes wild.

"Arnie, what are you doing?"

"This is the only way," he said, his voice breaking with emotion. "This is all Trevor's fault. I hope he's burning in hell." The bitterness in his voice shocked her. "You can't imagine the things I did for him. The secrets I kept. I should have known I couldn't trust him."

Her heart jumped to her throat. Oh, my God. She was shaking her head, telling herself this wasn't happening.

"And now I'm the one who has to pay the price.

He took Rachel from me after taking my father's last dime. It killed him, you know, losing everything." He looked in the rearview mirror again. Fear seemed to deform his face. She could hear him breathing heavily.

She started to turn in her seat to look back again to see if anyone was following them, but suddenly Arnie hit the brakes. The sports car went into a sideways skid in the middle of the road, tires screeching, smoke billowing. She could see out over an old cherry orchard, see the lake way down at the bottom of the steep mountainside past the orchard.

Jill let out a scream as Arnie hit the gas. The sports car leaped forward and then dropped over the edge of the pavement. For a moment she thought he'd lost his mind. But then the tires came down hard on a dirt road that cut through the trees of the orchard and down the mountain.

Jill felt as if she was falling as the sports car roared down through the tunnel of trees, the headlights flickering on the dark green of the branches, dust boiling up behind them.

Clinging to the door handle, she shot a look at Arnie. His face looked feral in the dash lights, eyes wild, teeth bared as he wrestled the wheel, fighting to keep the car on the dirt road between the trees.

Moonlight flickered through the clouds, and she saw the lake coming up fast—and the cliff at the end of the road, dropping to the water below.

"Arnie, don't do this! For God's sake!"

But Arnie didn't slow. In fact, he kept the gas pedal to the floor. "This is the only way."

"My God, what are you doing?" she cried over the roar of the engine.

The car continued on down, the cherry trees blurring past. Her pulse thrummed in her ears.

"I told Trevor," Arnie said. "Please don't get my dad involved in any of your schemes. I begged him. 'No, buddy, I wouldn't take a chance with your old man's retirement. Come on, what kind of guy do you think I am?'" The perfect mimic of Trevor's voice startled her. "I trusted him. My dad invested everything, thinking Trevor was going to make him rich. It killed him. When he realized he'd lost everything, his heart couldn't take it. All those years of working under some guy's car, grease under his fingernails, all those years…"

The limbs of trees smacked the windshield and scraped the roof loudly.

"Trevor deserved to die," Arnie went on. "He got what was coming to him."

A weapon. She had to stop him. She grabbed for the wheel and he backhanded her, knocking her against the door. She reached the latch on the glove compartment. The compartment door flopped down, spilling everything. A black ski mask tumbled out and landed on the floor at her feet.

"It was you," she whispered hoarsely, then looked up to see that they were about to go over the cliff and plunge into the lake below.

At the last minute, Arnie turned the wheel and hit the brakes. Jill saw the cherry trees coming at her. A large branch hit the windshield, shattering it. She could hear the limbs slamming into the car, feel the car start to roll in the soft earth between the trees, then flatten out, still moving.

When at last the car stopped, Arnie threw open his door and stumbled out. Shaken, she groped for her door handle, pulled it. The door fell open and she was out and running almost before her feet hit the ground.

She heard the pounding of his feet behind her. He was close, very close. She could hear his ragged breath, almost feel it on her neck.

She stumbled and almost fell. She felt the brush of his hand through her hair and dodged to the right. The wrong way. It led to the cliff.

He tackled her and took her down hard, knocking the breath out of her as they fell. He quickly got up, dragging her to her feet and pulling her toward the cliff—and the lake below.

"This is the only way out," he said as she tried to fight him with her fists and kicked at him.

"No!" she screamed. It couldn't end like this. Mackenzie Cooper's face flashed in her mind and she cried out for him.

His arm around her chest, his free hand covering her mouth, Arnie dragged her the few yards to the edge of the cliff.

They teetered on the rim and she looked down, feeling the cold, wet air blowing up from the water. She thought she saw a light below her in the water, but realized it was lightning—a storm was approaching. Thunder rumbled somewhere out on the lake. Just like the night Trevor was murdered.

She tried to stop Arnie, but he was too strong. He picked her up and held her out over the edge of the cliff, out over the water, then he swung her body outward and released her.

She grabbed for him, got nothing but air. In that microsecond, she hung, suspended at eye level with him as lightning lit the sky around her. She thought

she glimpsed regret in his expression. Sorrow. He teetered on the edge of the cliff as if to jump, then turned
to look back, his face twisting in terror as if he saw
Trevor's ghost behind him.

Then Jill was falling. She hit the water, the force
of her fall driving her deep into the cold darkness of
the lake.

At first she saw nothing, felt only the all-encom-
passing liquid prison. Then she saw light above her.
Her lungs screaming for air, she started to swim toward the surface, toward the shaft of light that sliced
through the clear water.

She made the mistake of looking down and saw the
source of the light. A car rested at an angle on the bottom, its headlights shining upward through the water.

The driver's-side door was open, the dome light
on, the driver still behind the wheel, her hair floating
around her face like a dark aura.

Jill let out a cry, swallowing water, losing critical
air. Frantically, she swam toward the surface, following the shaft of light pointing upward from her red Saturn's headlights, the image of Rachel Wells bound to
the steering wheel with duct tape branded on her brain.

As she neared the surface, she saw Arnie's body
above her, the water dark around him, the side of his
head smashed in.

She kicked away from him and broke the surface at
last, gasping for air, choking on the lake water she'd
swallowed, choking on the fear that still clutched at
her chest.

From above her, Jill thought she heard someone cry
her name. She swam toward the rocky shore, praying
she wasn't imagining the sound of Mac's voice.

CHAPTER FOURTEEN

IT WAS LATE afternoon by the time the sheriff let Mac go into Jill's hospital room. He stopped just inside the door, shocked at the sight of her lying on the bed, so small, so pale. White as the sheets around her. Her eyes were closed, her lashes dark against her cheeks. His chest constricted at the sight of her.

He'd been so wrong. So very wrong. He closed his eyes as the pain and anger engulfed him, recalling what he'd read in the sheriff's report from Jill and Brenna's statements.

The sheriff had concluded that it had been Arnie who'd killed Trevor. After all the years of taking everything that Trevor dished out, Arnie had finally had enough when Trevor stole Rachel from him. He blamed Trevor for his father's heart attack, as well, but Rachel, it seemed, had been the last straw.

The sheriff had found evidence that led him to conclude that Arnie had also killed Rachel. But not before she'd made the call to Jill, which had brought Jill and Brenna down the lake road to meet her. Arnie must have been lying in wait. He shot the tire out on the van, attacked Brenna, then, wearing the black ski mask Jill had found in his glove compartment, gone after Jill.

When she'd gotten away and run, it was believed he

must have gone to his car and come back, pretending
he just happened on to her.

By the time Charley Johnson had called from the
Kalispell Police Department to say that the skull was
a positive match for a teenaged girl who'd disappeared
nine years ago, the case was already closed.

More of the dead teenagers' jewelry had turned up
in a safety-deposit box Trevor Forester kept at the bank.

Trevor was believed to have killed all eleven girls
over the years. Arnie Evans was dead now, too. The
coroner concluded that Arnie had hit his head when he
fell from the cliff and was dead by the time he hit the
water. Jill was just lucky to have survived.

"Mac?" She opened her eyes as if sensing him in
the room.

He tried to smile. It hurt. As he moved to the side
of her bed, he had the same feeling of failure he'd had
when his wife, Emily, had died of cancer. Helpless. The
pain excruciating. Unbearable. He'd promised himself
he would never care that much again.

"I'm so sorry," he said, taking her hand. Her skin
was surprisingly warm. He tried to think of the right
words, but he knew there weren't any. He'd failed this
woman. Failed himself. Worse, his feelings for her were
killing him. "If I hadn't left you and Brenna…"

She shook her head. "You had to help Shane. I
was the fool, taking off the way I did. Thank God,
Brenna's all right."

He nodded. Arnie had only knocked Brenna out and
dragged her into the pine trees. She'd suffered a slight
concussion and a few scrapes and bruises.

"I know why you're here," Jill said, her gaze locking with his. "You came to say goodbye."

He nodded, unable to speak.

She smiled, her eyes filling with tears. "It hurts to care so much about someone. I understand that. I understand why you can't let yourself do it again."

So she knew about Emily.

"I guess you heard—Shane and Zoe have decided to go to college together," she said. "They're going to the junior college in Kalispell, so Zoe can still work part-time at the bakery. They're in love."

"Yeah." He let go of her hand and stepped back. "I'd better go." There was so much he wasn't saying. Couldn't say. Best left unsaid. And yet it was hard to leave. As he turned and walked to the door of her room, opened it and went to step through, he couldn't help himself. He glanced back.

His eyes met hers, all the feeling they'd felt that first night arcing like lightning across the room, warming him to his center. And then he left and the door closed behind him.

MAC HAD ONE stop to make on his way out of town.

Nathaniel Pierce greeted him. "I figured you'd be by today." He motioned Mac inside. "Do you have time for a drink? Or do you just want your pay before you leave?"

He grinned at Mac's obvious surprise. "Summer's almost gone. Your job's over. Nothing can keep you here now. Not even a woman. Not even Jill Lawson, it seems."

Mac took the last two twenty-dollar gold pieces from his pocket and held them out to the man. "That makes all twelve, right?"

Pierce nodded slowly as he took the coins from him.

"I guess that concludes our business. Now, about that drink…" He walked to the bar in the massive living room and filled two glasses from a decanter.

Mac watched him. "I know why you hired me," he said as Pierce offered him the drink. "You already had ten of the coins back and you could have gotten the other two as easily as I did. Probably more easily. But you didn't want Marvin or Shane. You wanted that fourth man. The shadow on the videotape you said you didn't notice."

Pierce held out one of the filled glasses. Mac took it and watched Pierce walk over to a small antique desk. He opened a drawer, took out a check, closed the drawer and crossed to Mac to hand him the check.

Mac took it and glanced at the amount. More than triple what he normally charged. "I know you killed them—Trevor, Rachel, Arnie. I can't prove it, but I know you did."

Pierce lifted his glass as if in salute, then took a sip. "Greed killed them."

"If greed killed, you'd never have been born," Mac said, putting down his untouched drink. He tore up the check and let the pieces fall to the highly glossed hardwood floor. Then he turned and walked out of the house.

He headed his truck down the lake road away from Flathead, away from Jill, telling himself he was doing her a favor by leaving. But he hadn't gotten far when he realized just how wrong he'd been. He slowed the truck, feeling a pull on him stronger than any he could remember.

Damn. He had to go back.

His cell phone rang. He clicked it on, thinking it

might be Jill, disappointed when it wasn't. It was a friend he'd called about Pierce's gold coins. Mac had been curious just how much three lives were worth.

"Those dates you gave me of the two coins," his friend said. "Those are worth about two hundred bucks apiece."

"What?" Mac said, braking and pulling off the road. "I guess I should have told you. They're part of a twelve-coin set."

"Wouldn't make any difference. Those are common years. Even if you had the missing years, they'd all be worth about two hundred bucks, or about fourteen hundred dollars in total."

Mac felt his pulse pound. "You're sure?"

"You wouldn't have called me if you didn't think I knew my coins," his friend said. "Anyway, I have the book right in front of me."

Mac thanked him and clicked off, then floored the pickup. Pierce had lied. Mac wasn't sure why that surprised him. The coins weren't rare. So what the hell had getting them back been about? Just simple vengeance?

Mac remembered what Shane had said about Arnie thinking there was more in the metal box than just the coins and if there had been something else, Trevor had it. His heart leaped to his throat. Oh, God, he had to be wrong.

BRENNA CAME IN shortly after Mac left Jill's hospital room. "I heard they were releasing you and I figured you'd need a ride home."

"He's gone," Jill said, and finally let the tears come.

Brenna rushed to her. "Oh, sweetie." She hugged Jill, gently rocking her.

The nurse came in and shooed Brenna away, saying Jill needed her rest. The sleeping pill gave her nightmares. Or maybe the nightmares were just from the past few days and everything that had happened.

Jill awoke with a start a couple of hours later, and for a moment she thought Mac was in the room with her again. He wasn't. He was gone. Gone from her life. Leaving her empty inside and lonelier than she'd ever been, mourning what could have been.

The doctor released her, and Brenna drove her to the bakery. Zoe and Shane were there, along with Jill's father and his woman friend Darlene and a bunch of Jill's friends, all gathered to welcome her home.

Although seeing them lifted her spirits, she still felt empty inside, as if some part of her had left with Mac. Darlene had baked a cake, which she cut and which Zoe served with coffee.

Darlene was petite and gray-haired, with twinkling blue eyes and a cheery disposition. Perfect for Jill's father.

The phone rang every few minutes. Jill didn't feel like talking to anyone right now and asked her father to take messages. People were calling to wish her well. Other calls were from reporters from other newspapers wanting interviews, he said.

Jill looked through the array of flowers and cards that had been sent. Many of them were from her regular customers. She was deeply touched.

"This one has a note on it that says you have to read the card before eight-fifteen," Darlene said, and glanced at her watch. "You're barely going to make it."

Eight-fifteen? Jill took the card from the large

bouquet of red roses, hope soaring through her as she ripped open the envelope and read:

Jill began to cry.

"Is it bad news?" Darlene asked, sounding concerned.

Jill hugged her. "No, it's wonderful news."

Zoe came up and read the card over her shoulder. "Too cool," she said. "You'd better get moving or you're gonna be late. Take my car."

MAC FLOORED THE GAS. It hadn't been about the coins. Or revenge.

His breath escaped in a rush. "No." He'd felt from the first that everything about this was wrong. He'd known. On some level, he'd known.

Pierce had his coins. Shane said he thought something else was in the box. But whatever it had been, Trevor must have taken it.

The sheriff's report. Jill's words: "Arnie said someone was after him, trying to kill him. He'd seemed so afraid."

But she hadn't seen anyone and in the end concluded Arnie had just pretended they were being chased so he could get her to the same spot where he'd killed Rachel Wells. But Mac knew better now. Arnie had been trying to save Jill by throwing her into the lake.

Arnie hadn't fallen or jumped. Pierce had probably struck him with something. If Mac hadn't gotten to Jill when he did, if he hadn't seen the skid marks on the road, then the van with the flat, if he hadn't gone back to the skid marks, driven down through the orchard…

Mac watched the headlights eat up the pavement.

He dialed the hospital. Jill had already been released. He called her home number. No answer. He dialed information. Got her father's number. No answer there, either. Information gave him Zoe's number. The phone rang and rang, and finally it was picked up. He could hear rock music. "Zoe?"

The music stopped with a suddenness that was both comforting and jarring.

"Hello," she said with a giggle, her attention obviously elsewhere. Shane must have been with her.

"Do you know where Jill is?" he asked.

"Mac? She went to meet you."

What? "Meet me?"

"Yeah, she got the note you sent with the flowers."

He'd never sent a woman flowers in his life. Not even Emily. He wished now that he had. That he'd had the sense to send them to Jill with a note telling her to meet him.

"Where was she meeting me?"

Zoe let out another giggle. "You should know."

"Where?"

"At the Foresters' lake cottage."

He hung up. He wasn't far from the Foresters'. He could be there faster than the sheriff's department could get there. And unlike the deputies, Mac knew what to expect when he got there.

As she stepped into the dark cottage a little before eight-fifteen, Jill sensed Mac near her—just as she had that first time. Only now something was different. At first she didn't know what. Then she caught the faint scent of his aftershave.

Mac hadn't worn aftershave that first night. In fact,

she couldn't remember ever smelling it when he was around her. He always smelled of soap and sunshine.

"Mac?" Her voice sounded tight, nervous even to her. She heard the scuff of shoes on the tile floor. He was close. Close enough he could touch her. She felt a chill, a combination of desire. And fear. Something felt wrong. She'd been so excited that Mac had come back. Excited he'd wanted to make love again in the cottage. That he'd changed his mind about the two of them.

She stepped back, banging into the door she'd just closed behind her. "Mac?" The urgency in her voice seemed only to send her fear escalating. "Turn on a light. You're scaring me."

There was a whisper of sound in the pitch blackness, then a light flared from the corner, momentarily blinding her.

She blinked. "You're not Mac." She was feeling for the door handle behind her, her blood pounding in her ears, and yet she was telling herself there was no reason to be afraid.

The man before her was no homeless person off the street. In fact, he looked as if he belonged here. He wore gray jeans, a white polo shirt and deck shoes, and he was sprawled in a chair, a glass of red wine next to him on the end table.

"Sorry if I scared you," he said. He seemed amused, rather than upset, that she'd just walked into the cottage. "I'm a friend of Alistair's. I'm staying here tonight, keeping an eye on the place. I was just enjoying watching the lake in the dark," he said as if anticipating her question, and smiled. "I can see you're disappointed that I'm not this Mac you were looking for. Sorry."

She was the one who was sorry. And confused. Where was Mac?

The man rose gracefully from the chair. "I don't think we've ever met." He held out his hand. "I'm Nathaniel Pierce and you, I know, are Jill Lawson." His smile broadened at her surprise. "I've seen you around and heard volumes from Alistair. He's quite a fan of yours."

She tried to relax, but felt strung tight as piano wire as she reached for his hand. She told herself it was from her disappointment. Her surprise to find someone other than Mac in the cottage. In the dark.

His larger hand enveloped hers and she felt a jolt of something like…fear. Her gaze flew up to his. She knew she'd never met him before, but something about Nathaniel Pierce seemed familiar. "I should be going." She tried to free her hand, but he held on to it.

"So soon? What if your…Mac shows up? Why don't you join me in a glass of wine while we wait for him?" His gaze held hers as securely as his hand trapped hers in his.

"No, thank you. Maybe he's waiting for me by the house."

"I wouldn't be so sure about that, Jill."

A shaft of ice cut down her spine at the change in his voice. She'd heard the voice before. Her heart hammered in her ears. He was pulling on her wrist—just as he had fourteen years ago that night beside the lake road. The night he'd tried to give her a ride.

"No!" She brought her free hand down hard on his wrist, breaking his hold, and bolted for the door. But he was right behind her. He hit the door with his palms, slamming it shut with a thud, one hand on each side of her.

"Did you like the roses?" he whispered.

She didn't breathe. Didn't move.

"You know, I'd forgotten about you," he said in that same whisper. "It had been so many years. You were the only one who got away. Really messed up my summer. Quite a few of my summers. I had to leave after that, get rid of that car. I did love that car."

She remembered the car and him. It had taken her years before she could sleep without a night-light because of him.

The realization made her fear spike. It hadn't been Trevor who killed those teenaged girls. And those years when no girls had disappeared were when Nathaniel had been gone. Her legs were jelly. She had trouble taking her next breath. There was no one around but them. No one to hear her scream. Nathaniel Pierce had killed all those girls. She'd been the only one to get away.

And now he'd caught her.

"I didn't know who'd robbed me until Heddy was telling me about the antique ring Trevor had bought you. She knew I'd always been interested in jewelry and had some expertise—I'd taken enough of it off girls' dead bodies." He laughed, a bloodcurdling sound. "Heddy wanted to know what it was worth. She was probably wondering where her son had gotten the money for such a ring. I almost laughed in her face."

He pressed Jill closer against the door with his body, his face next to hers. "I asked what other presents her dear son had given you. She told me about the silver charm bracelet. She thought it was sweet. *Sweet*. The bastard was giving you jewelry that belonged to my girls, the jewelry I'd taken off their bodies after I'd… enjoyed their youth, their innocence, their last moments of life."

She shuddered.

"What else did Trevor give you from my stash?"

She shook her head.

"Don't lie."

It had been dark that night when the car stopped to pick her up. She hadn't really noticed it—nor had she seen the driver's face in the dark. Later she recalled there was no light inside the car when he'd stopped for her. He had turned off the dash lights. He would need to work in the dark.

He crushed his body against her. She could feel him reaching for something. The next thing she knew, he slapped a wet rag over her mouth and nose. She fought the smell. She fought him. But not for long.

JILL AWOKE TO a blinding white light. The pain in her head assured her she was not dead. That and the rock of the boat and the sound of him breathing over her.

She closed her eyes tightly as the light moved closer and she felt his hands on her again. It wasn't until he'd lifted her in his arms and carried her out of the boat that she opened her eyes and saw that he wore a headlamp.

As she followed its beam, she saw where he'd brought her. Her heart dropped like a stone.

The old mansion on the island stood stark against the night sky. Suddenly she couldn't get enough air through her nostrils. She began to panic, her breathing shallow. Tiny flecks of light danced before her eyes. She was going to pass out again.

He stopped, shifted her in his arms to free one of his hands and ripped the tape from her mouth.

She gasped at the pain and began taking large gulps of night air. Sobs rose from her panic and she was crying and gasping.

He carried her up some stairs, the steps groaning under them from the weight. The smell hit her first. Rotting decay. Then the whine of the wind as it moved restlessly through the empty structure.

She'd feared where he was taking her the moment she'd seen the house. All the years of hearing the stories about Aria Hillinger. Her beauty. Her tragic life. And worse, her tragic death. The stories about people hearing a woman's screams coming from the island. Jill's blood turned to ice when she realized those had been real screams over the years. Young women who'd been carried up these same stairs to their deaths.

He put her down on the edge of the fourth-floor balcony, but his hand remained on her neck, his fingers biting into her flesh. The railing was gone.

Jill was so close to the edge she could feel the wind blowing up the side of the house into her face. All he had to do was straighten his arm and let go of her neck and she would be airborne. This time, the fall would kill her because she would land in the rocks below, not in the water. Not in the water as she had when Arnie had thrown her off the cliff. Oh, God, Arnie. It had been Pierce after him. Arnie had saved her life.

The wind blew back her hair, stole her breath. She tried not to panic. Tried to think. But she knew as she teetered precariously on the edge of the deck that she stood no chance of besting this man physically.

It was clear he had stood here many times before.

That alone terrified her. How many other women had stood here, knowing they were going to die? Jill could feel their fear as keenly as she could feel the evil inside these walls. Women had screamed for their lives. Just as she would scream for hers.

MAC REACHED THE cottage, saw Zoe's Beetle parked near the Foresters' dark house. No other cars. Pierce must have come by boat.

Mac was out of the pickup, running down the hill to the cottage, knowing he was too late when he saw the dock empty. He burst into the cottage, anyway. Would Pierce expect him to come back? Mac doubted it. Pierce thought he knew him so well. Pierce thought he would run from a woman like Jill Lawson as fast as his pickup would take him.

No, Pierce wouldn't expect him.

The cottage was empty—except for Jill's purse. Mac picked it up, held it to his face, the soft leather smelling of her perfume.

Why had Pierce left her purse behind? For the same reason he'd sent the roses and note? To make everyone think Jill had gone to the cottage to meet Mac? When she disappeared, the sheriff would be looking for Mac—not Pierce.

He rushed out to the dock. He and Pierce had stolen a few cars in their youth. Hot-wiring a boat would be a piece of cake. He jumped into the fastest of the Forester boats. Within minutes he was roaring across the water, headed for the island. He'd remembered something Pierce had told him about his mother one night when he'd been drunk and his defenses down. The next morning he'd sworn it was a lie.

But even then Mac had heard a ring of truth in Pierce's story.

"Katherine isn't my real mother. My real mother killed herself when she was young," Pierce had said. "Really young. My father doesn't think I remember her, but I do. I used to stand on the balcony with her. I used to worry that she would try to jump. She could never have reached the water from the fourth story."

"Did she jump?" Mac had asked.

"No. She hung herself."

JILL HEARD NATHANIEL PIERCE take a breath and watched him look out at the lake as he began to speak. It was some sort of a ritual, she thought.

"She was so beautiful," he said. "Childlike. She used to stand here and look out at the lake. She loved this room. I would stand here with her. Her hair was long and blond and she smelled of summer and something sweet like strawberries. Her arms were slim and she wore a bracelet my grandfather had given her. A tiny silver bracelet."

Jill's throat closed. Aria Hillinger. My God, he was talking about Aria Hillinger. Goosebumps skittered over her bare skin. Nathaniel Pierce had been the child. The child believed to have drowned or starved to death on this island.

"She loved me," Pierce said. "She was so sweet and innocent. You would see it in her eyes, as if her life was just beginning and nothing could hurt her."

He looked at Jill and she knew the ritual was almost over. Her fear spiked, a shot of adrenaline that sent her heart into overdrive.

Those other women, had they fought? Had they tried

to talk him out of killing them? Had they believed that they could come up with a way out of this?

"He found me," Pierce said. "My father. He'd finally come to save her, but it was too late. So he never told a soul. He was married, you see, to Katherine. So he brought me to her, made her lie. Katherine did anything my father told her. She pretended I was hers, hers and my father's. They just pretended my real mother never existed, that my father never had an affair..." His voice trailed off, the silence even more frightening. "But he bought up the island and all the Hillinger property."

He seemed to come back as if from a distance. "But I remember her. She was so beautiful. So young. Don't you see, she will always be young. My father is old now, a wrinkled, crippled-up old man who has suddenly developed a conscience. That's why he sold the island, you know. The old bastard knew what I'd been doing all these years but he didn't have the guts to try to stop me."

Pierce laughed, a horrible sound that held no humor. "He knew if anyone tried to develop this land, they would find the bodies. He was counting on that stopping me." Pierce shook his head, the headlamp swinging back and forth, making her stomach roil. "The old stupid fool. Now he is old and dying, but my mother will always be young. Just like you, Jill."

He began to take the tape off Jill's ankles. She watched him, gauging her chances of fighting him off physically once her hands were free. Bad plan. He was stronger, larger, and he'd obviously done this more times than she wanted to consider. She doubted anyone had gotten away from him. At least not for long.

"Of course, you will want to scream when the time comes," he said. "They all do."

She thought she heard a boat, but she couldn't see any lights. It sounded as if it was coming this way, fast. But Pierce didn't seem worried about it. He turned her around and that's when she saw the noose hanging from the rafters. He smiled at her surprise. "Let me tell you about asphyxiation," he said.

THE SOUND OF a boat grew closer. Still Nathaniel Pierce didn't seem to notice. Or care. Probably because no one came to the island, especially at night.

He dragged her over to the noose, the glare of his headlamp blinding her again. She tried to fight him— just as he'd obviously hoped. She heard a horrible sound and realized it was laughter. Nathaniel Pierce had thrown back his head and was laughing as he wrestled the noose around her neck.

The rope was coarse and chafed her skin. He tightened it around her throat, then stepped back to look at her as if posing her for a painting. Or a photograph.

Then he stepped close to her again, reached into his pocket and pulled out a silver charm bracelet with a tiny silver heart on it. He smiled with satisfaction as she saw the name engraved on it. Jill.

"It's yours," he said as he carefully clasped it on her wrist. "There, just as it should have been all those years ago. Fourteen, right?" His eyes sparkled.

She listened for the sound of the boat motor and realized she couldn't hear it anymore. Despair swept over her. The boat must have gone on past to the east side of the lake. She'd been praying that someone had seen the light from Pierce's headlamp. Would come to investigate.

But what fool would come to this island this late?

"Oh, you look so sad," Pierce said, lifting her chin with his finger and gazing at her face. "Just think, you will always be this age. Young. Not as young as you would have been fourteen years ago." He tsked. "Your own fault. You should have gotten into the car."

She tried to find her voice. If she could get him talking, she could buy herself a little precious time. "You killed Trevor, didn't you? And Rachel and Arnie and all those girls? Why?"

He shook his head as if disappointed in her, then walked over to where he'd tied the other end of the rope. She tried to run. To shake her head out of the noose. To get away.

He laughed again, clearly enjoying her delaying efforts. He pulled the rope. The noose tightened, then loosened again. "Are you sure you don't want to scream?"

She closed her eyes and thought of Mac, remembering their night in the cottage. She clung to that memory as Pierce jerked the rope tighter and tighter, lifting her off her feet. Mac was wrong. They would have been amazing together.

The rope cut into her neck, the pain excruciating. No air. She gasped, determined not to scream. Determined not to give Pierce that satisfaction, knowing it hadn't saved the other women he'd killed here, knowing it wasn't going to save her, either.

She could feel a different darkness. Stars glittered behind her lids. Then she heard it. The sound of footfalls thundering up the old wooden stairs. She opened her eyes.

Pierce had turned toward the sound, the headlamp shining on the landing at the top of the stairs.

Jill thought she only imagined Mac as he burst through the doorway, a gun in one hand, a flashlight in the other. She tried to call out to him, but the noose was too tight and she could feel herself passing out. She fought it with all her will. Don't give up now! Not now!

AT FIRST ALL Mac saw was the light shining at him. He dived to one side, expecting gunfire, and swept the beam of his flashlight across the room. The light wavered as it fell on Jill suspended above the floor, the noose around her neck.

Oh, my God! He was too late!

"Let her down!" he ordered, his voice breaking as he shone the beam of his flashlight on Pierce. "Let her down now!" He rushed over to Jill and lifted her, putting slack in the rope, all the while holding his gun on Pierce. But the man had tied the rope off and just stood watching as if with interest what Mac would do next.

"Untie the rope!" Mac yelled. "Or I'll blow your blue blood all over this room." He could feel a slight movement from Jill. She was alive!

"You don't want this woman or her mediocre life," Pierce said, the headlamp shining on Jill's face. "Why are you doing this? Can you imagine yourself making cinnamon rolls? She means nothing to you. Walk away, Mac. It's what you do best. Anyway, it's too late."

Mac put the first bullet in Pierce's right thigh. He let out a howl and dropped to one knee. "Untie the rope, Pierce. Now!" Mac's second shot only grazed

Pierce's other thigh. Pierce stumbled over to the rope and quickly untied it.

Mac lowered Jill to the floor and, keeping his weapon close, loosened the noose around her neck until he could get it over her head. She gasped for breath and tried to speak.

"Shh, you're going to be all right," he said. "Don't talk. Just breathe."

She pulled Mac nearer. Her whisper was harsh and painful sounding, and he realized it took everything in her to get the words past her throat. "He has a gun."

The headlamp hadn't moved from the spot where Pierce had dropped after untying the rope. Mac flicked the beam of his flashlight to it and saw that the headlamp lay on the floor, the beam pointed at him. Pierce was gone!

Still on his knees beside Jill, Mac shone the flashlight across the room. Pierce couldn't have gotten away that quickly. Not wounded as he was. Mac would have heard him if he'd run. But Pierce hadn't run. He'd moved like a big cat, a cat with only one purpose—destroying its enemy. And Mac was that enemy, he realized as he felt the gun stab into his neck.

Pierce knocked the flashlight from Mac's hand. It hit the floor, the beam illuminating the three of them. Pierce squatted down next to Mac and eased the weapon from his fingers, then tossed it away into the darkness. Mac stared after it, memorizing where it was in case he got the chance to go after it.

Jill lay gasping on the floor, her hand to her throat, her eyes wide and terrified. Not for herself, but for him, Mac realized as Pierce leaned down.

"Why did you have to come back?" Pierce asked,

squatting next to him, still pressing the barrel of the gun into his neck. "Why couldn't you just let this all end? She would have been my last, and then everything would have been forgotten."

"You're just kidding yourself, Pierce," Mac said, surprised by how calm he sounded. "You couldn't stop killing. Anyway, the cops know about the bodies you buried on this island. They're going to come after you."

Pierce laughed. "Nice try, old buddy, but they think Trevor killed those girls. Don't you just love the irony? Trevor stole my coins, not realizing what else I kept in that box. All my sweet things' jewelry. He didn't have a clue what he had. And now everyone believes he was the one who did those terrible things to those girls. It's too perfect."

"Not quite. Trevor and Arnie are dead. You can't blame this one on him or Arnie."

"I always get away with it," Pierce said, not sounding worried in the least. "I can make it look like you took off with her. Make sure someone uses your credit cards. I can keep the cops guessing for years until they tire of looking for the two of you."

Mac dropped his gaze to Jill. She motioned slowly with her head and his eyes followed the movement. She'd wrapped the rope loosely around Pierce's ankles as he'd been talking and now had the end, ready to pull it.

He gave only the slightest nod. She jerked the rope. At the same time, Mac drove his arm up, knocking the gun away. A shot exploded, echoing off the walls.

Pierce went down hard, his body kicking up dust from the floor as it hit. Mac dived for his weapon and was on Pierce before he could get up. He pressed the gun to the side of Pierce's head, and Pierce smiled up at him.

"You aren't going to kill me," he said. "It's not in you. And the bitch of it is, you know I can hire the best lawyer money can buy. I'll get off. Maybe a little time in a nice sanitarium. Then I'll be cured. I've gotten away with murder for years." The smile broadened. "I will again."

Mac could hear the coast guard boat nearing the island. "Yes, I know," he said to Pierce, and pulled the trigger.

Then he moved over to Jill.

Tears streaming down her cheeks, her eyes never leaving his face, she pulled Mac down and held him. He wrapped her in his arms.

"I knew you'd come back." Her words were a hoarse whisper coming from her injured throat.

He kept her wrapped in his arms as he watched the lights of the coast guard boat draw nearer and nearer.

EPILOGUE

JILL SAT ON the deck of her father's lake house and watched a sailboat move across the blue-green waters of Flathead Lake. She could smell the cherry blossoms on the slight breeze and hear her father and Darlene in the kitchen discussing their upcoming wedding.

Jill smiled at the thought of her father's happiness. It was matched only by her own. In the months since that horrible night at the Hillinger mansion, the memories had faded and blurred. Sometimes she still had nightmares but Mac was always there to hold her. She'd never felt safer. Or happier.

Mac had bought what Trevor had named Inspiration Island. He'd burned the old Hillinger mansion to the ground.

The remains of all the murdered young women had been removed and sent home for burial. At last their families could begin to heal. And Nathaniel Pierce was dead. He wouldn't hurt anyone ever again.

Jill turned at the sound of Mac's footfalls on the deck and smiled up at his handsome face. He stepped closer to her and she noticed he had one hand hidden behind his back.

"What?" she asked, laughing. Mac wasn't the kind of man who showered a woman with gifts. Thank goodness, she thought, remembering Trevor's.

"For you," Mac said shyly as he pulled the bouquet of wildflowers from behind his back.

Tears stung her eyes.

"I've never given flowers to a woman before," he said, dropping to his knees in front of her chair. "I wanted you to be the first."

She took the flowers, drawing him to her with her free arm. He kissed her neck and she felt that wonderful thrill she'd felt from the first.

And Mac *had* been wrong. When they'd made love again, it was more amazing than the first time. In fact, every time they made love was more amazing than the last.

Their spring wedding was huge and held at the church in Bigfork, overlooking the lake. The same church where Jill's father and Darlene would be married next week.

Mac had moved his P.I. business down from Whitefish and into a building he'd bought across the street from Jill's bakery. Zoe and Shane had moved into Jill's old apartment over the bakery, both of them working part-time while they attended junior college in Kalispell.

"I can't believe the change in Shane," Mac had said.

And Shane hadn't been able to believe the change in his uncle. "He's, like, human."

Mac had laughed and pulled his new bride to him.

They'd bought a place on the lake. From it, Jill couldn't see Inspiration Island. Mac said maybe someday they would build a camp on the island for kids. The island needed laughter. But first it needed to heal.

Alistair and Heddy Forester sold their house on the lake and moved away. Jill saw Alistair before he left. He looked like a very old man. He'd told her again how sorry he was. "I wish I could turn back the clock," he said, and shook his head, tears in his eyes.

"There is something we haven't talked about," Mac said now, drawing back from her.

She smiled at him. They'd talked for days after what had happened. Talked about his first wife, Emily. Her death. Mac's fear of loving again. His confession that he'd fallen for Jill that first night in the cottage.

They had taken it slowly, spending time together, talking about everything. That bond had been there from the beginning, though. It made it easy. It felt so right.

"What haven't we talked about?" she asked, looking from her bouquet of beautiful flowers to him. He'd put them in a small jar with water. The jar brimmed with the bright colors of spring. Like love, she thought.

"Kids," he said.

"Kids?" She thought he was talking about his plan for the island. But then she looked into his eyes and felt a jolt. "Kids?" she repeated, her eyes filling with tears. She'd been so afraid he would never want children of their own. He'd taken the first step by letting himself love her completely, knowing he could lose her, just as he'd lost Emily, just as he'd almost lost Jill that night on the island.

Mac nodded. "Jill, I want to share this. I keep seeing you holding a baby in your arms. This love of ours, it's so strong...." He shook his head, at a loss for words.

He knew life could irreversibly change in an instant. Sometimes all it took was a kiss. His life had changed that night in the cottage when he'd kissed Jill Lawson. He couldn't explain it. But she was right, whatever had happened was more than sex. Sometimes two people connected in a way that tore down all barriers and united them forever.

She leaned forward, cupped his face in her hands and pressed a kiss to his mouth. "Say the words," she whispered against his lips.

He pulled back enough to look into her eyes and smiled. He had no idea what the future held. But he was no longer afraid. Losing was the flip side of loving. But loving was worth it. Whatever time he had with Jill, he intended to enjoy every moment of it. He was no longer afraid of making the same mistakes his father had made. He wasn't his father. And Jill Lawson was like no woman he'd ever met.

"I love you." The words came out so easily. "I love you." He lifted her into his arms and spun her around. "I love you! And I want a baby!"

She was laughing, a wondrous sound, and he was laughing, too, holding her and spinning, the world spinning around them, the two of them dizzy with happiness.

As he stopped and let her slowly slide down so he could kiss her again, he looked into her eyes, promising to give her love, all the love now bursting in his heart. He kissed her, and then they were spinning and laughing.

He heard Jill's father and Darlene come out onto the deck.

"What in the world?" her father said.

"We've decided to have a baby!" Jill announced.

"Babies," Mac said, and kissed her. "Lots of babies."

Life changed in an instant. His had changed with one kiss.

* * * * *

New York Times bestselling author

B.J. DANIELS

introduces *The Montana Hamiltons*, a gripping new series that will leave you on the edge of your seat...

Available now! Available now! Coming 2015!

"Daniels has succeeded in joining the ranks of mystery masters."
—*Fresh Fiction*

www.HQNBooks.com

PHBJDTM

INTRIGUE
EDGE-OF-YOUR-SEAT INTRIGUE,
FEARLESS ROMANCE.

Use this coupon to save
$1.00
on the purchase of any
Harlequin® Intrigue book.

Available wherever books are sold, including
most bookstores, supermarkets, drugstores
and discount stores.

- ✂

Save $1.00
on the purchase of any Harlequin® Intrigue book.

Coupon valid until March 15, 2016.
Redeemable at participating outlets in the U.S. and Canada only.
Not redeemable at Barnes & Noble stores. Limit one coupon per customer.

Canadian Retailers: Harlequin Enterprises Limited will pay the face value of
this coupon plus 10.25¢ if submitted by customer for this product only. Any
other use constitutes fraud. Coupon is nonassignable. Void if taxed, prohibited
or restricted by law. Consumer must pay any government taxes. Void if copied.
Inmar Promotional Services ("IPS") customers submit coupons and proof of
sales to Harlequin Enterprises Limited, P.O. Box 3000, Saint John, NB E2L 4L3,
Canada. Non-IPS retailer—for reimbursement submit coupons and proof of
sales directly to Harlequin Enterprises Limited, Retail Marketing Department,
225 Duncan Mill Rd., Don Mills, ON M3B 3K9, Canada.

U.S. Retailers: Harlequin Enterprises
Limited will pay the face value of
this coupon plus 8¢ if submitted by
customer for this product only. Any
other use constitutes fraud. Coupon is
nonassignable. Void if taxed, prohibited
or restricted by law. Consumer must pay
any government taxes. Void if copied.
For reimbursement submit coupons
and proof of sales directly to Harlequin
Enterprises Limited, P.O. Box 880478,
El Paso, TX 88588-0478, U.S.A. Cash
value 1/100 cents.

® and ™ are trademarks owned and used by the trademark owner and/or its licensee.
©2016 Harlequin Enterprises Limited

BJDINC0116COUP

e didn't know how to deal with someone who didn't
em to want—or need—one damn thing from him.
specially after the ordeal of the past few weeks. He
dn't know how to relax anymore, how to sit quietly and
t a bowl of soup without waiting for the next blow, the
xt trick.

He knew his name was Dallas Logan Cole. He was
irty-three years old and had spent the first eighteen years
f his life in Kentucky coal country, trying like hell to get
ut before he was stuck there for the rest of his sorry life.
e was a good artist and an ever better designer, and he'd
ent the bulk of his college years trying to leave the last
estiges of his mountain upbringing behind so he could
art a whole new life.

And here he was, back in the hills, running for his life
gain. How the hell had he let this happen?

"I guess those are the only clothes you have?"

He looked down at his grimy shirt and jeans. They
eren't the clothes he'd been wearing when a group of

men in pickup trucks had run his car off the road a few miles north of Ruckersville, Virginia. The wreck had left him a little woozy and helpless to fight the four burly mountain men who'd hauled him into one of the trucks and driven him into the hills. They'd stripped him out of his suit and made him dress in the middle of the woods in the frigid cold while they watched with hawk-sharp eyes for any sign of rebellion.

Rebellion, he'd later learned, was the quickest way to earn a little extra pain.

"It's all I have," he said, swallowing enough humiliating memories to last a lifetime. "Don't suppose you have anything my size?"

Her lips quirked again, triggering a pair of dimples in her cheeks. "Not on purpose. I can wash those for you, though."

"I'd appreciate that." He was finally warm, he realized with some surprise. Not a shiver in sight. He'd begun to wonder if he'd ever feel truly warm again.

She picked up his empty bowl and took it to the sink. "The bathroom's down the hall to the right. Leave your clothes in the hall and I'll put them on to wash."

"And then what?"

She turned as if surprised by the question. "And then we go to bed."

Don't miss
BLUE RIDGE RICOCHET by Paula Graves,
available February 2016 wherever
Harlequin® Intrigue books and ebooks are sold.

www.Harlequin.com